NOT FOR WOMEN ONLY . . .

"Hot Prowl" by Mary Wings
Two women, one a cop answering a call, the other a San Francisco filmmaker who becomes the hostage of a junkie, prove it may be a jungle out there . . . but they're the hunters, not the prey.

"The Other Woman" by Wendi Lee
A female private investigator reluctantly agrees to take a "creep and peep" case spying on an unfaithful wife—and discovers she's not only in the middle of a lover's triangle, she's an unwitting accomplice to murder.

"Dust Devil" by Nancy Pickard
When a young mother runs off with her infant son, the baby's father hires a PI to track her down in what seems a straightforward custody battle but leads down a twisted trail of betrayal, psychosis, and murder.

"Where Is She? Where Did She Go To?" by Dorothy B. Hughes
Written espeically for this volume and completed shortly before the author's death, this period tale of jazz, Hollywood, and homicide is an atonal, dark, and brilliant riff on classic mystery writing.

AND MORE OUTSTANDING STORIES IN . . .

VENGEANCE IS HERS

VENGEANCE IS HERS

· ·

EDITED BY

MICKEY SPILLANE

AND

MAX ALLAN COLLINS

To John —
Thanks for asking me to talk & to hope you enjoy!

Best

Jan Grape
May 27, 1998

Ⓞ
A SIGNET BOOK

SIGNET
Published by the Penguin Group
Penguin Books USA Inc., 375 Hudson Street,
New York, New York 10014, U.S.A.
Penguin Books Ltd, 27 Wrights Lane,
London W8 5TZ, England
Penguin Books Australia Ltd, Ringwood,
Victoria, Australia
Penguin Books Canada Ltd, 10 Alcorn Avenue,
Toronto, Ontario, Canada M4V 3B2
Penguin Books (N.Z.) Ltd, 182–190 Wairau Road,
Auckland 10, New Zealand

Penguin Books Ltd, Registered Offices:
Harmondsworth, Middlesex, England

First published by Signet, an imprint of Dutton Signet,
a division of Penguin Books USA Inc.

First Printing, May, 1997
10 9 8 7 6 5 4 3 2 1

 REGISTERED TRADEMARK—MARCA REGISTRADA

CONTENTS

VENGEANCE IS HERS
An Introduction

. . . .

By Max Allan Collins

Tough crime fiction has frequently been labeled misogynist. It has been said that such [male] writers as Dashiell Hammett, James M. Cain, Raymond Chandler, and—yes—Mickey Spillane have betrayed a hatred for women by so frequently presenting black-widow villainesses. And when the women in the stories of these men were not black widows, they were helpless damsels in distress who needed a big strong man to save them. . . .

This charge is specious, of course—Hammett is the man who created witty Nora Charles, after all, and Cain brought hardworking Mildred Pierce to life. True, Chandler created his share of black widows and distressed damsels (and one memorable little sister) but they were a complicated and varied lot; when that great hard-boiled [female] writer Leigh Brackett adapted Chandler's *Big Sleep* to the screen, she had great fun expanding on his racy dialogue—Brackett's exchanges between Bogart and Bacall are the stuff movie dreams (and director Howard Hawks's reputation) are made of.

Spillane has taken the most and the hardest knocks in the misogyny witch-hunt—ever since Mike Hammer shot a certain female psychiatrist in her supple tummy at the conclusion of *I, the Jury* (1947)—and critics (few of whom ever seem to have read his work) often like to say that the murderers in Spillane's whodunit plots *always* turn out to be women. Actually, Spillane murderers are more often men, though a good share of murderesses (to use a now-sexist term) do turn up. Asked about this, Spillane has said, "What's the big deal? You got two choices." Sometimes the bad guy's a man—sometimes it's a woman. In *Vengeance Is Mine,* actually, there's a third choice . . . but that's another story, and another controversy. . . .

What few critics have noticed, but many readers (including Spillane's vast female readership) know, is that part of the writer's approach is to portray strong, larger-than-life characters, female characters definitely included. Spillane's female "bad guys" are as memorable (and memorably bad) as the males; and such female "good guys" as Mike Hammer's secretary Velda and Tiger Mann's lover Rondine are as two-fisted as they are beautiful. Velda is a licensed PI who was packing a rod when V.I. Warshawski was in grade school.

The charge of misogyny against hard-boiled mystery writers has become outdated, in part because so many women are writing hard-boiled mysteries, now. There are probably at least as many fictional female PIs walking Chandler's mean streets in the 1990s as men. Possibly more.

When Marty Greenberg and I got together with Mickey Spillane to discuss doing a series of anthologies continuing the short-fiction tradition of *Black Mask* and *Manhunt* magazines, one of the first notions we came up with was an all-female volume . . . with one male gate-crasher: Mickey himself.

And, since vengeance is the classic Spillane motif, the theme of this volume, as reflected in our title, seemed a natural. But don't look for any male-bashing herein: the assumption that women who write hard-edged suspense fiction hate men is as specious as the reverse.

Mickey's contribution to this volume is the provocatively titled "Sex Is My Vengeance," in which the author recounts a meeting with a prostitute in a bar. The woman tells her own tough yet poignant story, in a sensitive slice of life with a point of view that should surprise Spillane's knee-jerk critics.

All sorts of points of view are on display from the women writers who've contributed stories written especially for this unique volume. J. A. Jance gives us "One Good Turn," providing a twisty tale that is at once character study and thriller; Valerie Frankel climbs into the shoes and soul of a woman fighting a battle against herself, in the wonderful, terrifying "Pounds of Flesh"; Susan Rogers Cooper presents a deceptively simple tale of the battle of the sexes in "Family Tradition"; the always entertaining Joan Hess provides a rare short-story excursion into the southern hamlet of Maggody, where "Time Will Tell" how an act of vengeance does, or doesn't, go down; Barbara Collins chillingly demonstrates how a high-school prank can misshape the future in the darkly comic story of a lovely, deadly "Reunion Queen"; past disappointments and lingering high school memories also play a role in Sharyn McCrumb's perceptive portrait of a fan's enduring obsession with a minor-league pop star, "Among My Souvenirs"; reader favorite Margaret Maron maintains a cozy tone in the wonderfully nasty "No, I'm Not Jane Marple, But Since You Ask"; Mary Wings contributes telling character studies of two women, one the hostage of a junkie, the other the cop answering a "Hot Prowl" call; and in "Couldja Die," Annette Meyers contributes a startlingly original slice of life about the New York theater world, with a narrator who demonstrates (unintentionally) that civilized society has an ominous, savage undercurrent.

In a Spillane anthology, we must meet some private eyes, and L. J. Washburn's rousing historical Hollywood tale, "Pictures in the Stars," reveals in PI narrator Lucas Hallam the author's mastery of a male point of view; Wendi Lee (who, as W. W. Lee, writes a fine series about a male private eye in the Old West) presents "The Other Woman," in which we find a female PI taking on a nasty "creep-and-peep" case, feeling none too proud about it; S. J. Rozan's Chinese-American PI Lydia Chin encounters danger on the "Subway," an exciting tale about rape that is both troubling and insightful; Jan Grape's two-woman PI agency—G & G Investigations—earns "A Front-Row Seat" thanks to first-rate detection and a refreshingly human narrator; popular veteran Nancy Pickard presents a male PI while summoning a twisting "Dust Devil"; and talented newcomer Christine Matthews introduces Chicago private eye Susan Elliot in "Belated Revenge," a fresh look at the traditional detective-story theme of a family facing present-day tragedy due to tragedies long past.

We are also thrilled, honored, and saddened to present the last completed work of Dorothy B. Hughes. Her story "Where Is She? Where Did She Go To?" was written especially for this anthology, and finished shortly before her death in 1993. Her daughter Susie Sarna, also a talented writer, worked closely with Dorothy on this intriguing, vivid period tale of jazz, Hollywood, and—possibly—murder.

I met Dorothy Hughes, celebrated author of *Ride the Pink Horse* and *In a Lonely Place*, in 1981 at a mystery convention, the same convention where I met Mickey Spillane. Dorothy said (after witnessing our two-man panel discussion) that she found Mickey and me "cute." This unlikely designation is one I will always cherish.

We dedicate this volume to her memory.

SEX IS MY VENGEANCE

By Mickey Spillane

She looked at me with a wry smile then turned to the drink in her hand. "No prostitute has ever turned her back on society," she said. "All she did was accept it a little closer to her bosom."

"That's too philosophical," I told her. "You've thought that one out."

Her grin spread and for a moment she was real pretty. "I've had plenty of time to think. In this business you can stick fairly close to the subject and not get sidetracked."

"But is it true?"

"Yeah," she nodded. "It's true. It's the way I feel."

"What about the others?"

For a second her eyes flicked to the back bar mirror and automatically her hand went to her hair. "We used to talk about it. They feel the same."

"Used to?"

"We skip it now. We save the answers for the . . . clients."

The waiter came over with our order, served it with a flourish, and when he left I said, "You'd hardly expect the . . . clients to be conversationalists, too."

"You'd be surprised."

"Nothing surprises me, kid," I told her. "Now draw me a picture."

Once again I got that noncommittal, noncaring grin. "Do people always ask you where you get ideas for the stories you write?"

I nodded frowning. She was pretty shrewd at guessing games.

"Well, there's one question they always ask . . ." she hesitated, then: ". . . us." Her eyes grew empty before she went on. "One question . . . *'How did you get into the racket, honey?'*"

I pulled her back out of the dry taste of thought with, "You tell them?"

"Sure. Oh, sure. They get their money's worth. They want to hear some strange, sordid story so that they'll feel neat and clean by comparison and they get it. If you think you can tell stories you should hear some of the things I . . . *we* dream up."

"How much is the truth?"

"None," she said. "I never told that."

"Feel like telling me?"

"Would it help somebody?"

"Maybe. You can never tell. It's a rough world."

"Sure, I'll tell you. But first you got to ask me the right question."

She waited, watching me closely. But I was as shrewd as she was. I wasn't about to ask her *HOW* she got in the racket. That was easy. Anybody with a warped sense of values could do it.

I said, "Okay, kid, *WHY* did you become a prostitute?"

She grinned and I knew now that I was going to hear the right yarn.

I watched her, waiting, and maybe wondering a little what she'd say. From appearances, you couldn't tell at all. She was tall, brunette, dark-eyed, prettier than most and when we had walked into the restaurant a lot of men had followed her with their eyes. Her voice was the unexpected, soft with maturity, yet always concealing a laugh. For some reason there was no remorse, no anger in her makeup. If it had ever been there, at all, she'd learned to hide it deep where it wouldn't trouble her casual encounters.

The title of *prostitute* was a personally applied one in her case. She was a solo vendor, no part of an organized ring, no "club" member; still not a streetwalker or a bar biscuit. Her trade existed in a strata where "clients" wore gray flannel suits and advertising was done softly, but efficiently, in whispers. In her own way she was approaching the top levels of her field where there is no hope and the only way left is down . . . fast. And forever.

"It started in high school in upstate New York," she said. "I was a sophomore and running with the wrong crowd. Everybody else was a year or so older and a little more prepared for the fast life. They knew the answers. After a few wild parties I started on the way to being an unwed mother."

"The guy?"

"Prominent in school. Good family and all that. He denied it and his family backed him up, though up to that time he had done enough bragging around school about his little conquest."

"Did he . . . make any arrangements for you?" I asked.

She remembered back and laughed. "Yes, that he and his family did. And brother, did they do it well." She laughed again as if it were of no consequence. "They arranged for me to board out in reform school at Hudson for a year so no squawks on my part could besmirch the bastard's reputation." She stopped, then added, "Sorry for the swearing."

"Didn't your family help out?"

Something happened to her face. For the first time the bitterness showed through and the disgust was in her eyes. "The old man said it served me right. He beat me black and blue with his fists and would have killed me if he hadn't been too drunk to catch me when I got away." She stared past me, her eyes boring into the back of the booth. "He was always drunk. If ever I earned any money baby-sitting he'd grab it and blow it on a bottle."

"Couldn't your mother do anything?"

"Not a thing. She was scared of him, too. He'd beat her for any reason at all. A few times the neighbors had him arrested, but he'd just make it worse on us later." Her eyes went across the table to mine. "You just can't explain what it's like when there is no love in a family," she said.

And so the cause was explained very simply and accurately. With one sentence she had put her finger right on it. If you look at it closely enough she had analyzed the problems of the world. Two words. No love. But these things you don't see often enough. The meaning is obscure until you see the effect.

And effect . . . the reason to search for a cure, was what I wanted.

"This made you a prostitute?"

She shook her head slowly. "No. Not this. Many things."

"So?"

"Can I get vulgar?" she asked softly.

I nodded.

"You won't mind? It's just that sometimes I can't say it right. I have to speak in . . . *patois*. You know what I mean?" I laughed at her and she said, "I picked up the word at Hudson. My only accomplishment. They had a Canuck kid there with a big vocabulary."

"Shoot."

"The old man told me that I was nothing but a damn whore and if I had to do it to do it for dough, then he beat hell out of me and kicked me out. My mother tried to stop him and he slapped her." She stopped and took a deep breath. "And that ended her resistance. She left the rest up to me."

"He should have lived to be a hundred but right away," I said.

"Earlier." For a second she puzzled over it, her lip between her teeth. "I got out that night. I slept on the damn stoop. The next night I did some baby-sitting, made a dollar eighty and made the mistake of going in the house. I had another belt in the head, had my dough taken away with the old man accusing me of making it whoring. Did I tell you he was a real bastard?"

"You mentioned it."

"No, I mean a *real* one? Maybe he had a complex. Anyway, I was too young to reason it all out. Like the saying goes, I had the name, so I had might as well get the game. There was only one thing I hung out for."

"What's that?"

"The baby. I got him. Nobody was taking the baby away from me. They tried but it couldn't be done. I would have blown the whistle so loud on certain people if they had done it that the old town would have flipped."

I asked, "How's the kid now?"

"Good. He's raised properly. He's loved. Now that's all we say. Okay?"

"Okay."

"The town was a typical upstate town. It had three classes of girls . . . the good ones in the majority, those who sold it, and those who could afford to give it away. Like every place else, it had only one class of boys. They had access to all three. When they couldn't afford it they went with the good ones. When they could, they didn't."

"Great," I said. "One hell of a situation."

"Didn't you have it in your day?"

I laughed quietly. "Sugar, in my day a gal was safe. We rode bikes. The schoolyard was crammed with twenty-eight inchers. On a bike all you got into was a conversation. Maybe we thought we were hotshots, but we were mild ones. Real mild. We kissed and carried books. Rode babes on the crossbar if we had the nerve. Now the bikes are gone and the Buicks take their place. Conversation is only a by-product. The tough guy a while back is a patsy today. Like the poem reads, 'Seduction is a sissy's game, a he-man likes his rape.'"

"So you know what I mean?" She smiled.

"I've studied it objectively. I hate punks and the ones who raised them. I've been there watching fifteen-year-olds being indoctrinated into *horse* and I've creamed the slobs who did it. I've been shot up and smeared in the process but only when the odds were bad. The odds were so bad that I wound up in the lineup one time until they found out I was the only one who would testify."

She leaned forward and patted my hand. "You're nice," she said. "Now want to hear the rest?"

I said yes.

"High school was all kid stuff. This was the formative time. I was everybody's friend and they were mine. They commiserated with me for one reason. We always wound up sympathetically." She grinned real big. "Step one," she said.

"In our clean, righteous, one-party town, we had some men. Ah, such men. Big ones. Large men who ran our clean, little town. They ran the biggest crap games on the Hudson and were a drop for all upstate narcotics and track payoffs. They were big, they had dough, cars, and clothes. They had all the dames they wanted. In their own way they were even respected."

"So?"

"So some of them had had a yen for young girls. They even made it real pleasant and paid off in twenties and the younger girls felt flattered and suddenly financially secure. The thing that had ostracized them from family and friends became the means to introduce them to a new circle. That is, until the boom went down. Until a wife found out that a teenager was usurping the family cot. You know what I mean?"

I nodded again. "I know."

"It was tough. No place to go, no understanding to divide right from wrong. No home unless you want bruises and swollen spots."

"Really that bad?"

I got that funny smile again. "Really. He picked up a knife one night because I came in without any money. Look."

She held out her hand and across the palm was a livid scar from thumb to pinky.

"I grabbed the blade to keep him from killing me."

When she looked up she saw the question in my eyes.

"No," she said, "I wasn't that strong. He was drunk again. He fell down and I ran. That night he almost beat my mother to death."

"Why did you go back at all?"

This time her answer came quickly. It was fast and direct, and if there was any accusation at all it was in her tone. "Have you ever wanted to be loved? Have you ever needed someone, even a drunken bastard dad or a scared mother?"

I sat back and said, "This is your story, sugar."

"I'm beginning to wonder." Then she laughed again. "Okay, now we progress. You still want the *patois*?"

"Natch."

"So in simple I got kicked out. A visit to home was a challenge, a chance meeting with the old man direct combat. He tried to rape me, but I got away. He tried to get his friends to con me into a mob job, but I got away. You have the home picture now?"

"I got it."

"Swell. Now we go outside. At sixteen I beat out all

the liquor laws in a very easy way. You'd never believe it. I conned the bartenders. Then I conned the customers. I had me a living that was easy and . . . natural. You see, like a lot of men, I didn't have a definite trade."

I had to stop her. "Ease off. Too fast."

"Oke." And I got that grin again. "I could make the customers by making the bartenders first."

"All this under eighteen?"

"Man," she said, "you just don't know."

"Girl," I said, "you're crazy. I'm cop happy. I know. I've watched."

The smile tugged at her mouth, then went all the way across. "You're for real, man, aren't you?"

"I said I'd been shot."

"This story comes out you might get it again."

"I'll go for it. If I catch another one I deserve it."

"You travel loaded?"

"If I have to."

"So the large men up there promoted me. I didn't notice their smiles. They had big bills and a way of talking. They made me feel good. You know?"

"I know."

"Then I grew a little. All over big. You know?"

"I know."

"I was smooth, a looker, built. I knew what they wanted. You know?"

"I know."

"I sat in one day when they were arranging a big fall and when they made the fall and sobered up they remembered I had been there and was the soft touch in the deal and to get me out they shipped me."

"Cold?"

"Sure. What else? I didn't want the river. They were slobby enough to frame me out sideways. It would have worked with my history. You know?"

I said, "I know, stop the philosophizing and the *patois*."

"Hell, Mick, they would have cold cocked me into the Hudson."

"You ran?"

"Like crazy. I took the first ship out. Man, did I take it." She let the grin grow across her face. "You ought to know. I bummed a tenner off you to take the Dayliner down the river to my ship. Don't you remember?"

"The ten I remember," I said. "Who was your ship?"

"A narcotics addict who had already spent a session in Lexington [Kentucky] trying to dump the monkey. I had met him while I was still a pig, but he didn't care. He was ready to take care of me. He was the only one who would; the only one who cared enough. My family called him a damned spic, but he loved me more than they did.

"All his money went into me. He dressed me and fed me good. We had an apartment that put us both way up there and if Harlem had a middle class, we were it.

"Oh, we made big plans, the both of us. He was going to dump the monkey and I was going to back him up."

"What happened?"

I got the smile again. "The monkey was too big, too heavy. For more *H* he started pimping me into a routine. If we ate it was because I was lucky enough to cut out a few bucks for the table. The rest went for *horse.*"

"You put up with this?"

"Let's say I loved the guy."

I said, "Let's not. Love doesn't demand that."

"It was better than what I had."

"Was it?"

She shrugged. "So now it was all in earnest. No recriminations. No remorse. Either he felt too sick or too good to beat me. If he was sick I went out and hustled a buck under the marquees on TS and shacked in a joint along the upper forties. If he was happy we ate on the strip like biggies and shacked fancy together at a big hotel."

She stopped and toyed with her drink.

I said, "So go, girl."

"To where? He gets picked up with a load of *H* and shipped off to Dannemora. Hell, it wasn't an *N* deal they grabbed him on. They knew he was a pig and let him off with a small squeal. So he got Dannemora instead of Sing. You can laugh and write . . . but Mick, you can't miss the guy like I do."

"What happens when he comes out?"

"So guess. He goes back to *H* and pimping and I go back to you-know-what, only not in style."

I glanced up fast. "Now you're in style?"

"Only after an effort," she said.

"Your guy won't cure?"

"Never. He left me on relief in a tenement in Harlem. When he comes back he'll be set to ride again. The horse is big."

"Meanwhile?" I asked.

"Meanwhile things change. The relief lad comes around to find out if I'm qualified. At the moment, with all the problems, I'm not. But luckily I could see that he needed more relief than me."

"So?"

"So we traded. I got my extra relief; so did he. We were both happy. He came around regularly and as he upped my relief, I upped his." She paused and smiled. "Is the *patois* frightening?"

"Not to me."

"The politics, then?"

"To me they're all crumbs, honey."

"This one was my lucky break. He introduced me. He had friends upstairs who could cover his relief . . . uppances." She laughed deep in her chest and continued. "We got to be real friends. Before long I didn't need the apartment nor the relief."

"This, then, was a turning point?" I asked her.

"Another one. I saw the possibilities within my special limitations."

I made a face and shook my head. "That wasn't the right answer and you know it. There were other doors open. You could have gotten a job."

There was a sudden seriousness about her. "Perhaps. If I had moved far away. If I could have cut out from everyone I knew." She stared down at her hands. "There was always the present to consider . . . the immediacy of the moment. The child, money . . . a lot of things. And there was something about being . . . like I was. It shows through. Oh, not all the time, but it would come up."

Her hands made a furtive gesture of annoyance and for a second she nibbled at her lip.

She said, "You see . . . it wasn't only that I *had* to do what I did. It was . . . well, I really didn't object."

I just looked at her and waited.

"Oh, hell," she blurted, "I liked it that way."

"You just wiped out all your excuses, kid."

"Not quite, Mick. You only grow to like the things you become familiar with. They could have had another pattern ready for me."

"But when they didn't you turned your back on society."

She laughed again. "Like I said, that isn't the case. Society finds me . . . us . . . useful. My clients are now of the best. I can spot them brooding over a drink . . . lonely because home has no meaning for them . . . lost because they have been pushed away from someone they love . . . or just so happy to be away from some miserable situation where they come from that I am their rescue, their relief. No, as immoral as the situation might seem, this present society has a definite need for me. I take society right to my bosom where it finds a home."

"Which," I remarked, "doesn't say much for society. But there's still another angle. Although said society nestles on your bosom, it still finds your business illegal as well as immoral and sooner or later the ax comes down. Some of your erstwhile clients might even turn into your inquisitors."

"Mick, that will be the day." I got an impish grin and she reached into her handbag. She brought out a notepad and flipped it back a few pages so I could see the meticulous bookkeeping, the neat rows of names, places, and figures.

"My insurance," she told me. "Men have been known to develop sudden righteous streaks when under pressure and if I fall, they fall too. I've always kept a fine record of events that could shake people into keeping their mouths shut."

I picked it out of her fingers and leafed through it. Across the top it had in red pencil, *Volume 4*. On page six I saw the names of two persons I knew. You probably do too.

When I handed it back I said, "This could get you real killed, kid."

The chuckle again. "Only *you* know about it."

"So where do you go from here?"

"Future plans?" She mused a moment. "I don't go anywhere. I try to hold fast. I've learned every trick in the trade. When it has to be, there isn't a bellboy in the world who could spot me for what I am. Nor a cop, nor another woman. Not when I really don't want it to show. Right now I'm in a top bracket and playing the M and B game for what it's worth."

"Translate, kid."

"*Manufacturers and Buyers.* The money boys come in from out of town and are buttered up by the manufacturers with 'dates' who turn out to be good convincers. It's an angle that can get results when talk can't. Oh, it doesn't work on everybody, but if a guy is susceptible to this kind of bargaining it goes over great. As a matter of fact, I've seen plenty of O-T's hit the city panting like crazy. They've been thinking about it ever since they left home and they're never disappointed. Everything is nicely arranged, everyone's satisfied and everyone makes money. Prostitution has lost its cloak of shame and become part of big business."

"More philosophy?"

"Nope. A statement of facts. Remember, I'm close enough to know." A smile played across her mouth as she looked at me. "Right now I'm good enough to be accepted in the best of places. I'm welcomed as a lovely doll who has the peculiar facility of being able to speak the . . . *patois* . . . of the person she's with. It's something I've learned through my numerous associations. As I mentioned, when I don't *want* it to show, it doesn't."

"Look," I interrupted. "Are you happy with an arrangement like this? Is this the best you can do?"

For a long second she didn't say anything. She stared to one side lost in thought, her chin relaxed in her hands. Then she turned to me slowly and shook her head.

"I could probably do other things, if that's what you mean. However, I *am* doing the best I can in this particular business. And happy?" Her eyes got a little heavy lidded. "Yes, I'm happy. I feel good, let's say. I'm afraid, old boy, that I have a little touch of that old disease called *nymphomania*."

Now she leaned forward and there was something in her face that wasn't there before.

"I'm a sex machine now. That was the pattern I had to conform to a long time ago and what started out as something pretty rough turned into something I couldn't do without. Now I realize what happened . . . I began using sex as a substitute for love. It wasn't as satisfactory, but I never knew love to start with and sex wasn't too bad a replacement. It grew on me too. I liked it. I still like it. I find myself anticipating every night coming up like a tout does a horse race.

"I like to look at men and figure out just how they'd react if I walked in their room stripped to the teeth. I like to watch them shake all over when they know what's ahead if they're good boys. You know, some of them can't even breathe right. They choke on things and can hardly hold their hats in their hands. They get all catted up when they suddenly realize that I want to be in bed worse than they do and home and family stops existing for them. Between the bar and the bed they'll lick their lips chapped and turn into complete idiots at the sound of a sigh.

"And don't think it's only a few who get like that. Damn near every man is the same. They moralize like hell outside and cat it just as fast when the door gets closed. Do you think they're honest about it? Hell, I've seen remorse happen so fast to some of those self-righteous cats that after the steam is gone they turned on me like black widow spiders in reverse. They hate themselves but won't admit it and turn on me. I'm going to tell you something. I think it funny as hell to watch those cats flat out. I get a charge out of seeing them squirm and try to commit mental suicide. For a week maybe, they're going to have a sex hangover worse than any that ever came out of a bottle . . . then they'll come back catting again.

"No, I don't feel sorry for them. None of them can ever give me a bad time anymore. And besides, that big empty need that I have inside me gets filled up. Not all the way, but enough. When I sleep I sleep satisfied and not like the sorry kids who were in Hudson with me. I need men bad and I get men. For me, they do what I want them to do and they pay me besides. I can make them want me so bad that even with money on the side the old sex play turns into love. Imagine that? They pay off for love.

"That stuff I'm not buying. They're suckers who'll go for any old bait. If there's any love for me it's up in Dannemora and I'll wait for it to get back. Then we'll

see what happens. Who knows? Meantime I'm scoring.
I'm getting a bundle that will take care of the child and
pay for another trip to Lexington if the monkey comes
back again.

"I have a big one tomorrow. We met in a very toney
restaurant. He's sixty-seven years old and has been frustrated since the night after he got married. The guy's
real cat and if you saw him you'd flip. When he touches
me he comes all apart at the seams and what happens
to him in a bedroom would really make a story. Daytime
he runs a business that touches half of New York, but
when his turn comes he can hardly open the door to
the room but when I'm done with him he's as good as
brainwashed. Then I laugh at that old pig who was supposed to be such a big and sanctimonious individual. I
laugh and he doesn't even hear me. They should see
him now."

The tightness around her mouth relaxed and she sat
back. One hand was white where the other had squeezed
it too tightly.

"So that's the *WHY*," I said.

"What?" She sounded far off.

"The real reason you're a prostitute."

She frowned at me, puzzled.

"It wasn't a pattern. Anybody can jump out of a mold
if they want to badly enough. It *was* a lack of love on
the part of others only partially. If you had loved them
enough you could have overcome the situation."

"Now you're philosophizing."

"Could be, but listen. The real *why* has a vengeance
motive. You're getting back at them. The nymphomania
excuses things a little and the need for money for a 'right
cause,' the child, a cure for a drug addict, makes it easier. But actually, you're just getting back at them, aren't
you? They're paying off for the big mistake. They're
paying off for that year in Hudson. They're paying off
for the flat in Harlem, the bumps and the bruises."

Her nod finally came. "They're paying off good."

"Is it worth it?"

"First tell me something. You've been around. Those
eyes don't fool me. Is society any better than I am?"

"Not the society you know."

"Okay. Then it's not worth it. You have anything better in mind?"

I waved the waiter over for the check and laid a bill on the platter.

"I'll think about it," I said, "then I'll write you a letter."

"Do that."

"Thanks for all the talk, kid." I stood up and handed her her fox scarf from the hook. "Can I drop you someplace?"

She grinned real big. "You can, but you'd better not."

"Oh?"

"The client might not appreciate it," she said. "Just to the cab."

So we went outside and I whistled at a Yellow. We said so-long and it took her away to somewhere and for a few minutes I felt just a little bit sad about it. She and society. A great team. Society especially. Right off the corner a smelly drunk was stretched on the sidewalk. There was blood on his cheek. He could have been dead, but society didn't care. At the moment society was stepping over him with only a curious glance down. Then a cop came along and when I was getting in the cab that stopped the cop was getting him gently to his feet.

POUNDS OF FLESH

By Valerie Frankel

134   Fat, I thought as I looked down the length of my body. Fred and I were lounging on the couch in my Brooklyn apartment with the TV on. I breathed in and unbuttoned my jeans. I bought them a size small as incentive to lose weight. Never happened. I looked over at my fiancé and asked, "Am I . . ."

"No, you're not fat," he said without looking at me. "And that's the last time I'm saying it today." It was sticky and hot out. I hate July.

"Would you still marry me if I weighed two hundred pounds?" I asked.

"You do weigh two hundred pounds, don't you?" he said and snickered. I socked him hard on the arm. This from the guy who once said, When you gain weight, it shows in your legs. Our relationship barely survived that.

I watched him rub his bicep and said, "I hope that hurt." A friend of mine had a boyfriend once who told her that he'd prefer it if she lost weight. She responded by saying she'd prefer it if he had a bigger penis. Neither subject came up again.

Fred leaned over and kissed me on the lips. He said, "Yes, I'd still marry you if you weighed two hundred pounds." Then he grabbed what he called a fistful of Amanda. We snuggled deep into the cushions of my couch and felt each other up.

"*Attack,*" screamed the TV suddenly. "Attack the enemy!" We broke apart and turned toward the set. A tiny muscular woman in leotards with flaming red hair ranted and raged across a small stage. She did a few karate kicks. About fifty extremely overweight women sat in big chairs in the audience. Many wore (tight) housecoats from Kmart. The tiny woman stopped slicing the air with her feet and turned to face her crowd and the TV audience.

She introduced herself as Belinda Contral. Her voice was throaty and harsh, probably from all the screaming. "I was as fat as you once," she announced and pointed at a cowering brunette in a royal blue tent. A slide projection appeared suddenly on the white wall behind Belinda. The image: a mountain of a woman, redhead, sitting in a beach chair, waving by the side of a dirt road. Belinda stood to the left of the image. Everyone gasped.

"That's right," she confided. "That used to be me. I struggled with my weight for years. And, as you can see," she said, pointing at the slide projection, "my weight was winning. My years of dieting were—and were not—a losing battle." The crowd laughed. I laughed. Fred didn't. "But I learned to fight back," she continued. "I learned to attack fat with fresh water, fruit, and exercise. I fought hard and I won. Look at me now!" She kicked her leg high like a chorus dancer. No doubt she was limber. But water, fruit, and exercise? Hardly original enough to care. I turned back to Fred for more hugging and kissing.

"What helped me most was REDUCE—a specially created diet supplement," Belinda Contral added. That caught my ear. She went on to describe the formula that had been created by a team of Berkeley nutritionists. "I had a couple hundred pounds to lose, so I needed serious help," Belinda hawked. "I volunteered to be a guinea pig for the REDUCE scientists two years ago. In the first three days on the supplement," she paused, "I lost twenty pounds. Yes, believe it. And you can too." Then she pitched her whole package of inspirational videotapes, cassettes, CDS, her diet cookbook and, of course, the amazingly expensive REDUCE formula. The 1-800 number flashed at the bottom of the TV screen. Then the screen went black.

Fred had clicked off the set. He rubbed a dewy bottle of beer across his forehead. Strands of brown hair stuck to the sweat on the back of his neck. My air conditioner had broken and I decided not to get it fixed, partially out of environmental guilt, partially because I thought the heat might sweat a few pounds off me before our wedding next month. Of course, I didn't give that explanation to Fred. He would think I was being ridiculous.

"Maybe I should create a weight-loss system and go on TV," Fred suggested. "Here's the slogan—Eat less." He popped a potato chip in his mouth. "1-800-EAT-LESS. Think it'll sell?"

"You really are an insensitive clod, Fred," I said. Belinda Contral's number was 1-800-FAT-ATAK. I might as well investigate, I thought. It can't hurt to make a free phone call.

"You're not *thinking* of calling that number, are you?" asked Fred. "Look, Amanda, you don't need to lose weight. You're perfect." Fred kissed me. I could taste the beer on his lips. I licked them clean and kissed his face. I wondered briefly if human sweat had any calories. Then Fred made me forget about food for the next few hours.

136 I subtracted a pound because my hair was still wet. At 5 feet 6 inches, I should weigh somewhere in the neighborhood of 130. The tables at the doctor's office, though, have been getting more and more generous as the years go on. I might one day be listed as skinny. I laughed at the notion and stepped off the scale.

The wedding was in twenty-two days. My dress (off-white, silk) fit already. If I lost a few pounds there was still time for an alteration. I got dressed. Fred had kissed me good-bye while I was showering. I've long since gotten over feeling self-conscious when he sees me fully naked in dim light. But for an uncomfortable minute last night on the couch . . . I shook it off. My thighs were fine. 1-800-FAT ATAK. Belinda lost twenty pounds in three days. That was the first time I'd seen her commercial. I wouldn't be caught dead in her leotard outfit, but I had to admit—that woman looked good.

I made my living writing freelance magazine articles. I had two stories to worry about that day: the *Mademoiselle* article about nerd appeal and the *Cosmo* story about why it's okay to have sex on the first date. I tied my hair in a knot and sat down at my desk. I turned on my Mac. I stared at the blank screen. I flashed to the mental image of me and Fred dancing at our wedding in my parents' backyard in Short Hills, New Jersey. I was in my gown. It looked tight. The telephone loomed on my desk.

Nerd appeal. What do I love about dorks? I asked myself. 1-800-FAT-ATAK. Twenty-two days wasn't much time really. Anything advertised on TV had to be bullshit. I thought of my sister's wedding album, of that one picture of me in the ugly taffeta bridesmaid dress that made my arms look like ham hocks. I picked up the phone and dialed.

I got the promotional message: "You have just made the most important call of your life," said the throaty voice of Belinda Contral. "You have decided to change your ways. You have decided to take control of your life. You have decided to attack the enemy. To attack the fat. I did it. You can too. Hold please and wait for instructions on how to place your order. Have a pen and your credit card number ready."

I ordered two weeks' worth of REDUCE for eighty dollars. I didn't get the cookbook and calendar of Belinda in various karate poses. The formula arrived the next day by Federal Express. I took my first half-cup dose that evening. The stuff was white and thick. It tasted like cherries. I helped myself to another quarter cup for good measure.

142 One week later, I got in a fight with the laundry service woman. She'd cleaned all of my jeans in steaming hot water and then used the hottest drier temperature possible. I could barely squeeze into them. I hated tight jeans. They make everyone present slightly uncomfortable.

I'd been out so much that week: three editor lunches and two friend dinners. I couldn't resist splurging in restaurants, especially with everyone insisting I get dessert. I was getting married in just two weeks. I deserved to treat myself. I hadn't had time to prepare any at-home low-fat meals. Fred grilled a couple steaks for us at his apartment one night, but I'd hardly call that dietetic.

I peeled off my jeans in frustration and pulled on some loose boxer shorts. It was too hot out for jeans anyway. I was swollen from the heat. No air-conditioning. I counted back days. I was due to get my period in less than a week. That explained it, I said to myself. The heat, my period, the restaurant meals. The REDUCE box said that I might gain weight before I lost any. My metabolism would be a bit cockeyed and I shouldn't panic if the pounds didn't fall away immediately. I'll stabilize, it said.

147 Five pounds later, I was beginning to get scared. Fred has been sleeping at his place for the last few nights. He wanted to start moving his stuff in that night, but he hasn't seen me since I weighed 144. I called him at work and told him to not come over later. I felt sick. Cramps. I probably would tomorrow night too. Something was wrong. I felt clammy, light-headed, and ravenously hungry all the time.

I called 1-800-FAT-ATAK. I hoped the electronic message would eventually lead to an operator who could put me in touch with the executive offices. I impatiently listened to the message from Belinda, the 500 combination packages, all ordered by pushing the telephone buttons. The message never explained how to get a person on the line. I sat through the whole thing five times before I realized I hadn't missed it.

I checked the REDUCE box for a company address or another 1-800 number. I found an address for Contral Inc. in Elizabeth, New Jersey. I called information and got an out-of-service phone number. I called New York City information for the executive offices of Belinda Contral, Contral Inc., or REDUCE. Nothing. I called Berkeley University in California and was transferred about ten times before I confirmed that no team of nutritionists from the university or med school knew anything about REDUCE. I started to panic.

I got a grip by downing two Cokes and a couple Twinkies. I'd been a fact-checker for two years before I became a freelance writer. I can figure this out, I reasoned. I'll report it, like a story.

The first call I made was to *Consumer Reports*. My friend Jeanie worked there. I asked her to do a check on Belinda Contral or Contral Inc.

"Not the karate diet guru?" she asked. "You drank that REDUCE?"

"I'm afraid so."

"Contral Inc. is under investigation by the FDA. They're testing REDUCE. It doesn't look good." Jeanie went on to explain that they'd gotten a few thousand complaints from customers who were actually gaining weight on this REDUCE formula. Apparently, Contral aired her commercial only three times, all in the last week. The spot had been pulled by the Fox Network advertising sales people because of the FDA investigation. The 1-800 number was still active, though, pending the FDA report.

"I've gained thirteen pounds," I confessed. "My wedding is in two weeks."

Jeanie sighed. "Get a doctor, Amanda."

My head was spinning. I hung up and cried myself a little cry. I was stupid. I hated that I'd been swindled because of my fat obsession. I was a sucker. I'd been duped by a fraud who knew I couldn't resist. I wondered if that fat woman in the slide had really been Belinda. It couldn't be. If she'd been fat, she would never take advantage of other overweight people.

I cried into the kitchen. My appetite did not suffer in the stress. While I prepared a juicy roast beef sandwich, I called my father, a doctor. I asked him for a referral to an endocrinologist in the city. He was concerned, but I told him it was for a friend. Then he told me how beautiful the impatiens look by the patio and that the tent man was there all day, measuring the yard. I forced excitement into my voice and told him that sounded great. We hung up and I made an appointment for the next day with Dr. Judith Schwartz at NYU Medical Center on First Avenue.

I spent the rest of the day trying to get a line on Belinda Contral. I spoke to the DVM, the New York City Department of Consumer Affairs, and the advertising sales department at the Fox Network. I know the network had to have a billing address at least, but they wouldn't give me anything. At one point, I slammed the phone down and gave myself a blood blister. Insult to injury. I put the remaining REDUCE in a bag to take with me to the doctor's office.

I went to bed early. I couldn't fall asleep. When I lay on my side, I could feel the new fat on my belly shift and hang toward the mattress. Because of the weather and my weight gain, I've been wearing loose-fitting sundresses with no stockings. My legs chafed when I walked. Red spot has sprung up on my inner thighs and they itched. I've also noticed a different smell to my body. Not unpleasant, just different. I hated these changes. I tossed and turned.

At three in the morning, I got out of bed and ate the leftover Chinese food from dinner as I wondered if the REDUCE was responsible for my increased appetite.

155 I didn't think it was possible to gain eight pounds overnight by having a midnight snack. Not only did the gain show on the scale, I was horrified by the difference in the mirror. In the past, I sort of knew in my heart that I hadn't been fat-fat. I was borderline chubby. But now, I was fat. No question. I was twenty-five pounds overweight, by even the most generous weight tables around.

I took a deep breath and tried not to get down on myself. I made a promise that I'd never be vain again. I was going to see the doctor in an hour. She'll give me a pill and everything would be okay. I actually smiled as I got dressed in the same ankle-length sundress I'd worn for the last couple days. My bra cut into the fat on my back. It restricted my breathing. I stuffed my swollen feet into sandals. I bit back tears and left my apartment. My legs chafed and my butt jiggled as I walked toward the subway. A few blocks along, I was distracted by the crash of doors bursting open at P.S. 54, the Brooklyn Heights junior high school. Students spilled out onto the street. A group of boys walked toward me.

As I passed them, several of the boys cupped their hands over their mouths and made a sound—"Moo," they said. The others tittered. I was too shocked to react while it was happening. I turned around to look. They were staring back at me, pointing and laughing.

That's when I realized that other people can see this. I hadn't left my apartment in a few days and I'd sort of gotten to the point where I didn't believe what was happening to me. I thought I was making it up, that it was some kind of hallucination. Now the nightmare was confirmed. Moo, they said. I was a cow. I stumbled down the subway steps and fell against the turnstiles and cried.

My loose flesh jiggled with each wrenching sob. A train pulled into the station just as I recovered. People struggled to get around me, pushing and muttering under their breaths. I could see the contempt in their eyes for the fat lady blocking their way. I'd looked at fat people before and felt a strange relief that I wasn't one of them. I waited patiently for all the people to pass me before I squeezed myself through the turnstile. If only the Mars bar I bought on the platform tasted as bitter as I felt.

163 Eleven days until the wedding. The doctor didn't do much of anything but take my blood. She'd have results in a few days. I should stop taking the REDUCE. That I'd already gathered. She gave me a mild thyroid stimulant. I double dosed myself.

To be on the safe side, I made an appointment with the tailor who'd done the alterations on my gown. I told her that I might need one more fitting and that I'd come in exactly one week before the wedding. Four days to lose—my God—thirty pounds. My wardrobe now consisted of cutoff sweats and a few button-down shirts Fred had left at my apartment.

Fred and I had a fight the night before. He showed up at my place after work. Uninvited. He said into the buzzer, "Amanda. Buzz me up." He'd left his keys at work, thank God.

"Fred, I told you not to come over tonight." I was terrified that he'd see my fat through the walls.

"I need to see you," he said. "We haven't spent the night for a week."

"I just don't feel well," I said. "You don't want to catch my cold before the wedding."

He was irritated. "I miss you, Amanda. I don't give a shit about your cold." Then, in a soft voice, he said, "I want you." I pictured him leaning against the speaker, pressing the talk button. I bit back a sob.

"I want you, too, but I just can't let you in. Soon. I promise."

He said, "Look, Amanda, is there anyone up there?"

I was shocked. "No, of course not."

"If I find out someone's up there, the wedding is off."

I shouted into the speaker, but he'd gone. I took another thyroid stimulant. I got the spins and passed out in the kitchen after polishing off the potato salad leftover from my deli dinner.

173 I'd decided to view this as some kind of weird science experiment. I can now fit into nothing but my bathrobe. It gets hot as hell in the apartment, especially with the robe on. I'd walk around naked, but I have two full-length mirrors.

I haven't left my apartment in three days, not since I went to the doctor's office. I've had to order in all my food. I was only using the restaurants that took credit card numbers for deliveries. That included the Chinese place, the Mexican restaurant, the pizza joint, the rib joint, and the diner. My mother called me every day and asked me if anything was wrong. I sound funny, she said. Just nerves, I told her. Just prewedding jitters. She then told me about how many outlets the band needed and that the gardener came that day to mow the lawn.

Fred was becoming more and more difficult to keep away. His lease was up at the end of the month and he wanted to get moving. He was currently buying the story that I want to stay apart until the wedding night so that it'll be special for us. I'd always loved Fred's sentimentality but I lost a little respect for him when he believed the lie.

I've come to discover what the strange smell was—sweat. I'd never sweat so much in my life. I would get so thirsty from dehydration, I'd have to drink another Coke. My neck and wrists had grown so thick that I'd taken off all my jewelry (I'd had to remove my rings—including my engagement ring—ten pounds ago). None of my shoes fit because of my swollen feet so I couldn't leave the house even if I wanted to. I'd broken out on my chest, back, and face. I credited the sweating. My stomach was so stretched that I found myself getting hungry every hour. I'd gone through the entire bottle of thyroid stimulants. I couldn't bring myself to work on any magazine articles.

Instead, I turned on the TV to watch the soaps. The phone rang. I prayed it wasn't the *Cosmo* editor.

"Hello?" I asked.

"Amanda Bennet?"

"Dr. Schwartz, thank God it's you."

"Amanda, listen to me. I want you to come to NYU immediately." She was a forced calm. Was I dying? I burst into tears. "Amanda," she said, "call a car service and come here right away. I'm going to help you. Can you call a car?" She spoke to me as if I were a child.

"I'll be there as soon as I can."

184 I'd been at the hospital for two days. I was relieved to be wearing the comfortable hospital gown—no bra—and not any constrictive clothes. I checked my machine a couple times, but I'd stopped returning calls. Editors called about stories. Fred was frantic. Jeanie from *Consumer Reports* said there was a class-action suit in the works against Belinda Contral. She had the lawyer's address and phone number if I wanted it. Would I mind if she gave him my number? No calls from anyone connected to or with information on Belinda Contral herself.

When I first arrived at the hospital, Dr. Schwartz gave it to me straight. She'd had my gynecologist fax over my medical history. Did I know I had a hypoactive thyroid? I told her I assumed so, or I wouldn't have blown up like a zeppelin in two weeks. She meant, did I know I had a thyroid condition before taking the REDUCE? I shook my head. She handed me the box of REDUCE I'd given her. She pointed to a paragraph in small print on the bottom of the box. I read it out loud: "If you have a hypoactive thyroid or any other kind of thyroid condition, please consult your doctor before using."

I said, "I didn't read this."

"Your thyroid has been yanked in so many different directions—you haven't abused the prescription I gave you?" I nodded yes. "That's what I thought. I'd like to put you on an IV, get you on a liquid diet and keep you here for observation for a few days. I'm afraid the incredible weight gain in such a short amount of time has put a strain on your heart. Your blood sugar is sky high, as is your cholesterol. You're twenty-eight years old and on the verge of a heart attack." Attack. Fat attack. The words screamed in my ears.

I said, "I'm supposed to get married in a week."

Dr. Schwartz frowned. "Do you want me to call your fiancé?"

"No," I said. "He won't understand." Would he? I wondered. Was I underestimating Fred? He'd told me he would still marry me if I weighed 200 pounds. From the way things have been going, I'd be up there come the wedding day. I told Dr. Schwartz I'd call my parents myself.

180 I was "stabilized" and had actually lost four pounds. I felt a glimmer of hope and rescheduled my appointment with the tailor to two days before the wedding. I warned her that I'd gained some weight. I hoped I'd lose the fifty pounds in the next four days, though I knew in my heart that wasn't possible. Then again, I didn't think it possible to gain fifty pounds in two and a half weeks.

I finally called my father and told him what happened. He was furious. I pretended to hear concern in his voice. He asked if the wedding was off and I told him no. I was losing the weight and Fred loved me for me, not for the useless size 8 dresses that hung in my closet. I called up Jeanie and told her where I was, not to worry, everything would be okay.

My dad must have called Fred, because he showed up at the hospital the next day with flowers for me. My dad must have warned him, too, because he didn't run screaming out of my room when he saw me. I smiled and cried even. I hadn't lied. I'd been sick and now I was getting better. He kissed my forehead and cried too. He asked me how long it would take me to lose the weight. I couldn't make a guess. A few months. Years. But it didn't matter, he said. He loved me and he'd stand by me.

I was happy for a few hours after he left. The lawyer Jeanie told me about called and asked me to join the class-action suit. He reported that over two thousand people have had similar experiences with REDUCE. The FDA examination of the stuff proved that it was actually a thyroid suppressant that would make the user *gain* weight. He believed the whole thing was a scam to make sure people ordered more REDUCE when they didn't see immediate results. Belinda herself claimed yesterday that she'd been rooked too. She was just a struggling actor—real name Maggie Reardon. She had disassociated herself with the company and insisted she knew nothing of the scam.

I asked the lawyer for a business address for the company. He waffled, but eventually gave it to me. It was the same address on the REDUCE box in Elizabeth, New Jersey. The lawyer knew their phone had been disconnected—they were trying to avoid angry callers. He gave me the unlisted number.

178 Dr. Schwartz sent me to my parents' place in Short Hills two days before the wedding after conferring with my father. I wasn't trusted to spend the time alone in my Brooklyn apartment. Dad was to administer my medication and monitor my caloric intake. My mother cried when she saw me. My father couldn't bring himself to hug me, he was so clearly disgusted. Nonetheless, the tents went up in the backyard and the caterers set up extra stoves in the garage.

I kept my appointment with the tailor. She nearly fainted when I walked in. She said the alterations couldn't be done in two days. She'd have to slice the gown wide open and add several panels to the bust, the waist, the arms. It couldn't be done. I begged her to try and made her an offer she couldn't refuse. She agreed to it and we left it at that. I'd pick up the dress the morning of the wedding.

Fred called to make sure everything was okay. He confessed to feeling betrayed by my lies. I apologized and meant it. He accepted. We said we loved each other and that we couldn't wait to get married. I thought I heard some hesitation in his voice, but I chose to ignore it.

In forty-eight hours, I'd be a bride.

180 I bounced a couple of pounds up the scale on my wedding day. I blamed my midnight sneak assault on some of the premade hors d'oeuvres my mother had stocked in the fridge. My mother cried in the morning when she saw how many dumplings and stuffed mushrooms I'd scarfed. I promised her I wouldn't eat another thing ever again, as long as I lived.

I went to pick up the gown. It looked pieced together with visible seams and tacking. The tailor had tears in her eyes when she handed over the dress. I tried it on. I looked like a massive off-white silk elephant. The tailor sighed and said, "It was so beautiful once." I didn't feel a tingle of guilt. But depression, yes. That began to set in when I pulled off the highway to grab a Big Mac on the way home from the tailor's. What was wrong with me? I was on the verge of a heart attack, I was wearing a (tight) housecoat my mother picked up at Kmart, and I was still stuffing my face. No wonder Dr. Schwartz didn't trust me. I certainly couldn't trust myself.

182 The wedding was one hour behind schedule. According to Fred's parents—they'd been horrified to see me—he should have arrived hours ago. My mother had nearly bitten her lip clean off, and my father kept staring at my fat and muttering, "Thirty thousand dollars."

I wasn't an idiot. When the phone call came—Fred was at the airport about to board a plane for San Francisco—I wasn't surprised.

"Amanda, I'm so sorry," he said.

"I won't be fat forever, Fred," I said.

"The doctor said you might. She said you can't control your eating and that your thyroid gland is totally wrecked."

"It's not my fault. That woman, Belinda Contral. She swindled me."

"She didn't put a gun to your head and make you pick up the phone."

"I did it for you," I accused. But I knew that was another lie.

"This isn't easy for me either, Amanda," he said. "I'm losing you too."

I realized then that Fred was gone forever. He'd never come back to me after this. And the simple fact that he was leaving me because I'd gained, what, fifty little pounds? Come on. He said he'd marry me if I weighed 200 pounds. I wasn't even close to that. I said, "You promised, Fred." I looked down the length of my wedding gown. Fat, I thought.

"Good-bye, Amanda," he said and hung up.

185 The guests were informed of the horrible news and everyone went home. They still had a Saturday night stretched in front of them. Some of my friends wanted to stay and help me, but I couldn't take their staring. I sent them home and felt lonelier than I thought possible. I was left with ten thousand dollars' worth of pâté, wedding cake, champagne, and the angry, hurt faces of my parents. I'd ruined it for them, clearly. I'd ruined it for me. I went up to my old bedroom with a large platter of salmon, roast beef, and goat cheese and locked myself in. While I ate, I thought. My life had been destroyed in a mere three weeks. All because of the REDUCE. I remembered I had the phone number of Contral Inc. in my purse. I called it from my room as I munched sun-dried tomato toast. The phone rang and rang. Finally, a woman answered and said, "Jimmy, is that you?"

"Hello?" I asked. The voice was throaty and harsh. I wasn't sure . . .

"Jimmy? I'm going to kill you if you don't get your ass over here." It was her. Belinda Contral. The actor who said she had nothing to do with the company. Taking calls at the business number. In Elizabeth, New Jersey, three exits away from Short Hills on the Garden State Parkway. As she continued to berate this poor Jimmy fellow, I flashed to that commercial. Fat attack. I lost the weight, you can, too. The slide of her—not her—three hundred pounds ago. Belinda karate-kicking her slim muscular legs. She's never been fat. I knew it now in my heart. I hung up the phone and grabbed my purse.

My mother was weeping softly in my father's arms in the living room. They didn't seem to notice me take the car keys out of my mother's purse. I got in the Subaru and drove south, toward Elizabeth.

I got to the office building in twenty minutes. I was still wearing my wedding gown. The building was unlocked. There was a reception desk in the lobby, but I didn't see anyone around. I didn't sign in at the desk. I didn't notice any surveillance cameras in the lobby or in the elevator. I got off on the sixth floor. The office door was locked. I pushed the bell and, sure enough, Belinda Contral answered the door.

She was tiny—even smaller than she looked on TV. She couldn't have weighed more than 100 pounds. She was about five feet two or three. Her red hair was cut in a bob that flattered her cheekbones. She was an attractive person. She was wearing a pair of jeans and a tank top. I used to wear that same outfit every day when I could button my jeans.

She cocked an eyebrow at my wedding gown and said, "The office is closed on Saturdays. If you want to place an order, call 1-800-FAT-ATAK. Fight the enemy. Attack the fat." She started to close the door in my face. I leaned my weight against it and pushed my way inside. I closed the door behind me.

She said, "What the fuck do you think you're doing? Get the fuck out of here."

"You ruined my life, Belinda Contral."

"Oh, Jesus, another one. Listen, fatso, I didn't do a damn thing but go on television. If you really wanted to lose weight, you'd eat less and exercise more. But you wanted the quick way out. No work. All easy."

I thought of Fred and his 1-800-EAT-LESS idea. I said, "My fiancé left me because of you."

"It isn't my fault you're lazy."

I said, "You took advantage of all of those people."

"I didn't do anything."

"You scammed all those people," I said. "And you're going to pay."

Her face contorted in anger. "Nothing is going to happen to me, you disgusting fat piece of shit. You make me sick. You stink of sweat. You're revolting. I'm sorry you think I did this to you, but I've got news for you, honey. You did this to yourself. And you'd better get your disgusting fat ass out of here before I call the cops."

My anger was surfacing now. Fred leaving me. My wedding, ruined. My parents. I took a step toward her. She backed away, scared, uncertain. I felt a tinge of power rush over me. I took another step. Belinda squared off like she was about to karate chop me. I said, "If you want me to leave, you're going to have to make me."

Without missing a beat, Belinda kicked the air, not two inches from my face. I'd raised my arms to block the blow and somehow caught her ankle. I lifted her leg and flipped her. On her back on the carpet, she kicked me in the knees and I fell on the floor right on top of her. I heard something crack as I landed on her rib cage. She started screaming.

I flashed to when Fred and I first heard her commercial on TV. We'd been kissing. I felt a few tears roll down my round cheek. I barely heard the snap of bones or her gurgles and choking sounds. I heard only the words, "Attack the enemy," screaming in my ears. I bounced up and down on Belinda as she struggled to push me off. I outweighed her by eighty pounds. No contest. After a few minutes, there was no fight left in her. I got up and noticed the blue tint to her skin. It matched the spun sugar flowers on my wedding cake.

A bookshelf leaned against the wall behind us. I pulled it down and it fell right on top of Belinda's body. I found a tissue on top of the desk to wipe the tears and sweat off my face and to clean the buzzer and door handle.

I walked out of the office building and found my car. Instead of heading back to my parents' house, I drove south, toward the Jersey shore. I felt a sudden desire to touch the Atlantic Ocean. After about ten minutes, I caught my breath. That slaying had been quite a workout. I must have sweat off at least a couple pounds.

ONE GOOD TURN

· ·

By J. A. Jance

Was she out there again, waiting for him? Gary Spenser wondered. Probably. Most likely in fact. When did that woman sleep?

The second question was one Gary Spenser couldn't answer. He had no idea. It seemed to him she was always there—always outside whatever place he happened to be, always waiting for him.

Lurking was more like it. Wherever he went, he found himself listening for the distinctive idle of the engine on her hand-controlled, wheelchair-equipped Vanagon. Every morning when he left the house to go to work, the now-familiar van would be there waiting for him. Since Gary preferred working the early shift, the van's driver did, too. Her van would follow his Toyota 4–×–4, keeping it well within sight from the time Gary left the condo's garage in downtown Seattle until he pulled into the Boeing lot in Renton.

In the afternoons, after work, he would find the van and driver waiting for him once more, parked just outside the plant gates when he got off shift and headed home. After retracing the morning route, she would park her blue and white Syncro in the handicapped zone directly in front of his building. She was such a permanent fixture in that spot that some of Gary Spenser's neighbors probably thought she lived in the same building.

And her shadowing of Gary Spenser didn't end there, either. In the evenings, if he went out for dinner or to have a few beers, she would be lying in wait for him still—her eyes scanning restlessly for him over the top of some unread newspaper or book. She made no attempt at subterfuge or subtlety. No, she brazenly parked her van outside his various but usual hangouts—the bars or restaurants, the grocery stores or movie theaters—where he squandered his precious hours of leisure time.

What a pain! And what the hell else did Nyla Pollock want from him anyway? According to the judge's sentence, Gary Spenser had long since paid his debt to society. He had been forced to take out a loan at the credit union in order to cough up enough cash to pay the outrageous fine. And he had worked off his two hundred hours of community service by answering telephones at the local drug and alcohol hot line. Except for driving to and from work—which the sentencing judge had expressly allowed—Gary Spenser was walking, wasn't he? Even a crazy woman couldn't ask for much more than that.

For the tenth time that evening or maybe even the twentieth Gary Spenser fought back the urge to get up and walk over to the dirty, neon-framed window of Spike's Place. He had to battle the temptation to look outside and see for himself whether or not she was there.

Even without looking, he knew she would be. Of course she would. In his mind's eye he could see Nyla Pollock sitting hunched over her van's steering wheel like some dangerous female vulture—waiting for him to step out of line so she could dive down out of the sky and nail Gary Spenser's poor, hardworking ass to the ground.

Think again, bitch, he thought to himself. You're not going to catch me doing anything wrong. Not tonight, and not ever.

Without being asked Spike Malvern fetched Gary another beer, bringing it from the tap at the far end of the bar and setting it in front of Gary. Spike paused long enough to light a cigarette.

"So, is your girlfriend out there again tonight?"

When Spike asked the question, he intended it as a bit of harmless conversation, but Gary Spenser's stony silence warned the bartender that he had gone too far. Spike hated like hell to offend one of his best customers. That was bad for business.

"Want me to check for you?" he offered.

"No. Forget it!" Gary Spenser replied shortly. "Just leave me alone, will you?"

"Sure thing," Spike replied.

The bartender retreated down the bar, leaving Gary Spenser to stew in his own solitary juices.

What's the matter with me? Gary wondered. Why not let Spike look? And why am I so damn touchy about it?

Maybe Nyla Pollock really was beginning to get to him. No, it wasn't Nyla herself so much as it was the idea of Nyla Pollock and the pressure of wondering about her: Would she be there or not? And what was she going to do? And when?

It mystified Gary that not getting up to look out the window should use up so much energy and take such a tremendous amount of willpower. How could not looking be harder than looking? And what the hell difference did it make if he verified her presence with his very own eyes or if Spike did it with his? And why did he need to know in the first place?

The series of questions buzzed around in his head like a swarm of angry bees. Killer bees, he thought wryly. Just like Nyla Pollock.

The whole thing was crazy anyway. Looking or not looking—it didn't matter. After all, she had been there waiting for him everywhere he went for months now. Why would tonight be any different? Why agonize over it? What was the matter with him?

It was impossible to explain—even to himself—why Gary Spenser needed so desperately to see whether or not she was out there. What kind of fool went around checking on ghosts? And Nyla Pollock seemed far more like a ghost than she did anything else.

Gary had spoken to her in person only once although they had seen each other daily for months now. In the beginning, she had been nothing more than a vaguely threatening presence—disturbing, but not a clear and present danger. Now, a year later, although nothing in Nyla's outward appearance had changed, Gary Spenser was taking her far more seriously.

He was bright enough to realize that if anyone had changed, he had. Against his will, he had somehow let her into his life—his consciousness. He found himself wondering about her wherever he went—whatever he did—at home or at work, at all hours of the day and night. She had become an unwanted fixture in his mind. Sometimes he seemed to be viewing life through her eyes, not his, interpreting his actions through Nyla Pollock's frame of reference.

No wonder he wondered about her. No wonder he had to fight the obsessive compulsion to check whether or not she was there. The urge to check and the ever-increasing difficulty in resisting that urge had become symbolic of the running battle between himself and that unwelcome third-party in his head. It seemed as though Nyla's presence was similar to a newly broken molar. Checking on her was like running a tongue over the rough edges of a freshly cracked tooth. He did it not because it would do any good and not because it didn't hurt, but simply to confirm the fact that the broken tooth existed—that it was real.

So was Nyla Pollock, Gary Spenser thought grimly. Inside his head and out of it. She existed all right. In spades.

Unlike so many other times, however, on this particular occasion Gary succeeded in resisting the compulsion to look. He did it by resorting to a simple mind game, by playing a clumsy but effective trick on himself. He pretended that someone had superglued his worn Levi's to the equally worn orange vinyl cushion on Spike's rickety bar stool.

The mental picture of someone with a chrome-and-vinyl bar stool stuck firmly to his ass trying to walk unobtrusively to the window definitely struck Gary Spenser's funny bone. Not only did it keep him from moving, but it caused a snort of laughter to bubble to the surface. He stifled the sound as soon as he could, burying it with a phony cough. After all, he didn't want his cronies in the bar to think he was the one who was crazy.

Polishing off the last gulp of his latest beer, Gary hunkered down on the stool and tried to shut out the racket from a noisy bunch of rowdies at the far end of the bar.

Those guys were the real drunks, Gary Spenser thought bitterly. He knew for a fact that each and every one of them had at least one DWI, and they were all still driving their own cars whenever and wherever they damn well pleased. Where was the justice in that?

One of them—a guy close to Gary's age who at that very moment could barely stand up on his own two feet—was pontificating at tedious length about why the Seattle Mariners—thanks to this fairly new group of local owners—finally had a shot at the pennant. Two of the drunk's buddies said it would never happen.

Who the hell gave a damn? Spenser wondered irritably. No matter who owned the Mariners—local or not, foreign or not—Gary Spenser personally considered them a worthless team of losers who would never win anything but a permanent berth in major league baseball's bottommost basement.

Impatiently, Gary raised his empty glass and caught Spike's eye.

"Hey, barkeep," he called. "Leave those guys be and hit me again."

Spike extracted himself from the baseball debate and brought yet another Miller Draft with him when he came down the bar. Anxious to know if all was forgiven, he set down the foaming glass and ignored the stack of bills and change sitting on the bar next to Gary's elbow.

"This one's on the house," he said.

Spenser nodded his thanks.

"Can't you do something about her, get a court order or something?" Spike nodded significantly toward the door. "I mean that woman follows you everywhere you go. Seems like harassment to me. Isn't it illegal? I thought the guys down in Olympia just passed a law about that."

Gary shook his head. "She never says a word to me, so there's been no threat. Until she does—threaten me, that is—my lawyer tells me I haven't got a leg to stand on."

"What a bummer," Spike murmured sympathetically. "It's not like you did it on purpose or anything."

"No," Gary agreed. "It wasn't on purpose at all."

In fact, he still didn't know exactly how he had hit Bryan Pollock's Honda. The accident had happened just over a year ago now on a Friday night. Gary had stopped off for a drink or two or maybe three after work. He had spent the better part of the evening at a little joint down in Renton—a fern bar not far from the plant.

Maybe he had stayed there drinking longer than he had intended. And maybe he had indeed had a little too much to drink, but he sure as hell wasn't that drunk. Not falling-down drunk like those baseball freaks down the bar.

Gary had tried to explain the whole situation to that officious jerk of a snot-nosed cop—had tried to tell him that the glare of the setting sun had somehow blinded him for a fraction of a second. But that pushy little creep of a cop was only interested in one thing—giving Gary the damn Breathalyzer test. Which he had flunked. Royally. Big deal.

But if the medics had been a little more on the stick— if they had worked the damn jaws of life better and faster—maybe the damn kid wouldn't have died. Sure some of it was Gary's fault. Spenser knew that, and he was sorry it had happened. In fact, he had told Nyla Pollock that very thing, face-to-face, in the courtroom, just before the judge sentenced him. But she hadn't given him any kind of acknowledgment or answer. From the look on her face, she might have gone stone-cold deaf. She had just sat there in that motorized wheelchair of hers, staring up at him in the same vacant, lifeless way she did now—every single time he saw her.

"Got a light?"

A low-pitched but pleasant female voice jarred Gary out of his solitary contemplation. Startled to have someone else intrude on his private thoughts, Gary Spenser glanced to his right to see a well-built young woman in short shorts and a skimpy halter top sitting on the bar stool next to his. She was gorgeous—summer-bronzed— and much, much too good looking for Spike's Place.

One look at her convinced Gary that she must be from out of town—California maybe—and had wandered into Spike's sleazy Pioneer Square establishment by mistake. No one who looked like that ever came into Spike's on purpose.

She must have been sitting there for some time since the cocktail glass in front of her was already almost empty. She tapped the end of her cigarette on the bar.

Despite all that had happened to him, Gary Spenser hadn't managed to give up drinking. However, he had quit smoking. Completely. Spike's yellow Bic lighter was lying on the counter, well within reach, but Gary made no effort to pick it up.

"A pretty girl like you shouldn't smoke," he said pointedly. "It's bad for your health."

"So's drinking," the young woman returned.

With an indifferent shrug, she got up, walked around Gary to the lighter, lit her own cigarette, and then returned to her original place at the bar. Gary more than half expected her to make a big issue of it, but when she blew the first plume of smoke into the air, she sent it swirling down the bar away from both of them.

That's something at least, Gary thought. You couldn't expect young kids to be even that polite most of the time.

"Touché," Gary said, lifting his glass to her in mock salute before taking another sip of beer.

She returned the favor with a raised-glass salutation of her own. "Here's to you," she countered.

It wasn't exactly the beginning of a beautiful relationship, but Gary had to admit she was an amazingly beautiful piece of ass. It intrigued him to realize that he was actually noticing a woman for a change—that he was even interested. After all, in the past year, he hadn't exactly gone out of his way looking for female companionship. Why bother?

For one thing, it was too damn cumbersome to explain why, if a date wanted to do something that took them outside the immediate downtown neighborhood, they would have to take her car and she would have to drive. Not only that, with the extra damn king's ransom he was having to pay in auto insurance premiums these days, he couldn't afford to date much. He was too damned old fashioned to expect a woman to go dutch treat. As a consequence, he had read a lot of books from the Seattle Public Library, and he had watched hell out of his damn television set.

"You live around here?"

Gary looked up to see that the young woman's surprisingly green eyes were frankly appraising his reflection in the smoke-hazed mirror behind the bar. Her hair was an unruly blond cloud haloing out around her head. A mischievous but not unpleasant smile played around the corners of her generous, crimson-colored lips, allowing occasional glimpses of straight white teeth.

This girl was a looker all right, even just from the

neck up. And in her revealing halter top, she wasn't bad from the neck down, either. Not by a long shot!

Gary jerked his head in the general direction of his building—a relatively new and moderately priced condo development a stone's throw away from the Kingdome. He liked living downtown, and his building wasn't bad as long as the Mariners or the Seahawks weren't playing a home game. Then getting in and out was an absolute nightmare.

"Just down the street a ways," he said. "How about you?"

"I'm from San Diego," she answered. "Up here on vacation. Somebody at the hotel said I should take in the Seattle Underground tour."

"Did you?" Gary asked.

She took a drink, made a face, and nodded. "I bailed out halfway through. Who cares about walking through musty old buildings and hearing that they had to put purple glass in the sidewalks so dirty old men wouldn't hang around underneath and look up women's skirts? since when is *that* news?"

Since when indeed! Gary Spenser had been surreptitiously examining the girl's shapely legs, but he stopped that now. Abruptly.

"Where are you staying?" he asked.

"The Edgewater. Ever heard of it?"

"The Beatles stayed there once," he replied informatively, trying to impress her with his knowledge of local history and color.

"Who are the Beatles?" she asked. But then, when Gary started feeling his age—hemming and hawing around in confusion and trying to explain, she relented and laughed it off.

"Hey," she said with a grin. "Don't get your sweat hot, mister. I was just teasing. The Beatles may have been a little before my time, but I'm not stupid. I do know who they were. And yes, the desk clerk—the same fool who sent me down here for the Underground Tour in the first place—also told me they stayed there. It must have been something if people in Seattle still talk about it after all these years. Or doesn't much happen around here? How long has John Lennon been dead anyway?"

"I don't know," Gary Spenser answered, shaking his

head and feeling every one of his fifty-two years. "Seems like a long time."

Meanwhile, he was busy computing the years in his head. How long was it since the Beatles broke up? If this girl was that young—and she did seem like a girl not a woman—what the hell was she doing talking to an old guy like him in the first place? Was she a hooker or what? Could be, although she didn't seem to have any of the hard, sharp edges your professional whores usually had. And none of them ever bothered with the regular denizens of Spike's Place. They all knew in advance there was no percentage in it.

Gary upended his glass and raised his forefinger. As if operating on radar, Spike caught the classic barroom signal.

"Another?" he called from down the bar, turning away from the Mariners conversation—both a little drunker now as well as a little louder.

Spenser nodded. "And bring one for the lady," he added.

"Thanks," she said.

"The name's Gary," he told her casually. "What's yours."

"Bree."

"Isn't that some kind of high-toned cheese?"

"Different spelling," she answered. "It's short for Breeze. My mother was one of those aging hippies—tie-dyed shirts, love beads, and all. It could have been worse, I suppose. She could have called me Moonbeam."

They both laughed at that. Gary was glad the girl seemed to have a sense of humor. So many women didn't.

"So what's fun to do around here?" she asked.

"You here by yourself?"

"Pretty much."

"What does that mean?"

"It means I flew up with a girlfriend from work—another dental hygienist. We had planned this trip for months, but she must've got into some kind of bad food yesterday. Today she's sick as a dog. We were supposed to drive up to Mount Rainier this morning—breakfast in Paradise—but I didn't want to do that all by myself. And it didn't seem fair that, after spending all that money, I should have to stay around the hotel room and hold her hand while she barfed her guts out. There must be something more fun to do than that.''

Gary smiled inwardly and took the drink Spike pushed across the bar to him. He could think of one or two fun things himself, he thought wryly. Maybe even more than one or two.

He turned slightly and examined the young woman's classic profile. Her fine-boned features seemed oddly familiar to him somehow, although he couldn't quite place her.

"I know this must sound like the oldest line in the book," he said, shaking his head, "but it seems like I've seen you somewhere before."

"Do you happen to have a dentist in San Diego?" she returned brightly.

"Nope. Mine's in the Medical-Dental Building right here in downtown Seattle."

She tossed her mane of hair and laughed. "Well then," she said with a smile, "it must be a case of mistaken identity."

They both drank in silence for a moment or two, then he caught her regarding him somewhat more seriously.

"So," she said determinedly. "Would you like to go do something or not?"

Before answering, Gary Spenser took another long drink of beer. It was a feeble and entirely unsuccessful attempt to conceal both his growing confusion and his fear. Because that was the bottom line. He really was afraid, and he didn't know how to react.

If you spend your life living with a shadow, you don't have to worry about the shadow's reaction to the passing of the hours or to what goes on around you. The faithful phantom at your feet grows long or short, thin or fat, dark or light, depending on the hour of the day, the angle of the sun, and the prevailing weather. But Nyla Pollock wasn't nearly as predictable as a shadow. Nor as harmless, either.

This was one of those tricky, mine-filled areas between Nyla Pollock and himself that Gary Spenser had never before cared to test or even recognize. That was the other reason he hadn't done any dating in the past year. Plain and simple, he had been afraid to. He hadn't dared.

What if his appearing outside the confines of his own

apartment with a woman—any attractive woman—was enough to push Nyla Pollock over the edge? After all, her only son would never have an opportunity to do any of those same things—to find and court a woman. To marry her and perhaps sire a child.

Not that Gary had any preconceived notions about getting it on with this young woman—of getting lucky and maybe making a baby for God's sake. Not even likely! But still, at the relatively ripe old age of fifty-two, the heretofore unused fatherhood option was still open and available for Gary Spenser. At what would have been age twenty-four, it wasn't an open option for Bryan Pollock, and it would never be again.

"So what are you, gay or something?' Bree demanded, sounding irritated that her question had thus far been ignored. She had signaled Spike for yet another round of drinks. Once he delivered it and picked up the money, Bree swilled hers down as though it was water. Gary still had half a glass of beer left in the one drink. His next was lined up and waiting for him on the bar.

Gary downed the remaining half glass and pulled the new one in front of him while his ears burned bright red in humiliation. He had been carefully pacing himself all night long. If she hadn't started talking to him, he would have called it a night and headed home long before now. He had hurried the last beer or two more than he should have, and they had hit him pretty hard—a lot harder than he would have expected.

Maybe it was true. Maybe he couldn't drink the way he could when he was younger. But he wasn't going to sit there and let this little slip of a girl drink him under the table. And insult his damn masculinity in the process.

"I'm not gay," he answered huffily, "which I'd be happy to demonstrate if you have either the time or the inclination. I just have this little problem, that's all."

"Problem? Like a disease you mean?"

My God! Where were girls coming from these days? "No disease!" he answered sharply.

"What then? Are you married? I notice you're not wearing a ring."

"I'm not married," he said. "But I could just as well be. You ever heard of MADD?"

"The magazine?"

"No. Not that one. Mothers Against Drunk Drivers. They're this group of radical women—mothers most of them—who want to get all the drunk drivers in the world off the road."

Bree nodded. "Oh, yes. I have heard of them. They've all lost kids in drunk driving accidents, right?"

"Right. I was in an accident like that last year. I was driving. A boy was killed—a twenty-three-year-old kid by the name of Bryan Pollock who had just graduated from Seattle University. His mother's van is parked right outside. In the handicapped zone. She follows me everywhere I go."

In the hazy mirror, the reflections of their two pairs of eyes met and held. "You mean she follows you around like in one of those creepy old James Bond movies?"

"Just like." Gary nodded.

"But is she dangerous? I mean, does she carry a gun or anything?"

"I can't tell, and there's no way for me to find out. All I know is she's always there. Sometimes it feels like she's deliberately trying to drive me crazy."

Bree reached over and let her fingertips graze Gary's upper arm with a light, feathery touch while her eyes glowed dark with sudden sympathy.

"I think that's terrible," she asserted, "tormenting you like that. I'm sure you feel bad enough about it already."

Expressions of sympathy from strangers weren't common occurrences in Gary Spenser's narrow sphere of experience. The girl's unthinking yet open gesture of empathy touched him in a way he couldn't possibly have anticipated. A thick lump formed in his throat, making speech difficult.

"I do," he croaked almost inaudibly. "God knows I do."

Bree reached down and picked up a purple-and-yellow-striped canvas bag that had been resting unnoticed on the grimy hardwood floor between her rickety bar stool and Gary's.

"Gather up your money," she ordered in a way that implied she wouldn't accept no for an answer. "We're getting out of here. You and I are going to go someplace else and have some fun. I thought I needed cheering up, but you're in a hell of a lot worse shape than I am. Come on."

Gary chugged the rest of his beer, left five bucks on the counter for Spike, and jammed the remainder of his change into his pocket.

"Is there a back way out of this joint?" Bree was asking.

"Sure," Spike answered. "Out through the alley past the Dumpster, but . . ."

"That's the way we're going," Bree announced flatly. "And if anyone comes looking for my friend here, tell them he wasn't feeling well and that he's holed up in the head." She finished by giving Spike an exaggerated, green-eyed wink.

"Gotcha," Spike answered with a conspiratorial grin. "It's about time somebody woke Poppa Bear up and dragged him out of hibernation."

Once Gary allowed himself to be pulled upright, it took a couple of steps before his ungainly legs and feet got workwise, but with Bree's solicitous guidance, he stumbled clumsily toward the bar's back door. Outside in the alley she led him past two more drunks who were loudly debating the ownership of a bottle of Thunderbird. Keeping to the alley, Bree took Gary two full blocks away from Nyla Pollock's waiting van before they cut across First Avenue and headed over to Alaskan Way.

After the warm stuffiness and stale, cigarette smoke-encrusted atmosphere of Spike's Place, the fresh air along Seattle's waterfront seemed delightfully cool and refreshing. Summer-warmed salt water from Puget Sound lapped gently against creosote-saturated pilings, giving off a sharp, pungent odor. Late in June, it was still not quite dark at nine-thirty at night. The streets thronged with tourists out using the long warm evening hours to laugh and spend money and have a good time.

Had Gary Spenser been born in a later era, he might have been worrying about AIDS and condoms right about then, but like that guy in the old country-western, shit-kicking song, Gary Spenser was still lost in the fifties. Instead of thinking about "safe-sex," he was suffering from a terrible case of what television's Dr. Ruth would refer to as "performance anxiety."

What if he tried taking Bree home to bed, and he couldn't get it up? Or, worse yet, what if after months of celibate living, he got so excited that he went off way too soon?

Gary Spenser may have been out of the game for a while, but he was sure he wasn't misreading the signals. Bree was interested in him all right. Interested and eager even. Gary Spenser was determined to measure up to her expectations. But what he needed most right about then was time enough to sober up slightly before push came to shove.

"Have you ever taken a ferry ride?" he asked.

As soon as the words were out of his mouth, he wanted to take them back. What if she thought him hopelessly romantic or stupid or maybe a little of both?

"A ferry ride?" she responded. "Where to?"

He shrugged. "Out across the Sound. Over to Winslow or Bremerton. The city skyline's beautiful at night. We could walk onto the ferry, take a round-trip, and end up right back here later on."

"How long would it take?"

"An hour or two. It depends on whether we catch a Bremerton or a Winslow. We'll take whichever one leaves next."

"Sounds good to me," Bree answered enthusiastically. Gary Spenser breathed a heartfelt sigh of relief.

The two of them were the last two walk-on passengers before the Winslow Ferry, the "Sealth," sounded its horn and began to pull away from the Coleman Ferry Dock.

"There's your hotel," Gary pointed out when the Edgewater's huge red "E" came into view. "You can hardly miss it."

"Hardly," Bree agreed. Reaching into her purse, she pulled out a pack of cigarettes. She lit her filter-tip with one hand cupped carefully around a match to ward off the stiff ocean breeze. When the wind ruffled her hair, she shivered.

"You're cold," Gary observed. "We can go inside where it's warmer."

Bree shook her head. "No. I like it out here, really. It's just that it's a lot cooler up here than what I'm used to."

Without another word, Gary shrugged his way out of his sports jacket and slipped it over Bree's cool, bare shoulders. Then they both leaned against the guardrail on their elbows and watched as the downtown Seattle skyline receded into the night. For some time they were forced to share the rear upper deck with a busload of Japanese tourists who kept the deck alive with noisy talk and snapping photo flashes.

"You're right," Bree said eventually. "It really is beautiful out here on the water. Thank you for inviting me."

Gary tried to sound casual. "I had almost forgotten about it myself," he returned. "I haven't done this in years. It always takes visitors from out of town to get the locals to play tourist."

"This accident thing has been really tough on you, hasn't it," she ventured.

Gary hung his head. "Yes," he allowed. "Yes, it has."

For a time neither of them spoke. There was only the comforting rumble of the ferry's powerful engines and the rush of water churning in the ship's wake.

"Tell me about him," Bree urged quietly.

Gary looked over at her. He could have played stupid and pretended he didn't know what she meant. He had no idea how it had happened, but he realized that somehow the two of them had already moved well beyond the realm of casual conversation.

"I don't know if I can," he answered uncertainly.

"Try," she said.

Except for oblique remarks to Spike or some other barkeep now and then, Gary Spenser had avoided discussing the issue of his accident almost entirely. But now, standing on that pulsing ferry deck and talking with a complete stranger, he was finally able to talk about it.

"Bryan Pollock was evidently a good kid," Gary said huskily. "His crippled mother's only child, for one thing. He was a top student and a gifted basketball player. Not good enough to make it in the pros most likely, but he played first-string collegiate ball from the time he was a sophomore. When he graduated from Seattle U., he had already been accepted by three different medical schools."

"What a waste," Bree murmured. "No wonder his mother's upset."

"No wonder," Gary Spenser agreed ashamedly, hanging his head. And for the very first time since it happened, he really was ashamed of what he had done. He made no attempt to spew out his usual string of self-justifying excuses.

"And I don't blame her," he added. "I mean, I understand her beef, but I just wish sometimes she'd leave me alone and let me get back to my own life. Know what I mean?"

They were standing very close together now, leaning out over the rail. The tour guide had long since herded his camera-toting group inside, so Bree and Gary were alone on the upper deck, standing just beyond the pale yellow glow of the overhead lights that both lit and warmed the outside benches. After another long silence, Bree tossed away the glowing stub of her latest cigarette, sending it arcing into the water. Then, without a word, she leaned over and kissed Gary Spenser on the cheek.

It was a gentle, caressing type kiss—the kind a mother might give a small boy as she put him down for an afternoon nap.

"First you have to forgive yourself," she said quietly.

He looked over at her, surprised and shamed by the sudden sting of tears in his eyes. In all the preceding months, he had never cried. Not once. God knows he had felt like it a thousand times over, but the tears had refused to come. Now they did, cascading down his cheeks, dripping off his chin, making him feel like a damn fool. And a wimp besides.

"Maybe that's her problem, too," Bree said thoughtfully.

"Nyla Pollock's problem?" Gary managed at last while dragging a handkerchief out of his pocket. He blew his nose in noisy, foghorn fashion then mopped his damp eyes and wet face. "You mean she can't forgive me because she can't forgive herself?"

"Something like that."

"But what is it about Nyla Pollock that needs forgiving?"

"Who knows?" Bree returned with a shrug. "Everybody has something like that. We all do."

"Even you?"

She nodded. "Even me."

The ferry was curving in toward Winslow now, moving along beside the narrow band of lights that marked the opposite shore.

"How old are you?" Gary asked when he was able to speak again.

"Twenty-five. Why?"

"If that's all the older you are, how did you get to be so smart?"

"My mother was a child," she answered evenly. "Having a parent like that makes you grow up fast."

Gary nodded. "Maybe so," he agreed, "but how come you can be smart without being hard? So many women are these days, especially the smart ones. Some of them are so damn tough it's a wonder they don't shatter into a million pieces."

"I guess I'm lucky then, aren't I?" Bree returned with a smile, and she reached over and kissed him again.

Only this time it wasn't a motherly kiss on the cheek. The moon came out from behind a high-flying cloud and bathed the ferry's roiling wake in a silvery wash of light, but Gary and Bree were blind to its glowing phosphorescence. They were totally absorbed, wrapped in each other's arms, their lips and tongues melding and exploring.

When they broke apart, Gary Spenser was shaken and breathing hard. His face was as flushed as if he'd been drinking shot after shot of straight Jack Daniel's. But the sudden heat that flooded his body had nothing at all to do with alcohol. For the first time in months he felt absolutely sober.

"My God," he whispered in wondering gratitude. "I had forgotten what it felt like to want someone. To feel happy. To be alive."

Bree pulled away from him a little, but only far enough to look up into his eyes. "See there?" she asked with the impish grin once more playing on her face. "Didn't I say you needed cheering up?"

Wrapping her arms around his neck, she drew his face down close to hers once more and fastened her hungry lips against his. The bite of tobacco was sharp on her tongue as it darted in and out between Gary's upper and lower teeth. When he tasted it, the flavor was as tantalizing as forbidden fruit, and the sensation excited him almost beyond bearing.

Lost in another series of long, impassioned kisses, neither one of them noticed the ferry was slowing to a stop until the loud, raucous horn blasted into the night air around them, announcing the ferry's arrival at the Winslow dock.

Startled out of their necking, Gary and Bree jumped apart guiltily and then convulsed with laughter like a pair of giddy teenagers.

There was hardly anyone waiting at Winslow to make the return trip to Seattle. It wasn't long before the ferry started to move once more. Only one or two intrepid tourists ventured upstairs and outside, but they quickly retreated belowdecks, put off by the chill of the stiff evening breeze.

Lost in their own world, Gary and Bree were impervious to the cold. They stayed right where they were, not even bothering to move to the forward portion of the deck.

"Do you like to dance?" Bree asked suddenly

Gary shrugged. "Dance? I guess so," he said. "but I haven't done it in years, and I'm not very good."

"Let's dance."

"But how can we? There's no music."

"Watch this."

She knelt down and fumbled in the bag that had so far spent the entire ferry trip parked between their feet on the deck. She pulled something out of the bag and handed it up to Gary. When his fingers closed around it, he discovered he was holding a small, palm-size portable radio.

"It's a good one," Bree said, straightening up. "We should be able to get something decent on that. Does Seattle have any old-time music stations?"

"KIXI is the only one I know of," Gary said, fumbling stupidly with the dials. "It's an AM station. I forget the frequency."

"Here," she said, taking the radio from him. "Let me try."

For half a minute or so she fiddled with the buttons and dials. Soon the strains of Frank Sinatra singing a wonderfully apropos "Strangers in the Night" wafted around them.

"How's that for knowing how to pick 'em?" she asked with a laugh.

"That's great," Gary agreed. "Couldn't be better."

He took her in his arms, crushing her tightly against his chest. They danced, swaying gently in time to the music, one golden oldie after another. Once a green-jacketed ferry employee stuck his head out on the deck. Seeing them, he disappeared without a word.

"Ferry workers have to be exceptionally discreet," Gary said with a laugh. "I'll bet they see it all."

"I'll bet they do," Bree agreed.

Finally, as Seattle's skyline began to come into clearer focus, Bree seemed to tire of dancing. She led Gary over to the benches. Easing himself down onto one, Gary started to pull Bree down beside him, but she slipped out of his grasp.

"What you need now, my friend, is a good neck rub."

"You sound like a doctor dishing out a prescription."

"Maybe I am," she replied. "With all due humility, I'm very good at it. People say I have strong hands."

With that, she placed herself directly behind him, and stood there with her feet spread wide apart. She grasped the tops of his shoulders and began kneading them as though they were lumps of bread dough. Gary Spenser sighed. He closed his eyes and relaxed, giving himself over to her touch while months of stress and strain seemed to drain out of him.

This is one damn fine woman, he thought. Where the hell has she been all my life?

"Do you think you can?" Bree whispered softly.

She leaned forward and pulled his head back until he was resting against the soft, sweet swell of her breasts. Feeling her against him like that, Gary Spenser could barely talk, let alone think.

"Can what?" he managed, trying fuzzily to follow the conversation.

"Forgive yourself."

"Oh, that."

It was hard to form the words—like trying to speak a foreign language and make your tongue wrap itself around strange, unfamiliar sounds. In order to speak at all, he finally had to lean forward and pull away from her entirely. He sat with his head bowed as if in prayer. His voice, when it came, was choked with emotion.

"Maybe I can now, Bree," he said softly. "With your help, maybe by God I can."

Those were Gary Spenser's last words. His very last thoughts. He barely felt the razor-sharp blade of the six-inch knife that plunged deep into the back of his neck, severing his spinal cord and exploding the precious, life-sustaining medulla. His bent neck and massage-slackened muscles offered almost no resistance to the searching, deadly blade.

There was no time to respond or fight back or even cry out. It was over far too quickly for that, although not quite quickly enough to suit Bree. For what seemed like forever, his dying body heaved and leaped in space. It took all of Bree's considerable strength to keep him from flying off the bench. Only muscles honed by years of constant weight lifting made that possible.

At last the dreadful twitching stopped and Bree was able to take stock. She was proud of this almost blood-less kill, but still it wasn't entirely clean. Experience had taught her that killing never is.

Careful not to touch his shoes or any other smooth surface that might hold prints, she pulled his heavy legs up onto the bench and eased him into a reclining position. She covered him with his own jacket and closed his eyes. She found the empty beer bottle she had kept in her bag for that exact purpose. Carefully taking it out of its cloth wrapper, she pressed it into his hand and closed his flaccid fingers around it. Then she stood back and admired the total effect.

Gary Spenser looked just the way she had intended— like some hapless bum who had befouled himself while in a drunken stupor. With him reeking like that, no one would come too close to check on him. At least not right away.

Only when she was completely satisfied with her work did Bree pause long enough to carefully wipe off the knife. Then she walked over to the edge of the rail. Making sure no one was watching from the lower deck, she heaved the weapon as far as she could out into the blackened waters of Puget Sound. By then the ferry was starting to slow down for its return approach to the Coleman Ferry Dock.

Bree made her way downstairs, stopping in the rest room long enough to make sure no lingering blood or gore remained to betray her. She was clean. Everything had gone just the way she had rehearsed and planned. Now that it was over, she felt cool and calm. She was careful to be neither the first passenger nor the last off the ferry.

Once safely on land, Bree walked swiftly back to Spike's Place in Pioneer Square. It was early still—not yet closing time. Bree was relieved to see the blue and white Vanagon still parked in the handicapped zone. That was good. In the intervening ninety minutes or so, someone was bound to have noticed the van sitting there with an older woman waiting patiently inside. One or two of those witnesses would no doubt come forward, giving Nyla Pollock an airtight alibi at the time of Gary Spenser's death.

Bree slowed as she approached the van. She liked the name, Bree. It sounded sophisticated, somehow. She wished she could keep it as her own, but that was out of the question. Someone in the bar might have overheard her using it.

Not until she was within twenty feet of the van did her tight, disciplined calm desert her. This was the telling moment—the encounter she had dreamed about and looked forward to for almost three years now—from the first moment she had known for sure she was adopted.

Like disgruntled children everywhere she had always hoped to be a foundling. After all, how could the woman so stupid as to name her only child Moonbeam actually be her real mother?

But the knowledge came to her late. It was only as a twenty-two-year-old and during her parents' ugly divorce proceedings that she had glimpsed the truth. Her adoptive father, outraged by his paltry divorce settlement, had decided to get even with his wife by spilling the beans about their only child. And that was how Moonbeam—"Beamie" as she preferred to be called—discovered that the aging flower child who was supposedly her mother—a woman with far more money than brains—wasn't her "real" mother after all.

It had taken two more years, but with her adoptive father's underhanded help, Beamie had at last been able to learn Nyla Pollock's name. Then, having finally discovered her birth mother's identity and location, Beamie had been shocked to read that very same name emblazoned in all the newspapers in the aftermath of Bryan Pollock's fatal automobile accident.

The rest of it—giving Gary Spenser his just deserts—Beamie had figured out entirely on her own.

She inched closer to the van. In her secret dreams and fantasies she had planned for this meeting with her birth mother in minute detail, seeing it as an emotion-charged, loving reconciliation. Now, after what she had done, Beamie knew that imagined encounter could never be.

Beamie stopped walking altogether, inches from the driver's window. The older woman sitting inside the vehicle had fallen fast asleep. For a moment Beamie was tempted to leave Nyla Pollock just that way. She studied the older woman's face for several long moments, noticing the inarguable similarities between them, realizing that there was far more than a slight resemblance between Nyla Pollock and her abandoned daughter.

Taking a deep breath, Beamie rapped sharply on the driver's window with the back of her knuckle, startling Nyla awake. Beamie motioned for the other woman to roll down her window. Nyla did so, but cautiously, like a city dweller.

"Who are you?" she demanded through the inch or so of cracked window. "What do you want?"

"I have a message for you," Beamie returned. "He wanted you to know that he's sorry."

With that, she turned and walked away.

Behind her, Nyla rolled the window down the rest of the way. "Who's sorry?" she called into the night. "What are you talking about?"

But Beamie didn't turn or answer. Instead, she melted silently between the buildings with a native's adept knowledge of the terrain. A half block away she slipped into one of her own several cars long before Nyla Pollock was even able to start hers.

Once in her astral silver Mercedes 300 CE, Beamie pulled the gray canvas shopping bag out of the obnoxious yellow-and-purple-striped one, placing the latter inside the former. The blond wig came off and disappeared into the gray bag as well. The green contacts popped out one by one. She would flush those down the first available toilet. She slipped a navy blue sweatsuit on over her shorts and halter top and exchanged her sandals for a pair of worn Nikes. The sunless Germaine Montiel tan had come to her safely out of a bottle from Nordstroms. It would disappear all by itself in a day or two.

Finally, shaking out her own long, brunette hair Beamie started the powerful engine of the Mercedes coupe and signaled to pull out of the parking place. Always a careful driver, she checked over her left shoulder just in time to avoid being struck by Nyla Pollock's blue and white Vanagon, which came careening wildly down the one-way street.

The older woman, probably searching in vain for a strange female apparition, drove past the Mercedes without giving Beamie a second glance. And that was just as it should be. No one would ever have to know about this. Just as they didn't know about Beamie's adoptive mother, either.

Realizing she would never see Nyla Pollock again, Beamie felt a sharp tug of loss as the taillights of the speeding Vanagon swung out of sight around a corner and disappeared into the night. Beamie's birth mother would never know how her gift of life had been repaid. How, in a world ripe with casual violence and teeming with legal injustice, for once the tables had been turned. She would never guess that her unwanted child—the tiny daughter she had given up for adoption twenty-five long years earlier—had sought Nyla Pollock out in order to become the willing instrument of her birth mother's revenge.

It was a shame, Beamie thought, as she shifted the Mercedes into gear, that no one would ever explain to Nyla Pollock how it was that one good turn deserved another.

BELATED REVENGE

By Christine Matthews

"After she found her grandfather's body, Dana was never the same."

Rena Mancini scooped the tears from her eyeballs. I offered a tissue but she only shook her head. Her large hands continued to rub her eyes, then smoothed the wetness into her cheeks.

I hadn't seen her or her husband in over fifteen years and it would have been great visiting with them now if the circumstance weren't so depressing. But, you know that saying: "What goes around comes around"? I guess Dana ended up where she deserved to be and I can't say I was feeling badly for anyone except her poor mother.

As I waited for Mrs. Mancini to stop crying, I noticed Mr. Mancini was still quite dashing. My mother and I would wonder, between coffee and soap operas, what this handsome man saw in Mrs. Mancini.

She'd gotten even shorter over the years and her face lay in soft wrinkles like a silk dress in need of ironing. She was the gruffer of the pair and had a third grade education. Instead of complementing each other, they contradicted. But it had always been evident that Mr. Mancini adored his wife.

"Mrs. Mancini . . ."

"Rena," she corrected.

She'd been my second mother ever since I was five. I felt embarrassed confessing my inability to think of her now as a pal. So, I chose the easiest way around the situation and avoided calling her by any name.

"I don't understand why you came to me. I thought you retired to Phoenix."

"We did. Moved there right after you girls graduated from high school. But Dana stayed in Chicago. Got her real estate license and was making good money . . . until she married that loser."

Dana and I had been best friends forever. We'd met our first day in kindergarten, played together after school almost every day, and talked on the phone when we were out of each other's sight.

I loved going over to Dana's house. She was a blond, blue eyed, pampered little girl and owned every toy imaginable. Mrs. Mancini would make spaghetti dinners, all the while telling us stories of coming to America on a big ship with her parents. She claimed that was the first time she'd had her teeth cleaned—while onboard. I still remember the gory details about how a dentist supposedly scraped tartar from her teeth with a knife. Sweet woman—awful teeth.

"Your mother and I kept in touch. She told me how you went on to college and married Jon. He was such a nice boy. Dana always liked him."

I bet she did. Jon was the reason I hadn't seen Dana since our senior year in high school. She'd made a play for him while I was away on vacation. I stood in my living room, holding a stupid souvenir from Mexico, listening to Dana tell me how Jon had taken advantage of her.

Later, Jon told his version and I believed him. We got married, then separated. People grow up, things change, but I'd never worked through my resentment for Dana.

So many plots I'd conjured to insure she suffer for stealing my trust. And after hearing news through friends of friends that Dana had married an alcoholic, divorced, and then taken to the bottle herself, I sadly admit, it made me feel vindicated.

But this?

"Paul reminded me you'd gone into investigation, Susan. He heard it from Mrs. Trama."

Chicago may be a big city, but like anywhere else, it's made up of neighborhoods that breed gossip.

Paul finally decided this was his cue and came to life. "And since we were here to visit our oldest daughter, Arlene, we thought we'd look you up. What better person to help our Dana than her best friend from the old neighborhood."

Mrs. Mancini's body and head trembled in agreement.

"Where's Dana now?"

Mr. Mancini answered. "At a sanitarium, near Schaumburg. It's close to Arlene's house so she can visit whenever she wants. Dana's been there since last spring. Almost a year now."

"And what do you need from me?"

Paul set down his coffee mug. He stood and looked out the window. The view from my office, located in the spare bedroom of my apartment, looks out over the large parking lot of a discount furniture store. He watched a truck unloading sofa beds and then spoke.

"I'm sure you remember when the old man died?—well, Dana became depressed, withdrawn after that."

"We were about ten?" I asked.

Mrs. Mancini picked up the story as her husband continued watching the furniture truck. "Just barely. It was three days after Dana's tenth birthday. We'd gone shopping. When we came home I thought Papa was sleeping and sent Dana to wake him for supper.

"She got about halfway up the attic stairs when she saw her grandpa laying on the floor in his room. She screamed. It was too dark to really see anything. Thank God she was spared that."

Mr. Mancini walked to his wife's side and bent to offer comfort; my mind wandered back up Dana's attic stairs and to her wonderful train set.

The tracks were mounted on a piece of plywood that was the size of two large dining-room tabletops. Her father had painted it dark green and added a small village. Plastic evergreen trees dotted the landscape and tiny people stood waiting on a miniature platform. There was a tunnel, street lamps that lit up, and when the train came into the station you could press a button and the engine whistled and blew circles of white smoke. As much as I loved that train, Dana loved it more. She'd do anything to play with it. Even walk by the bedroom where her grandfather had killed himself.

Every time I came to visit, she'd point out the bullet hole and tell me how the slug had passed through his head and into the ceiling. Every time we wanted to play with the train she'd point and recite and never, never, even once did she let me work the controls of that train. Not even once would she let me hold the panel of buttons. Not even once did she let me blow the goddamn whistle. And still I came to that house and still I listened to her story.

Mr. Mancini shuffled back to his chair. "Her grades suffered. She cried a lot. We had to take her to the doctor for depression. And the migraines started."

"And now she's in Oak Hills. They started her on shock therapy last month." Mrs. Mancini sniffled.

"I still don't understand why you need me." I hoped I didn't sound rude.

"Because . . ." Mr. Mancini leaned forward, speaking slowly as if I was deaf and he wanted me to read his lips, ". . . because all the doctors in the world won't be able to free her from the guilt she's been stabbing herself with for over twenty years. Dana needs to be free of this, know that her grandfather's death had nothing to do with her, nothing at all."

I shifted my weight in the swivel chair behind my desk. "I didn't know she felt responsible; she never showed much emotion."

"Don't you remember the time she said her grandfather's ghost came to visit when she was taking a piano lesson?" her mother asked. "Dana had such a crush on that Edelman boy then."

"Stephen." I smiled. All the girls loved Stephen Edelman. Myself included.

"Yes. He's the one.

"Well, she was at the piano and said she was asking her grandfather how she could get this boy to like her. All of a sudden a key on the piano started playing. All by itself."

"She told me it was B natural," I said. "That her grandfather was telling her to just be herself and Stephen would like her."

"And it helped." Her father beamed. "She dated Stephen for quite a while after that. All the boys were crazy for Dana."

My resentment flared up again but I didn't tell them I'd been dating Stephen first. I found out about a year after he broke up with me that Darling Dana had been sharing all my confidential fears and gently stirring in a few of her own until Stephen figured I was more than he bargained for. But even after I'd found out the truth, I refused to believe my best friend would do something so terrible to me.

"What Mr. Mancini and I need from you is proof. Something to convince Dana she was not responsible for her grandfather's death. He'd yelled at her earlier that morning. She'd left a toy or something on the floor and Papa almost fell. He was angry. But she needs to know that had nothing . . . nothing at all to do with his death." Mrs. Mancini was all business now. Her tears had dried, her shoulders stiffened and her hands were still, folded on her lap.

"How about the death certificate?"

"We had several copies but the insurance company and the funeral home and social security, they all needed one and we can't find another anywhere."

"I'll call the Hall of Records. It should take a few days to get a copy."

"We'll be in town for a month," Mr. Mancini said. "You can reach us at Arlene's."

"I'll see what I can find."

"Do you need something up front? A retainer?"

I patted her hand. "This is a favor for some dear friends."

"No, friendship and business do not mix." Mr. Mancini pulled out a brand new eelskin wallet. "Here. Is this enough?" He laid two one-hundred-dollar bills on my desk.

"That's fine." I picked up the money and put it inside a small drawer.

"Well," I said, standing, "let's hope this does some good."

"Oh, one thing more," Mrs. Mancini said as I followed her to the door. "Maybe you could find time to visit Dana at Oak Hills? I know she'd love to see you. I don't mean to mix business with friendship but . . ." She looked up at her husband sheepishly.

"That's for Susan to decide."

I hesitated. "I'll try."

*   *   *

I didn't try that hard. In fact . . . not at all. The first thing I did was exactly what I'd told the Mancinis I'd do. I called the Cook County Hall of Records and asked for a copy of the death certificate for Louie Grigoletti. There was a ten-dollar fee involved and the document would be sent out within the week.

Spring wasn't showing itself as quickly as previous years and I was suffering from cabin fever. I decided to visit the old neighborhood. It was only a thirty-minute drive and maybe a blast from the past would stir up some ideas.

I headed for Michigan Avenue. Not the section that cuts through downtown Chicago flanked by elegant stores, no, the end of Michigan Avenue that runs through the old neighborhood in Roseland.

As I drove down the street, I saw the bus unload three high school students. They stood in front of the Karamel Korn Shop. I couldn't believe it was still there. They shoved one another, then started to concentrate their bullying efforts on the smallest, a black boy who looked like a freshman. He saw me watching and embarrassed, started shouting.

"You got a problem, lady?"

I steered down the hill, away from the group, and hid my grin. Things change, I guess, but most often they stay the same. That was certainly true of the attitude on the south side of Chicago contained within these blocks where I'd walked, cruised, and just hung out.

I turned left at Palmer Park and went past the library until I came to Dana's street. Her house was the smaller of the two situated on one oblong lot and it skimmed a cluttered alley. I couldn't park my car in front because it was a bus route; parking was prohibited.

A vacant lot occupied the space where Dana's cousin had lived. I maneuvered between the broken glass and stray pieces of wire and parked. Locking the door, I realized the sun was casting my shadow at a 3:30, after-school angle. And I was ten years old for that half block walk, avoiding the cracks in the sidewalk, careful not to break my mother's back by stepping on any.

I swear it was the same metal gate that hung on two rusty hinges. I remembered swinging back and forth on it, chanting: "In came the doctor, in came the nurse, in came the lady with the alligator purse."

Then I was standing in front of the weathered old house. Badly in need of paint, it had always looked haunted. I'd never once seen Mr. Mancini do any work on the place. The lawn was laced with ruts where bicycles made their summertime journey route from the back door to the front gate. A kid started screaming, "Mommy! Mommy! There's a lady in our yard! Should I call 911?"

A young woman came to the back door; it opened onto the side of the house and she held the screen shut as she shouted.

"You lookin' for something?"

"Sorry," I apologized weakly, "I didn't mean to scare your daughter."

"Never mind her."

I walked closer to meet the woman's eyes.

"I'm Susan Elliott."

She waved a damp dish towel at my extended hand. "Yeah, fine, so what do you want?"

I cut the preliminaries. It was obvious this lady meant business. "I'm a private investigator and I'm working on a case for the family who used to live in this house. It's very important that I look around—take a few notes for the police."

Even though the police would never become involved, and it really wasn't necessary I look around, a few intimidating words thrown in at the right time usually stuck to the brain of those standing in the way. The scowl covering her pimpled face turned to a smirk. She'd surely heard the words "police," and "Private Investigator" but wasn't convinced enough to let me enter.

"You got ID?"

"Sure." I climbed the bottom two steps, digging through my purse until I found my wallet. "Here."

She moved her lips as she read to herself. "Can't be too careful," then held the door open for me.

The house smelled of baby poop. Cabinets were spotted with handprints, the floor sticky with something red, probably Kool-Aid, and when she offered me a seat, I told her I'd only be a few minutes and just needed to walk through the house.

"Well, I'll take the kids out front so's you can concentrate." She scurried out the door with a baby in one arm, a toddler in the other and a girl of about five, hanging onto her mama's dirty shirttail.

"Thanks."

You always hear how people return to a childhood scene and things seem smaller. There's always that rare exception. This house felt just as large and empty as it had all those years ago. The floor creaked and not one hint of welcome showed itself. The woman out in the front yard must have threatened her kids with sure death if they disturbed "the law." Except for the ticking of a clock in the front bedroom, the place was shrouded in silence.

After I'd walked through each room and delayed myself downstairs as long as I could, I backtracked to the kitchen and opened the door leading upstairs to the attic.

Automatically my hand went to the cord hanging above my head and a low-wattage bulb lit the uncarpeted, steep stairs. I counted six steps and stopped. Because there was no wall, to my left, enclosing the staircase, my eyes were level with the floor. I could see the door of the small bedroom. The view was exactly as it had been that evening when Dana discovered her grandfather's body.

I continued up the stairs, ducking as I neared the pitch in the ceiling. I went straight to the bedroom and opened the door. Expecting to find it as I had found everything so far—the same. It was startling to see the walls had been painted black, decorated with Day-Glo posters of Guns N Roses and Ozzy Osbourne.

The ceiling was also painted a matte black and if there had been a leftover bullet hole, by now it surely had been patched over. I dragged a red plastic milk crate out of a corner and stood to poke my fingers across the low, cob-webbed ceiling.

Near the light fixture, my nail caught and inserted an entire index finger into the hole. Then I got off the crate and stood over where Grandpa Louie's bed had been. Holding my hand to my head, I cocked a thumb and aimed at my temple. One clean shot entering the right side of the head, exiting the left and the bullet would have planted itself in . . . the wall.

Strange.

There was no way the bullet could have lodged itself into the ceiling unless the old man had been lying down. I bent myself into several positions and couldn't come up with one that the arthritic man could have managed.

I distinctly remembered the funeral director talking to us, explaining how lucky for everyone that "Grandpa still looked like himself." My nightmares had been narrated by that soft-spoken undertaker for years. Always patting my hand. and when he put that alabaster figurine into my small hands he said, "This is what death feels like. Cold and hard."

Each time Dana took me upstairs we followed our routine. She'd tell me the story of finding her grandfather and point out the bullet hole in the ceiling. She'd explain how there hadn't been much blood. I'd ask a new question and then we'd slam the door and run over to watch the miniature village light up and the signalman wait for the next train.

A child's memory, of course, is questionable. And all those years in between have adjusted my recollections. But when something is reinforced the way each visit to Dana's imprinted the tragedy into my impressionable brain, I grew up never questioning that Louie Grigoletti had shot himself in the head. But if the bullet had entered Louis Grigoletti's head at an angle required to penetrate the ceiling near that light, then part of the top of his head had to have been splattered on that ceiling.

I was curious now. More curious than when I was ten years old. Suddenly all the hazy moments were almost coming into a sharp focus and I wanted to see Dana again. I wondered how much she had changed. Would she be glad to see me? Was she a bonafied nut case and would she even recognize me? I decided to check in with her parents first.

Mr. Mancini answered the phone. He told me his daughter Arlene and Mrs. Mancini were out shopping.

"I just wanted to tell you I visited your old house. It felt odd going back . . ."

"I don't like to remember that place. Rena wanted to stay. It was the only home she'd ever known. With the war, coming to America when she was so young. Then when her two older brothers joined the rest of the family . . . That house, that neighborhood, it all meant security to her."

"You're not even a little bit curious about how it looks?"

"No." I knew this line of questioning was leading to a dead end.

"Well, if you can tell me where Oak Hills Sanitarium is, I think I'll visit Dana tomorrow."

"That's good of you, Susan." Mr. Mancini seemed genuinely happy. "Dana loves to have visitors. Just take Meachum Road for about three miles; it's right past the hospital."

"Is it a big white building, surrounded by a wrought-iron fence? I always thought that was a hotel."

Mr. Mancini laughed. "For what they charge it should be a first-class resort on the Riviera. Any word on the death certificate?"

"I called about it right after you left the other day. It should be here by Friday at the latest."

"Fine. I'll tell Rena you called. Oh, visiting hours are only from one o'clock until suppertime. Do you need any more money?"

"No, I've only made a few calls."

"Guess we'll wait to hear from you then. And, Susan . . ."

"Yes?"

"I want to thank you. I know you and Dana had some differences, your last year of school. She never told me the particulars but there was a definite change after graduation. Fathers aren't as dense as you might think."

At that moment I liked Mr. Mancini even more. "I never thought you were dense."

"I just wanted you to know I'm aware this might make you uncomfortable. Rena and I think of you as one of our own. And poor Dana needs a friend now."

The lobby of Oak Hills Sanitarium was tastefully decorated in varying shades of beige and green. Potted trees gave the large room an outdoorsy feel. The receptionist wore a linen suit and smiled through perfect white teeth as I approached her desk.

"You can wait over there." She pointed to a row of

wicker chairs. "I'll page Ms. Mancini. She's expecting you?"

"No."

I turned and walked to seat myself on the chair nearest the door. Maybe I wanted to be close to the exit in case Dana got violent. After all, her mother had mentioned shock therapy. I fidgeted with the strap of my purse while reassuring myself this wasn't a mistake.

"Ms. Elliott." The receptionist waved for my attention.

"Ms. Mancini will meet you on the veranda. Just go out those doors."

Veranda. I hadn't actually ever heard anyone say that word let alone sit on one. I thanked the woman and pushed open the French doors leading outside. At least twenty oversized rocking chairs lined the porch. The afternoon had turned into a full-blown spring day; the view was gorgeous. Apple trees were in blossom and the wide yard was planted with daffodils and tulips. A wind chime tinkled in the warm breeze. I settled into one of the rockers and with each push backward, my feet left the porch and my stomach jumped a little.

"You look good."

Her voice startled me and I stood up.

"So do you." I wasn't lying. There was no need to lie. Dana Mancini looked great. A few wrinkles around those big eyes but the teenager I remembered was still inside there and we hugged each other hello.

I could feel her heart pounding against my chest and a part of me was glad she felt uneasy. She'd earned so many uncomfortable moments I was glad I was there to watch.

Finally we held each other at arm's length and she silently nodded her approval. She stared at me for a few moments more and then broke free to sit in the rocker I had occupied. I sat to her left and we both faced toward the flower-spotted yard.

I finally broke the silence. "Long time no see."

She didn't laugh. "If my parents hadn't called you, I guess it would have been even longer."

"I've wondered about you a lot." Not with much affection and I still didn't feel any guilt about that.

"You could have picked up a phone anytime. You could have called Arlene."

"The phone works both ways, you know. My name hasn't changed and I've lived at the same address for . . ."

"Six years." Her head bobbed as she rocked slowly. Her voice hadn't betrayed one emotion and my irritation gave way to surprise.

"It'll be seven years in August." It seemed important I get in the last word.

She was weary and still avoiding my eyes asked, "Do you even remember what it was that we fought about?"

"Yes. It was the lies you told about Jon. It took me a long time to realize you'd deliberately set out to hurt me. And later, when I was willing to try and get past all that, I found out you'd lied about so many other things I just couldn't forgive you anymore."

I waited for Dana to argue and was again surprised when she didn't.

"I lied a lot back then. My therapist says it was to cover up my insecurities, my loneliness, blah, blah, blah . . . there's a million reasons why I did what I did. I don't blame you for not wanting to see me. There was a long period when I didn't want to see myself anymore either." She held out her arms, and showed me scars on both wrists.

"Why? You got anything you wanted; your parents adored you . . ."

"They pampered me; they protected me; I was their pet. I got everything they could afford and nothing they were free to give. I hated them. I still do."

"But . . ."

"Grandpa was different. He understood. We were so much alike."

Dana stuck both hands into the pockets of her white cardigan. I was startled when her voice rose. "I lied about that, too."

"About what?"

"Grandpa . . . he didn't kill himself."

Stunned, I turned back to the view. Dana wedged her feet under the rocker so her chair couldn't move.

"You shouldn't believe me. No one does. There's no way I can make anyone believe me and it's driving me totally . . ." She started rocking again and this time pushed herself back and forth at a more frantic speed. ". . . completely, forever insane."

I stood, bending down to grab the arms of her chair. "Why would you lie? You were only ten? I remember everything you told me, all those times, all the stories. I even went back to your old house and the bullet hole is still there, in the ceiling. Remember all the times you pointed it out to me? All the goddamn times you told me about finding your grandfather?"

Her sad eyes finally stared into mine. "I did it. They tried to make it look like suicide. Only I knew the truth but I was a spoiled selfish kid. Who'd believe me, right?

"Now I'm in here. Aren't you happy about that one? Rotten, bitchy Dana, she finally got what she deserved. Isn't that what you thought? What you've been thinking ever since my loving, adoring parents came to you for help?"

I leaned against the railing in front of Dana's chair. My breath seemed to have been sucked out of me and I needed support. Finally, after digesting the information she'd thrown out at me, I started in with my own questions.

"If this is true, why would your parents come to me, allow me to dig into the circumstances regarding your grandfather's death? Why would they risk anyone finding out? Why is their only concern in all this that you have some peace of mind?"

Dana rocked back and her mouth laughed up toward the sky until her eyes filled with tears.

"Peace of mind! There was never any peace in our house. Didn't you wonder why Arlene was never around? They fought all the time. Grandpa heard them; he wasn't deaf. He'd cry and I'd sit with him and I'd cry. Rena would get mad and Paul would get mad that Rena was picking on me, and on and on it went."

I'd forgotten Dana referred to her parents by their first names and her voice colored my black-and-white memories.

"Until that afternoon you went shopping."

"We never left the house. Rena was so angry that day. Grandpa wanted meatballs for dinner and Rena said he'd get what he'd get. They fought and finally Grandpa went upstairs for a nap. On the way, he tripped over my Raggedy Ann. He kicked her out of his way and scolded me.

"Rena had always hated Grandpa. She blamed him for having to leave Italy when she was small. She blamed him for everything bad that ever happened to her. And when Grandma died and Grandpa had nowhere else to go, Rena let him come live with us but he had to stay out of her way.

"Paul just ignored Grandpa but every time Rena complained, Paul would shout that it was her father and she had a responsibility.

"Rena came upstairs about an hour later and woke Grandpa up. They started arguing all over again. I ran in to try and break them apart. Grandpa was crying, holding his cheek and asking how his own daughter could be so cruel. I ran and hugged him.

"That's when Rena went crazy, she started screaming that he'd stolen her little girl away from her and he couldn't have me. Grandpa got scared. He opened the top drawer of his dresser and I saw a gun. He only wanted to keep her off of him. He didn't even pick it up."

The image of Rena Mancini as a screaming banshee was one I would never be able to imagine. To me, she was the warm, loving mother. As I listened to Dana I rejected her crazy accusations that would force me to rethink my childhood and recast the good guys and bad guys. But she spoke with such sincerity . . .

"All of a sudden, Rena was pointing the gun at Grandpa, screaming how much she'd always hated him. He just sat on the bed."

The words started coming slower and we both needed a rest from the truth—at least as Dana perceived it. She rubbed her temples. My head pounded and my stomach clenched. I took a deep breath of the clean air scented with cut grass.

"So." I spoke slowly, still trying to sort through it all. "Your mother had the gun and your grandfather never fought for it? Touched it?"

"Not until later. Rena finally calmed down. She said she hated both of us for making her life unbearable. She said she wished we were both dead. That's when I got hysterical and Rena aimed the gun at herself.

"I screamed and grabbed for it the same time Grandpa did. But I was younger and quicker. I held tight, so afraid to let go. A shot went off. The stupid thing just exploded in my hand. Grandpa dropped to the floor.

"I killed him."

"This is all so hard to believe. Too hard. Everything's changed if what you say is true. It makes all my memories . . ."

"What about mine? I swear, Susan, you're the most selfish person I've ever known. How many things are exactly as you remember them? Tell me! How many?"

I answered without hesitation, "Your old house is exactly as I remembered it. Even the bullet hole in the ceiling."

"Yeah, well, I guess that was the only bit of truth in the whole story."

"So, if your parents altered the truth, why did they come to me to help you?"

"Stupid, stupid Susan. They know you believe the story almost as much as I did. And they also know you don't particularly like me anymore. You're their ally."

A recorded announcement instructed that visiting hours were over and would all visitors please leave through the east entrance.

Dana and I walked toward the front door, never touching each other with our hands or emotions. I still didn't like her and I could tell she hadn't grown any fonder of me.

"I'm expecting a copy of your grandfather's death certificate. Your parents didn't have one. Maybe that will have something that I can use as an opening and get them to explain all this. I'm still not sure what I believe."

"It doesn't matter what you believe, I know I've told the truth. Oh, could you give a message to my parents for me?"

"Sure. What is it?"

She politely held the door open. "Tell them not to come back here. I don't ever want to see either one of them again." She slammed the door with such force I thought the glass would break.

* * *

I spent the next few days sorting through what I believed to be true, what I knew to be true, and what I hoped would end up false. When Louie Grigoletti's death certificate arrived, I called Mr. Mancini right away.

"Could you and Mrs. Mancini come over to my place this afternoon?"

"Did you see Dana?" He didn't seem to hear what I'd just said.

"Yes. Wednesday afternoon."

"Did she say anything about us? Did you upset her?"

"Why don't you just drop by and I'll tell you everything."

"My wife can't come." Mr. Mancini started to sob. "She's in the hospital. After we tried visiting Dana and got turned away, Rena was so upset she started having chest pains. Her heart, it isn't strong. They're keeping her in for a few days to take some tests. Keep her quiet. This is upsetting her so."

"Are you okay?"

"I'm just hoping you can find something, some little something that will reassure Dana and help Rena relax, too."

"I'll come to you. How's two o'clock? I'll drive out to Arlene's; the death certificate arrived today. We can discuss what I found."

"Fine. I'll be here all day. I can't go to the hospital until later."

"Is there anything else I can do?" I felt helpless.

"No. I'll see you soon."

A middle-aged woman answered the door and I assumed it was Arlene. Because she was so much older than Dana and married at an early age, I'd never really known her.

"Susan?" She looked just like her mother.

"Arlene?"

We laughed and nodded and she let me into her large split level. Obviously she and her husband were doing very well.

"Dad's in the kitchen. But before you talk to him I'd like to know how Dana's doing?"

"I thought you went to visit her regularly. Your parents gave me the impression they put Dana in Oak Hills because it was close to you."

"Oh no, that was just a coincidence. Mom has a way of making things seem nicer than they actually are. Sit. We can talk awhile. Dad's having lunch and watching a baseball game. The Cubs, I think."

"You sure he won't hear us?"

"Positive. He doesn't even know I answered the door."

"Good, then tell me how your grandfather died. I need to hear your version."

Arlene looked confused. "My version? Well, I was eighteen and married. I would have done anything to get out of the house. Mom and Dad fought all the time. When Grandpa came to live with us, things really got unbearable.

"Then one night, Mom called and told me she'd been out shopping with Dana and when they came home, Dana went to call Grandpa for supper and found him dead. He'd had a heart attack."

"A heart attack? Did you go to the funeral?"

"Oh no. I hate things like that. I just couldn't go and Mom and Dad said it was better if I stayed home and didn't get everyone else upset."

"So you never saw your grandfather's body?"

"No."

"When's the last time you saw Dana?"

"Sometime before she went to Oak Hills. We're not close. Mom's always kept me up on Dana's news. She told me how Dana felt responsible for Grandpa's death because she'd had an argument with him that day. She's obsessed about it ever since. Mom and Dad never get any peace."

"Thanks. Do you think I can see your father now?"

"Sure." She stood and went to the kitchen, never looking back.

Mr. Mancini followed Arlene back into the room. She carried a tray set with coffee for two. "I'll just leave this and you can talk in private."

"No, I'd like you to stay."

"Pop, is that okay with you?"

Mr. Mancini nodded. "Fine." He smiled toward his daughter.

I pulled the document from my purse. "Mr. Mancini, this morning I received your father-in-law's death certificate. I think you should see it."

"My eyes aren't that good with these glasses. I need new ones. Why don't you just read it to me, tell me what you found."

"Well . . ." I looked to Arlene, watching her face for any change of expression. "According to this, Louie Grigoletti died from a self-inflicted wound to the heart, a gunshot wound."

"What?" Arlene looked shocked. "That's got to be a mistake. Grandpa died from a heart attack. Isn't that true, Pop?"

"No. That's the story we told you, sweetheart. And anyone else who would listen."

"What do you mean, the 'story'?"

"We were trying to protect Grandpa's memory. He killed himself, honey. And you know the church considers suicide a mortal sin."

"Are you aware that Dana thinks she killed her grandfather?" I directed my question to Arlene.

"Killed him? Why would she think that when he had a heart attack . . . no, you said he killed himself . . . so how could she think she had any part in this? Pop, explain this to me."

"Dana didn't have anything to do with it. Your mother and I have been trying to tell her that for too many years to count."

"When I spoke with her the other day," I said, "she told me there had been a gun, a struggle, and a shot was fired. She claims that her hand was on the trigger when a bullet entered Mr. Grigoletti's head and exited into the ceiling."

"What? Oh my God!" Arlene was hysterical now.

"Susan, Arlene, listen to me."

We both sat back and waited.

"Rena is not the easiest person to live with. You know how agitated your mother can get." He stared at Arlene until she nodded her agreement.

"Her papa used to know all the right buttons to push to make her crazy. Every time they had a fight, the old man would storm upstairs and threaten to kill himself. Well, this particular afternoon, Rena was too tired to plead and beg his forgiveness. When she didn't hear anything she assumed he'd fallen asleep. She went to check on him, he was awake, and the arguing started again. The crazy fool finally opened a drawer to show Rena he had a gun.

"Dana ran into the middle of the argument, they all ended up struggling for the gun. Rena still gets confused when she tells me about this part. I was at work so I have to believe her. Dana was too young to know any better and Louie was dead by the time I got home.

"After Rena made sure the old codger was alive, she ran down to get Dana and show her Grandpa was fine. She made her come back upstairs, but by then, the old man had come to, found the gun, and shot himself in the chest.

"Dana saw the blood and went into hysterics. Rena called me at work and I came home to that crazy house. Louie was already cold by the time we decided what we'd tell the police. We rehearsed Dana until she repeated our story."

"Don't you realize what you did to Dana?" I asked Mr. Mancini. "Can't you see the damage you and Mrs. Mancini have done?"

"But Louie couldn't have been buried in sacred ground if the church knew the truth. We had to think of his soul first."

Arlene left the room, disgusted.

"You understand, don't you, Susan?" Mr. Mancini still looked convinced he'd done the only thing he could in that terrible situation.

I wanted to make him feel better but my shock was too great. "I'm not a Catholic, Mr. Mancini. And even if I were, I think I'd have to take care of my little girl before anyone else."

"Rena and I did what we thought was right. It hasn't always been easy, but we've managed until yesterday when Rena broke down. Now I'll have to take care of things myself."

"I need to know one last thing." I was still curious. "Why did you hire me? Why didn't you just tell Dana the truth, show her the death certificate yourself?"

"She may be my daughter but I've never been able to get close to her. She's a strange kid. I thought she'd believe you because you don't like her either and she'd know you're not trying to make her feel better but just doing your job."

I tried calling Dana at the sanitarium—she wouldn't accept my calls. I tried visiting her but she wouldn't see me. I mailed a copy of the death certificate to Oak Hills, it came back unopened. Dana chooses to blame herself for her grandfather's death. I'm smart enough to know there isn't anything else I can do for her.

The Mancinis returned to Phoenix after Mrs. Mancini was well enough to travel. They phoned several times—I haven't returned their calls.

Arlene plans to try to see Dana and explain everything. I wished her luck.

Revenge is a strange thing. Once you get it, you're never sure what to do with it.

COULDJA DIE

By Annette Meyers

On a gold chain in the dark olive hollow of her throat she wears what looks like a five-carat diamond. Almost equal-size carats stud each earlobe. Her dark hair is cut pixie, but the back is longer and curls up under her ears, emphasizing the white glitter lobes.

She is not unattractive, but her lips are a thin, hard line. Her suit is simple, well-cut taupe linen. Everything else is gold and diamonds.

She is telling a woeful story. Their Mercedes stops dead in the Lincoln Tunnel shortly before five that day. The car is packed with her furs, her mother's furs, her mother-in-law's furs, for storage, Italian food she's made for the party, just a few small things she spent a full day preparing.

The police are lovely, wonderful, pushing them through the tunnel to the Mercedes dealership, which is so conveniently nearby.

"You should have gotten a diesel," she reports the cop as saying. "I have a diesel."

"Couldja die? My own Mercedes broke down this week, too," she says to me. "We think we were sold bad gas."

I nod sympathetically for a two Mercedes-Benz family.

"I tell you," she says, "getting stuck in the Lincoln Tunnel just before five o'clock, I did a lot of praying, as only a Jewish girl who converts to Catholic can . . ." She crosses herself several times. "And we got a cab . . . can you imagine at that hour . . . with all the food and furs? Couldja die?"

Moments ago, when they are standing at the arched

entrance of the hotel ballroom, I am certain she is looking for me. Her sharp, dark eyes flick over the room, searching. When they find me, the "ahhhh" is almost audible.

We met at Monte's annual celebration exactly two years ago, and again last year, only a few short months after Barbara's awful death. I'd come alone because Zack was on the road stage managing yet another touring company of *Fiddler on the Roof.* Actually, I was going to beg off because I'd spent a frustrating day talking to potential investors about Sandy Kingman's new musical. I'd taken an orthodontist and his wife to lunch, had drinks with two sleazy investment bankers, who do deals—whatever that means. I kept telling them to look at Sandy Kingman's track record. There are no guarantees in show business. One bad review from the *New York Times* and you might as well fold up your seven-million-dollar tent. I am sick to death of the litany.

Sandy was in his I-am-an-artiste mode. He'd been rereading his press clippings and decided he wouldn't have anything to do with raising money—it was beneath him—and wouldn't even let me trot him out for a blessing and a handshake to a five-hundred-thousand-dollar investor. I can tell you, I was beat. But when I called Monte expecting to get his answering machine, he'd picked up the phone and wouldn't let me beg off. He'd even sent a car to pick me up at the office. You should have seen Sandy's face when the doorman called up and said my car was waiting. It's hard for him to think that his slaves live well.

That was last year.

This year Zack is in Minneapolis with a company of *La Cage Aux Folles.* A job's a job, he says, and I'm sure he's right, but I have become a stage widow and more and more a camera observing the smorgasbord of life instead of participating. Which is okay for now, I think because being married to Zack is always turbulent. With him on the road, the seas are temporarily calm.

"We almost didn't make it . . . would you believe that Joey got a case at the beginning of the week? Couldja die? I said to the judge at the barbecue—he always has this big barbecue at the beginning of the summer—well, I said to the judge, we have a very special affair to attend in New York on Thursday, so I don't want you to keep Joey—you know, of course, Joey's the county prosecutor—later than Thursday noon. And that's what he did."

Joey, a tall, dark, nice-looking young man, comes over now with a drink for Karen. He does not seem at all embarrassed by the wealth of information coming lickety split from the lips of his Jewish-Catholic convert wife. In fact, he's a bit of a wuss, no snap at all, and it's hard to imagine him as a prosecutor. And I wonder how the county prosecutor is able to keep his wife in diamonds and furs.

"Yeah," he says. "I really thought we might not make it."

"I'd just gotten back from a business trip and gone for a swim," Karen says. "We have an Olympic-size pool and a high brick fence around our property . . . and I heard the telephone ring. Luckily, I had plugged it in at the pool, so when Joey called me that he was on his way, I jumped in the shower, got dressed, and was waiting for him when he got home."

"Then we got stuck in the tunnel," Joey says. "Did she tell you about the tunnel?"

"Yes," I say. This guy is unreal, I think. How did he get his job anyway? On the other hand, he's got a nice smile and maybe that's all you need in New Jersey.

"But we made it. Boy, was I crazy when we got stuck in the tunnel. I thought we were going to get killed. But the cops were so nice . . ."

"I told them who you are, Joey," Karen says. She points a bony finger at him. "So they should have been nice. But they were nice anyway, even before I told them."

"Well, I'm glad you made it," I say. "I was just about to leave so I'm glad to have seen you again." I've become the world's best liar.

"You're not leaving," she says, clutching my arm. "Oh, don't go," she says. "We just got here . . . and I wanted to talk."

Last year she'd talked my ear off telling me her life story, that her parents were Holocaust survivors who met in a displaced persons camp after World War II, where they'd married and where she'd been born. I heard how her father had made a fortune in the black market and when they came here, he'd had their bulletproof Rolls shipped over, too. She'd taken one look at Joey in high school and she's been holding on for dear life ever since. She tells me she has this little job as a sales rep for a cosmetic company so she gets to travel from time to time.

"I'm afraid I must go." I am edging away. "I have another appointment. But we'll see you again. Very soon, I hope."

"Oh, yes," Karen says. "Joey and I come in very often now since Marcia is seeing Monte. I did that, you know. We brought them together. She's going to move in with him. They're supposed to get married, but Monte keeps putting it off. Marcia calls me . . . she's so unhappy about it . . . what with the kids, you know, they're having a hard time adjusting to the city and the change in their lives. And I feel so guilty about it because I brought them together."

It is five years now that the kid brother of a gal I knew at college referred Monte to me, and I'd introduced Monte to Sandy Kingman, my boss, because Monte had a rather interesting musical that he'd written—book, music, and lyrics. And Sandy actually toyed with the idea of working with Monte, directing and producing. But Sandy must have sensed, he's good at that, that Monte was not malleable, and Sandy just can't work with strong, opinionated people, no matter how creative they are. He's not named Kingman for nothing.

So Monte did *Blink Your Eyes* himself and the rest is history.

Unlike Sandy, Monte always remembers who his friends are, and while he's never told me in so many words that he is responsible, invitations are always coming in for openings, for screenings, for nightclub acts. Books and record albums are often in the mail.

Monte is a directing, writing, composing talent the likes of which the entertainment world has rarely seen. Everything is balanced like the street musician playing ten different instruments all at once, but he is no street musician. He is a money machine, an industry by himself. Last year he won three Grammies, and two of his singles logged thirty weeks apiece on *Billboard*'s singles chart. Everybody and his uncle is trying to get on his band wagon, but Monte remembers old friends.

The only thing he can't balance is his personal life. But then, let's be serious. How many of us can?

Karen says, "But I know it will all work out for Marcia. She just worships Monte."

"I like Marcia," I say. "And she and Monte seem good together. Perhaps it will all work out. He's gun-shy, after what happened with his first marriage."

"That's the difference, you know," Karen says. "That Barbara was all wrong for him. She was just like his mother. He should never have married her. If I'd known him then, I would never have let him do it. And, by the way, we knew all about Nancy, of course we did—and she was wrong for him, wrong, wrong. You know, Joey and Monte went to college together."

"I know," I say, having heard the story in depth last year.

"And we all met again in Barbados, when Monte and Barbara were on their honeymoon. But Marcia is so right for him; I can't think about it not working out," she says.

"I really have to go now," I say.

"Listen," she says, breathing intimacy, "you ought to come to Atlantic City. We live fairly close. You would be very well taken care of . . ."

Fat chance, I think, but I say, "Well, we've never really thought about going to Atlantic City." I'm such a phony.

"Please come, you must come," she says. "Tell her, Joey, she must come. You must come." She puts her hand on my arm. "I know you'll enjoy it. We can do so much for you . . . we have connections."

I edge over to Monte, give him a hug and kiss. He's talking to three other people. He puts his arm around me and gives me a squeeze. He's gotten suave with his success, brusquer. He's been spending more and more time on the Coast. "Wonderful party," I say.

"Do you all know Sunny Browning?" he asks, sort of throwing it out, as if they should all know me.

Actually, my birth certificate says Sunshine. Would you believe my parents have one giddy moment and I get stuck with Sunshine for life?

"You must come," Karen calls to me, gesturing madly. "Monte, tell her she must come . . . we have connections . . ."

"What's all that about, Sunny?" Monte asks me.

"Oh, she wants us to come to Atlantic City," I say.

"What for?" Monte dismisses it, dismissing her.

Monte is full of his success, in the nicest way. He is generous and warm. And very busy. His career has taken off and the business part of his life is going great guns. But it's still hard to see him as a lover. He doesn't stay still long enough.

Oh, yes, when we first met him years ago, he looked a little like the actor Stallone, but now he has thickened, lost some of his hair, and has a distracted look about him. His mind may well be elsewhere, working on a deal, perhaps. With success he has lost his vulnerability, in that he is no longer boyish.

But he has energy and the kind of rough-hewn charm that come with a blue collar upbringing and a good education.

"I met that cute little friend of yours," Sandy Kingman says to me out of the blue one Monday morning. I've just come in from a weekend in Cincinnati with Zack and his wandering troupe of bus-and-truck freaks. I am so wasted I can hardly open my eyes. I should know better than to drink sea breezes because gin makes my insides rust. And drinking with actors while the stage hands are striking the set, preparing to move on to the next lousy hamlet can be hazardous to your health.

So I stare at Sandy through slits of lids because it hurts to see daylight, and he's drinking his coffee with a dollop of Ferna Branca, his usual, grinning at me like he knows something I don't know.

I can't stand it when he gets like this. It's like dealing with a bad kid.

"What cute little friend?" I ask. Truth to tell, I have no cute little friends, I hate cute little people, and all my friends, as I am, are a bit long in the tooth. And that's not cute.

"You know, the cosmetics rep who's married to the D.A." Sandy puts his feet on his desk, and I see he's taken to polishing his soles.

"Now, that's a good one. I have no cute little friend,

married or not to a D.A., and no one I know would be an Avon lady."

"Well, she sure seems to know you. She's crazy about you. That's all she could talk about."

"A lot of people are crazy about me," I say, gracefully deflecting his innuendo. "Where'd you meet this cute friend of mine?"

"Atlantic City. We went down to see Liza's new show, and there she was, cute as a button, at the next table. She recognized me and came right over and introduced herself."

Atlantic City, I think. D.A.? Somewhere in the back of my fogged-up mind it begins to come to me.

"They were sitting with Eddie Colangelo." Sandy sounds impressed.

"Eddie Colangelo? The name is vaguely familiar. Am I supposed to know him, too?"

Sandy is gleeful. "I love it when I know more than you do, Miss-know-it-all."

It's true. He just loves getting the drop on me because, truth to tell, I'm a news junky. I read everything, books, magazines, newsletters, not to mention newspapers, watch NBC, ABC, and CBS, at different times, of course, and top it all off with CNN, when the first three are not spouting forth. So he's got me. "I give up." I bestow one of my better smiles on him. "Who is Eddie Colangelo?" I try not to be testy, otherwise that's all I'll hear about for weeks.

"He's only the hottest lawyer in the country."

"Oh, yeah, I remember. Blame-the-victim murder. Drugs. Kidnapping. White-collar crime. *That* Eddie Colangelo." I put my thumb against my nose and push. "The boys."

Sandy looks peeved. "You knew all the time."

"I don't deny that." I'm good at this, pretending. And with Sandy, to hold your own, you always have to keep him a little off balance. I have also just figured out who my cute little friend must be. "Karen Bonaventura." That Sandy, he has no taste at all in women.

"How do you know her?"

"Her husband, the D.A., and Monte Morgan went to Villanova together. I've met her only two or three times. She's hardly cute or my friend." I am getting more and more annoyed as I speak, and my head is thumping to beat the band.

Sandy sits up. "Well, anyway, I think she's really cute. She brought Colangelo over and introduced him. He said he wants to be on our list, so you should call him. He says he has connections."

"I'll bet. He and Karen. Couldja die?"

He looks at me funny, not getting it, but Sandy never gets a joke unless he's telling it. I don't know why I bother.

The three women who have been a part of Monte Morgan's life for the last seven years have all been attractive and smart. But none as smart as Marcia.

We first meet Marcia the night Monte speaks to my students about what a composer looks for in a producer. I am teaching a course on producing for the commercial theater, at St. Vincent's College.

"We'll have dinner afterward at Pirandello's," I say when I confirm the date and give him directions to my classroom.

It's a hot, hot New York night; the discussion is lively; the window air conditioner is humphing and thumpfing. We are all sweating, Zack, Monte, and I, as we come out on the steaming street near Washington Square Park. We are a little high from the experience of the last two hours. It's almost ten o'clock. Pirandello's is just around the corner. The Village is throbbing with people, mostly weird, many young, and it might as well be daylight, for down here no one recognizes night.

The bar area of Pirandello's is crowded and noisy, and since our table is not ready, we stop to have a drink. A tall young woman begins talking to Monte. He buys her a drink. I nudge Zack and he shrugs. It seems as if she is making a pickup. But Monte talks to us and talks to her as if she is with us.

When we are told our table is ready, the young woman comes along with us, and we suddenly realize that she is with Monte, that he has asked her to meet us at the restaurant.

We sit down at our table, and Monte says offhandedly, "Oh, this is Marcia."

Marcia smiles uncertainly.

"Where did you park the car?" Monte asks.

"Not far from here," she says, "on West Fourth Street."

Imagine the shock of it. The three of us are to have dinner. To our knowledge, since Monte and Barbara split up, Monte's lady is Nancy. Nancy is supposed to have joined us, but Monte says she is working. We have known Nancy for almost a year, all the time she is Monte's lady. Now who is this Marcia, and where has she suddenly popped from? Add to that, it doesn't seem a new thing between them.

I feel sorry for Marcia then. How uncomfortable for her to be dumped into the evening without a by-your-leave. And how strange for us. I am celebrating the successful final session of a series of classes in a program I originated. It is presumptuous of Monte to insert a stranger into our celebration.

Yet Monte does odd things, but not cruel—only careless things, and he is a loyal friend. So one tends to forgive him.

While we eat I sneak a closer look at Marcia. She has very fine, delicate features, white translucent skin, dark hair, probably very long, rolled and bound in a severe chignon. She is dressed simply, but well, in a dark silk dress. And she's very exact: nails perfect, every hair tightly in place. How imperfect a relationship with Monte must be for her. For Monte is not a man to commit, certainly not after what happened with Barbara.

At this time Monte is still married to Barbara, although it's more like on again—off again. They met when Barbara was a singer-dancer in *Blink Your Eyes*. She is a small-boned, hyperactive girl, dark, with a great mass of dark curls, pretty like Lois Lane, and very obsessive.

"I buy my bread in the Village," she tells me, "and pasta fresh in Little Italy and . . ." She spins off urgently how she goes to the source for the very best of everything, pure foods, perfect silver, china, glassware, and linens.

There is a huge Italian wedding in Boston, where Barbara is from, and from the beginning, things seem to go wrong. Monte's success is apparent; Barbara's career is going nowhere.

We have dinner with them several times before they

are married, but it is their first dinner with us after their marriage that tells all.

Monte is very quiet—tentative almost—very unlike himself, and Barbara is vivacious, burning and crackling like a Roman candle. When he says something—any-thing—Barbara contradicts him, argues, criticizes. Her eyes flash. It is as if she is on speed. She wears us all out. With relief that the evening is almost over, I whip out my special dessert, chocolate mousse.

"I have the best chocolate mousse recipe," she says. "It's Julia Child's. I'll send it to you."

"I have Julia Child's chocolate mousse recipe in her book," I say. Just between us, giving me dessert recipes is like carrying coals to Newcastle. This is my specialty. I am one swell baker. Before I got involved with Sandy Kingman, I used to bake for the local restaurants. I am one of the best, believe me.

Monte is looking very uncomfortable.

"It's not the same," Barbara says. "This is from her television show."

"I have that book, too."

"You don't have this one. It's different," she insists. "I'll send it to you."

When they are gone, I say to Zack, "I thought they'd never leave. I'm exhausted." It's been an awful evening.

"She's a ballbreaker," Zack says.

"I don't think they're going to make it," I say.

Barbara, sure enough, sends me her special Julia Child chocolate mousse recipe, and would you believe, she's right. It is different, and it is better.

And I am right. Six months later Barbara and Monte split up. And it is bitter and vindictive on her part. She takes a job touring, has an open affair with one of the actors, and when that doesn't turn Monte into a scream-ing maniac, she tries suicide. It is all too much hot and furious emotion for Monte, who seems to thrive on peace in the home, and a less dramatic emotional life. Obviously, living with Barbara is somewhat like living on an erupting volcano. I am no stranger to volcanoes. Zack is no prince, but then, who is? There are no princes in this world.

A few months later we're walking up Third Avenue after a nice dinner at one of the Italian cafes and we run into Monte. He's just come from admitting Barbara to Lenox Hill, and he's wrecked. He looks bewildered. Barbara has gone from manic to depressive. Lithium is not working. She refuses to believe there's anything wrong with her. It's all Monte's fault. Everything is.

When she is released she decides she doesn't want their apartment for herself, she wants to get back together with him. He's being noncommittal and she goes into the bathroom and cuts her wrists and starts screaming as if someone is killing her.

Monte is beside himself. He just doesn't understand what's happening. He lives, as do most of us, in a world of parameters. Certain lines of raw emotion are not to be crossed, not even between husband and wife.

Barbara's wrists heal and, what do you know, she moves back into the apartment. It's like old times. Monte invites us to dinner. Barbara doesn't come out of the kitchen, where she appears to be creating a masterpiece of culinary delights with the maximum of noise. Monte apologizes for the racket and opens a bottle of Chardonnay. His hands shake so that he sets the bottle down on the coffee table.

"I—" he begins.

"Almost ready," Barbara calls from the kitchen frequently, but it is another hour before dinner is served. Several times she comes out and redoes the table setting. "You never get it right," she says to Monte. To the room at large she says, "He never gets it right. I always have to tell him what to do."

As I remember, she serves up a four-course banquet in an obsessive furor with a running account of where she bought everything and how she created this perfection. And perfection it is, but Monte is shrinking until he is almost not there.

We can hardly wait to escape.

Months pass. I meet Barbara coming out of Gracious Home carrying a long oblong package. She is wired and burning with a kind of lunatic enthusiasm.

"I'm so glad to see you," she says. "Come with me." She has a lock on my arm.

"I'm late for an appointment," I protest.

"No, I insist you must." Her voice is frantic. "I just

ran out for a minute because I didn't have everything I needed."

If you think I'm not curious, you're wrong. I am fascinated. I have to see what she is up to. So I let her propel me to their apartment. "Where's Monte?" I ask as we get off the elevator.

She is unlocking the door awkwardly, the package still under her arm. "He's in California. He's having an affair, and I'm leaving him." She flings open the door and pulls me in. "Don't tell me I'm wrong. I know you're always on his side."

The apartment looks strange. Everything they own appears to be lined up on the floor and table in stacks and piles. "I'm dividing everything evenly," she says, furiously tearing the paper off the package. It's a saw, a big one, and an architect's rule. She begins on the sofa, measuring halfway.

I watch stunned as she begins to saw through the brown velvet fabric, raising dust and down. "Barbara, stop. What are you doing?" She keeps sawing. "Stop. This is crazy. You don't have to do this."

Barbara looks up but doesn't stop. "I knew you would take his side. Get out of here." She is quite mad.

I am out the door eager to get away, but I run smack into Monte downstairs. He is carrying a briefcase and looks exhausted.

"What—" he says. He is surprised to see me.

"Monte! I thought you were in California."

"Why would you think that?"

"Barbara. Monte, she's upstairs cutting the sofa in half."

He looks sick. "I've got to go."

"I'll come with you."

"No, please. I'll take care of it. I'll call you."

He doesn't, but we live in a small community of theater people, and we hear that Barbara is back in the hospital.

I am returning from a backers' audition in Baltimore and spot the screaming headlines: ACTRESS MURDERED. It's front-page news in the *News* and the *Post*. We get calls from friends. Have we heard? TV runs amok with the story, keeping everyone up on the investigation for weeks, as do the tabloids. Only the *New York Times* refrains. Barbara has been murdered, shot to death. She has been out of the hospital for only two weeks. Peace had reigned. She'd had shock treatments and she'd responded well.

Zack is home for once, surprise, surprise, and we call Monte, but we get the answering machine with Barbara's hyper greeting and her best wishes for a nice day.

We read in the papers that although Monte is the principal suspect, he has an alibi. He was in the middle of a recording session. Barbara had obviously known her killer. . . . Maybe she had brought someone into the apartment. It was, we heard, something she had done before. Monte would come home and she'd be with a strange man.

All this leaks out to the press, and Monte's life is pored over by strangers. Sandy Kingman loves each new lurid chapter and is constantly flapping the latest story under my nose. "People in glass houses . . ." I warn him, but he thinks it's all a big joke. He never takes other people's pain seriously, particularly if he knows the person.

The notoriety puts Monte's new album at the top of the charts. Sandy is so jealous, he can't stand it.

The judgment is murder by person or persons unknown.

Monte is devastated by the tragedy and the manner of it, but then there is Nancy. Sweet, earnest and undemanding, uncompetitive, pretty, all her edges softer than Barbara. Had she been there for Monte while his marriage to Barbara was breaking up? Take a guess. You'd be right. She'd appeared in his last musical as a pit singer.

Nancy is also an actress, so perhaps their relationship is never going anywhere. But at the time, none of us knows that, certainly not Nancy. She and Monte are always together. She is his helpmate, his hostess, his friend, trusting and loyal.

Monte is working on a new project, and Zack and I are invited to a reading, held, incredibly, in the same living room where Barbara was murdered. It is eerie. Nancy has sent the invitations and is acting as hostess. She is a gentle presence, always looking to Monte for affirmation. I note with comfort that the mouthy Karen with her gold jewelry and diamonds and D.A. husband are not in attendance.

Tim Tipper is there. He's come from London after a huge success in the National Theater to direct Monte's new musical revue. Tim and his lover, who will design the sets, have quickly become close chums of Nancy and Monte.

"Isn't she a love," Tim says fondly of Nancy after she finishes singing the first-act finale, a lovely ballad. Monte has outdone himself with this score.

Monte looks happy with Nancy, but he's never been a hugger or a kisser, not even with Barbara, so if one were to ask a stranger who in this room is Monte's girl, it would be difficult to tell. On the other hand, whenever we see Monte now, he is with Nancy, but there are no dinners at the apartment or even with the four of us at a restaurant. Still, they are a couple.

So when we meet Marcia—abruptly—we are astounded. And it is definitely a relationship of some import, that is clear.

When Monte's company gives its annual party that year, both Nancy and Marcia are there, but it is decidedly Nancy's territory, and Marcia sits on the sidelines with her friends, Joey, the county prosecutor, and Karen, the Jewish-Catholic convert-cosmetics rep. They have, it seems, introduced Monte to Marcia, who is divorced and has two young children. And it seems, Monte and Marcia like each other.

Marcia stands well outside show business, and after all those years with actresses, maybe Monte finds her lack of ambition in the area refreshing. It is fairly obvious that Marcia knows about Nancy, but does Nancy know there is a Marcia? One doubts it.

I like Marcia. She is clearheaded and intelligent. And she is patient. Unlike Nancy, she is not a girl, but a woman.

We have dinner with them, a second time. It is different. We are all very comfortable with one another. We sit down and after looking over the menu, Monte orders for Marcia.

"Wait a minute," she says, laughing. "That's not what I want."

"Oh," he says, looking puzzled. "Sorry." But he

doesn't think much about it, and goes back to talking with Zack.

I am complaining about the cost of renovation we are planning to do in our apartment.

"I know," Marcia says. "When we started the loft, it was supposed to be so simple."

"Are you doing some building at home?" I ask innocently.

"No," Marcia says, "we're building a loft in the apartment for my children. Monte and I are living together."

"Marcia, how nice," I say, genuinely pleased, but still shocked that Monte had not said anything about the major change in his life. "Since when?"

"August," she says. It is now early October. "Didn't Monte tell you?"

"No." I turn to Monte, interrupting him and Zack. I shake my finger at him. "Monte, you're terrible. Why didn't you tell us that you and Marcia are living together?"

"Oh, yeah," he says. "I forgot."

But he didn't, doesn't. He avoids.

And what about Nancy?

"It was dreadful," says Joan, a friend of Nancy's and Monte's, when we meet some months later on the IRT subway platform. She's with Tim Topper and his lover. They are going to the theater, as are we. "I just don't— can't—think of Monte in the same way. He was terrible to her. He made her all sorts of promises and then turned his back on her."

"But we first met Marcia over a year ago. Didn't Nancy realize there was someone else?"

"Over a year ago! My God! This was going on a lot longer than we suspected," Joan says. "He is even worse than we thought. He did an awful thing to Nancy. He was our friend, too, and I have trouble dealing with that. And then after the accident—"

"What accident?"

"Don't tell me you haven't heard? Nancy was in a terrible accident when she was in Kennebunkport. It was hit and run."

"My God—" I look at Zack who shrugs. He doesn't know any more than I do.

"She had the offer to do *Cats* in stock. She didn't

want to leave Monte, but he said not to worry about him. It was a great opportunity. Nancy thought they would get married . . . we all thought . . . it was understood."

"How is Nancy? Where is she now?"

"I thought I told you. Nancy is dead."

Time passes. We all lose touch with Monte sporadically. He's busy and so are we.

Meanwhile, Sandy—like a dog with a bone—keeps nagging me about calling Eddie Colangelo because we're still short a million and we're eight weeks from rehearsal and Colangelo's connections could come in handy.

"Dirty money," I say.

"I'm not particular," Sandy says. "I've got a show to get on and art will out."

Sandy's got this idea that he's an artist, and therefore, the world owes him a production.

I'm not an artist, except in raising money, which Sandy thinks is crass, unless he needs it, which at the moment, he does. So who am I to argue?

I bite the bullet and call the mouthpiece, which I am now calling Colangelo because it makes Sandy squirm.

The mouthpiece, it turns out, talks like Anthony Hopkins. He says, "Let's discuss it. I'll send my car for you. You can spend the weekend."

You'll never guess where he is. Right. Atlantic City. He keeps a suite at the Kismet Palace.

"Well, I—" I'm not cool.

"Strictly business, my dear," he informs me.

I want to kill Sandy, but he's gone off to the Coast to audition a movie starlet or two, or whatever he does when he's playing producer. And pretty soon I'm settled back in a stretch limo the length of a lap pool sipping champagne from a tulip glass and watching McNeill/ Lehrer on my own private box. And we're speeding down the New Jersey Turnpike like there's no tomorrow. A girl could get used to this. And it sure beats the express bus from the Port Authority with the canasta players in the polyester pantsuits.

Before I leave I get Zack on the phone in Denver to tell him where I'll be. I need a little reassurance—don't ask me why—but I'm leaving my element, going into a strange one and I have the willies. Did I say I'm talking to my husband Zack on the phone? Wrong. I get the volcano instead, who screams at me, "That's why you called? To drive me crazy?"

How can you drive someone crazy who's already there? I ask you.

Anyway, I get down to Atlantic City on Friday night, and there's a message from the mouthpiece to enjoy my evening and to meet him in the coffee shop for breakfast at ten the next morning. Coffee shop? Is he kidding?

A cute bellhop in a musical comedy uniform takes me up to my room and confides he's an actor.

"How nice," I say. "But aren't you a distance from Broadway?"

"Yeah, well," he says, "I can make a bundle here in tips, and you can't live in New York without a bundle."

Don't I know it.

He shows me into a room as big as my whole apartment and hands me an eight and a half by eleven manila envelope.

"What's this?" I ask, giving him three bucks to get my overnighter back.

"You're down as a show business VIP," he says, "so I'm giving you my picture and résumé. I can sing."

"But can you dance?" I say.

He looks crestfallen, and I feel like a jerk. "Just an old show-biz joke," I say. He must be from Omaha.

After he leaves I take a bath in a marble tub the shape and size of the fountain in front of the Plaza, nude marble nymph and all, and crawl into a circular bed done up in satin sheets. I fall asleep calculating what sheets cost if there are a thousand circular beds in the hotel.

At ten o'clock the next morning, I'm standing in a coffee shop that looks like a bordello. Crimson flocking on the walls, rhinestones embedded in the counter, mirrors everywhere. A few bleary-eyed types are sitting like zombies at the tables ingesting caffeine for the next assault on the gaming tables. I have a thick legal envelope full of offering circulars and partnership papers, and I'm rehearsing my sales pitch as a leggy blonde in satin short shorts and little else shows me to the mouthpiece's table.

And what do you know, the mouthpiece is not bad looking. Sort of a slick Bobby De Niro. He gets up when he sees me coming. I should send Sandy and the volcano to him to learn manners.

Pretty soon I'm giving him my caveat emptor speech over my coffee cup about how if you can't afford to lose, you can't afford to invest, which you may think is ill advised in this situation, but I have found it disarms people, even mouthpieces.

"I'm not a rich man," he says.

You could have fooled me, I think.

"But I have connections. And I respect the quality of the musicals Sandy Kingman does. So you can count me in for five hundred."

Five hundred? Did he say five hundred? My brain says he can't mean that in dollars.

"Five hundred thousand minimum," he continues. "Maybe more." He's pouring tea for himself from a little pot. The mouthpiece drinks tea, talks like Anthony Hopkins, looks like De Niro. "Of course, there's just one thing I'll want—"

"Do you want a credit?"

He looks startled. "Credit?"

"I mean, associate producer or something like that?" They usually do when they put up this kind of money.

"Not at all, my dear," he says. He wants access to tickets. The best. Whenever he needs them, which will be often.

"I think we can arrange that," I say thoughtfully. We damn well can arrange that.

He writes a check with a Mont Blanc pen in this neat parochial school cursive while I sit there and then he signs the partnership papers, and believe me, I am about as cool now as I can get. I want to signal the waiter to bring me a phone so I can call Sandy at the Beverly Hills Hotel, but I am not that crass. I can hardly wait to get out of there and back to New York.

But the mouthpiece has another surprise for me. What a nice guy. He's arranged for me to join him for dinner and Shirley MacLaine's new show tonight. So what can I do? I spend the day at the pool getting golden, reading galleys for Sandy. It comes with the job. You see, Sandy doesn't read. I'm his eyes. I read galleys and manuscripts, playscripts and synopses, and tell him what I think, which I never have any trouble doing. He thinks

I'm an intellectual because I grew up in a bookstore. Literally. My father was Paul Browning of Browning's Bookshop on Madison Avenue.

In the evening I put on my little black knit with the stretch sequinned bodice, which I'd stuffed in the suitcase the last minute—because you never know—and present myself in the ballroom or theater or dining room, whatever they call it, and guess what? You're probably ahead of me.

Yes. There's my cute little friend Karen Bonaventura sitting at the mouthpiece's table with the D.A. and a short fat Vegas comedian whose name I can never remember.

"You should have told me you were coming," Karen says, scolding me as if I am a naughty child but she loves me anyway. Her mouth is a wound. "But I forgive you now that you're here."

She's an intense bone, encircled in a field of static. The cosmetic company she reps for turns out to be owned by a Colangelo client. Such a small world.

The conversation is inane. I have a great steak and too much champagne. Shirley dances up a storm. I love Shirley because she started on Broadway, and she's one of the great characters in an essentially characterless world.

"Monte and Marcia," Karen says when I make my excuses: early departure, important meeting in the city, and all that rot. "He should marry her. He promised he would. Talk to him." She puts her claws on me like a bloodsucker. Bloodsucker? I've definitely had too much champagne.

I can spin straw into gold, and I can do without Atlantic City, but I've got a check for a half million in my bag and signed partnership papers. I guess you can say I've come up a winner—or Sandy has, and nothing, repeat, nothing, is going to bother me.

Another year passes, and Monte has not married Marcia, but I begin to think he may.

And Karen says to me with a certain smugness, at the annual party, "Oh, yes, Monte was seeing Nancy four days and Marcia three days for a long time. Marcia worships him." Her eyes flick nervously from side to side, and she licks her lips with a small sharp tongue. She leans closer to me. "They're supposed to get married, but he isn't doing anything about it. I just hope I won't have to feel guilty about introducing them. I do, you know. I've done a lot for them. They'll never know how much. I mean, he will marry her, don't you think? Tell him," she says, clutching my arm. There is desperation in her voice now. "Tell him to marry her. He'll listen to you. Tell him to marry Marcia."

PICTURES IN THE STARS
(A Lucas Hallam Story)

By L. J. Washburn

Hallam felt as out of place as a horned toad in a ballroom.

He looked at the scientific equipment surrounding him, lifted his eyes to take in the great curving dome far above his head. A big slice was opening up in the dome, and as it widened, the lights in the place began to dim. Stars winked into view through the opening in the roof. The faint hum of electric motors came to Hallam's ears.

"I think you'll be interested in this, Mr. Hallam," the white-coated man beside him said.

Hallam didn't say anything, just nodded and fought down the vague nervousness that was gnawing at him. He was used to open spaces, and being inside a massive building like this bothered him some.

"There you are," Dr. Bauer said, bending and gazing through the eyepiece of the great telescope. After a moment, he straightened and offered, "Take a look."

He stepped away from the telescope and Hallam took his place. Bending awkwardly, Hallam looked through the eyepiece. The stars, which should have been mere pinpricks of light, suddenly seemed to leap at him.

"What do you think?" Bauer asked.

Hallam hesitated a moment, then rumbled, "Mighty impressive." He didn't add that he preferred looking at the stars from the open range, rather than through a 100-inch telescope.

The call from Dr. Bauer asking that he drive up to the Mount Wilson Observatory near Pasadena had come as a surprise to Hallam. He wasn't sure why an astronomer wanted to talk to a private detective. He had arrived just as Bauer and his staff were getting ready to open the dome for the night's work, and Bauer had requested that Hallam wait a few minutes until things were underway. The offer to let Hallam look through the giant telescope had come on the spur of the moment.

Lucas Hallam was a big man, tall and broad-shouldered. His hands were large, and his craggy face with its long gray mustache added to his rough appearance. He wore boots and jeans and a tan-colored cotton shirt with the sleeves rolled up. He had a suit and a Panama hat that he could wear when he had to, but he hadn't expected to be working today. Bauer's call had come late in the afternoon.

Hallam wasn't going to turn down work. It had been several weeks since he had had a client, and he hadn't done any movie work since falling off a horse and twisting his knee while doing a picture with Hoot Gibson. He'd had surgery on the knee a few months earlier, and luckily it wasn't hurt bad, just enough to keep him off a horse for a while. The Hooter was a good kid and had offered to find another part in the picture for Hallam, but it would have been a nonriding job, and Hallam wanted none of that. The knee was considerably better now, though, and Tom Mix was starting a new picture the next week. Come Monday morning, Hallam would take a *pasear* down to Gower Gulch and try to pick up some work there.

That gave him four days to devote to whatever job Dr. Bauer had for him.

Hallam stepped back as one of the white-coated assistants hurried past him, bent on some errand. The young man bent and looked through the telescope, then muttered something under his breath and scribbled some numbers on a piece of paper. None of it made any sense to Hallam.

One of the other young men walked up to Dr. Bauer. He had tightly curled red hair and blue eyes that looked out intensely from his pale face. "Is this the detective?" he asked Bauer.

"I told you I would handle this, Garrett," Bauer said stiffly. "I appreciate your concern—"

"Kevin's my friend," the young man interrupted. "I want to help in any way that I can."

Clearly, Bauer was annoyed that Garrett had broken in while he was speaking. "If there is anything you can do, I will be sure to let you know," he said. "Now, if you will excuse us."

He wasn't asking for permission, but rather dismissing the young man. Garrett started to say something else, then closed his mouth and stalked away. His behavior didn't strike Hallam as a smart way to act around the fella who ran the place.

"Perhaps we should go to my office, Mr. Hallam," Bauer said.

Bauer led him to a small room on the far side of the building. In a round structure like the observatory, there weren't any corners. When Bauer flipped on a lamp on his desk, the light seemed bright after the gloom of the big main chamber.

The office was full of books and papers, but they were neatly in place for the most part. There were several maps on the walls, maps of stars that Hallam supposed represented the solar system or the galaxy or something.

Bauer sat down behind the desk and waved Hallam into a straight-backed chair on the other side. He clasped his hands together and asked, "Are you familiar with the stars, Mr. Hallam?"

"Only to find my way around by them," Hallam replied. "You ride enough back trails, you get to where you can steer by 'em."

"The stars have been my life's work. I have been the director of this observatory since its opening in 1904. That is more than twenty years of my life, and before that I studied and observed the heavens all over the world. I have even discovered a few stars and named them. Perhaps by looking up so much, however, I have lost track of what is happening down here on the ground."

Hallam said nothing, waited for him to continue.

"Well," Bauer said after a moment, making his voice more brisk, "I suppose I had better tell you why I called you, Mr. Hallam. One of my assistants here at the observatory, a young man named Kevin Jeffries, seems to have . . . disappeared. I would like for you to look for him."

Hallam frowned. "Most folks go to the police about a missing person."

"I know that." Bauer nodded. "But I have a feeling that Kevin would not want me to do that."

Hallam felt his curiosity perk up. "Why not?"

The astronomer looked down at his desk, then back up at Hallam. "I suppose you could say that Kevin is keeping a secret. He would not want all the publicity that would result if it was known that he was missing. I am afraid the newspapers would make quite a sensational thing of it."

Bauer fell silent again, and Hallam waited a minute before asking, "You goin' to explain that, Doctor?"

"Our conversation is confidential, correct?"

"Legally it ain't, not until you hire me, but when a man asks me to keep shut about something, I generally do it."

"Kevin's father is Thornton Jeffries."

Hallam grimaced. That simple statement explained a lot. Though he hadn't been in southern California at the time, he had heard the stories of how Thornton Jeffries had become almost an overnight millionaire when oil was found on his property years earlier. Since that time, Jeffries had done nothing but get richer. Oil, orange groves, real estate during the land booms . . . Thornton Jeffries had a hand in all of them.

"Didn't know Jeffries had a son," Hallam grunted.

"I do not think he is overly proud of Kevin," Bauer said with a sigh. "He had in mind that Kevin would eventually take over the family business, but Kevin had no interest in such things. He wanted to be an astronomer instead. His father never understood."

"How long's the boy been missin'?"

"Two days. Thirty-six hours, actually. He was here Tuesday night, but he did not come in yesterday or today."

Hallam leaned forward, hunching his shoulders slightly. "Reckon you're right about the newspapers," he said. "They'd have a high old time with a story like this. But you know that boy could be in bad trouble, him bein' a rich man's son and all."

Bauer sighed again, his weariness evident. "I realize that, Mr. Hallam. It is possible that he has been kidnapped or robbed or—Lord knows what might have happened to him."

"You sure he ain't just off doin' something on his own?"

"He would have told me if he could not come in," Bauer said. "He was very serious about the work we do here, not a frivolous young man like so many you see these days. Besides, he has a special project of his own that he has been working on, an important project. When he was not here Wednesday, I tried to call him and did not get an answer. The same was true today. I am very worried about him, Mr. Hallam, but I hesitated to call the police. Kevin wants to be out of his father's shadow, to make it on his own. That is why I decided to hire a private detective."

Hallam nodded slowly. "Reckon I could look into it for you," he said, coming to the decision as he spoke. "Not unless you agree to something else, though."

"I am prepared to pay any reasonable fee—"

Hallam cut him off with a wave of a big hand. "If I haven't turned the boy up by tomorrow night, I want you to report this to the police. That's the condition."

Bauer considered briefly, then nodded. "You are right, of course. But you will give the case twenty-four hours?"

Hallam nodded again and stood up. "I'll need his address and telephone number. Don't suppose you've got a picture of him?"

Bauer shook his head as he wrote on a pad of paper. He tore the slip off and handed it to Hallam. "There is his address and number. I can give you a description of Kevin. He's tall and rather thin, with dark hair that is usually parted in the middle." A slight smile touched Bauer's face. "Recently he has been attempting to grow a mustache, as well. So far, he has not been too successful."

"He got any friends that you know of?"

"That young man who was talking to me outside, Garrett Alderson, is his best friend, I suppose. They have known each other for quite some time."

"What about women?"

"Really, Mr. Hallam, how would I know? Oh, there was one young lady up here one day. Kevin was showing her the telescope." Bauer coughed discreetly. "I imagine that Garrett could tell you her name. He was here that day, too, and I gathered that he was also interested in the girl."

"What about the boy's father? You checked with him to see if he knows where his son is?"

"I called the Jeffries estate and asked if he was there. Whoever I talked to, a butler I suppose, told me that Kevin has his own house. I already knew that, of course. The man said that Kevin had not been there for several months."

"You didn't tell anybody there that Kevin's missin'?"

Bauer shook his head.

It seemed to Hallam like the astronomer was taking an awful lot of responsibility on himself in this matter. The cops should have been notified, and the boy's family sure as hell should have been told. Those were decisions that weren't up to him, though. Bauer had made them already. Hallam's only decision was whether or not to take the case, and he had already made up his mind on that one.

"Reckon I could use your office to talk to this Garrett Alderson?"

Bauer stood up. "I will ask him to step in here."

He went out, leaving the office door open, and a few minutes later, Garrett Alderson appeared there. "Dr. Bauer said you wanted to see me, Mr. . . . ?"

"Hallam, Lucas Hallam. You and this Kevin Jeffries were friends, right?"

Alderson nodded. He said, "Kevin and I met at Stanford. We were both studying astronomy, and we used to help each other out on the work."

"You have any idea where he might've got off to?"

"None at all," Alderson replied with a shake of his head. "I think if Kevin had been planning to go away, he would have told me about it."

"The other folks who work here, do they know he's missin'?"

Alderson shrugged. "I suppose they've noticed he hasn't been at work, but as far as I know, Dr. Bauer and I are the only ones who are worried."

"Does Kevin have any other friends besides you, somebody who might know where he is?"

"He always kept to himself . . . No, sir, I can't think of anyone."

Hallam reached up and rubbed his jaw thoughtfully. "How about this gal who was up here, the one who was lookin' at the telescope? You know who she is?"

Alderson's eyes dropped, and he seemed uncomfortable as he answered, "Her name is Elena Fleming."

"She Kevin's girlfriend?"

"I suppose you could say that."

"But you're a little sweet on her yourself, ain't you?"

Alderson glanced up, his gaze meeting Hallam's again. "I used to go with her," he said sharply. "In fact, I introduced her to Kevin. But that was after she and I had broken up."

"Hold on, son. Didn't mean no offense. You know where the girl lives?"

"She has a house in Pasadena, not far from Kevin's place." Alderson frowned at Hallam. "Are you going to get her mixed up in this?"

"Just thought I'd ask her a few questions. She might know more of what was on the boy's mind than anybody else."

"I suppose so," Alderson said grudgingly. He gave Hallam the girl's address, then said, "Is there anything else?"

"No, I reckon that's all for now," Hallam said. "Thanks for talkin' to me."

Alderson paused in the door. "I hope you find Kevin, Mr. Hallam. He's a good friend, and I wouldn't want anything to happen to him."

"I'll give it my best shot, son."

Hallam wasn't sure how good his best shot could be in this case, though. As he pointed his flivver back down the winding road that led to the base of Mount Wilson, he thought about what he had been told so far. It wasn't much to go on, but it was enough to stir up some unpleasant speculations.

Anytime someone with a rich relative vanished, the

most obvious possibility was kidnapping. Kevin Jeffries
had kept his relationship to his father pretty quiet, but
someone could have found out and decided that putting
the snatch on the boy would be a good way to get some
money out of old Thornton Jeffries.

If that was the case, there would be a ransom demand.
Hallam would nose around awhile, try to turn up something on his own, but if he was unsuccessful, he would
have to go to Kevin's father and find out if he had
heard anything.

He had to go back through Pasadena anyway to get
to Hollywood. Might as well stop by Kevin's house and
take a look around, Hallam thought.

It was a small, neat bungalow on an avenue of small,
neat bungalows, well lit by streetlights. Hallam eased the
flivver to the curb and stopped in front of the house
Kevin Jeffries was renting. He killed the engine, waited
a minute before he got out and shut the door softly.

There was light in the house, a soft glow that was
there, then gone, then back again.

Looked like someone was searching the place with
a candle.

Hallam reached through the open window of the car
on the passenger's side and opened the glove box.
Coiled up inside was an old-fashioned holster and shell
belt, and inside the holster was a long-barreled Colt
Peacemaker. Hallam slid the weapon from the holster
and then dropped the belt back on the car seat. The
smooth walnut grips of the Colt felt good against his
callused palm.

He went across the yard toward the house, moving
with an efficient grace unusual in a big man.

The front door was locked. Hallam went to the side
of the house, moved along it silently to the back. There
was a screened-in porch there. That door was unhooked,
and the door leading into the kitchen was open, too.

Hallam paused just inside the house, letting his ears
work, picking up small sounds that told him the intruder—the *other* intruder, he thought wryly, since he
hadn't been invited in himself—was in the front part of
the house. His eyes had adjusted enough to show him
vague shapes where the furniture was. Hallam started
through the kitchen, toward the rooms where the other

person was. Suddenly, he saw the glow of the candle again, filling a doorway. He stopped in his tracks, the Colt coming up to cover the door as the glow became stronger.

The soft scrape of a shoe behind him was all the warning he had.

Hallam started to whirl, but he was just a little too late. Something hard bounced off his skull, staggering him. He lashed out with the Colt, not wanting to shoot, and caught a glimpse of a face in the dim candlelight filtering in from the other room and the glow from a streetlight coming through a side window. The blow missed, and he heard a grunt of effort as the other man swung again. This time the sap didn't hit him a glancing blow. It connected solidly, and Hallam went down as pain exploded behind his eyes. He felt the Colt slip from his fingers, but there was nothing he could do to stop it.

He didn't go under completely. He heard a man's voice rasp a curse and then the sound of running footsteps. Hallam forced himself up on hands and knees, trying to ignore the fierce pounding in his head, and started to feel around for his fallen gun.

The overhead light clicked on, blinding him, and something sharp came down painfully on his hand. He jerked back, heard a female voice exclaim, "Oh!" Then, "Don't you move! I've got a gun, and I'm not afraid to use it!"

Hallam looked up, blinking, trying to make his eyes start working again, and slowly focused on the shape standing over him.

It was a good shape, young and trim and curved in the right places, topped with an attractive face and a shower of thick brunette hair. The girl was a looker, and she was truthful, too.

There was a gun in her hand, a small revolver, and it was pointed right at Hallam's head.

"Hold on, miss," Hallam said, keeping his voice calm. He didn't like the wild look in the girl's eyes. "No call to go pointin' that hogleg at me. I mean you no harm."

"Wh-what are you doing here?"

Moving slowly so as not to spook her, Hallam drew in the hand she had just stomped with a high-heeled shoe. There was a small cut on the back of it. He said, "Reckon you'd be Elena Fleming."

She looked surprised. "How did you know that, Mr. Hallam? And what exactly are you doing lying on the kitchen floor?"

Now it was Hallam's turn to be surprised. He asked, "Do I know you, miss? You do look a mite familiar."

Elena Fleming smiled a tight smile but didn't lower the gun. "We haven't actually worked together, but I've heard about you."

Hallam nodded, remembering suddenly that he had seen her on the set of a Doug Fairbanks picture. "You're an actress."

"Just bit parts so far, but that's going to change," she said with a positive tone. "But that doesn't explain what you're doing in Kevin's house."

The gun hadn't moved an inch during the conversation. Hallam said in an even tone, "I'm also a private detective. Actin' is just a side job for me. That Dr. Bauer feller hired me to look for Kevin Jeffries. And as for why I was lyin' on the kitchen floor, as you put it, some sneakin' snake-in-the-grass hit me on the head."

The barrel of the pistol finally sagged toward the floor as relief washed over Elena Fleming's features. "My God, I thought you were one of the kidnappers!" she exclaimed.

Hallam figured it was safe to stand up now. She was holding the gun loosely, her arm hanging at her side. He got to his feet, scooping up his own Colt and tucking it behind his belt.

"You know for sure Kevin's been kidnapped?" he asked, his voice sharp.

Elena shook her head. "But he wouldn't just disappear without telling me. We're . . . we're engaged to be married. We have no secrets from each other. Something unexpected—something bad—must have happened to Kevin."

"That's the way it looks to me, too, but I haven't had a chance to do much lookin' into the matter, yet. Mind tellin' me what you were doin' pokin' around his house in the dark?"

"I was checking to see if he had come back. I came over last night, after Kevin didn't call me all day, but there was no sign of him. And I've worried so much since then I had to come back over. Besides, someone has to feed his fish."

"Fish?"

"Kevin has an aquarium with tropical fish, some quite rare species, in fact," Elena said. "Would you like to see them?"

Hallam's knowledge of fish extended to hooking rainbow trout out of a high mountain stream and pan-frying them, but that was about it. "I'll take your word for that," he told her. "How'd you get in?"

Her features began to turn crimson as she blushed. "Really, Mr. Hallam . . . Kevin and I *are* engaged. I have a key."

Hallam reached up and carefully touched the knot on his head, wincing as pain radiated from it. "Did you see anybody when you came in tonight?"

Elena shook her head. "The house seemed empty. If there was anyone here, he was hiding from me."

"Why didn't you turn the lights on?"

Elena laughed shortly, but there was no humor in it. "You haven't met Mrs. White yet, I take it. Kevin's next-door neighbor?"

Hallam shook his head, and damned if it didn't hurt.

"She seems to think that Kevin is her son. At any rate, she treats him like he is. And she doesn't approve of me at all. I didn't want her to see a light and come over here thinking Kevin was home. Why, if she knew I had a key to his house, the poor boy would never hear the end of it. She'd tell him I was just a brazen, shameless hussy! You know how some people feel about actresses."

That made sense to Hallam. He said, "You didn't find any sign of Kevin havin' been here yesterday or today?"

"None at all."

"Are any of his things missin'? You know, like clothes and a bag?"

"I couldn't find anything at all missing. Oh, Mr. Hallam . . ." Her voice cracked slightly. "I'm so worried about him."

"Don't you fret none," Hallam said, reaching out

rather awkwardly to touch her shoulder. "We'll find that feller of yours, and I'm sure he'll be just fine."

"I hope so."

Hallam kept the rest of his thoughts to himself. Now that his head was a little clearer, he recalled the face of the man who had hit him. Even though he had seen the features only for a split second, something in the back of Hallam's mind had thought they were familiar. Now, in the last few minutes, he had finally dredged up the memory and put a name with the face—Myron Dart.

And Myron Dart was nothing but hired muscle, a strong-arm man for Walter Tyrone.

Who was damn near the biggest crook in Los Angeles at the moment, if you didn't count the politicians.

Nope, Hallam thought, things didn't look too good for Kevin Jeffries, and they were getting worse by the minute.

It was a toss-up where Hallam would find Walter Tyrone. Tyrone frequented the best nightclubs in Hollywood, and there were plenty of them. After he and Elena Fleming left Kevin's house rather quickly so that Mrs. White next door wouldn't get suspicious, he sent Elena home with a promise to get in touch with her right away if he found Kevin or discovered anything about him. Then he looked in at the Cocoanut Grove and the Montmartre Cafe before getting lucky at a relatively new nightspot called the Red Top. A half-dollar got the parking lot attendant to admit that Tyrone had gone into the club earlier in the evening, in company with "one red-hot mama, lemme tell ya," as the youngster put it.

Hallam nodded, headed for the door of the club.

He expected to be stopped, and he was. The doorman, a beefy type whose shoulders strained the fabric of his gaudy red coat, put a hand on Hallam's chest and said, "You ain't goin' in there dressed like that, buddy. This ain't no cowboy saloon."

Hallam put a sorrowful look on his face and shook his head. "Mr. Tyrone's goin' to be powerful upset when he finds out you didn't let me in, pard," he said. "I got an important message for him."

"You can give me any message you got. I'll see that it gets to Mr. Tyrone."

"Nope, can't do it. This here word's got to be delivered personal-like." Hallam seemed to brighten. "Say, ol' Myron come in just a little while ago, didn't he, sort of worked up?" Without waiting for the doorman to respond, Hallam went on quickly, "Tell him I got news about Kevin. Can you do that?"

"Sure, sure," the doorman muttered. He stepped inside for a few moments, then reappeared. "Just wait right here, buddy. Don't run off."

"Don't intend to," Hallam said.

He hooked his thumbs in his belt and stood waiting, and as he did, he looked around the nightclub's entrance. There was a curving driveway with a red canopy over it directly in front of the heavy wooden double doors. Small windows were set in each door, but they had smoked glass in them and could not be seen through. Hallam had been inside the Red Top a couple of times, though, and he knew that beyond the small foyer was a big room, sunken a couple of feet below ground level and filled with the usual tables and chairs, with a bar along one wall, booths along the other, and a bandstand and tiny dance floor at the far end. The club's primary distinguishing feature was its huge skylight of blood-red glass. Lights mounted on the roof shone down through the glass, casting a red glow that moved around the club as the motors mounted on the lights made them rotate. It was a fancy gimmick in a town noted for fancy gimmicks. The place was popular now, but once the novelty of it wore off, the stars and starmakers of Hollywood might find themselves a new watering hole.

The entrance doors slapped open abruptly, and Myron Dart strode out, a scowl on his face. He was as broad as Hallam but not quite as tall, and his bald head had ugly ridges of flesh running from above his ears around to the back of his skull. In an angry voice, he demanded, "Where's this gink lookin' for me?" then his gaze fell on Hallam and he exclaimed, "You!"

Hallam had his feet braced, and the muscles of his shoulders bunched as he brought a knobby fist up and slammed it in the middle of Dart's startled expression.

All the power of Hallam's body was behind the punch, and with a howl, Dart flew back through the swinging doors, hit the drop-off where the main room of the club stepped down, and fell flat on his back. Women started to scream. Hallam didn't pay the commotion any mind. He brushed past the doorman, who was too stunned to stop him, and strode into the Red Top.

Myron Dart was trying to get up again, and at the same time was reaching under his coat. Hallam hooked his arm with the toe of his boot, jerked it away from the butt of the gun in Dart's shoulder holster, then let his foot come down on the wrist. Dart yelped as bones crunched together.

"Don't like it when somebody uses a sap on me," Hallam told him, pressing down a little harder. "Where's your boss?"

"Right here," a voice crackled. "What the hell are you doing, mister?"

Hallam looked up to see a well-dressed, handsome man with sleek dark hair standing next to a table, his clean-cut features mottled with rage. Still seated at the table, her mouth open in shock, was one of the most beautiful women Hallam had ever seen. He recognized her right away—Gail Sumner. She'd played a few second leads, and according to the gossip Hallam heard around the lots, she was poised for bigger and better things. A big publicity push was just getting underway.

"You'd be Walter Tyrone, I reckon," Hallam said to Gail Sumner's escort. "Seen your picture in the paper a time or two."

"Who the devil are you?" Tyrone demanded.

"Name's Lucas Hallam."

"I don't know you, Mr. Hallam, but that's my personal assistant you're assaulting, and I demand that you stop it right now."

"This personal assistant of yours—" Hallam looked down at Myron Dart, who was writhing in pain. "Reckon thug'd be a better word for him . . . Anyway, he clouted me with a sap earlier this evenin', and I didn't take kindly to it. I want to know why he was hidin' in Kevin Jeffries' house and waitin' to hit folks on the head."

Before Tyrone could answer, Hallam heard rapid foot-steps behind him. A glance over his shoulder told him that the doorman had recovered his wits enough to come after him, but Tyrone jerked up a hand and motioned the man to a halt. "Wait!" Tyrone snapped. "I want to talk to this man."

"But Mr. Tyrone . . ." the doorman said, clearly confused. "The way he came bustin' in here and all . . . I've already called the cops."

"Call them back," Tyrone said smoothly. "There's no need to involve the police in this, Jerry."

"Well . . . okay, Mr. Tyrone." The doorman sounded disappointed that he couldn't waltz a little with Hallam before the arrival of the authorities.

Hallam figured Myron Dart was in enough pain to not be a threat for a few minutes, anyway, so he got off of the man's wrist and said to Tyrone, "The way you're throwin' orders around, could be you own this place behind a front man or two."

Tyrone slipped a cigarette in his mouth and lit it with a gold lighter. "Could be," he admitted. "Or maybe not. That's neither here nor there. What's your connection with Kevin Jeffries?"

Dart curled up on the floor, holding his injured wrist and making little moaning sounds. Hallam stepped around him and came closer to the table where Tyrone stood and Gail Sumner sat. Right from the start, there had been several ways of playing this. He could have been subtle and trailed Tyrone for a while, but that might have taken too long. The fracas with Myron Dart, short-lived though it had been, had cut right to the heart of things, and that was the way Hallam liked it.

"I'm lookin' for Kevin," he told Tyrone. "His boss hired me to find him. Seems the boy up an' disappeared."

"You're a private investigator?" Tyrone sounded surprised.

Hallam nodded.

"Lucas Hallam," Tyrone mused. "I believe I have heard of you after all, Mr. Hallam, now that I think about it." He reached inside his coat, and when Hallam tensed, Tyrone smiled and said, "Relax, Mr. Hallam. I'm reaching for my checkbook."

That wasn't what Hallam had expected. He wasn't prepared for what Tyrone said next, either.

"I'd like to hire you myself. I'll double whatever Dr. Bauer is paying you to find Kevin, on the condition that you notify me first."

Hallam blinked. "You want to hire me? Shoot, I figured you kidnapped the boy."

"Why in the world would I do that?" Tyrone sounded genuinely startled by the suggestion.

Hallam hesitated before answering. This hadn't gone like he had anticipated. He had figured Tyrone would get all huffy and deny knowing anything about Kevin Jeffries. Now, Tyrone not only wasn't running scared, he seemed to want Kevin found as much as Dr. Bauer and Elena Fleming did. There were only two possibilities, Hallam finally decided: either Tyrone was behind the boy's disappearance, in which case he already knew that Thornton Jeffries was Kevin's father, or Tyrone hadn't had anything to do with it. Either way, Hallam didn't see any harm in revealing the connection between Kevin and his father.

"The boy's daddy is Thornton Jeffries," Hallam said.

"Really?" Once again, Tyrone sounded honestly surprised. "I had no idea."

"Then why do you want him found?"

"The young man and I have, ah, some business dealings to conclude," Tyrone said.

"What kind of business does an astronomer have with a high-class owlhoot like you?"

Tyrone chuckled. "You misjudge me, Mr. Hallam, just like the members of the press and our local police departments do. I'm just a businessman, an entrepreneur, if you will. A promoter." He put a hand on the soft flesh of Gail Sumner's shoulder, which was left bare by the low-cut silvery gown she wore. The dress went well with her platinum hair and deep blue eyes. "At the moment, I'm promoting Gail here. You could say she's my current project. But only in a business sense, of course."

"Of course," Hallam agreed heavily, not believing that for a second. "That still don't tell me why you're lookin' for Kevin Jeffries, or how come that goon o' yours was lurkin' around his house."

"I'm afraid some things will have to remain confidential until the time is right to announce them, Mr. Hallam. That's the way of business, after all. Everything at the proper time." Tyrone gestured softly with the checkbook he had taken from his coat. "Now, about that offer I made to you . . .?"

Hallam shook his head. "Don't think so. I already got a client. But I'll be keepin' an eye on you, Tyrone, so don't try nothin' funny." He jerked a thumb toward Dart, who had pulled himself into a sitting position but still had his sore wrist cradled in his lap. He was staring up at Hallam with hatred in his eyes. "And keep that fella clear of me, or next time there'll be worse trouble."

"Myron won't bother you anymore, Hallam. I can assure you of that."

Hallam turned to walk out. The club had cleared of patrons when the trouble started, leaving only the puzzled musicians on the bandstand to witness the confrontation between Hallam and Tyrone. He ignored the doorman's glare as he went out to his flivver, got in, and drove away.

Well, it had felt damned good to pop that Dart fella in the snoot, Hallam mused, but other than that, he couldn't see that he'd done a bit of good. Kevin Jeffries was still missing, and while the most likely suspect in his disappearance was not yet in the clear—Hallam wasn't stupid enough to take everything Tyrone had told him at face value—the waters had still been muddied up considerable. If Tyrone wasn't behind Kevin's kidnapping . . . hell, if there hadn't been any kidnapping at all . . . then where in blazes *was* the young astronomer? And if Tyrone had been telling the truth, what sort of connection could Kevin have with a shady character like Tyrone and a lovely young actress like Gail Sumner?

Elena Fleming was an actress, too, and pretty enough without being as spectacularly beautiful as Gail. Elena had never had the benefit of a publicity push like the one Gail was beginning to get, either. Other than that, there were some similarities. Maybe Kevin had a fondness for pretty young actresses, and maybe just because he was engaged to Elena, that didn't mean he might not be mixed up with somebody else like Gail. In which case Tyrone could have gotten wind of the affair and had the boy taken out and done away with. Men like Tyrone tended to get mighty possessive at times, Hallam knew, especially where women like Gail Sumner were concerned.

That would explain why Tyrone hadn't known about Kevin's father being Thornton Jeffries. If Tyrone had regarded Kevin solely as a romantic rival to be rubbed out, he wouldn't give a hoot who the youngster's father was. He'd just have Kevin killed and be done with it.

Hallam shook his head. He was doing a lot of speculating, but he couldn't prove a bit of it. Not only that, but the vague theory he'd come up with didn't really explain why Myron Dart, Tyrone's hired muscle, was hanging around Kevin's house. Dart's presence there made it look like Tyrone really was looking for Kevin. It was enough to make a fella's brain hurt, Hallam decided, and when that happened, the best thing to do was to head for the high country and clear your head.

He turned the flivver toward Pasadena. Mount Wilson was the closest thing he was going to find to the high country in these parts.

Evidently Dr. Bauer and his staff had finished their work for the night and gone home, because the parking lot around the observatory was empty when Hallam pulled in there an hour or so later. During the drive up here, he had been over and over the facts of the case, skimpy as they were, but he still couldn't make them add up to anything else other than the two possibilities that had already occurred to him—either Kevin Jeffries had been kidnapped by someone after a hefty ransom from his father . . . or Walter Tyrone had had the youngster killed in a fit of jealousy over Gail Sumner. That last theory was really stretching things, Hallam thought, but he couldn't afford to ignore it.

He parked his flivver, killed the engine, got out. The observatory would give him a quiet spot to think, and it was certainly pretty up here. He had told Dr. Bauer that he didn't know much about the stars except how to steer by them, but that wasn't strictly true. Many a night on the trail, he had lain in his bedroll and watched the great canopy of the sky spread out above him. To anyone who had spent a great deal of their days and nights outdoors, the sky was a source of endless fascination. Hallam had always enjoyed looking up at the stars, and that was what he did now. Everyone from the ancients on down had known that there were pictures in the stars if you looked close enough. Hallam had seen them himself. They were always shifting, ever changing, but they were there.

And if you got tired of one picture, you could always look at the stars from a little different angle and see a picture that was totally different. . . .

That thought burst through Hallam's brain at the same instant as the great dome of the observatory began to slide open.

Hallam wheeled around in surprise, hearing the faint grinding hum of the electric motors that operated the dome. In the starlight filtering down, he saw the split opening up in the center to give the telescope within access to the night sky. He had thought the observatory was deserted, but that dome wouldn't be opening by itself.

Bauer had said that Kevin Jeffries was working on a project of his own, a special project that was potentially quite important.

Maybe Kevin had come back to the observatory to finish it up, Hallam thought as he started toward the domed building.

The door was unlocked, he discovered when he got there. That made sense; as an important assistant to the director, Kevin likely would have had a key to get into the place. Hallam slipped in as quietly as possible, and that was pretty quiet considering that he'd been taught how to move by an old Apache. However, the noise of the motors was louder inside, and it would cover up any faint sounds he made.

There was a small light burning off to one side of the telescope, but other than that the cavernous space was dark. A slender figure in a long white coat moved around over there, near the eyepiece, then bent to peer through it as the dome's aperture reached its maximum. The man straightened, made notes on a clipboard, looked through the telescope again.

Hallam ambled up behind him and said, "Howdy, Kevin."

The figure in the white coat yelped in shock, threw the clipboard up in the air, and spun around, backing up quickly against the unyielding mass of the telescope. Hallam recognized him from the description—the dark hair parted in the middle, the wispy mustache. He was Kevin Jeffries, all right, no doubt about that.

"Who . . . who are you?" Kevin asked with a gulp of nervousness.

"Name's Lucas Hallam. I been lookin' for you for a few hours now, but I got to admit it seems longer. You got a lot of folks worried about you, son. I figured you was either dead or kidnapped."

Kevin swallowed again. "You . . . you're looking for me? Why?"

"That's my job. I'm a private detective."

"Oh, God." Kevin's fright grew visibly. "You're not working for . . . for *her*, are you?"

"Her?" Hallam repeated, a frown of confusion on his face. "You mean Gail Sumner?"

"No! I'm talking about Elena!"

"Elena Fleming? Well, she's mighty worried about you, but she ain't footin' the bill for my services, if that's what's got you spooked. I'm workin' for—"

Hallam broke off as a sweeping beam of light washed through the door he had left open behind him and played over Kevin's face. Hallam jerked his head around in time to see the last flicker of the headlights as the car outside came to a stop.

Kevin yelped again, and as Hallam turned back toward him, the young man lunged toward the small lamp that was set up on a nearby table and swept it off onto the floor. The bulb broke with a popping sound and darkness fell over the interior of the observatory. Hallam heard the swift patter of feet as Kevin ran off into the gloom.

A flashlight beam lanced through the blackness. "Kevin?" a voice called. Hallam recognized it as belonging to Walter Tyrone. "Kevin, are you in here? Come on, lad, no one's going to hurt you."

Hallam bit back a curse and edged to the side. Maybe Tyrone had followed him up here, maybe the so-called promoter had come on his own. Either way, it didn't matter. What was important was keeping Kevin alive.

"Hallam?" That voice came from another part of the observatory, and Hallam knew its owner, too—Myron

Dart. "You in here, Hallam? I saw your car outside, and you ain't gettin' out until you and I settle up for that poke in the snoot, you son of a bitch!"

"Take it easy, Myron," Tyrone snapped. "The important thing is finding Jeffries."

Hallam wished he'd brought the Colt from the car, but it was still in the glove box. He'd have bet the farm that both Tyrone and Dart were armed.

"Walter, where are you? I don't like the dark!"

That complaint made Hallam's frown deepen. Gail Sumner? Had to be. But if Tyrone had come up here to kill Kevin Jeffries, he wouldn't have brought Gail with him, would he? Not unless he wanted to make sure she understood what would happen if she ever went behind his back with another man again. But Hallam had just about discarded that theory . . .

"Just stand still, Gail," Tyrone said impatiently as he swept the flashlight beam around. "If you want to do something to help, see if you can convince Kevin to come out."

"All right, I will," Gail Sumner said, and Hallam could hear the pout in her voice. "Kevin! Please, sweetie, nobody wants to hurt you. We just want your help, like you promised."

Tyrone added, "And if it's a matter of money, I don't mind increasing the payment, Kevin. How about a thousand dollars instead of five hundred?"

In the darkness, Hallam gave a little shake of his head. This was getting more confusing than ever. What could a young astronomer do that would be worth a grand to a slick operator like Walter Tyrone?

And when the answer occurred to him in the next instant as he remembered his conversation with Dr. Bauer, he muttered a heartfelt, "Oh, hell!"

That was a mistake. With a rush of footsteps, Myron Dart charged him, shouting, "Gotcha, cowboy!"

"Myron!" Tyrone yelled, but it was too late now.

Enough starlight filtered down through the opening in the dome for Hallam to make out the shape of Dart lunging toward him. He ducked under the wild roundhouse punch that Dart swung at his head and stepped closer to slam a fist into the thug's midsection. It was like punching the wood-paneled wall of the Red Top.

Dart grunted and flung his arms around Hallam in a bear hug. Both men went down.

Hallam twisted as he fell and managed to land on top of Dart. He brought a knee up, but Dart took the blow on the thigh. Dart growled, and Hallam felt his ribs starting to give a little as Dart increased the pressure. Hallam ducked his head and slammed the top of it into Dart's face.

Dart's nose must have been swollen and sore from the punch Hallam had landed earlier in the evening, because he let out a howl and loosened his grip enough for Hallam to get an arm free. He whipped another punch at Dart's face, aiming by instinct, and connected with the man's prominent jaw. Hallam's other arm came loose then from Dart's grip, and as he heaved himself up so that he was sitting on Dart's chest, he clubbed both hands together and lifted them over his head, ready to smash them down in a blow that would end this fight.

Lights came on all over the observatory, blinding Hallam. He heard Kevin Jeffries cry raggedly, "Enough! That's enough, dammit! I wish I'd never even seen that blasted star!"

Myron Dart suddenly bucked underneath Hallam, throwing him off. Hallam rolled and came up onto his feet as his vision started to settle down a little. Dart scrambled upright and jerked a gun from inside his coat. As he leveled the pistol at Hallam, Tyrone shouted, "No, Myron! Blast it, don't shoot him!"

Dart's hands trembled a little as he trained the gun on Hallam. "Aw, come on, Mr. Tyrone," he pleaded. "I got to!"

"No! This isn't like the old days, Myron. We're legit now, remember?"

Hallam stood very still as Dart struggled with the conflict between his instinct and his boss's command. Finally, he lowered the gun and muttered. "Hell, hell, hell! You don't know how close you came, cowboy. You just don't know."

"Reckon I do," Hallam said, trying not to breathe too big a sigh of relief.

Kevin Jeffries strode out into the center of the floor toward Tyrone and Gail Sumner, who stood nervously with the promoter's arm around her shoulders. She had added a silver fox stole to her outfit and looked just as lovely as the last time Hallam had seen her.

"Legitimate," Kevin said with scorn in his voice as he faced Tyrone. "Does that include sending your strong-arm man to beat me up so I'd be sure to do what you wanted?"

"I've explained that, Kevin," Tyrone said, forcing himself to sound patient. "That was all a mistake."

"Ha! Reverting back to your true nature, I'd call it."

Hallam wanted to tell the boy to walk lightly around Tyrone and Dart, but Kevin was too mad to listen to him.

"Do you know how much trouble you've caused me?" Kevin demanded. "Do you have any idea how I've spent the past two days? I've been hiding! I sat in the bushes at Griffith Park most of the day today, and I'm covered with insect bites!"

Hallam knew Griffith Park and the Bronson Canyon area from the hundreds of Western pictures he'd worked on there as a stunt player and riding extra. But he never would have thought of looking for Kevin Jeffries there. It was a good thing he'd wandered back up here to Mount Wilson tonight on a hunch . . . maybe. He and Kevin weren't out of the woods yet.

Kevin put his haggard face in his hands and said around them, "The worst part has been dodging that crazy woman. I never should have told her what I'd found . . . and then you and that girlfriend of yours show up and make everything worse!"

Hallam came over and put a hand on Kevin's shoulder. Everything he had heard so far had confirmed the theory that had sprung into his mind earlier, but he had to know for sure. "You discovered a new star, didn't you, son?" he asked. Kevin nodded jerkily, and Hallam went on, "And since you found it, you get to name it."

"It's a perfect gimmick," Tyrone put in. "He names the star after Gail—one new star named after another one, get it? Hell, with something like that going for us, I can get Gail plenty of ink in every paper in town. Hell, across the whole damn world!"

"But Elena thought the star ought to be named after her," Hallam said. "After all, she's the gal you're engaged to, Kevin, so I reckon I can see her point."

"I am *not* engaged to her! She's the one who wants

to get married, not me. But when I told her about the star, nothing would satisfy her until I'd promised to name it after her." Kevin swallowed and turned a sick gaze on Hallam. "She carries a gun, you know."

"I know. She pointed it at me earlier tonight." Hallam turned to Tyrone. "Look, you can't force the boy to name that star after Miss Sumner here, and you can't bribe him, either. He found the thing, and he's got the right to call it whatever suits his fancy."

"Oh, I wouldn't have minded naming it after her," Kevin said. "And the money would have come in handy, since I'm trying to stay independent of my father. It's just that Elena—"

"Yes, Kevin?" The new voice came from the entrance of the observatory. It was shrill and high-pitched and Hallam knew it was going to be nothing but trouble. "What about Elena?"

Everyone turned around sharply to face Elena Fleming, who stood just inside the entrance with the same pistol in her hand that she had threatened Hallam with in the kitchen of Kevin's house. Kevin's eyes widened in terror, and he ducked around the telescope, shouting, "Somebody stop her! She already took a shot at me yesterday!"

Elena jerked the gun toward the spot where Kevin had disappeared and pulled the trigger. With a wicked crack, the pistol sent lead ricocheting off the telescope while Hallam, Tyrone, Dart, and Gail Sumner dove for cover.

"You traitor!" Elena screamed at Kevin. "I thought you loved me, and then you tell me you're going to name *my* star after that . . . that hussy just for money!"

As he crouched on the other side of the telescope, Kevin protested, "But I told you that thug threatened me, Elena! I thought I had to go along with them or they'd kill me!"

She advanced steadily toward the massive apparatus, the gun unwavering in her hands. "I come up here hoping and praying that I'd find you safe—and then here you are with that . . . that woman! I'll show you who you should have been scared of! How dare you trifle with my affections?"

This whole mess had gone from dangerous to crazy

back to dangerous, Hallam thought as he knelt behind one of the desks scattered around the big room. A few feet away, Dart was hiding behind another desk, and he had his gun out again. On the other side of the room, Tyrone and Gail had taken shelter behind a large rolling blackboard with a star chart pulled down from a roller at the top of it. Future editions of that chart might include a new star, Hallam thought, but Kevin Jeffries wouldn't get to name it unless somebody did something about Elena—and soon. There was no place else for Kevin to hide, and she would have a clear shot at him again in a matter of moments.

"Don't worry, boss," Dart called across the room to Tyrone. "I'll take care of that nutty dame!" He sprang to his feet, leveling his pistol at Elena.

Hallam didn't stop to think. Elena Fleming was more than a little touched in the head, no doubt about that, but Hallam couldn't stand by and watch her being gunned down. He launched himself across the space between himself and Dart and slammed into the back of the man's legs. Dart's pistol blasted, but the shot whined off into the shadows in the upper reaches of the dome, his aim ruined by Hallam. A split second later, Elena spun toward him and fired.

Hallam heard Dart grunt from the impact of the slug as he tumbled backward. There was a bloody patch on the shoulder of Dart's coat, and his face was pale. Hallam had seen more than his share of bullet wounds over the past fifty years or so, though, and he figured Dart would be all right if he got some medical attention fairly soon.

Kevin screamed as Elena fired again. Hallam raised himself enough to see that Elena had him cornered, backed up under the cylindrical body of the giant telescope until he couldn't go any farther. The next shot wouldn't miss.

Hallam scooped up the gun Dart had dropped when Elena shot him. He stood up, the pistol seeming to rise of its own accord as he lifted his arm. Elena was standing at an angle to him, pointing the gun in her hand toward Kevin. It was going to be a difficult shot, but Hallam didn't think about that. When there was a gun in his hand, Lucas Hallam didn't have to think.

He just let his instincts take over and fired.

As it turned out, he missed, but only by a little. Shooting a gun out of somebody else's hand was a hell of a tricky proposition, no matter how often Tom Mix or Buck Jones did it in the movies. But the bullet grazed Elena's forearm, tearing the sleeve of her blouse, leaving a bloody streak on her arm, and making her drop the gun. That was just as good and, once Hallam stopped to think about it, even more spectacular than shooting the gun itself. Either way it got the job done, and as Elena reached for the fallen gun with her other hand, he got to her and kicked it across the room. She turned on him, screaming and hooking her fingers into claws, and he figured it was time to break that rule of his about not hitting women.

He clipped her on the chin with a loosely balled fist and she sat down hard, stunned.

"God Almighty!" Tyrone exclaimed as he peered nervously around the blackboard. "Are you all right, Hallam?"

Hallam's nerves were still jumping around like a barefoot kid on hot bricks, but other than that he was fine. He nodded and said to Kevin, who was staring in horrified fascination at Elena, "I reckon you'd better call the cops now, and an ambulance for ol' Myron over there. Hope none o' them slugs flyin' around here hurt that telescope."

Kevin gulped as he looked down at Elena. "Will . . . will they lock her up?" he asked.

"For a while, I reckon they will. But they'll likely let her out again one of these days, so if I was you, son, I'd start thinkin' about who I was goin' to name that star after."

"He's going to name it after Gail, of course," Tyrone said as he emerged from behind the blackboard, bringing the obviously shaken actress with him, while a pallid-faced Kevin went over to Bauer's office to use the telephone.

"No!" Gail said abruptly, jerking away from Tyrone. She pointed a shaking finger at Elena and went on, "That lunatic would have come after me next! I don't want a star named after me, Walter, I really don't! Can't we just forget the whole thing?"

"But, baby, think of the publicity! You can't just throw away an opportunity like this!"

Hallam tucked the guns in his belt, hauled Elena to her feet, and went outside with her to wait for the cops and the ambulance. All the fight had gone out of her, and he didn't think she'd give him any more trouble. He left Tyrone and Gail squabbling behind him and stepped out to take a deep breath of the clean night air and look up at the stars.

Yep, there were still pictures up there, and as far as Lucas Hallam was concerned, the little pinpricks of light didn't even need names. The stories they told were enough.

Kevin Jeffries surprised them all, Hallam found out later. An old cowboy and private eye might never *be* a star, as far as the movies were concerned.

But he had one of the real things with his name on it, anyway.

NO, I'M NOT JANE MARPLE, BUT SINCE YOU ASK . . .

By Margaret Maron

I do appreciate your letting me come talk to you like this, Doctor. As I explained over the phone, this new book I'm researching has a character who's undergoing psychotherapy and since I've never been to a therapist, I—

Oh no, no, no, I don't mistrust the profession. Not at all. It's just that I've never needed it. Like surgery. I've never had an operation either. If you're basically sound, the need for surgeons, like the need for therapists, never arises, right?

Good! I'll try not to take too much of your time. Just meeting your receptionist and seeing the sort of books and magazines you keep in your waiting room has been a big help. What I mainly need from you now is some technical jargon to sprinkle over my book for verisimilitude, so why don't we pretend I'm a new patient. What are some reasons I might consult you?

Oh?

Oh my goodness! Really?

How do you spell that last one?

No, no, I think those are quite enough to start with. One thing, though. I don't see a couch.

No couch? But I thought therapy was always— Okay, from that smile, I'd guess you therapists have to deal with as many misconceptions as mystery writers. People usually think I'm either Miss Marple or another Jessica Fletcher. In your case, I'll bet being a woman helps. At least your patients don't expect a Freudian beard and a Viennese accent, do they?

So! If you were going to treat me, I'd come in, perhaps curl up in this really comfortable chair (such a restful shade of blue! Did you use a local decorator?). And we'd just sit here? Looking at each other and talking face-to-face? How . . . um . . . *interesting.*

Well, no, it's not that I'd be embarrassed exactly, but it's like the Catholics, isn't it? I think it's so wrong-headed of them to phase out the confessional. Not that I'm Catholic. Actually, I was brought up Southern Baptist, but I've always thought the confession booth itself was such a good idea: that you could go sit in the darkness and whisper your sins through a grill, into a priest's ear, and be absolved without ever seeing his eyes. I don't understand how any Catholics could feel comfortable sitting across the table from a priest and telling their sins in broad daylight. I mean, how could you look him in the eye? I've always been such an eye-contact person myself and if I were going to talk to you about *my* psychoses and neuroses—oh not that I *could*, of course. As I said before, I simply don't have any. I've always been physically and mentally healthy as a horse.

Just look at the kind of books I write.

If readers ever give much thought to the persona behind my books, they probably think I'm a nice, down-to-earth, nurturing female. I don't write violent, glitzy pornography; good is usually rewarded in my books; evil is usually punished. My way of writing may not be mean-streets graphic enough for some tastes, but it *is* very straightforward.

I hope that doesn't sound too smug? Or bland? But when I write of mayhem and murder, it's certainly not to sublimate unfulfilled appetites for color, violence, or a darker side of life. No indeed. What you see is what you get. I'm just your basic boring beige.

Well, yes, I suppose even beige occasionally has to decide whether it's going to complement black or white, and I won't say there haven't been one or two instances . . . okay, three maybe if you count my sophomore year in college. But I'm sure you don't want to hear—

You do?

No, that's okay; I'm used to people saying I must have the mind of a murderer. I *have* killed a lot of people. Only on paper of course. Never in real life. Although . . . come to think of it, that college incident might amuse you—a sort of busman's holiday?—and not just because you're a woman but because the outcome was based on an introductory psychology course that I had to take to fill my social studies requirements. The professor did a classic experiment on us that—

But maybe I should put it in context by first telling you about my roommate, Janelle Denby. Cute as a June bug and such a dear person.

As freshmen, we'd been assigned the same room by chance, but it was a lucky chance and we've remained friends ever since. We would have roomed together the whole four years if she hadn't dropped out in the middle of our sophomore year.

No, not to get married, though I admit that's what a lot of young women from my generation did. Me, for instance, but not till my junior year. No, Janelle quit because she was raped and she just couldn't seem to shake it off.

That's what they used to expect of us, if you can believe it: that rape wasn't much more serious than a broken arm; and when the body healed, the mind should forget. But I really don't think many women ever do, do they? She eventually went back and got her degree from an all-girls' school, but she could never put herself in a man's hands again, and so she never married.

Never had a child either, of course, and she used to talk about wanting four. Such a pity. She'd have been a wonderful mother. She just loved children.

Date rape's a buzz phrase for the nineties and it's good that women are braver today about speaking out when it happens to them; but years ago, things were different. Especially in those small southern towns where I lived till I was twenty. You're too young to remember and Raleigh's gotten a lot more sophisticated, but back then rape was something to smirk about. And more shameful for the victim than for her attacker. Look at the callous advice we got—*"When rape is inevitable, honey, just lie back and enjoy it!"*

No woman ever said that, did she? I was really encouraged when that politician got nailed to the ballot box last spring for coming out with that awful saying. And wouldn't you know he'd be from the South? Texas, wasn't it? You could tell what era *that* good ol' boy grew up in.

Anyhow, as I started to tell you, rape in the late fifties was usually considered the woman's fault. She asked for it, they said. Men were subject to certain natural urges that any really *nice* girl could keep under control. If not, she must have been dressed provocatively, or she'd let him go too far to expect him to stop, or what was she doing there alone that time of night anyhow?

Even college did nothing to change that early mind-set. It was part of our culture. Unless a girl came back to the dorm hysterical and bloody, it would be whispered that she only cried rape because the housemother had questioned her sternly about her disheveled appearance. (Back then housemothers took the term *in loco parentis* seriously. They literally did act like a parent.)

But Mrs. Flaxton had been making cocoa out in the kitchen that night in October when Janelle signed herself back in and got upstairs without being noticed. As sophomores, we were beginning our first year in Kirkland, an upperclass dorm.

I'd been reviewing for a quiz in that psych course with Liz Peterson, a junior who lived on the third floor, when Janelle burst through the door and immediately locked it behind her. She was a mess. No lipstick, knee socks crumpled at her ankles, her plaid cotton dress a mass of wrinkles. And she was so upset that she couldn't even tell us what had happened at first, just whimpered like a whipped puppy as she tore her clothes off and reached for her robe.

Her lips were swollen and there were bruises on her arms. I thought she'd taken a bad fall or been knocked down by a car or something, and I said, "You're hurt! I'll get Mrs. Flaxton."

"No!" she cried. "You can't— Nobody. Please, Maggie, nobody!"

She was shaking so violently that Liz pulled the cover off my bed and wrapped her in it and we held her until she'd calmed down enough to tell us that she'd been raped and Mrs. Flaxton mustn't know or she'd be kicked out of school because it was Tuesday.

Oh, I know that must sound ridiculous to you. It was ridiculous to us, too. Nevertheless, other than study dates at the library, sophomore girls (and yes, we called ourselves girls back then) weren't allowed to date except on the weekends. And going off-campus at night without signing out really was an offense that could get you suspended.

That's what Janelle had done. Between whimpers, she told us that she'd signed out to the library but had arranged to meet Buck Woodall down by the lake in a wooded park that served as a buffer between campus and the edge of town.

"Buck Woodall!" said Liz. "What on earth were you doing out with *him*?"

"I thought we were just going to walk along the lake in the moonlight," Janelle sobbed.

I was bewildered. Janelle and I had met Buck Woodall on the tennis court a few days earlier. He was a journalism major and something of a big name on campus. School paper, baseball team, student council, you name it. Incredibly good-looking with a slow bashful smile, dark sexy eyes and, yes, a reputation as a wolf with eight hands; but we forgot about that as soon as we met him because there was nothing crude or ungentlemanly about his approach. He was so smooth, a real dreamboat. I was just as smitten as Janelle, but when he put the moves on her I'd backed off and watched enviously while he turned all that charm on her.

"Oh, you poor schnook," said Liz. "Haven't you heard that he tries to get in the pants of every girl he dates? He keeps asking me out, but I wouldn't trust him for Sunday tea at the college chaplain's."

Liz was from up North and, as a junior, she was also our fount of campus wisdom, but this was the first time she'd mentioned Buck Woodall. She made up for it though in the next two hours.

It took her that long to tell us all she knew about him because Janelle went through all the classic rape responses: she locked herself in one of the two shower stalls with a douche bag and a quart of vinegar I'd stolen from the kitchen, and she stayed there with the hot water tap on full for a half hour until our communal bathroom was a cloud of steam. When she finally came out, she threw up twice, then went back for another twenty-minute shower. And still she felt dirty. When others on the hall grumbled, I said that she was trying to steam off the beginnings of bronchitis.

In between Janelle's bolts to the bathroom, Liz told us one story after another about Buck Woodall.

I probably don't have to tell you, Doctor, how he operated. I'm sure you've had too many women sit right here in this very same chair and tell you how it began with sweet talk and gentle kisses that gradually got more urgent and then when she—or in this case, Janelle—tried to put on the brakes . . .

No, the only thing new about date rape is the term itself. It may be a cliché these days, but back then— Oh God! I can't begin to tell you how frustrated and angry and helpless we felt that night.

And not just that one night. We seemed to be under constant sexual siege and there was nothing we could do about it. It was like the campus flasher.

Oh, yes, we even had one of those.

From the movie theater downtown, the most direct route back to the girls' side of campus was along Magnolia Lane, and then a right onto Longleaf. Longleaf was quiet and dimly lit. No houses. Just a lot of trees. On one side was a low stone wall backed with tall bushes where the park and lake fanned out to border the college. Stone steps led down an unlit path to the lake, and the lake was a popular place to hang out on the weekend. In fact, that's where I saw my first Frisbee.

Near the end of our freshman year, we heard rumors that a flasher had begun lying in wait at the intersection of Magnolia and Longleaf, and when he spotted any girls coming back to campus alone, he would suddenly appear under a Longleaf streetlight, expose himself, and then disappear into the bushes.

The first few times it happened, the girls reported it to the police, but they couldn't give good descriptions; and when the police rounded up some local known deviants, no one could make a positive identification. Eventually, someone in the police department must have talked to the Dean of Women, who talked to the dorm mothers, who each called a dorm meeting and explained that while men who exposed themselves were nasty perverts, they were basically harmless. As long as we never walked that route alone at night, we'd be perfectly safe.

In short, don't call the police again unless we were positive that we could pick our tormentor out of a lineup of look-alikes.

It was bad enough that the police didn't take exhibitionism very seriously, but the prevailing attitude about rape was even worse. If Janelle tried to have Buck arrested, it'd be her word against his. Too, her reputation would be forever smeared while his would actually be elevated—especially among guys who thought a woman's place was on her back anyhow. The old double standard. He's a stud; she's a tramp.

When I think how victimized we were—how—how—

Oh, thank you. A glass of water *would* be nice. No, no, I can hold the glass myself. See? My hands have almost stopped shaking.

I'm fine.

Really.

Isn't it silly of me to get so angry after all these years?

Especially since we actually got some poetic revenge. Even the way it happened was ironic.

You see, on our own, as part of a term-long research project, Liz and I'd been charting the appearance of the flasher. We tracked down rumors, found most of the girls who'd been accosted, correlated their descriptions with every known factor, from time of night to day of the month, and eventually came up with a recurring pattern that seemed to be based on the full moon. We'd actually predicted his appearance the month before and had missed him by one night. This month we were determined to nail him.

In the meantime, Liz and I'd read everything we could find about passive sexual perversion. The police had told our dorm mothers that such men never physically assaulted their victims, and the textbooks more or less backed them up. Liz and I had originally planned to go flasher-hunting alone, but after what happened to Janelle, we decided we needed more people.

That was my job. The full moon was two days away

and on the evening in question, I rounded up three other girls who were willing to skip the books and go see *Gigi*.

The moon was just rising as we came out of the movie and bought ice cream cones for the walk back to campus. By the time we turned into the street that led past the park, the moon had cleared the trees. Sarah and DeeDee had seen *Gigi* the week before and were trying to remember all the words to the duet between Hermione Gingold and Maurice Chevalier, while Miriam and I were debating whether we could hold out for marriage if a Louis Jourdan ever propositioned us in that sexy French accent.

Even though I made sure Miriam and I were in front of DeeDee and Sarah, I honestly didn't expect anything to actually happen, and I was as startled as they were when we suddenly noticed a man leaning against a lamppost almost a block away. DeeDee and Sarah stopped singing, and our footsteps slowed.

Everyone had described the flasher as someone young enough to be a student, and this man was certainly dressed in the campus uniform of the late fifties: chino slacks, madras shirt, a windbreaker draped loosely in front of him on his arm. Think Kingston Trio or early Pat Boone.

Now we didn't want to look like timid idiots in case he really was a student waiting for someone to come out of the park, so we kept walking. After all, flasher or student, he was all the way across the wide street from us, his back was half turned, and he acted as if he barely knew we were there.

We had just decided he was okay, and were making sheepish jokes about unwarranted nervousness when he suddenly turned, moved his jacket aside, and exhibited himself to us in all his swollen glory.

Startled, we froze for a moment; Miriam gasped and DeeDee gave a nervous titter. Even though I'd spent two days going over in my mind exactly how I meant to respond, I was so shaken that it took me a moment to react. Then adrenaline kicked in, and I shook my fist at him and yelled, "You rotten creep! Who the hell do you think you are?"

"Maggie, stop!" cried Miriam as I started running across the deserted street.

"Call the police!" I shouted back over my shoulder. "This is one time we're going to have a close-up description."

The flasher was almost as startled as my friends. Evidently, no girl had ever given chase before; and after a split-second hesitation, he took off like a shot rabbit, over the low stone wall and into the bushes.

As I swung myself over the wall, I could hear him crashing through the underbrush back toward the campus. "Stop!" I yelled. "Somebody stop him!"

If it'd been the weekend, there might have been two dozen students necking on the grassy slopes to help me chase him. On that Thursday night, the woods seemed deserted. The moonlight was so bright though, that as I cut over to the paved path that led from the steps at street level down to the lake, I spotted something lying on the ground just where the path made its first turn.

A man's windbreaker.

Jubilantly, I grabbed it and raced up the steps where Miriam and DeeDee were anxiously waiting. Sarah had hurried on ahead, they said, to call the police.

"He dropped his jacket!" I said, shaking it over my head triumphantly. "But I saw who it was and you know him, too."

"Who?" they cried.

"You'll never believe it. *I* don't believe it—Buck Woodall!"

"*Really?*" DeeDee was incredulous. "He's in my journalism class. Are you sure, Maggie?"

Miriam didn't know Buck except by sight, but I saw her eyes widen as she compared our flasher's shadowed features to Buck Woodall's face by daylight.

To do the police justice, they came quickly when Sarah told them I'd gone chasing the exhibitionist. They played their flashlights over the windbreaker and, sure enough, the initials B.W. were inked onto the brand label, followed by what later proved to be his student ID number.

The campus police arrived about then. DeeDee knew that Buck lived in Cameron Hall, and both patrol cars pulled up by the door of Cameron just as Buck came strolling up the walk as if nothing had happened.

He kept insisting that nothing had, but they hauled

him over to our dorm and made him stand under a streetlight while DeeDee, Miriam, Sarah, and I looked him over from half a block away.

"That's him," I said.

"Gee, I don't know," said Sarah. "I thought the guy had on light chinos."

"No," I said. "Don't you remember how white his— how white he was against those dark pants? And he had on white bucks, too, even though it's October. I thought he looked familiar. When I got closer, right before he turned and ran, I definitely recognized him."

"Yeah," said DeeDee. "Buck was wearing those white shoes in class this afternoon."

"You're right, Maggie," said Miriam. "It's him, all right."

"You're willing to swear to that?" asked the city policeman.

"Yes, sir, I am," I told him.

"Me, too," said Miriam and DeeDee.

"God, I can't believe it," said Sarah. "Buck Woodall the campus flasher? And after all that Don Juan bragging he's done."

Despite Buck's denials, the police took him downtown and booked him. The story was all over campus before midnight and psych majors had a ball theorizing about his sexual neuroses. All his boasts of earlier victories suddenly seemed like lies, and several girls got their reputations back that night because people thought exhibitionists "couldn't do it" with a real girl. Anyhow, being a stud was one thing; a flasher was something else entirely.

Believe me, Buck's stud-standing couldn't have fallen any lower than if he'd suddenly been caught wearing black lace bra and panties.

Of course, he tried to say he'd been out with someone that night, but the girl he named denied it categorically.

No, it never came to trial. This *was* the South, remember? His parents hired a lawyer and got it hushed up. Well, hushed up legally. Some genies never go back in the bottle, thank God. Buck tried to finish college in another state, but enough people knew so that the story followed him there, too. His journalism career never went anywhere. Last I heard, he OD'd in some boardinghouse down at the beach.

* * *

You look puzzled, Doctor. What did that psych experiment I mentioned earlier have to do with this? My goodness, you *do* pay attention to every word, don't you?

It was a classic experiment, so I'm sure you're familiar with it. I forget where it was originally done, but I suspect it's still being used out there somewhere. Anyhow, the way it works is that you have a professor in the middle of a classroom lecture when suddenly the door bursts open and in rushes one person followed by another who threatens the first person with a weapon. There's a loud scuffle and they rush out again, whereupon the professor asks everyone in the classroom to write an account of what just happened: describe the victim and the assailant—which was white, which black; the weapon and was it fired; how many blows were exchanged, et cetera.

You remember how most students muddle race, dress, and physical appearance? And how almost nobody ever realizes that the assailant isn't carrying a handgun? They'll describe that banana as everything from a pearl-handled automatic to a Colt .45.

Well, when my professor pulled the experiment on us, our class had to come up with one single description that all agreed with. The interesting thing was that, even though several of us started off thinking we'd seen one thing, after a while, we found ourselves remembering it as two of our most vocal classmates described it. They were so positive and they kept reinforcing each other until the rest of us fell into line and said, Yep, that's how they were dressed, all right; that's the kind of gun he carried.

Those two were in on it with the professor, of course, and they proved to the rest of us that when several people aren't sure of something, a positive person can actually make them accept his version of an incident.

I couldn't have done it without Liz, though. She had to maneuver Buck very carefully that night so that no one saw them go down to the lake together. She had to pretend to be chilly so he'd drape his jacket over her shoulders, then drop it where I could find it, and string him along till she heard me yell.

But you know what, Doctor? Telling you this has reminded me that Janelle was in therapy for several years; so I won't take up another single minute of your time. She'll give me all the details I need for my new book. Thanks anyhow.

How do I feel about what I did? Fine. Why not? It even gave the real campus flasher such a scare that we never heard from him again.

Oh, I see what you mean: you think I might be carrying around a load of guilt because I helped wreck Buck's life? Good Lord! Didn't he ask for it? So why should *I* feel guilty? Besides, I told you: I'm healthy as a horse.

Physically *and* mentally.

Just read my books.

THE OTHER WOMAN

By Wendi Lee

She had drab, brown hair, big dishwater-colored eyes—
the kind you see in Keane paintings—and her chin was
almost nonexistent. She wore the sort of froufrou dress
a girl from the Midwest would think was the height of
sophistication with its full cabbage-rose print skirt, puffy
sleeves, and large, square linen-and-lace collar. I'm no
Paris fashion plate myself, but I know a silly-looking
dress when I see one.

I stopped studying Eleanor Monahan from across my
desk and leaned forward. "Just what can I do for you?"

Eleanor shrank into her chair as if I had hit her instead of asking her a reasonable question. But she managed to summon up the courage to tell me why she was
there. "Well, Miss Matelli—" she said, lisping slightly.

I winced. "Call me Angela."

She hesitated, then dutifully repeated my first name.
"Angela. I want someone followed."

Aha, I thought, the scorned wife. I appraised her
again. It was possible, I thought, but she didn't have a
ring on her finger. Boyfriend, maybe? I had done background checks on quite a few boyfriends and fiancés for
a number of paranoid women.

Normally I don't like to take, as I call 'em, "creep-
and-peep" cases. Ever since I was involved in a high-
profile case that earned me a lot of press about a year
ago, my caseload had been full up. But with the reces-
sion in full swing, things were slowing down. With next
month's office rent in mind, I asked, "Who is he?"

"Not a he," Eleanor replied softly, "a she."

Her lesbian lover? I could feel my eyebrow arching

involuntarily. I couldn't picture Eleanor hanging around a gay bar with some biker babe.

She caught my wry expression, blushed, and hurriedly explained, "My lover's wife. I think she's having an affair."

That was a shocker, but I managed not to drop my jaw. She looked to be more the type who attended tent revivals on a regular basis than the kind who would be having an affair with a married man. When I think of the "other woman," the image of a sleek sophisticate comes to mind, not the plain-Jane sitting in front of me. I grabbed a stubby pencil and began scribbling. "Start at the beginning."

Eleanor had met Roger J. Hugo a few months ago. She'd been the costume designer for a summer stock production of *The Taming of the Shrew*. He had played Petruchio and during his costume fittings, he'd seduced her. They had been seeing each other once a week ever since the production ended.

"I'll be thirty years old next week," she said, her voice breaking, "and I'm still single."

"Have you thought about leaving him and taking up with someone already single?" I asked, dismayed. "The odds of him leaving his wife aren't in your favor." The last time I looked, I hadn't seen a sign on my office door that read DIVORCES R US. Despite how nice the money would be, I got a creepy feeling about this job from what little she'd told me.

Eleanor leaned forward with an imploring look. "He's on the verge of leaving her and he's left her before. I love him. I'd be good for him."

"Aw, gee, I don't know," I replied. "I'm not sure I want to get involved in breaking up a marriage just on that basis—"

"She's cheating on him," Eleanor cut in sharply.

I bit my tongue. It would be too easy to point out that Eleanor's main man wasn't exactly Mr. Fidelity. "How do you know?" I asked, making doodles on my notepad. I resigned myself to the fact that if I didn't look into this matter, some other less scrupulous private eye would take this girl to the cleaners.

"I saw Cynthia, his wife, at a restaurant about a month

ago," Eleanor explained. "Roger and I were already seated when she came in. She looked straight at us."

"Didn't he see her?"

"His back was to her. The tables were filled up, but she had walked in as if she were looking for someone. When she saw us, I expected a big scene. Instead, she got this panicked look on her face and left the restaurant in a big hurry."

I had to admit that it was strange behavior for a wife who clearly saw her husband with another woman. Usually a woman who discovers her husband is having an affair will do one of two things: she would let him know she'd caught him in the act, whether at the restaurant or later at home or, if they had an open marriage, she'd have continued doing what she was doing without blinking an eye—she might even stop by the table for a friendly chat with her husband and his mistress. But a woman who turns and walks out with a sheepish expression on her face is not a woman who wants her husband, cheating or not, to know about her affair.

When I asked Eleanor why she had waited so long to do something, she shrugged and dabbed at her swollen, red eyes. "I had only seen her once before. I kept thinking I'd made a mistake, that maybe it hadn't really been her in the restaurant. But just the other day, I saw her again, and it was the same woman. I kept wondering why she hadn't filed for divorce. She must have been meeting a lover when I saw her at the restaurant."

"I suppose he doesn't know any of this," I said, getting a nod of confirmation in return. It was clear to me why she hadn't told him—she was afraid he wouldn't believe her.

"No, he doesn't. And when he finds out, he'll blow his top," Eleanor replied. "Roger has a very bad temper." She sat there, hands folded carefully in her lap like a young girl at church, a look of hope on her face. I could tell she was good at that sort of thing. "Will you take my case?" she asked softly, her eyes lowered. Don't tell me why, but I hate it when someone doesn't look me in the eye.

"I'll look into it." I was half hoping she would back out when she heard what I charged per day. But without batting an eye, she whipped out her checkbook.

As she handed me the check, I asked one more thing that had been bothering me. "Suppose I'm able to confirm that the wife is having an affair, and you present it all to Roger. What if it doesn't work out in your favor?"

She answered simply. "Letting him know will be reward enough." With that, she stood up and thanked me. Before leaving, she handed me a couple of photos of Cynthia Hugo, explaining that she had obtained them from Roger's Mercedes glove compartment.

I spent the next few hours doing a background check on the Hugos. They had bucks, big bucks. Roger Hugo was president of Hugo Manufacturing, a company that made plastic containers. Hugo money had not been made with the environment in mind. In fact, Roger had probably never even heard of biodegradable products.

Cynthia, whose maiden name was Bergdorf, was from old Newport stock and her family had a portfolio of Fortune 500 company stock that would make a stockbroker salivate. Since Cynthia's money had been used to build her husband's company into the conglomerate it is today, she owned the controlling share, fifty-one percent, of Hugo Products.

I started surveillance on Cynthia Hugo at six-thirty the next morning.

The Hugos lived near the Chestnut Hill Reservoir, just a few blocks off Chestnut Hill Avenue. Despite being located near a busy intersection, it was about as isolated as a house can get in a Boston suburb. Van Dine Court was an exclusive dead end with only four houses, all authentic Victorian gingerbreads on sprawling landscaped lots. The Hugo house was pale gray with black-and-white trim. Very toney.

Parking my Datsun 510 across from the Hugo residence, I figured my car wouldn't look too out of place in an area where the average annual income of a resident was in the high end of six figures. Residents would probably assume I was the hired help.

There were his and hers Mercedes sports cars in the driveway, one white and one burgundy. One glazed donut and half a thermos of Italian roast coffee later, a small, neatly dressed man with well-cut graying hair left the house and got into the white Mercedes. By my calculations, that had to be Roger Hugo. He wasn't handsome in a classic sense, but there was something attractive about him. Still, it was hard for me to picture him with mousy Eleanor.

When he had driven away, giving my car barely a glance down his long, thin nose, I had to wait another hour and a half before Cynthia Hugo stepped out the door. Grabbing my binoculars for a better look, I hunkered down so I wouldn't look so much like a spy—which, of course, made me look exactly like one.

Her photo had been unkind, adding about ten years to her face. In person, she looked like she was in her midthirties. Dressed in a straight black skirt and scarlet blouse with a black-and-white houndstooth pattern, her pricey little outfit went well with her auburn hair, blunt cut just above the shoulder, and crimson lipstick. I was willing to bet my retainer fee that her blouse was pure silk.

We spent the first part of the morning browsing through Bloomingdale's and Marshal Field. Eventually Cynthia Hugo ducked into Filene's basement sale. Every Boston woman, from Wellesley to welfare, shopped there. Even the wealthy love a bargain. It's the thrill of the hunt, and the triumph you feel when you walk out with a prize. By the time we left Filene's, I was carrying a bag with a leather designer purse and a little black skirt of my own, both marked down to twenty-five percent of the original price.

It was now twelve-thirty and she had bought out all the upscale department stores within walking distance. We headed toward the warehouse district. I was beginning to think that we were going to hit all the factory outlets as well, but she surprised me again by entering a bar and restaurant called The Stronghold. The name was familiar, but I couldn't quite place it. I took a small table in the raised part of the restaurant, overlooking Cynthia's table. She seemed to be waiting for someone.

The Stronghold had a rustic theme with exposed brick walls, rough-hewn wooden beams crisscrossing the ceiling, potted plants to give the customer that woodsy feel, and waitresses in jeans, flannel shirts, and hiking boots. I usually don't feel weird about eating alone in a restaurant, but I felt a little self-conscious here. The waitress who came over to take my order had light brown hair

piled haphazardly on top of her head, wisps of it framing
her round face, and wire-rim glasses. I felt like I was
back in the early seventies.

"Hi. My name's Flora and I'll be your waitress today.
Can I take your order?" she asked.

"I'll have a beer, whatever's on tap, and a pastrami
on rye with hot mustard."

She flashed a perky smile. "We have oyster stew
today. It's delicious."

"Oh, I think I'll pass," I said, handing her the menu.

"Are you sure?" she asked, wrinkling her forehead
and pushing her glasses up the bridge of her nose.

"No, thank you," I replied politely but firmly. I didn't
like to eat anything that reminded me of mucus.

She noticed my Filene's bag. "Been shopping today?"

I smiled coolly at her. "Yes," I replied pointedly, "and
I'm very thirsty."

She toddled off to get my beer. It occurred to me that
my waitress appeared to be flirting with me, but I didn't
have time to think on it very much. A thin black woman
was approaching Cynthia Hugo's table. She was striking
with her upturned nose and dark hair that rippled halfway down her back. Cynthia stood and they kissed—not
just a buss in the air, not just a peck on the cheek, but
a passionate kiss. I finally took a good, hard look around
me and made a brilliant deduction: there was not a single man in the place. I looked back at Cynthia and her
friend, their heads close together, their hands touching.
Then I looked around the dining area again, and realized
there were similar couples all around. Some detective
I was.

While I was ruminating on all of this, my sandwich
and beer arrived. As I ate my meal, a plan formed in
my mind. When my waitress came over to give me my
check, I smiled at her. While I paid, I racked my brain
for her name—was it Fauna? No, Flora.

"Flora," I began, feeling like a rat. She brightened.
"Listen, I have a favor to ask."

She carefully counted out change and handed it to me.
I waved it away—it was a generous tip. "I'm from the
West Coast," I said, lying through my teeth, "and I write
for a little publication there called the *Gay Times*. Sometimes we use pieces on the nightlife in other cities.

Would it be okay to take a few pictures for an article on this place?"

Flora frowned. "I don't see why not. Why don't I ask my manager." She gave me a soulful look before departing.

I watched Cynthia out of the corner of my eye. She and her friend were taking their time, pushing their salads around on the plates, touching each other's hands, the occasional kiss, playing footsie under the table.

I hoped my plan would work, but I felt like a heel for what I was about to do. After all, with a husband like Roger, who wouldn't find comfort in the arms of another woman? But I had to keep telling myself that this was no different than working for a wife who had an adulterous husband. Since the Hugos were both having affairs, Eleanor might be right—maybe this would just force the issue of divorce and when the dust settled, everyone would be happier in the long run. At least, that's what I kept telling myself.

Flora came bouncing back. Her manager was really excited that someone wanted to do an article on the restaurant. She didn't think the customers would have a problem because of the restricted circulation of the periodical.

I told Flora to thank her boss for me. She lingered a moment longer. "If you're staying over tonight, maybe I could show you around Boston and Cambridge. We could check out some other places for your article," she suggested in a shy tone.

I now felt about one millimeter high. She really was a sweet kid. Putting on my best disappointed look, I touched her arm. "Gee, I'd love to, but I have a plane to catch. There's a gay rights rally to cover in San Francisco." Flora pushed up her glasses and nodded, her face registering both disappointment and understanding. "But," I added, "the next time I'm in town—"

"Oh, yeah," she replied, brightening visibly. "Come on by and we'll do the town."

When she left, I took my camera out of my bag and began shooting random photos of the place, several with Cynthia and her friend in the frame, having a very cozy conversation. When I was halfway through the roll, I pocketed the camera and left the building. It was drizzling outside. I sprinted to my car and grabbed my new telephoto lens. In Boston, walking is easier than driving, and chances were good that The Stronghold was conveniently located close to Cynthia Hugo and her lover's love-nest.

I was loitering in a doorway across the street from the restaurant, my camera ready for action, when they left together a few minutes later. Like any tourist in Boston, I snapped a few photos and trailed them to a Beacon Street condominium, red brick, fenced in by wrought iron, with lots of character. When they disappeared inside, I entered the foyer and checked the names on the mailboxes. Two boxes listed male occupants, one box listed a married couple, but the name on the fourth box was A. A. Matthews. Most single women think it's clever to put just their initials on their mailbox and in the telephone book to discourage intruders and obscene phone calls, so I reasoned that this A. A. Matthews was Cynthia's friend.

I left the building and crossed the street, taking shelter in the doorway of another old building with character that had gone condo. I was having dismal thoughts about choosing a career that involved standing in the rain when the lights went on in the bay windows to the right of the entrance. The shades were up, and I could clearly see the front room. I fitted the lens to my camera and focused on the window. In the doorway to the living room, I could see the two women kissing intimately, peeling layers of clothing off each other in the heat of passion—until one of them noticed the view of the street. They didn't seem to take notice of me, but a moment later, the shades were drawn. At least I had gotten my shots.

I was drenched by the time I got back to my office. Eleanor Monahan, clutching her purse with the intensity of a mother awaiting word about an injured child, was waiting for me. "I just thought I'd stop by," she explained in a faltering voice. "It was on my way to the subway."

I mustered up a cold smile and led the way into my office, Eleanor trailing the raindrops dripping off my anorak. Inside, the radiator was pinging, a sign that it was working, and my warm office smelled like stale coffee and rancid chicken and mayonnaise. I remembered throwing away half a chicken salad sandwich the other day—apparently the building's janitorial services hadn't bothered to clean my office last night. I made a mental note to have a talk with the building manager.

Once I had shed my damp jacket and was settled in my chair, I gave her a full report. I tapped my camera. "It's all in here."

Eleanor was leaning forward with an eager expression, and for a moment, I forgot how lackluster she normally appeared. "When can you get the pictures developed?" she asked, blinking. Then she waved her hand as if she were erasing a thought, and her chair creaked from Eleanor practically bouncing up and down in her seat. "No, no, maybe you should just give them to me and I'll get them developed. I know a good place."

I shrugged and handed her the roll. Getting film developed was time-consuming and an extra expense for the client. If she wanted to do the honors, that was fine with me. As she placed the film canister in her handbag, Eleanor's eyes gleamed with the good news.

"This is better than I had hoped," she replied, elation shining in her face. Why shouldn't she be happy? After all, she was about to destroy several people's lives on the very slim chance that Roger Hugo would want her when the dust had settled. More likely, he would despise her for bringing it to his attention. But who was I to pass judgment? I was no better than she was, profiting from someone else's misery.

She stood and shook my hand, then left the office with a determined look on her face. This was a woman who was out to get the man she loved to give up his wife for her—at any cost.

I shook my head, wondering if I'd done the right thing. This was one job I didn't want to repeat.

A few uneventful days had passed when I got the phone call. I had spent the better part of that day playing two-fisted poker—and I wasn't winning.

"Matelli," I said into the phone.

There was no immediate response, but I could hear a man shouting something unintelligible on the other end. "Hello?" I repeated, louder this time.

There was a thunk, as if the caller had dropped the

receiver, then I heard heavy breathing. I was beginning to think it was an obscene phone call when a woman lisped, "Miss Matelli? Angela?"

"Who is this?" I asked sharply, not in the mood to play twenty questions.

"Eleanor. Eleanor Monahan. I hired you last Tuesday."

Oh, God, I thought. She's been dumped and now she's going to dump on me. I didn't want to hear this.

"What happened?"

"I showed Roger the photos. I told him about Cynthia and the woman on Beacon Street. He—he got really angry. He hit me and left, saying that he was going to kill her."

I sat up. "What do you want me to do about it?"

"You can probably stop him before he does something stupid. Please," she said with an urgency in her tone. "You've got to get down there right away. Roger went to the Beacon Street address."

"I'm on my way," I told her. "Meet me there." I hung up. I wouldn't normally ask a client to go into a dangerous situation, but I figured that by the time he reached his destination, he might listen to Eleanor. And if we both failed, I decided to bring a pal along—my Smith & Wesson .32 automatic.

The condo's security door was propped open. An invisible ice cube ran down my back, sending chills up and down my spine. I took out my weapon and jammed a clip into place.

A. A. Matthews's door was open just enough for me to slip inside. I stood in a small entryway, a full-length mirror on a wide open closet door reflecting part of the living room. There were no lights on inside the apartment, and the sunlight was no longer hitting the front windows. A dim, gray light filtered into the room. I could see a shape on the floor, but I couldn't tell if it was a rug design or something else.

I walked in slowly, my gun preceding me, and took in the scene. The first thing I noticed was the musty smell of death. An end table and a chair had been knocked over in a struggle. There were three people in the room—or should I say, two people and one body. Cynthia Hugo was the rug design I had seen in the mirror. She was sprawled in the center of the room. I was too late. Cynthia Hugo had been strangled. Her lover lay unconscious on the floor near the sofa. There was a trickle of blood from a cut on her temple. It looked like she would be out for a long time.

Roger Hugo stood over his wife's body. A weak light seeped through the window, casting Hugo's ghostly shadow across the grisly scene. The only thing to do now was keep him from handling too much of the crime scene. I slipped my gun back in my purse.

Having seen Hugo only once before outside his home, I wouldn't have recognized him here if I hadn't known the situation. The artfully cut and blow-dried hair from a week ago was now in disarray, as if someone had tried to tear it out. His polo shirt was ripped at the neckline and he had deep scratches on his face and neck.

"What happened?" I asked quietly. I didn't bother to introduce myself.

Hugo didn't seem surprised that a complete stranger was in the room. "I killed the bitch," he replied calmly, his gaze locked on his wife's body. "She was cheating on me. With another woman. Can you believe it?"

I choked back my reply. It seemed unnecessary to remind him that he was having an affair as well. The floor creaked and I turned to see Eleanor standing in the doorway. She took in the scene slowly with a sharp intake of breath and her hands fluttering up to her face.

"What are you doing here?" Hugo asked from behind me. I couldn't see his expression, but the steely tone of his voice told me he wasn't happy to see her.

"I just came to see if Angela got here in time," Eleanor replied in a strange tone. If I didn't know any better, I'd say that she sounded almost triumphant. I wondered why a woman would be happy about her married lover killing his wife. With the hint of a smile, Eleanor added, "I guess she didn't. Your temper got the better of you this time."

I felt as if I'd walked into the middle of a movie. Before I could ask what was going on, Hugo spoke again. "So you came here to gloat, is that it?" I looked at his flushed face, a muscle in his jaw pulsated.

"Wait a minute," I said. "I thought you two were lovers."

"We were," Hugo said acidly, "but I dumped her about a month ago."

It took me only a moment to put it together. I turned to stare at Eleanor. She no longer looked like the shrinking violet who had come into my office a week ago. The narrowed, glittering eyes, the sly cat smile told me that she had engineered all of this. And I'd been the sucker who put it all into motion.

"You told me about his temper," I said to her, "but you didn't tell me the affair was ended. I would never have taken the job if I'd known that."

"Of course you wouldn't," she replied lightly. She crossed her arms, a satisfied smirk on her face. "But you're the detective. You should have checked out my facts."

It took two seconds to get to her. I hauled her up by her coat lapels until she was nose to nose with me. "You used me," I said, angry at her, angry at myself. She was right, of course. I had been sloppy. I was just as much to blame for Cynthia Hugo's death as Roger Hugo and Eleanor. Roger would go to prison. My license might be in jeopardy if the police felt inclined to pursue the matter. But Eleanor would be able to walk away from this without a blemish on her record. She had orchestrated it all, but had done nothing that could be construed as illegal.

She pulled away from my grasp and straightened her collar, her expression betraying no emotion. "Roger taught me that everyone gets used at one time or another," Eleanor replied in a hard voice. Then with a giggle, she addressed Hugo. "I got you good, you son of a bitch. You're going to spend the rest of your sorry life in prison. This is better than I'd hoped for."

Hugo was behind me, so I was caught off guard, thrown against a wall of bookshelves. Several books rained down on my head. Hugo launched himself at Eleanor. In the feeble light, I could see that although Hugo was small, he was powerfully built. His face was red with fury, making him look almost demonic. Eleanor struggled in his grip, her eyes wild with panic, her nails tearing at the clamp he had on her shoulders.

I tried to get up, but my ankle had twisted when Hugo shoved me, and I collapsed back against the shelves. I tried again. Taking it slowly, I pulled myself up. Hugo was sitting on Eleanor's prone figure, strangling her with his bare hands. I thought he was going to succeed, but Eleanor reached into her coat pocket and pulled out a gun. I tried to warn Hugo, but the blast covered up my yell. His body jerked once, then hung suspended for a moment, his hands still tight around her neck. Gasping for breath, she managed to shoot him again. Hugo collapsed on top of her in a heap.

Sobbing and coughing, she tried to push him off, but her gun hand was pinned under his body.

Eleanor threw me a weary, pleading look. "Help me get him off."

I tested my ankle. It felt all right, but I knew it was sprained and I'd pay later if I didn't get some ice on it soon.

Eleanor started to whimper and struggle. "Angela, please. Help me."

I limped over and looked down at her. Hugo's blood was soaking the floor around them. "I'll go call the police," I said before I turned and hobbled out, leaving her pinned under the dead man.

WHERE IS SHE? WHERE DID SHE GO TO?

By Dorothy B. Hughes

It was that year of the concert. There would never be such a one before or again. Nor even faintly resembling it. I read about it in the evening news some ten days before it was scheduled. Not a big story, not a flashy ad, no pics, just a small news story in the Entertainment section. I didn't wait for Skye to come home, I called him at once. He is in the Music Department at our university. I knew he'd be in his office by 3:40 answering students' questions. Classes break at 3:29.

"Skye!" I trilled his name. If it's possible to trill Sk's. "You can't imagine!"

"Then you'd better deal it out one syllable at a time. What's happened?" Skye's speaking voice is a beautiful baritone. Of the same quality as a french horn. Or a silver clarinet. That's why I married him. I've told him so from our first date. "Guess who's going to do a concert three weeks from now!"

Quite obviously he had not even looked up from his student papers of the day. "Can't guess. Inform me."

I breathed in deeply, exhaled, and repeated the exercise. For control. "Louis Armstrong! That's who!" In the '40s and '50s Louis was the finest player who'd ever blown a horn. And, believe you me, there's never been a finer one since. Nor will be. Louis is a horn genius. No disputing.

"Who's on piano?" Skye asked, beginning to catch the excitement I'd breathed out.

"Count Basie, that's who! And on trombone, there's Zad."

Zad was Whiteman's trombonist. He played with all the great bands and big jazz groups, if they were lucky enough to sign him up in advance.

"And . . ." I withheld the final touch, the maraschino cherry atop the incredible confection. The beyond belief perfection of this musical evening to come. I worded it slowly, every syllable distinct, every sound a chime. "And the singer is . . . Ella. Ella herself!!"

I had him with that. His eyes must have widened to doughnut size. His golden brown eyes. A match for his Santa Monica beach tan. He ordered, "Get hold of Edward, Liz. Ask him to pass the news to the Winivers. Wyn's on location, his agent will know how to reach him. This will be bigger than Dizzy's."

We'd made the Dizzy Gillespie opening just two weeks prior, at a club down on lower Vine. Dizzy was the new jazz singer, fronting his own band, who was causing so much excitement. He played horn, but not like Louis. No one plays like Louis, Gillespie had a voice like a crazy crow and all the jazz crowd flipped for it. His first appearance was SRO from the time it was announced. Those Vine Street clubs are rather on the small side.

We were three couples who made all the new jazz concerts in Hollywood, the ones that played Kansas City Jazz. Kansas City, Mizzoura. (And let that St. Louee French-speak, "Missouree" get lost.) Yes, Skye and I were born and raised in Kansas City. It was jazz then. And now. Forget about Chicago. Chicago was never Southern and jazz is Southern Deep South. Only someone from down south can play jazz the way it should be played. It doesn't matter if the music is black, white, or tan. It has to be Deep South.

We had been four couples but Forrest, our lead clarinet, was on location in South America. He's still in bit parts but he'll make it out. He's not only a real actor, he's common sensical about steering his career. His wife is with him. She's into bits also.

Edward was a cameraman with Paramount, he and Skye had been university friends. His wife, Cluny, a Paramount blonde, was a line dancer with the studio. In Hollywood then, almost all our crowd worked for the pictures one way or another. Edward was a caring person, once a friend, always a friend, to risk a cliché. Edward and Wyn had been boyhood neighbors and school friends to boot, and no matter his drawbacks today, Edward would not discard him.

I put off calling Edward because I knew he would take for granted that I was also getting in touch with Wyn. He was the one who brought the Winivers into our well-integrated music group after Forrest left. Wyn was rather more than somewhat dim. He could fake jazz or copycat it, but it was not intrinsic with him. It never would be. He didn't have the right roots. Even if he did claim Missouri Jazz as his swaddling lullaby, he was a Kansan from the bridge of his nose to his nasal inflections. He had lived in New York since a toddler. His father was a prominent Eastern banker or industrialist.

And that nonwife of his! Frangi! Pronounce the g squashed, short for Frangipani. She was a real dimout.

When, nudged by Edward, I called Wyn, the response was as expected, "You can just bet Frangi and I will be there. With bells ringing!" Not wedding bells. None of us knew the exact status quo of Wyn and Frangi. They lived together, sort of. It wasn't commonplace then. Certainly not in Missouri, which for the most part was as old-timey in mores as the Puritans from whom the good Methodists of our state had evolved. A Missouri singsong always concluded with "Give Me That O-wold Ti-ahm Ree-li-junn," even on campus sing-a-longs.

Our music men had a rehearsal that night. The wedding selections were not familiar to Wyn. Edward had arranged waivers for him to play with the group in the weekend. They were playing a wedding in Universal City. Because Edward was a constant friend to friends, engagements were steered his way whenever friends could. It didn't mean big money but at least it was recognition of our group's aspirations. Moreover, they played below scale, helpful to young couples who wanted special dress-up wedding memories but hadn't enough money to hire an entrepreneur of such things. Of the four, only Skye was Musicians Union as yet. The Musicians Union has always been a strong one, an important and respected one, even way back then. And how can you join a union without credits? And how can you get credits without a union card? I used to ply my uncle with those questions when I first met Skye.

My uncle had more than once been president of the Kansas City Musicians. He would explain patiently each time, he was a most caring man, "You get experience playing with your school groups. If you're good, there'll be some Union Father or Big Brother who hears you and will use you on waivers now and again. Before you know it, you'll have enough credits to play with a union outfit. It's up to you to get yourself noticed as a coming top man."

My uncle had been in the union since his school days. His society orchestra was one of the special dance orchestras in our town. He played classical piano as well as jazz. Like my own Skye. But neither had ever aimed at being a concert pianist. That takes money and a special dedication. Without the first, they couldn't have dedication.

Wyn wasn't bad musically. His sax had content and fiber, and he could double on a banjo, mandolin, or guitar, although with nothing like Edward's precision or imagination.

The key of C was too intricate for Frangi. She didn't play any instrument nor was expected to. She sang her version of the blues. The idea of her in the same room with Ella was heresy. I counted on Wyn to have enough musical sense to explain to her in one-syllable words like, "No!" that you don't drone an obligato to a featured singer. If he didn't, and if Edward didn't, I'd do it myself.

Once I'd handled the phone calls, I decided to go for the tickets right now. It was sure to be a sellout. The news item had mentioned that The Broadway was handling the reservations at present.

The Broadway, an adjunct to the main store in downtown L.A., was at the corner of Hollywood and Vine. The manager made a practice of handling local attractions to save theater or concert goers from having to drive to downtown.

In those days you could park right on Hollywood Boulevard. There was always room at the curb except when the annual Santa Claus Parade was on or some similar big event. I drove in, parked right in front of The Broadway, bought tickets for our four couples and was back home in time to have five o'clocks ready for Skye before he returned home from the campus.

After Skye scanned the tickets, he asked, "At what club are they playing?" I'd asked the same question at The Broadway's box office.

"They haven't found a club yet. The good ones are all booked past next weekend. Louis's group is at some new spot on Hollywood Boulevard just before the Vine intersection."

"I don't remember any club there," Skye puzzled.

"I don't either, but you know Hollywood. Places come and go. Anyhow, The Broadway ticket man said they told him the entrance staircase is almost right across from Musso Frank's. The address is on the envelope." I concluded, "I'm going even if they're playing out on the streetcar tracks and I sit on the curb."

"Take a cushion," Skye advised.

All the next week, I anticipated with rising excitement, simply unable to believe they'd be such a starry configuration from a little piece of cardboard I'd bought at our own Broadway shopping mart.

Came the night. Edward was going to be late getting home in time to make it. So Skye and I would pick up Cluny and him, too, if he was ready by then. The four of us usually shared a ride.

What we didn't expect was the others. Could we also accommodate Wyn and Frangi? It seems that Wyn's high-class fancy foreign roadster was having one of its temperamental fits. Not unusual. Its high fine-tuning of parts must have been arranged to support high-fine mechanics. In fine shape, let me say. These experts must have lived in Beverly Hills in a Louis B. Mayer mansion if their hourly fee was an indication of their income. Of course we'd share the ride. As long as the Wyns were ready to leap into the car as we drove by their door. There would be no delaying tonight while Frangi changed her attire because it didn't "seem" right, a frequent assertion of hers. Actually she must have been quite insecure as she never felt right after viewing what other women were wearing. Yet she was the fashion plate, not us simple folk.

Everything clicked. Edward had made it home. Although still damp from his shower, his hair was combed and he tied his four-in-hand as he followed Cluny out their door. The Wyns were on their doorstep. Edward must have warned Wyn they'd better be.

Via Sunset Strip we rolled onto Hollywood Boulevard by 7:30 P.M. The concert was scheduled for 8:15. Schwab's, bright and busy as usual, was the official greeter for the boulevard. And with her first glimpse of Schwab's, Frangi piped up, "Can't we stop just a minute at Ess and Tee's?"

The S&T fulgent identification square was just past the drugstore, a few paces down the block.

"There isn't time," I said distinctly and perhaps menacingly. That's what Skye later called my voice.

"There's plenty of time," Frangi informed me. That was one of the main irritants of Frangi's nudge for her own way. She could and did count the minutes accurately. The rest of us were attuned to guesswork. "We have forty five minutes and we can be there in five." She brooked no nonsense from women. They weren't enticed by her as men were, this she knew plenty well.

S&T's was a relatively new place. It was more suited to the Strip of those days, than to the Boulevard. Just a storefront of a place, dressed up with fancy new furnishings, gilt-legged tables and chairs covered in rose pink imitation satin. A gilt-edged bar extended all the way to the small dance area at the rear presided over by a mammoth and thunderous-decibeled jukebox. The place was popular with the studio extras who couldn't afford the Strip. It wasn't so much a drinking place as one in which to meet up. There you'd find your friends, male or female, and learn the latest gossip of the other studios. Frangi had her claws and fangs ready to grab onto anyone connected with the studios. So far no takers. She'd have liked to be discovered the New Star but she'd settle for entrée through the extras gate. If one rising star allegedly had been discovered sipping a soda at Schwab's, Frangi would have been there as a daily routine, as it not that even she knew that you don't get anywhere stealing another's act. And so she frequented S&T's where she was flip enough to be accepted even by Skip and Tory, neither of whom particularly liked females cluttering up their place.

"I just want to drop in and see who's expected tonight."

Drop in and rub up every male in the place to find out what's shooting late tonight.

"There is not time," I repeated, loud and clear. "With a new destination, one whose seating arrangement we don't know, or how many tickets have been sold for— we are going there *now*," I emphasized. "You can drop by S&T's after the concert and find out who's there."

She didn't continue with her wants, she evidently knew she was getting nowhere and wasn't about to. Wyn of course was of no use. He had obviously been trained early to "keep quiet and it'll all go away." Either that or he never was interested in her sudden ideas.

So we progressed down toward Vine, found a good parking spot near The Broadway entrance and witnessed young Norm, our drummer boy, parking his van by habit nearer a lighted intersection, which the police patrolled. He kept his drums and other equipment locked in his van.

Norm's wife didn't often have a chance to join us. She had three under-five-year-olds at home and, we strongly suspected, a fourth on the way. Strange how some young couples never find out what's causing babies until it's too late. The Norms couldn't afford the ones they had, much less additions. He had a good job in some machinery factory but no matter how good, a family of six or more costs. He was a nice kid, no chance to go to college of course, but intelligent, a reader and happy natured. If he could only play a sax we could get rid of Wyn and Frangi.

Regrettably, Edward parked right smack next to Rosenda's street-front showcase window. I could almost feel Frangi's deep groan of desire. Frangi was the only woman I've ever known who could wear a Rosenda creation. All sticks and bones on a small-scale frame. Rosenda designed originally only for the studios. She opened the first Rosenda's Atelier to dispose of her dress models at a price no tyro could afford. Being pricey and abetted by what was Hollywood taste at the time, she became fashion stylish. Before Nolan was conceived, before Chanel became a number, fashion quivered over Rosenda's designs. Wyn had money but not enough for Frangi to shop at costly Rosenda's. Frangi seemed to think that money came out of a spigot in their backyard. Wyn did not indulge her idiosyncrasy. No one could have except possibly the master of the mint.

The current creation had the place of honor at the left side of the show window. This creation was indeed beautiful, worthy of Frangi's reaction. It was composed of quivers of lace, tarnished lace. Not gray, not black, not musty, not earthy. The adjective "funky" had not yet been developed. It would almost have been too descriptive. Even if you couldn't afford a Rosenda, and few women could, not being built like Pinocchio, you could ooh-ahh over what she had fancied. Her creations deserved to become high fashion. She designed, cut patterns, and used needle and thread delicately in her large blunt fingers.

Following the Broadway's ticket information, we advanced to the open doorway between Rosenda's and the department store. A flight of wooden steps, uncarpeted, led up, up, up, with its old wooden handrail, unvarnished, to grasp onto for assistance. There was no entrance lobby, no arrows pointing the way. No visible door with transom above, with a street number on it.

But Musso Frank's was directly across the street as I had been told it would be.

As the rest of us moved to the stairway entrance, Frangi did not. She continued to stand outside Rosenda's show window, seemingly mesmerized by Tarnished Lace. I truly could not fault her—the dress was exquisite. And it would fit her. It was made for someone all bones as she was. If it could have fit me, I think I'd have done the same as she. But it never could have, not with a million years of diets. And I'm only a size twelve.

Our group was starting upstairs—clatter, clatter, clat . . .

"Come on, Frangi," Wyn called.

Her reply, as was normal with her, was, "Go ahead. I'll follow."

By then, Norm had joined us. So we had thud, thud, thud, interspersed with the clats. Norm was a hefty youth.

There was no landing, you just kept on going up. At the top there was a door forward, ajar. We walked in. No one was there. But there was a Bechstein baby grand by the south windows. There were music racks here and there, some with music sheets in place. Drums were arranged to the left of the piano.

"Who's on drums? Krupa?" Norm asked. Not too hopefully. I don't think I ever heard Norm ask any question hopefully. Poor kid. So far he didn't expect much of life and hadn't received much. Except a wife and three kids or three and a half.

I told him I didn't know. The Broadway ticketer didn't know either. He only knew it wasn't Krupa as he was tied up with a San Francisco band this weekend.

"But he's sending his Number One fill-in," I assured Norm. "He'll be good. He wouldn't be working with Louis and the Count if he weren't one of the best."

"I'd like to play behind Louis," Norm said with a sigh. A sigh almost as potent as Frangi's when she first looked upon the Tarnished Lace.

But before any one of our musicians could follow on that, Wyn had entered the room, had looked it over and emitted a chunk of laughter. "It's a damned rehearsal hall!" he announced.

And it was. Not any bigger than a classroom at the college. Around the other three walls were square wooden tables, three tables on each side of the hall and two centered, opposite the musicians' placement. Each table had four wooden chairs, the sort used in study and rehearsal halls.

Being first arrivals we took the two center tables. Edward and Skye pushed them together and set our chairs around them. There was nothing on the tables, not even an ashtray or setups nor what passes for silver in clubs. Nothing.

We weren't alone long. A tall towhead, mid-young fellow in blue shirt and a pair of worn khakis joined us. "I'm Ralph," he introduced himself. "Do you have your tickets or do you want some?" A small pack held together by a rubber band was visible sticking up in his shirt pocket.

I informed him, "We have them. I bought them at The Broadway as soon as I read in the paper about the concert. There's one more of us downstairs," I added, then asked, "Is it all right to put these tables together?" Which we'd already done of course.

"For sure," he said. He placed a plastic pad scenic

with New York City in front of each place. "I'll bring tumblers and napkins."

By now several other couples had arrived and were choosing tables.

"But I'm sorry to say we have no kitchen. There wasn't time to arrange for that." He brightened. "But we'll have an early intermission—a long one, so you'll have time to bring something over from Musso's if you want. We've arranged with them that we'll bring back the hardware."

It was Skye, scanning our tickets, who posed the question, as profs are wont to do.

"How does it happen they're not playing one of the Vine Street clubs?"

Ralph was apologetic. "All the clubs had bookings before Louis and his manager decided to break in the act here before they travel it across country to New York. This hall was all that was available for opening tonight. They'll get a club later—they'll be here another week—down on Vine, their manager is negotiating. It's not a big one but if nothing else opens, it will do." He repeated what I'd heard at The Broadway. "Watch the papers. They'll be running a big advert in the dailies and the trades."

"We won't need the big club dates," I boasted. "This is greater than any planned concert. We'll be right with them, face to face in this room."

"You're musicians?" Ralph hoped.

"The men are," I supplied. I'm sure he relaxed on that. Only musicians would respect other musicians individually in this sized room.

Edward began, "We have a little band . . ."

At which moment in walked Frangi. No, not in Tarnished Lace. But obsessed with the memory of it. Of course one look and our helper reacted as all men do on first sight of her. Before they find out that behind that unreal mask of her face was a more or less empty head.

Wyn was asking Frangi as if it were no more than idle curiosity, "Where have you been?"

There was no way to overhear the answers, only the questions gave a clue.

The musicians were entering through the door at the rear and we quickly sat down at our table.

There was Louis, big smile, carrying his trumpet, and lifting a free hand in greeting. And there was the Count also in smiles, his piano bench placed just so. And there was Zad, another big smile as he towered over all of them and us. They were all dressed as casually as Ralph. Only the substitute drummer was unsure of the territory. Even that young Louis would never have been unsure of anything, not with his trumpet in hand. They settled into place, tested tuning. And then, ever so softly, Louis began the lead-in to "Black and White and Blue."

Intermission was a necessity. A person can tolerate only so much ecstasy before taking a deep breath. We trooped down the staircase, wordless, gulping the mild evening air as it drifted to meet us. With an audience of so few, all could spread out a bit, some were strolling the half block down to Vine, others idly walking the curb toward the other corner. There wouldn't be time to duck across to Musso's for a drink.

Ralph, too, had changed his tune before he opened the doors to the hallway. He'd made another of his apologies, evidently from backstage orders. "We won't take too a long an intermission. There's too much more program to come."

As yet Ella hadn't joined the band. There would be Ella and Louie in one of their spunky duets—Ella and the Count in some of their rarely heard solo material.

Ralph also told us, "I'll ring this bell when the second half is ready." He let it ding for us. It was a child's playtime bell.

"We'll be listening," I assured him. I for one wouldn't go beyond its sound.

For those who hadn't smoked during the music, intermission was the time to light up. The evening air began to be mingled with the good herbal scent of tobacco. And Edward had ducked across and returned with some icy cans of Bud.

Frangi didn't stay with our group, she headed straight for Rosenda's, as could be expected. Although Wyn and Edward had their backs to the showcase window, I was watching. Once Frangi went inside, she momentarily disappeared, then reappeared with Rosenda herself in tow. They came across to the Tarnished Lace creation. Rosenda lifted it with a creator's care, held it almost tenderly in her work-blemished fingers, as she led the way, presumably to a dressing room. On that I was right.

Frangi emerged in the masterwork as if it had been designed for her. Rosenda remained a respectful but watchful rear. From their unheard dialogue, I presumed she wanted to wear it outside to show to Wyn. To dislodge a few more thousand dollars from him to make Lace her own.

Rosenda was in no way going to permit that. She made this obvious by the violent arm gestures and facial negations on both sides of the unheard dialogue.

And Ralph's bell dinged.

All of us clack-clacked upstairs obliterating any and all outside distractions. We were returning to a once-in-a-lifetime musical memory.

As we settled again around the wooden table, I queried Wyn, "Where's Frangi?" I spoke quietly, to avoid stirring up a heap of useless discussion in our party. That could come later.

Wyn sort of looked over his shoulder, obviously expecting no answer from the rest of the audience, then shook his head. "I don't know," he said. And added, "With Rosenda, I suppose. She'll be along."

Well, she wouldn't be readmitted unless she appeared soon. No theatrical offering has an open door for stragglers once the curtain is up. Even an imaginary curtain. I didn't explain this to Wyn. Quite evidently he was used to her doing her own thing without his interference. And just as obviously, he couldn't care less.

The musicians were entering their half of the hall casually, each taking his place by his own music rack. Ella was sort of in the background behind the piano. Quite as if she didn't belong with them and was just there to attend the important guys. She wasn't glamorized, her navy blue daytime dress was only adorned with a white collar and cincture.

Without any preamble, Louis lifted his trumpet to his mouth and began a hushed introduction to the classic "Wang Wang Blues." When he reached the chorus, he picked up the tempo ever so slightly. I'm sure I wasn't the only one who had noticed that Ella had come up beside him so that together they sequed into the chorus,

"Wang, Wang Blues . . . Wang Wang Blues . . . My baby's gone and left me with those Wang Wang Blues . . ." dragging out the "Blooo-oos" in harmony.

It was only the beginning of a musical night that no one who was in that rehearsal hall would ever forget.

What came after wasn't important. It, too, was unforgettable. But it could not tarnish the greatness of this night of the blues.

And the extras. Such as "Twelfth Street Rag," our Kansas City song about that shoddy downtown cross-street. The entire troupe jazzed that one up to the fullest meaning of jazz.

And the finale! The oldest classic in the blues book. The one that affixed St. Louis, even if on the Mississippi, as a Missouri river town as was Kansas City. The "St. Louis Blues," with Ella bringing tears to your eyes with "I hate to see (one, two) the evening sun go down . . . (2X4 beats)," and Louis joining her with the heartbreak, ". . . Because my baby's gone and left this town. . . ."

The finale sent us down again into the night, silenced. Words are trivial after the sublime.

Frangi was not waiting for us, was not in sight outside or behind the glass of show windows. And Skye and I were responsible for seeing the couple home.

Wyn said, "I'll go see if she's still in Rosenda's." The lace dress was again behind the show window.

I told him, "I'll go in with you." I didn't think Rosenda would want a man prowling around her dressing rooms, certainly not near midnight and obviously near closing time.

Wyn didn't care if I joined him, he'd have been even more pleased if I'd taken on the whole look-around.

When we went in, Rosenda was right there jangling a ring of keys. "We are closed," she stated. "We close at midnight."

I explained to her, "We're not shopping. We just want to know if his wife is here. Frangipani . . ."

"That one with the licorice stick hair?" Rosenda was defensive, ready to take on all comers.

"She didn't come up to join us at the concert after intermission. She had been trying on your lace dress."

"She is not here," Rosenda erupted. "I tell her to get out. And you know what?"

Of course we didn't. So we waited. She still had the ball in her corner.

"She started to walk out with My Dress on her!! My twenty-seven-thousand-dollar dress!" She managed to continue after a shaky breath. "I did not let this happen." Again the deep breath for control. "She said her husband would buy it for her, maybe so much dollars down, so much next payday until the twenty-seven thousand dollars is all paid!!"

Now she was shrieking, "I tell her I do not sell my dresses like Montgomery Sears. I create!! You pay and the dress is no longer mine. But not until you pay!!!"

It took her longer than a brief moment before she regained self-control. "But this dress is not for sale!" she said quietly. This was somehow more menacing than her temper tantrums had been. "It is created for those Frenchies who are doing business with Em-Gee-Em." In those days, MGM was king of the motion picture jungle. "Not just that one." She brushed off Em-Gee-Em. "All the big studios want Frenchie dresses. And I am to create for them. My Tarnished Lace I create for those Frenchies who are taking it back to Paris for the big showing. And I go with them to instruct their seamstresses how to make something so fine for other studios. I create! They sew!"

Wyn said, "Let's go—she isn't here."

I should have liked to examine the dressing rooms but that certainly wasn't possible tonight with Rosenda having hysterics. Perhaps I could get back tomorrow and see if Frangi left any clue as to where she was heading. But obviously I wasn't thinking intelligently. If at all. Of course she'd be home, probably was by now. She would have solicited a ride from one of her Hollywood Boulevard coven.

At this hour, nearing midnight, traffic wasn't heavy. Our car stood alone at the curb and we boarded it. Skye managed a turnaround and we headed toward the West Strip. As we crossed La Brea, Wyn asked, "Would you mind dropping me at S&T's? She's probably waiting there."

We were practically there and Skye pulled over. There was ample curb parking here as well as down by Rosenda's. The No Parking signs never fazed any of the Hollywood Boulevard regulars. At midnight the police weren't on a ticketing cruise.

Before we stopped, Wyn had said, "You needn't wait."

And I had said, "She may not be here."

And he had said, "She may have been here and left a message with the boys."

"Suppose she isn't and hasn't been?" Skye asked.

"It's no problem," Wyn assured us, "there are any number of friends who'll be here. They'll give me a lift, they have before."

So this wasn't new, Frangipani going off on her own. He thanked us, and dropping him, we drove on home. But I wondered to myself how much longer Wyn would take these humiliations. He wasn't that sort of man, he had as much personal esteem as she had—or better to call it self-pride. Somehow Skye and I did not discuss the situation then or after we reached home. Possibly like myself, he did not want to—the word again—to tarnish the early glory of the evening.

Midweek Cluny telephoned me. "Edward's getting the boys together for a rehearsal this evening. At our place. Wyn will be there. I made sure of that before calling you."

"I'll be there." I thanked her. "Is it an early?"

"No one could get away for one of those six o'clocker's. He's calling it for seven-thirty. You've been wanting to talk with Wyn, here's your chance."

"Frangi hasn't returned?"

"As of last night, she hadn't."

I had a class tonight but I could borrow notes from one of my classmates. I'd been taking a class now and again hoping to pick up enough points for a master's. If I made a serious foray on points, I might be able to make it the same time Skye took his doctorate. Trouble being I was always letting things interfere with my schooling, then vowing Neveragain. Neveragain is too late and don't I know it? But tonight was an essential requirement.

The wives were always invited to sit in at rehearsals. Edward called us the Critics Corner. Cluny and I usually made it. We lived near each other, and she and Edward had no children to be kept awake by the music.

Somehow our men seemed to think it bad form to ask personal questions about someone's family. All that she or I ever learned from our husbands was that Frangi had not returned. Wyn and Edward met daily, working at the same studio, and Edward and Skye always talked the day over come cocktail hour.

I would go to the rehearsal and I would ask personal questions. How could Wyn take umbrage when he had lived openly with Frangi, bringing her to all our get-togethers, making no bones about the lack of a marriage? And how could he dismiss her so erratically? There were several questions I had in mind.

When Skye came home from the campus that afternoon, I told him of Cluny's call and that I planned to be at the rehearsal to have a chance to talk with Wyn.

"You won't learn anything new," Skye said. "None of us has. Wyn thinks that Rosenda is responsible for her absence."

This was something I hadn't heard since the night of the Tarnished Lace.

"What do you think?" I asked him.

He hesitated before answering. "Ed and I don't think so. We think Wyn is the one who caused her to disappear that night."

"You don't really think . . ." I couldn't finish the sentence.

". . . that she hasn't returned because she can't?" This was too impossible to contemplate. "We don't think. We only wonder about what could have happened."

With this night's revelation from Skye, you can be sure I was at Cluny's rehearsal hall early. Norm came next but of course he wasn't in on happenings. He was too young and too family burdened to be part of the Wyn crowd.

Wyn arrived, as carefree as he'd always been. Greeted Cluny and me in our sideline chairs, and she almost at once took off with some excuse of having to check on the refreshments she was planning.

At once, I asked him, "Has Frangi come back?"

"Not yet." He tossed off the words as if she'd just gone around the corner for a pack of cigarettes.

"It's almost a week." I looked, and was, puzzled. "But where can she be?"

"Well, she has a lot of friends. She could be staying with any of them."

"But . . ." By then I was thoroughly disoriented. ". . . why wouldn't she call you?"

He shrugged. "She could be sleeping. She could be making rounds with a friend." One sting of the tongue, "Male or female."

It took me a bit of time to face reality. I asked then, "Have you tried to find her?"

"Certainly not," he emphasized. "Of course not," as if I were weak-witted. "You know Frangi does her own thing. She doesn't want anyone interfering with her life."

"Why don't you call her family?"

"I don't know anything about her family. I don't know if she has a family. She's never mentioned them."

I was baffled. I always knew the two of them were strange, but not that strange. Nobody was. "Maybe something happened to her," I rather stammered that.

Wyn ignored it. "She'll get in touch when it suits her," he said.

"If she can."

Those three words erased his carefree act at once. He said flatly, "You think Rosenda took care of her."

"You mean did something to her?" I asked it as if that had never occurred to me.

"Rosenda was mad enough." And Wyn added, "You don't know how Frangi can be. You want to kill her."

And did you? I couldn't broach that query even to myself. Of course he didn't. He was young, he was careless, but he wasn't vicious. Besides, he never would have considered that as an escape from her. It would have been bad form.

He'd had enough. Without an excuse or needing one, as this was rehearsal night, not a party, he took himself off to where the men were tuning up, inventing new riffs and talking music, not his way of life. I had in mind to question him further, but to no avail as he left as soon as rehearsal ended. It was nigh midnight so none of us lagged around.

Skye and I didn't bring up the Wyn and Frangi situation as we drove, nor did we later at home for we were too tired to talk and the alarm clock would be going off too soon to propel us into yet another day.

But I had come to a decision, either presleep or in-sleep that night. I didn't care what Wyn did or did not intend to do. I wasn't ready to cancel out Frangi just like that. No, I didn't like her, I'd never liked her. She wasn't one of our sort. But none of that mattered. Our likes and dislikes were definitely did not matter. When someone was in trouble we helped. And I felt certain that Frangi was in trouble. Wyn obviously did not think so. Doubtless he knew her better than the rest of us but if he was not going to take steps to find her, I was going to make a try at it.

We had a small police department over on Santa Monica Boulevard, an offshoot of the Hollywood full-scale station. I decided to go over there and find out if they handled missing persons. If so I would report her as missing.

Of course by the time I reached the building, I drove on by. I'd had time to think on the short ride. The officer would need to know more than I knew. I could just see him, pen in hand, reading from the Missing Persons Fact Sheet or whatever it would be called.

"What is her family name?

"Where do her parents live?

"What is her social security number?"

And then a page of questions about the man she'd been living with. I couldn't throw Wyn to the wolves that way.

I realized I knew nothing whatever about Frangi. She never talked of the past as most of us do, having memory perk up at an odds-and-ends remark about our family members, and school-days and school parties and travel vacations. Nothing. Never did she give even a monosyllable about where she came from, what she recalled of early days, about where she'd lived in Hollywood before she found Wyn. Perhaps Wyn had none of the answers either. It may have been why he wasn't taking steps to find her. If he had tried.

As I drove into The Village I had another idea. We have in our neighborhood, as in many towns these days, a giveaway news sheet, The Shoppers Guide, which is supported by local advertisements as to grocery specials, and variety store specials, and what's at the movie houses, and what activities for the public are happening at the U that week along with news of local events and newsworthy goings on of local citizens. The paper is found in racks at the doorways of various advertisers. Shoppers pick up a copy for the ads, and read the other sections because they're interested in local happenings.

I knew where the office was. Not only that, the editor was Jack, who had been in one of Skye's journalism classes before his graduation a year or so ago. The merchants have free parking lots as street parking is scarce to nonexistent, so I parked and walked back the two blocks to the news office.

Jack was there at the front desk as usual. After our greetings I asked him if he ever had knowledge of missing girls in and around our parts.

"There's always missing girls being as we're next door to Hollywood," Jack said. "They come out here hoping—expecting—to get into The Movies. When they don't make it, they disappear. Go back home, most do, but some—I suppose they lost face at failing to make it—don't go back home. We get inquiries."

"I've another," I told him. I sketched it briefly—no names—a girl living with a friend of Skye's who hadn't turned up since she left our crowd on concert night. I mentioned Rosenda and said how I personally didn't believe she had anything to do with it but that she and the girl had had an altercation and our friend wasn't around when the concert was over and we were all ready to head home. And she'd never returned.

Jack was unbelieving. "You don't think she went back to Rosenda's and she did away with her? Come on, Liz. She's a successful business operator in Hollywood. For years!"

"I don't. No I don't, Jack. But certain others of the crowd—the girl's live-in, for instance—do think Rosenda knows the answers."

"They should ask her."

"Perhaps they have. Though I doubt it."

"Well, they won't get a chance for some time. She's gone off to Paris, employed by some of the fashion big-wigs to give instruction to some of their workers. There was a big article in the Fashion section of the *Times* last week."

Jack reached for his yellow pencil and scratch pad. "Give me her name and I'll keep my eyes open for a news story and my ears open for local gossip. And drop in whenever you're over here. Any emergency info, I'll call you."

I explained I'd be by frequently with taking courses at the U and Skye a professor there.

"Okay, keep in touch. It's not always hopeless, Liz. Some of them talk it up with friends and the info is passed to other groups and, as I run a local gossip shop, they pass it to me."

And that was that. I felt relieved of a sense of guilt I'd realized I had been carrying since that night. The night we drove away from Hollywood. Why had we listened to Wyn's summation: "She'll find her way home. She always has."

Always. Over and over. But at night, a girl alone, and on Hollywood Boulevard. Always a possibility of trouble.

Another week went by. I dropped in on Jack over and again. But I never spoke Wyn's name to him or any outsider. It wasn't Wyn's idea for her to stay, it was hers, openly stated to him but for all of us to hear. *"You go along, I'll get home."* And yes, all of us knowing she'd have plenty of rides from friends at S&T's. That was factual.

Had it been a walkaway from Wyn? Was this a behavior repetition of how she'd come to move in with Wyn back then when it happened? None of us could ask Wyn about that, he wasn't the sort who'd talk unless he instigated the conversation.

Another week, another rehearsal. This time I didn't go, we were having special pre-exam material. I had the car, Skye was being transported by Edward, so I was at home when he returned.

And he had incredible news to tell. Not that anything was incredible where Wyn and Frangi were concerned.

"Wyn's going back to New York," Skye told me, like a by-the-way. "To be married."

"To Frangi!" I yelled it though I wasn't three paces away from where he was seated on his side of the bed.

"Not to Frangi. Frangi has never come back."

"What—tell me. TELL ME!" I settled on a footstool I'd pushed over to his knees.

"He's engaged to a girl back east. Formal engagement last spring. On the *Times* Social pages. Wedding set for September. Late September. Fashionable wedding date. I was put off until Lillia—Lillia Doucker—finished being finished at finishing school. From knowledgeable sources like Edward, the Douckers are up a peg or so financially from the Winivers and more important, are socially pegged higher.

"Anyhow, Lillia finished Miss Educational Topspot and her father let her choose a graduation present. She decided on two weeks in Paris. Her best friend got a matching gift from her Daddy Gotrocks—and off they went. So Wyn decided it was a good time to come out to Hollywood. He'd always fancied being a movie actor—which of course was anathema to his parents— but he'd been working and saved his money and came out for some know-how from his best college friend Edward. Which is how he got to be an extra and made it to some minor—very minor roles in some oversized musical productions. Edward had some clout at the studio and Wyn did have expensive looks, apparel, and musical knowledge.

"Before the two weeks were used up, Lillia and her friend had discovered two of their boyfriends were also in Paris and one of them had brought his boat."

"A yacht?"

"We don't say 'yacht,' " Skye explained, a la Wyn. "Only the lower classes of yachtsmen say 'yacht.' In OUR crowd, we say 'boat.' "

"And so . . ."

"The boys invited the girls to join them on the boat to cruise the Mediterranean ports of Africa and Europe. It was moored at Les Sables. The cruise took more than a month."

"Don't tell me," I interjected, "that this hadn't been planned from scratch. How come she's not marrying the boat man?"

"She can't," Skye explained pontifically.

"He's married?"

"Oh no," Skye scoffed. "She can't because he went to the wrong prep."

"You're kidding."

"I'm quoting. Quoting Wyn when Cluny asked the same question. 'There are good preps and poor preps.' The boat man didn't make it into a good prep like Eton. You understand, you have to be registered at birth to the ones that are good. Like Wyn's prep. Either boat man's family wasn't socially up or they didn't have the money for a good one when he was borned. Anyway, Lillia and her parents wouldn't even consider the fellow who had the yach . . . boat."

"So now Wyn and Lillia will marry and live together, not happily ever after, but socially correct ever after," I said. And asked, "What about Frangi?"

"She probably knew about it all along. From the time she moved in with him. And probably located his successor at some of the parties they attended. Higher ups on the picture level than extras. And knowing it was nearing time for his return to Lillia, managed her own affairs to her liking."

I couldn't exactly fathom it. Why that night? She could have moved out anytime along the way, he wasn't at home that much. Wyn was a social—not society—a *social* creature. He wasn't a bad sort. He was just one of those eternal boys. One who never outgrew the stud book of prep school

Cluny called the next week. "There'll be a rehearsal, probably Friday. They're trying out some new sax players. Wyn's gone."

"Already?"

"He left Saturday. I'm to tell Frangi when—if—she returns. He asked us to keep her things in our storeroom until her return."

"Any clues there?"

"None. But she wouldn't leave all that behind. You should see her wardrobe. All the best silks and linens and sequins. Even some touches of mine. And jewelry!! She took the best with her, of course—the diamonds and pearls. She always carried those, remember? But the gold and silver pieces!! And she left a bank book—savings—she'd been tucking away, I figure, since she moved in with Wyn."

"Maybe she won't come back, Cluny."

"You don't mean . . .?"

"No, I don't. What I mean is, she may have upped herself financially. Lots of odds-and-ends riches in a Hollywood crowd. Maybe she decided to be an old man's favorite instead of her usual young man's sweetheart. Of course I'm just supposing."

"I do the same. But will she ever return? Sometimes it gives me shivers. Either she took herself away or . . ."

"Or there's Wyn and Rosenda."

And mutually, we changed and avoided the subject.

It was the next week at Jack's News that I dropped in quite early before campus. He was ready to go places, gathering the tools of trade.

"Liz," he greeted, "there's bones along the road down San Diego way. My cop friends gave me a pass to cover it."

"Instead of the dailies?"

"I think it's so they can work without being shoved aside by big-shot reporters. They'll inform the press later 'through channels.' " He directed me out back to his coupe and we headed to the highway going south. But we didn't stay with it long, we were off and curving to a back road.

He knew the territory and after about an hour, he sequed off to a real side road, one that had orchards growing in fields, and even some fields of fodder. And not an hour on that road, we could see the activity at hand. Ambulance, stretchers, and attendants loading. Squad cars with numerous police doing the things policemen do when searching answers. One of the officers came up to the driver's window to Jack. "Over there," he directed.

Offhand Jack motioned at me, muttered, "My assistant," or it sounded like that, and came around to open my door. I went with him. Before we reached the roadside where the ambulance attendees were gathering, I saw the woman. Not in a million years could it be Frangi. It was an oversized woman, in T-shirt and jeans that once were light blue. I didn't see her face, I didn't want to. I didn't want to think about Frangi being thrown away as this woman had been.

I managed to sidle to the edge of one of the groups to wait for Jack.

"Not your missing friend?"

"No." I shook my head. "Frangi was small, all bones. Nothing like this big woman."

"I'm glad of that," he said. Maybe he'd hurried me so he wouldn't have to talk of our destination: bones at the side of the road. And he, hoping it wouldn't be Frangi while I was there.

I told Skye all about it that evening. From the time I'd approached Jack, and all the days since, hoping to hear something of her.

I said, "Maybe she did go with the Frenchies to Paris."

"Maybe," he agreed.

"I don't know how she could arrange it that easily."

"She was experienced."

"I suppose."

"By the way," he said, yawning big, "you know this is our summer to do Provence."

"I hadn't forgotten," I told him. "I've just had other things on my mind."

We had toured Normandy two summers ago, and he'd planned Provence for the next tour. He rents a car and drives the back roads. He is on the search for folk music in all countries and communities. His dissertation will include words and music and backgrounds. It will be a major book in music matters.

"I don't suppose we can have a few days in Paris before we start Provence?"

"Maybe two days?"

"At each end," I said. I didn't know if I'd get anywhere but I could try to query the fashion designers—in my high school French and their lack of English—even the best of them, I'd discovered on earlier Parisian visits, take pride in speaking Franco-English.

At least I could try. To stop thinking about it. She'd turn up. Everyone turns up. I just hoped I wouldn't keep my eyes attuned to the verges all the time we were driving Provence. All the rest of my life. At home. And abroad.

She'll turn up. Without my watching for her. People can't just disappear.

FAMILY TRADITION

By Susan Rogers Cooper

I thought of Jeff, sleeping, his mouth half open, spittle wetting the pillowcase. He would stink of beer. He always stank of beer. I thought again how easy it would be to slit his throat or beat him to death with his own baseball bat or shoot him with the gun he kept under his pillow.

I looked to the bathroom ceiling, above the tub where I lay, counting the tiles. There was no need, really; to count the ceiling tiles. I knew how many there were. One hundred and eighty-seven. Not counting the half tiles on the north wall. I knew exactly how many there were, but continued to count them every night he locked me in. On those nights when my behavior or my body didn't please him. It was strange how he was rarely too drunk to throw the bolt home, making me a prisoner in my own bathroom, the burglar bars on the windows making me think of the *Birdman of Alcatraz*.

I counted the tiles, over and over, because if I didn't the thoughts would come. The memories.

"Daddy, where's Mommy?"

"Shut up and go to bed."

"But where's Mommy?"

The sting of his hand on my face, the pain of his booted foot against my spine.

"I said get to bed or you'll be in the basement with her, you little bitch! Now go."

He threw the pancakes, already buttered, syrup thick on the plate, against the counter. The plate cracked and dough, butter, and syrup slid down the counter and onto the floor.

"How many fuckin' times do I have to tell you? Done, bitch! Cook 'em done or don't feed 'em to me!" he screamed.

I knelt down to pick up the pieces of china and food. I heard the scrape of his chair against the linoleum and tensed. He grabbed me by the hair, hair I keep short for that very reason. But there was enough. Enough hair to pull me up and shove me against the stove.

"I've got a fuckin' presentation this morning! And you care more about your floor than me! How the fuck am I supposed to do my job with an empty stomach?"

He was in my face, breathing on me, the toothpaste breath little better than the beer breath of the night before. He slapped me hard in the face. But open-handed. He wasn't really angry. Just pissed. He grabbed my arm, shoving me forward, away from the stove.

"Fix me something to eat!"

I went to the cupboard and took down a box of corn-flakes, got a bowl, the sugar, and the milk. I set them before him.

"Jesus! I'm supposed to do my work on cereal!" He shoved the box of cereal, the bowl, the sugar, and the milk to the floor and got up, moving purposefully toward the door. Turning, he looked at me. "Do you think you could possibly fix your hair and put on some makeup before I get home? You look like shit."

I nodded my head.

"What?"

"Yes," I said weakly. He started for the door. "Jeff," I said.

He turned around. "What?"

"I just wanted to remind you my mother's coming on Friday. For the weekend . . ."

"No," he said, studying the clasps of his briefcase to make sure they were closed.

"But you said . . ."

He looked up. His face was pleasant. "I changed my mind. Are women the only ones who can change their minds?"

I didn't say anything.

"Karen, I asked you a question. Are women the only ones who can change their minds?"

"Of course not."

"Then . . ." He shrugged and opened the door to the garage.

"But she's planning on coming, Jeff . . ."

"Tell her something's come up. I don't want her in my house snooping through my stuff."

"She doesn't do that . . ."

He turned toward me. "Are you trying to make me late? Are you trying to make me look bad at work?"

"No . . . of course not . . . it's just . . ."

"Tell the old bitch something came up. Okay? Can you handle that?"

I nodded my head.

"Karen!"

I looked at him. "Yes," I said. "I'll tell her something came up."

He smiled. "Good. And don't forget to fix yourself up before I get home. You've been looking like a lesbo lately. That short hair and no makeup."

"All right," I said. I went to the door and watched him walk to his car and get in. There was no bomb in the car. I didn't know how to do that.

Dr. Turner washed his hands with a solution at his sink. "That's a nasty bruise on your leg, Karen."

I smiled. "I'm getting clumsy in my old age. I ran into the frame of the bed when I was vacuuming."

"And the one on your back?" he asked, looking into my eyes.

I looked down. Away from his gaze. "I fell down the stairs."

He sat down on the stool he'd used while giving me my examination. Patting my knee, he said, "Well, I guess you already know the answer to this." He smiled. "I'd say you're about four weeks pregnant."

I felt the blood drain from my face. I was sure the home pregnancy test had been mistaken. I'd been so careful.

"Mommy! Mommy! You're bleeding!"

"Hush, baby, help me get up."

"Daddy! Mommy's bleeding!"

"Shut up, I can't hear myself think." I watch him swig
his beer, turning up the volume on the televised baseball
game.

*"Help Mommy get out to the car, Karen. I need to go
to the hospital."*

"Is my baby brother or sister okay?"

*"Help Mommy stand up, honey . . . oh, oh, God,
no . . ."*

I turned the water off at the main tap under the sink,
then opened the top on the toilet tank and pulled the
flush handle, watching the water slowly drain from the
tank. When the tank and bowl were both empty, I
opened the economy-size bottle of Grandma's Ammonia
and poured it in the tank. Carefully, I put the lid back
on, rearranging the flowers on the top in the precise
order Jeff liked. I lifted the lid to the toilet bowl and
poured in most of the bottle of Clorox. I closed the
open window and then sprayed the bathroom with air
freshener to mask the odor of the bleach.

I used the duct tape from his toolbox to seal the windows, making sure the curtains covered them.

I put the bottles of Clorox and the Grandma's Ammonia back in the cabinet and went into the bedroom. I
got out Jeff's pants that he used to work on the car and
an old T-shirt, pulled out an old pair of socks from his
drawer and his stained sneakers. Then, along with a
large bath towel, I put them in a bag and put the bag
under the bed. Then I went into the kitchen to start
dinner. And wait for Jeff.

I heard his car pull up and went to the door to wait for
him. I was wearing his favorite sweater without a bra,
the way he liked. I had on his favorite pants, the ones
that were so tight they cut me in the crotch. I'd curled
my hair and put on makeup, heavy on the eye shadow
and mascara. The way he liked. He walked to the door,
opened it, and looked at me. He smiled and leaned over
to kiss me.

"Um, you look good enough to eat," he whispered in
my ear.

I smiled. "Thank you."

He stroked my back, under the sweater. "Turn off the stove," he said.

When he was through with my body, he rose from the bed and went to the bathroom. I waited until the door closed behind him.

"Jesus, this bathroom stinks!" he yelled.

"Sorry, I was cleaning earlier," I called back, jumping from the bed and reaching under it, with the bag from under the bed in my hand, I tiptoed to the door, leaned my ear against it, listening. I heard the sound of his water, then the sound of the toilet flushing. I threw home the bolt, pulled the towel out from the bag, and rammed it against the bottom of the door.

I heard him gasp. I heard him hit against the door. "Karen .."

I heard his body fall.

Half an hour later, I threw back the bolt, removed the towel, and went into the room, a cloth covering my face. His eyes were opened, the vivid blue dull and glazed over. The skin on his body was blistered and red where the chemicals had burned him. Gingerly, I lifted his arm and felt for a pulse. There was none. It worked out well that he'd wanted to use my body before he went to the bathroom. He was naked now. I wouldn't have to undress him and take the things from his pockets. He'd already done that for me.

I quickly untaped the window and opened it, giving myself some safe air to breathe and took the used tape into the garage, throwing it away in the garage trash can, along with other bits of tape and wire and manly things.

I dressed him in the old jeans, T-shirt, old socks and stained sneakers, using a spray bottle filled with bleach to lightly dust the clothing, then I slipped his watch off his arm and put it with his things in his tray on the bureau.

I went to the closet in the bathroom and took out the Clorox and the Grandma's Ammonia, set them on the counter, and reached up and shut the bathroom window. Opening the door, I stood at the bedroom side of Jeff's body, and opened the lids to both cleaners, holding my breath. I knocked over the Clorox so that some spilled on the floor and put the ammonia bottle in Jeff's hand, tipped over. I left the room quickly, heading for the phone.

I sat on the couch in the living room. The tears flowed freely. They usually did.

"Mrs. Osborne?"

I looked up. One of the EMTs stood in front of me. I stood. "Is he going to be all right?" I clutched the EMT's arm.

"Ma'am, I'm sorry . . ."

"Oh, my God!" I leaned toward him and he held me. "What happened? I don't understand . . ."

"Looks like he was mixing cleansers. It happens sometimes. A chemical mixture . . ."

"It's my fault! If I hadn't been feeling bad he wouldn't have been trying to clean the bathroom for me! He doesn't do it often . . . he didn't know what to use . . . oh, God . . ."

The EMT sat me down on the couch. "Ma'am, we have to take him out now. Is there anyone I can call for you?"

I shook my head. "My mother's coming to visit for the weekend. That's why we were cleaning . . ." I put my face in my hands and sobbed. Drying my eyes on the sleeve of my sweater, I said, "She'll be here any minute . . ."

"You want someone to stay with you until . . ."

I shook my head again. "No, she's on her way now." I stood up and walked with him as far as the bedroom door, where the bathroom and my late husband lay beyond.

I waited until the two EMTs brought out the shrouded body. I touched the sheet that covered his face. "Jeff," I said, "Oh, Jeff!"

"Ma'am, we're taking him to the morgue. It's in the basement of Memorial Hospital," the EMT who'd held me said. "You won't need to come by until tomorrow."

I nodded my head and watched them carry Jeff's body out the door.

"The smell seems to stay forever," Mom said. "That's the bad thing."

She opened the window and waved her hand around the bathroom, shooing out the bad air.

"Mommy, what's that smell? What's wrong with Daddy?"

She puts her hands on my shoulders, gently pushing me out of the bathroom doorway. "Hush, Karen," she says. "Daddy's had an accident."

Walking back into the bedroom where I sat cross-legged on the bed, she said, "What's for dinner?"

I sighed, a tear escaping to my cheek. "I'm too distraught to cook." Stroking my stomach where my baby grew, I said, "If it's a boy, I think I'll call him Jeff, Junior."

"That'll be nice," Mom said. She patted my hand. "Buck up, honey," she said. "It had to be done. How about we go out to dinner?"

"Pizza?" I asked.

"Sounds great." We walked out of the house and toward her car.

Mom smiled. "You think Jeff's folks would mind if we buried him next to your father?"

A FRONT-ROW SEAT

By Jan Grape

I awoke on that cold wet March morning with a fierce sinus headache over my right eye. Things went downhill from there. I broke a fingernail and tore a run in my panty hose. I had to dress twice because I snagged my sweater and had to change. When I walked out the front door I banged my little toe against the potted plant I'd brought inside for protection from the cold. "Damn Sam." I limped out to my car and sank into the seat gratefully.

Some mornings should be outlawed, I thought, but I managed to get to the office which I own and operate with my partner, Cinnamon Jemima Gunn, at eight-thirty a.m. on the dot. C.J., as she's known to all except a few close friends, would have killed me if I'd opened up late. With the way things were going, death didn't sound half bad.

At nine a man pushed open the door with its distinct sign, G & G investigations. He stopped cold in the middle of the reception area and looked around as if searching for someone.

He wasn't handsome. His nose was too long and it hooked at the end, ruining his overall attractiveness. Dark, blue-black hair waved across his head and curled down over the tips of his ears. His eyes were blue-gray and crinkle lines radiated outward from the corners. He was probably no taller than five feet ten with a rounded abdomen and torso, like he'd rather sit in front of the tube and veg out than work out. I'd guess his age around fifty.

"May I help you?" I asked.

His navy suit looked expensive, but off-the-rack, and he added a floral print tie to spiff up his white shirt. He wore a black London Fog–style raincoat, open and unbelted, and a perplexed look.

"Do you need an investigator?" I asked when he didn't answer my first question.

"Is Mr. Gunn here?" His voice was husky, like he had a cold.

"There is no Mr. Gunn. Only C.J., but she's in court . . ."

"She? I don't understand. I want to talk to Mr. C.J. Gunn." His annoyance was obvious in his derisive tone.

"C.J. isn't a mister. C.J.'s a woman."

"I'll speak to your boss, then."

"I'm it." I smiled. "I mean, I own this agency. Well, C.J. and I are co-owners actually. I'm Jenny Gordon."

"You mean this detective agency is run by a bunch of damn women?"

"That's about it, sir."

"Well, shit." He turned, walked out, and slammed the door.

"Up yours, fella," I said to his retreating footsteps.

I didn't waste time wondering about him. It happened occasionally—some macho pea brain unable to hire a female private eye because of his own ego. I shrugged and turned back to the computer terminal.

Electronic technology baffles me. I think I'm a little intimidated to think a machine is smarter than I am. But C.J., who's a computer whiz, had set up a program for our business invoices and all I had to do was fill in the blanks, save, and print. I could handle that much.

G & G's bank account was dangerously low and unless we collected on some delinquent accounts or came up with a rich client or two, we were in deep doo-doo.

We'd worked too hard for that, but it meant sending out timely statements and following up with telephone calls. Our biggest headaches were large insurance companies that always seemed to run sixty to ninety days past due.

I got all the blank spaces filled on the next account and saved the file, but before I could push the button to print, the telephone rang.

"Ms. Gordon, this is Dr. Anthony Randazzo." The

husky voice was familiar. "I want to apologize for the way I acted a few minutes ago."

So, the piggy chauvinist was a doctor. His name rang a bell in my head, but I couldn't connect it. My first impulse was to hang up in his ear, but he kept talking fast—as if he could read my mind.

"Ms. Gordon, I've been under a lot of stress . . ." He laughed, sounding nervous not jovial. "Boy, does that sound trite or what?"

I waited, unsure if he expected an answer.

"I honestly am sorry for storming out of your office. I acted like some idiot with a caveman mentality. I need an investigator and your firm was highly recommended."

I'm not a die-hard feminist, but the emotional side of my brain was yelling hang up on this bastard while the practical left brain was reminding me we needed a paying client and the doctor could be one. I wondered who was wicked enough to send this clown in our direction. "May I ask who recommended you?"

"My niece works as a receptionist for Will Martin's law firm."

Oh, hell. Will and Carolyn Martin were counted among my closest friends. Good friends aren't supposed to send the jerks of the world to you.

"I've never met Mr. Martin," he continued, "but my niece thinks highly of him."

Whew! That explained it. When asked, Will automatically would have said, "G & G." Knowing this guy wasn't a client of Will's made me feel better. "Dr. Randazzo, perhaps I should refer . . ."

"Please, Ms. Gordon, don't judge me too quickly. My wife and I desperately need help. It's a matter of life or death."

Now that he was contrite he was much easier to take, but I still wasn't sure I wanted to work with him. "I'm not . . ."

"Please don't say no yet, let me explain briefly. Two months ago, I was involved in a malpractice suit. You probably heard about it."

The bell in the back of the old brain pinged. Anyone old enough to read or watch television had heard. Because of the high costs of health care nowadays, which the medical profession tried to blame on things like malpractice suits, the media had talked of nothing else. Randazzo was a plastic surgeon. A woman had sued him for ruining her face. She hadn't looked too bad on TV, but the jury awarded her a huge amount. Mostly for pain and anguish, as I recalled. The doctor had lost and lost big.

"Yes, I recall," I said, wondering why he needed a PI now. "But the lawsuit's over, isn't it?"

"Yes. Except for working out the payment schedule." He cleared his throat. "But I think our problem has a definite connection. I'm really worried and will be happy to pay a consulting fee for your time."

"I, uhmmm . . ."

"Would five hundred be appropriate?"

He got my attention. Five big ones would certainly help our bank account. I could probably work for Attila the Hun for five hundred dollars. Okay, so I can be bought. "Would you like to make an appointment?"

"If you're free this evening, my wife and I are having a few friends over for drinks and hors d'oeuvres. If you and Ms. Gunn could join us—whatever you decide to do afterward is entirely up to you, but the five hundred is yours either way."

"What time?"

"Seven, and thanks for not hanging up on me."

Dr. Randazzo gave me directions to his house and we hung up.

I had the invoices ready to mail by the time C.J. returned.

She remembered the Randazzo lawsuit. "Five hundred dollars just to talk?"

"That's what the man said."

"Are you sure he's not kinky?" A knowing look was on her cola nut-colored face and her dark eyes gleamed wickedly.

"Maybe. But he said his wife and other people would be there. It didn't sound too kinky."

"Hummm. Guess the lawsuit didn't bankrupt him if he's got five C notes to throw around." C.J. worked her fingers across the computer keyboard.

"He probably has hefty malpractice insurance," I said.

I watched as she punched keys and letters appeared on the monitor in front of her eyes. C.J. can find out the most illuminating information about people in only a matter of minutes. With my technology phobia I don't understand modems, networks, and E-mail and have no idea what it is that she does. I've also decided I really don't want to know any details.

"Let's just check on his finances. I'm sure he has investments, stocks and bonds, real estate and what have you. Never knew a doctor who didn't." A few minutes later she muttered an "Ah-ha. Looks like Randazzo was shrewd enough to put a nice nest egg into his wife's name, but his medical practice *is* close to bankruptcy." She printed up some figures, stuck the papers in a folder, and we closed the office and left.

Since my apartment is only a few blocks from our office and her place is halfway across town, C.J. keeps a few clothes and essentials there for convenience. We took turns showering and dressing.

C.J. wanted to drive. Since she liked to change cars about every six months she'd recently leased a Dodge Dakota SE pickup truck. As roomy and as comfortable as a car. But what she was proudest of was a fancy sound system, tape deck and CD player. She popped a CD in and turned up the volume.

A woman sang, "I wanna be around to pick up the pieces, when somebody breaks your heart."

"All right." I laughed and she raised an eyebrow. I picked up the box and read about the songs and the artists. These were golden oldies by Peggy Lee, Nancy Wilson, Sarah Vaughn, Judy Garland, and others. It wasn't her usual type of music.

"That's Dinah Washington," she said. "I knew you were gonna get a kick out of this one."

I'd been hooked on country music forever but a couple of years ago I discovered Linda Ronstadt singing ballads from the '30s and '40s. And the funny thing is, I remember my parents playing records and dancing to music like this. It's an early memory and a rare one with my parents having fun. Somehow my mother's long unsuccessful battle with cancer had wiped out too many good memories.

I listened to Dinah singing about her old love getting his comeuppance, and how sweet revenge is as she's sitting and applauding from a front-row seat.

"Cripes," I said. "That really knocks me out. I've gotta have a copy."

"I'll give you this one, girl, after I've listened to it."

The Randazzos' house was located in the hills above Lake Travis, west of Austin. After a couple of wrong turns we found the brick pillars that flanked the entrance of the long drive. The blacktop curved into the front of the house and ended in a concrete parking area. C.J. pulled up between a dark green Jaguar and a tan Volvo.

The Spanish-modern house was large and rambling, made of tan brick with a burnt-sienna tile roof and built onto the side of a hill. The arched windows were outlined in the same color tile as the roof and black wrought-iron bars covered the bottom halves. The Saint Augustine grass was a dun-muckle brown with little shoots of green poking out—normal for this time of year.

We got out, walked up to the ornately carved double doors, and I pushed the oval-lighted button beside the facing.

"Some joint," C.J. said, as we waited.

A young man dressed in a cable-knit sweater with a Nordic design and charcoal gray slacks opened the door. Late twenties, blond and blue eyed with a Kevin Costner smile. He was so handsome my breath caught in my throat to look at him.

When I said Dr. Randazzo expected us he frowned, but stepped back and said, "Come in."

We were in an entry hall that ran across most of the width of the front and was open-ended on both sides. I couldn't recall ever seeing a house where you entered into a width-wise hallway.

We were directly in front of and looking into a large square atrium. Behind the glass wall was a jungle of green plants, shrubs, and trees, with a spray of water misting one side. The darkening sky was visible through the roof and I saw a couple of small green birds flitting back and forth between some trees.

The scene was exquisite and several moments passed before I could find my voice. "I—I'm Jenny Gordon and this is C.J. Gunn. We were to see Dr. Randazzo at seven."

"I'm Christopher Lansen and I work with Tony Randazzo." His voice was nasal and high-pitched and it sure didn't go with his looks. "And I'm sorry, Tony isn't here at the moment."

"Oh?" I asked, "A medical emergency?"

"I don't think so. I mean, I don't know exactly."

"I'm sure Tony will be back shortly, please come in," said a woman coming into the hall from the right side. Her voice was soft and there was no trace of a Texas accent. She sounded as if she'd had elocution lessons and had graduated at the top of the class.

She was dressed in a soft blue silk shirtwaist dress, belted with a gold chain, and wore gold hoop gypsy earrings. She was tall and willowy with dark hair pulled severely back into a bun. She would have looked elegant except she hunched her shoulders instead of standing straight.

She had high cheekbones and almond-shaped dark eyes. There was a hint of Spanish or American Indian in her tight, unlined and unblemished face. Her age could have been anywhere from thirty to sixty. Probably has had a face-lift, I thought.

"I'm Marta Randazzo. Are you the investigators my husband hired?"

"Uh . . . yes," I said. "And please call me Jenny. My partner is C.J."

The young man put his hand on her arm. "Marta, why don't you go back inside and I'll talk . . ."

"No, Chris. I, I want to speak to them now." Her voice sounded tentative, as if she hated to contradict him. She turned abruptly and walked down the hallway toward the left, leaving us no choice except to follow.

"Mrs. Randazzo," said C.J., who was walking directly behind the woman. "I should clarify something. Your husband asked us over for a consultation only. He hasn't actually hired us."

Marta Randazzo entered a huge den/family room. At least half of my apartment could fit into this one room, but maybe it seemed bigger because of the glass wall of the atrium. Another wall was taken up by a fireplace large enough to roast a side of beef. The room's decor was in Southwestern Indian colors. Navajo rugs and wall hangings, Kachina dolls, framed arrowhead and spear points, Zuni pottery, turquoise and silver jewelry knickknacks were everywhere. In a small alcove to one side of the fireplace was a wet bar. A sofa, love seat and three chairs were covered in Indian-design fabrics.

It felt like déjà vu until I remembered I'd once been in a living room decorated with Indian things. Inexplicably, I couldn't remember when or where. "It's a lovely room," I told her. "I like it."

"Thank you." She motioned for us to sit, indicating the sofa, and she sat on a chair to our right. Christopher Lansen took a spot standing near the fireplace.

"I believe Chris told you Tony isn't here at the moment," Marta said. "He should be back soon."

But she didn't sound too certain. "I'm sure . . . I, uh, know he didn't forget you were coming. . . ."

Chris Lansen said, "Marta, I don't think . . ."

"Chris?" Marta Randazzo stiffened. "Let me finish, please."

Lansen turned away and walked to the window staring out into the darkness. His body language indicated he didn't like something she'd said or was about to say.

"Tony mentioned you were coming." Marta got up, walked to the mantel, ignoring Lansen, and took a piece of paper out from under a Zuni bowl. "He had me write out a check for you." She walked over and held it out to me.

I automatically reached for the paper and looked at her. I glimpsed a flicker of something in her eyes just before she turned and sat down, but then it was gone. Fear maybe? Or despair. I couldn't be sure.

The check was made out to G & G investigations for five hundred dollars and signed by Marta Randazzo.

"Mrs. Randazzo," said C.J. "Perhaps we should wait until your husband returns and we can talk to him."

"I agree," said Chris. He looked at Marta with a stern expression. Some battle of wills was going on between the two of them. "He'll be back soon." Lansen's tone was emphatic. "He and I planned to talk about the surgery I'm doing on Mrs. Franklin tomorrow. He wouldn't forget about that."

"Oh, you're a doctor, too?" I asked, hoping to ease the tension. He and Marta were definitely uptight.

"Yes. I'm an associate of Tony's. A junior partner."

"We could wait a little while for him if it won't inconvenience you, Mrs. Randazzo." I tried to hand the check back to her. She ignored it, so I placed it on the end table next to me.

"Please, call me Marta," she said. She jutted her chin slightly. "That check means you are working for *me*, doesn't it?"

"We're here on consult. That was my agreement with Dr. Randazzo."

"Then, in that case I'm consulting you. It must be obvious to you both . . . I should explain."

Chris Lansen cleared his throat and Marta Randazzo looked at him, her face creased with a frown. Her chin jutted out again briefly before she relaxed. "Jenny, C.J.? Would you like something to drink? Coffee or something stronger?"

"Coffee would be fine," said C.J. and I agreed.

"Chris? Would you go make coffee for my guests?" Her tone sounded like an order, but she didn't raise her voice.

He gave her a look as if she'd just asked him to wash the windows or something equally distasteful, but he left the room without speaking.

"Jenny, my husband has disappeared," she said when Lansen was gone. "I was taking a shower. After I dressed and came out here, Tony was gone. I assumed he'd gone for a walk, but that was at five o'clock and he still isn't back yet."

"Have you looked for him?" I asked. She reminded me of someone, but I didn't know who.

"Yes. Chris came over about six and when I mentioned I was getting worried about Tony, Chris got into his car and drove around looking. He didn't find Tony."

"Your husband walks regularly?" C.J. asked.

"Yes, if something is bothering him. It's his way of relieving stress. But he's usually back after about twenty to thirty minutes."

"Could his disappearance have something to do with why he wanted to hire us?" I noticed out of the corner of my eye that C.J. was poised on the edge of her seat.

C.J. got up, muttering something about going to help with the coffee and went in the same direction Chris had gone. I knew she was using the old divide-and-question-separately technique.

"Maybe," said Marta.

"Do you know why he . . ."

"Yes," said Marta. "Someone's trying to kill me."

"What makes you think someone is trying to kill you?" ·

"Someone followed me all last week. The same man I think, I'm sure it was the same car." She began twisting the hem of her skirt as she talked and I noticed bruises on her inner thigh near her left knee.

"After I became aware of this man," she continued, "I realized he'd probably followed me even before that. Then night before last that same car tried to run my car off the road. You drove up here and saw those treacherous curves. And the cliffs are pretty steep. I almost went over the edge. It scared me silly."

"Why would anyone want you dead?"

"I don't know, uh . . . maybe it's someone from the Davis family—wanting to get back at Tony."

"The Davis family?"

"The people who sued my husband."

"But why? They won their case."

C.J. and Chris came back into the room. He was carrying a silver serving tray with four china cups sitting in saucers.

Chris said, "My thoughts exactly. Why would anyone from the Davis family . . ."

"Money might not be enough," said C.J.

"What?" asked Marta.

"Revenge can be sweeter than money." C.J. sat on the sofa where she'd been before while Chris placed the tray on the coffee table. "Mrs. Davis feels she has suffered," she said. "And now it's Mrs. Randazzo who must suffer."

Chris carefully handed a saucered cup of coffee to each of us and then took his and returned to the fireplace. "That's what Tony thought," he said placing his coffee on the mantel. "But I think it's all hogwash."

"I know what you think, Chris. You've been vocal enough about it." Marta's voice got lower and that made her words sound more ominous. "You think I'm imagining all this, but you don't know. You just don't know." Marta began stirring her coffee, banging the spoon against the cup. "Tony believed me. And now something has happened to him."

"Oh, Marta," said Chris with a there, there, little lady tone. "Tony's only been gone a couple of hours. He's gotten sidetracked, that's all."

"Maybe he twisted his ankle and fell into one of the canyons," I said. "He could even be unconscious."

"I looked in all the likely places," said Chris.

"Maybe you should call the search and rescue squad," I said.

"Law enforcement won't be inclined to do anything until he's been missing for twenty-four hours or so," said C.J.

"I want to hire you to find my husband and find out who . . ."

The doorbell rang and Chris, without asking Marta, left to answer it. He acted as if this were his house not hers.

"Will you try to find Tony?" Marta asked, ignoring the interruption.

C.J. and I glanced at each other and I saw her imperceptible nod of agreement.

"Okay, Mrs. Randazzo," I said. "You've just hired us." I picked up the check. "Consider this a retainer for two days."

My partner, who believes in being prepared, said, "I have a contract with me." She pulled papers out of her shoulder bag, handed a page to Marta Randazzo who scanned it quickly, and took the pen C.J. offered, and signed it.

"Marta?" I asked. "Does one of the cars out front belong to your husband?"

"The Jag is his. My Caddy is in the garage."

"And the Volvo belongs to Chris?"

Marta nodded.

Chris walked in with a man and woman trailing behind. The man was stocky, about fifty with heavy dark eyebrows and a hairline that receded back past his ears. The strands left on top were plastered to his reddish scalp. He was dressed in a three-piece suit and looked as if he'd rather be anyplace else except here. He walked straight to the bar without speaking and poured a drink.

The woman came over to where Marta now stood. "Chris told us Tony is missing."

She was short with a voluptuous figure and blond Farah Fawcett hair. "Oh, Marta, you poor dear." The woman put her arms around Marta and kissed the air near Marta's cheek.

"I'm fine, Sonja." Marta recoiled from the woman's touch, but forced a smile. "I'm sorry, the party is canceled. Chris was supposed to call you."

"Oh, he came by about six-thirty. Said he was looking for Tony," said the woman. "He called back later and left a cancellation message on the infernal machine. I just thought we'd drop by on our way out to eat."

The woman noticed C.J. and I for the first time. She looked at Marta and said in a stage whisper as if we weren't there, "Are they from the police?"

"No, uh, Sonja Bernard." She nodded, and we stood. "This is Jenny Gordon and C.J. Gunn. They're private investigators."

The man who'd come in swayed over a double shot of amber liquid in a glass. I assumed he was Sonja Bernard's husband.

"Private dicks, huh?" he said and laughed uproariously. From his slurred words it was obvious this drink was not his first. "Don't think I've ever met a female dick before, black or white. How do?"

He took a big swallow and said, "Tough gals, huh? Do you carry guns? Which one is the dyke? I'll bet it's the black one."

"Bernie, don't be crude," said Sonja. "Their sexual preference is none of your damn business."

Marta's face turned red. "I apologize . . ."

I hated it, too, because I knew C.J.'s sharp tongue would slash and trash Bernie before he could stagger another step. And that was if she decided to only chew him up instead of knocking him on his can. My partner's an ex-police woman, six feet tall, and trained in Tukong Martial Arts. She could put him down and out.

I felt her body tense and spoke quickly, "C.J.? We probably should go." But I wasn't quite fast enough.

"He doesn't bother me, Mrs. Randazzo," said C.J. She smiled sweetly at the man, and then back at Marta. "His whiskey-soaked miniscule brain is ruled by his own penile inadequacy." Her next words were directed to me and spoken through clenched teeth. "You're right, Jenny. We must be on our way, but perhaps Marta will show us out. I have a couple more questions."

"What did she say?" asked Bernie. "Did she just insult me?"

"Of course, Bernie," said Chris, who walked over and took the man's arm. "But turnabout's fair play, wouldn't you say? Let's refresh your drink." Chris took the man's arm and turned him toward the bar.

The man needed another drink like a cowboy needed a burr under his saddle, but the maneuver had moved him out of C.J.'s reach.

The man followed, muttering something about how he'd bet a hundred dollars Tony was shacked up with a blonde someplace.

"I'm terribly embarrassed . . ." said Sonja.

"And I'm terribly sorry for you," I said to her.

Marta Randazzo looked as if she'd like to climb into a hole someplace, but she walked out of the room instead.

C.J. and I followed. Marta veered off into a small sitting room where we stood and asked our questions.

C.J. made notes as Marta gave us descriptions of the car and the man who had followed her. She hadn't seen the license number. She said the people who sued her husband were Ellen and Herbert Davis.

"First," said C.J. "We'll check the local hospitals and emergency clinics, in case Dr. Randazzo has been brought in unconscious. And we'll try to check up on who's been following you. It won't be easy without that plate number."

"Will you call? No matter how late?" Marta asked. "I mean even if the news is . . ."

"Yes," I said. "We'll call if we hear anything." She gave us a recent photo of her husband.

"This could turn into an all-night job," I said as we got into the truck and headed to town.

"Did you catch that last remark from old Bernie?" I asked.

"No, I was having too much trouble trying to keep from decking the guy."

"I figured. Bernie mumbled something about Tony being shacked up someplace."

"Which is why the police are reluctant to get involved in domestic squabbles," said C.J. "The missing usually turn up the next day looking sheepish."

"Did you learn anything from Chris?"

"Only that he knew his way around the kitchen."

"You think the Randazzos quarreled?"

"Didn't you see the bruises on Marta's neck?"

"No, I missed those, but I saw bruises on her leg. That muddies up the waters a bit, doesn't it?"

The next morning we drove to work separately in our respective vehicles. My partner is a morning person and her energy and excitement greeting a new day bugs the hell out of me. I needed time for my body to wake up slowly and the short drive without her helped.

Last night we'd checked all the emergency rooms without turning up the doctor. I'd called a friend, Jana Hefflin, who worked in Austin Police Department communications to see if her department had taken a call regarding a John Doe of anyone fitting Dr. Randazzo's description. She checked with the 911 operators, the EMS operators, and police dispatcher, all at APD headquarters. It was a negative on our man.

Finally, I called Marta Randazzo to report that there was nothing to report. It was almost two a.m. when we made up the bed in the guest room for C.J. and called it a night.

The new day was filled with sunshine and blue skies—reminding me of why I love central Texas.

Austin's built over the Balcones Fault, an ancient geological plate that eons ago rumbled and formed the hills, canyons, and steep cliffs around west Austin. The land west of Austin is known as the Texas Hill Country. The city's east side slopes into gentle rolling hills and fertile farm land. Our office is in the LaGrange building which sits on a small knoll in far west Austin near the Mo-Pac Freeway and from our fourth-floor office there's a fantastic view of limestone cliffs and small canyons to the west.

At the office, C.J. ran computer checks on the Davises. Ellen Davis had never sued anyone before and neither she nor her husband had a police record. She also ran three other names: Sonja and Hirum "Bernie" Bernard and Christopher Lansen.

Mr. Bernard had a DUI and a resisting arrest charge pending. He also had a couple of business lawsuits resulting in settlements. Sonja Bernard had called the police recently in regard to a domestic dispute. Dr. Lansen had one bad debt on his credit record and a couple of unpaid parking tickets. A bunch of ordinary people, nothing to set off any alarm bells.

C.J. learned from a friend on the computer network that Ellen and Herbert Davis had left three weeks ago on an extended vacation to Hawaii. "That lets them out as revenge seekers," she said.

"You got that right," I said, using one of her favorite sayings. I called Mrs. Randazzo to see if she'd heard anything. She hadn't, and afterward I made follow-up calls to the hospitals.

I told C.J. a trip to Dr. Randazzo's office might be helpful. "Maybe the doctor has a girlfriend and someone from his office knows about it."

"Maybe he even plays with someone from work."

Having spent a few years around doctors myself, I knew the long hours of togetherness sometimes bred familiarity. "This whole thing just doesn't make good sense to me. If Randazzo and his wife had an argument and he stormed out, why didn't he go off in his Jag, not just head out on foot someplace?"

"Unless," said C.J., "he wanted to stage a disappearance. That malpractice suit left him in bad shape financially except for those assets in his wife's name."

I liked it. "What if he has other assets, hidden ones, and worked out a scheme? What better way than just walk off? Leave everything. And if another woman is involved she could meet up with him later. Intriguing, huh?"

"Yeah, but what about someone trying to kill Marta? If the Davises are out spending their newfound money, then who?"

"So," I said, "Randazzo hired someone to scare Marta in order to throw suspicion off of his own plans."

We couldn't come up with any more ideas, so I left to talk to the doctor's employees.

Randazzo's office was in the Medical Professional

high-rise building next door to Seton Hospital on Thirty-eighth Street, a few miles north of downtown and only a fifteen-minute drive from my office.

Years ago, I had worked at an X-ray clinic in this building. My husband, Tommy, used to pick me up for lunch and we'd go around the corner to eat chicken-fried steak. The restaurant went bust a while back and of course, Tommy was killed a couple of years ago. Nothing stays the same, I thought, as I pulled into an empty parking spot and got out.

Randazzo's suite of offices were on the second floor. A typical doctor's suite. Comfortable chairs in the waiting room, popular magazines scattered on tables, and modernistic art prints hanging on the wall. A curly-top redheaded young woman, about eighteen, sat in the glassed-in cubicle.

Were receptionists getting younger or was I only getting older? After I explained who I was and what I wanted, I was asked to wait. Ms. Williams, the head nurse, would be with me in just a few minutes, I was told.

It was a good half hour before Ms. Williams called me. Her office was small, more like a closet under the stairs, but there was a desk and secretary-type chair. A telephone and a computer sat on the desk and file folders covered all the remaining space. She was about my age of thirty-five and every year showed on her face today. I'd guess a missing boss could upset routines.

"Ms. Williams, I'm sorry to bother you but if you'll answer a few questions, I'll get out of your way."

"Please call me Tiffany. Ms. Williams reminds me of my mother and I'd just as soon not think of her."

"I hear that," I said. "And I'm Jenny." Even though she didn't ask me to, I sat down.

"I don't know if you've talked to Mrs. Randazzo today, but she's hired my partner and me to try to find her husband."

"Wow, I've never talked to a private detective before. It must be exciting." Tiffany Williams ran her hand through her brown hair which was cut extremely short and was two shades lighter than my own chestnut color.

"It's not exactly like it is on TV. Most of my work

involves checking backgrounds on people. Nothing too exciting there."

She looked disappointed. "Dr. Lansen told us Mrs. Randazzo had hired someone to try to locate Dr. Tony. How do you go about finding a missing person?"

"Pretty much like I'm doing now with you. You talk to friends, family, and coworkers. See if they have any knowledge or ideas."

"I don't know where he's gone. I just work here."

"I understand. But sometimes coworkers overhear things and that chance remark might give a clue." She nodded and I continued, "Tell me about Dr. Randazzo."

"Tell you what?"

"What kind of boss is he? It helps if I can get some feel for the person. Did he seem unusually upset or worried about anything lately?"

"He's always upset about something. He's a very intense person. A control freak. He got upset whenever people wouldn't do as he said."

"You mean his patients?"

"Everyone. His wife, his employees, the hospital staff." Tiffany Williams began chewing her fingernails. They looked red and ragged as if she'd already spent a lot of time gnawing. "Everyone is afraid of him and no one would knowingly cross him—about anything."

"When I worked in X-ray I ran across doctors like that and I always called it the prima-donna syndrome. Some doctors let a little power go to their heads." Tiffany was nodding in agreement after her initial surprise that I'd once worked in medicine.

"Yes. And when a second doctor comes in and is so nice, you see how things *could* be."

"You mean Dr. Lansen?"

"Yeah, he's so easygoing, but a great doctor, too. The patients all love him and the employees, too." She thought a moment. "I think everyone responds to his kindness but that didn't go over with Dr. Tony."

"I can imagine. Do you know how Marta Randazzo got along with Dr. Lansen?"

"I don't know if I should say. It's not professional."

"I understand and I don't blame you. Let me tell you what I've observed and see if you agree."

She nodded and I said, "There's an undercurrent of something between them. It goes deeper than an . . ."

"Very definitely," she interrupted. "I think Chris hopes to get ahead by being attentive to Marta."

"That doesn't sound too smart or ethical."

"I never said Chris is an angel. He has his faults. He wants a partnership with Dr. Tony and he wants to reach the top as quickly as possible."

Okay, I thought, the young Dr. Lansen is ambitious. But was that enough to have caused Randazzo's disappearance? "How did Tony feel about Chris's ambitions?"

"Pleased as long as Chris kept Marta occupied."

"Oh?"

"Our patients are mostly female and women find Dr. Tony's bedside manner quite charming. If Marta's attention was elsewhere then . . ." Realizing she was saying too much, she stood. "I've got to get back to work. It's gonna be one of those days."

I stood also. "Okay, but one more question. Was there one lady Dr. Tony was especially close to lately?"

She walked to the door, looking as if she were a little girl who'd just tick-a-locked her mouth shut. She then sighed. "I probably shouldn't, but you'll find out anyway if you keep digging. Dr. Tony is having a relationship with a patient—or was. We all knew about it."

"Who?"

"Sonja Bernard, a neighbor of theirs. He did surgery on her and they got involved a few months ago. They were going hot and heavy and it was beginning to get sticky."

"Did Marta know?"

She nodded. "Chris let it slip but I'm sure it wasn't by accident. Chris always does things for a reason." Tiffany went out into the hallway. "I really do have to get busy."

"Okay and thanks." I turned to leave, but remembered something she'd just said. "You said Dr. Tony and Sonja *were* going hot and heavy?"

"Yes, but they broke up last week. And remember you didn't hear any of this from me."

"My lips are sealed."

On my way back to the office I wondered why Lansen had wanted Marta to know about Tony and Sonja.

Somehow, that didn't fit with my image of the young doctor on his way up. You can get fired for getting the boss's wife upset.

I pulled onto the street behind the LaGrange and Jana Hefflin from APD communications rang my car phone.

"Jenny, I've been listening in on a call one of my 911 operators is working. Dr. Randazzo was located about an hour ago—he's dead."

"Damn. What happened?"

"He was shot. Body was in a deep ravine about a half mile from his house. The police aren't calling it homicide yet, they're still investigating."

"You're sure it's Randazzo?"

"Yep. He had identification. Sorry, Jenny."

"Thanks, I appreciate it. I owe you one," I said. I knew Jana had an abiding affection for chocolate-covered strawberries made by a local candy company—Lamme's. I'd make sure she received a box the next time they were offered for sale.

When I got inside, I plopped in a customer chair in front of C.J.'s desk and told her our missing person had been found dead.

She was pulling apart sheets of computer paper as they came out of the printer. "Should we call Marta Randazzo?"

"We'll wait. The police have to make their notifications."

We discussed my conversation with Tiffany and when the printer's clatter abruptly stopped, C.J. held up the pages. "I came up with more info about Mrs. Randazzo. She comes from an old West Texas ranching family. She inherited more money than you or I could ever imagine.

"I think," she added, "Dr. Lansen changed horses in mid-stream. When he realized Randazzo was losing the lawsuit and the medical practice would go down the tubes, he figured Marta was his best bet. She's got enough money to set up two or three practices.

"And personally, I think young Lansen is involved right up to his pretty blue eyes," said C.J.

I thought about how Marta and Chris Lansen had acted when we were there. C.J. could be right. If Chris wanted to get ahead and if he felt Marta could help. But I didn't think Marta was involved. She had seemed genuinely worried about Tony's disappearance and, besides, I liked her. "No, I can't buy it."

"Why not?" C.J. prided herself on her judgment of people and she got a little huffy because I didn't agree. "Look, he's hot after the missus and he probably saw a quick and dirty way to take out the husband."

She was working up her theory hoping to convince me. "He probably began stalking Marta to use as a cover for his real target . . ."

When I said I couldn't buy it, I meant I couldn't buy Marta's involvement. I did have many doubts about Chris Lansen. "Possibly. He says he went out looking for Randazzo. Maybe he found him and killed him."

"The stalking tale could have been just that, a tale."

"What about your 'Good Buddy,' Bernard?" I asked. "His wife's infidelity could have sent him into a jealous rage. Or what about the woman scorned, Sonja Bernard?"

C.J. said, "Bernard might strike out in the heat of passion if he caught his wife with Tony. But he's a drunk and I doubt he'd have the balls to plan anything sophisticated.

"And Mrs. Bernard is out from the same mold as Randazzo. She's played around for years, but she always goes back to her husband. He needs her."

"Surely you didn't find that out from your computer," I said.

"No, I called Carolyn Martin, she filled me in on the Bernards."

My friend, Carolyn, who's hip-deep in society happenings, knew all about the skeletons in the jet-setters closets. If Carolyn said Sonja had the morals of a rock-star groupie, then it was true. "Okay, so where does that leave us?"

C.J. stared at me. "Back to Marta Randazzo. She's one cool bitch."

"No, I think she's putting on a front. Acting cool when she really isn't." The more I thought about it the more I felt I was right. "Marta couldn't kill . . ."

"Listen to you, Jenny, listen to that nonsense coming from your mouth. The husband abused her regularly, he played around—even had an affair with a friend." C.J.'s tone was curt.

"Chris Lansen and Marta Randazzo together," she

said. "They have the best motive and Chris sure had the opportunity . . ."

I thought about the vulnerability I had seen in Marta's eyes and was determined to give her every benefit of the doubt. "If Chris did it he was acting alone."

"No way. Marta is involved, believe me. She was fed up with her husband." C.J. shook her finger at me and raised her voice. "Randazzo acted like a horse's ass routinely. Now he's lost his medical practice—suddenly, Marta and Chris both see a solution to all their problems."

"Dammit, we don't even know yet that it was murder. Maybe Randazzo killed himself. What do the police say?"

C.J. shrugged.

"Take it from me—if Randazzo was murdered Marta didn't do it." I stood and walked out of the reception area and into my inner office, slamming the door behind me.

Once inside I started cooling off immediately. I've always been that way. I can get angry enough to chew nails, spout off, then quickly my anger subsides. When C.J. began to get angry with me, I should've backed off. It was stupid and I knew it.

My partner can stay mad for hours—days even. The only way to head it off was to try and make her laugh. If I could get her to laugh things would smooth out quickly.

I stayed in my office for about five minutes, rehearsing what I would say to C.J., but when I went back out to her desk in reception—she was gone.

She'd left a note saying she'd gone to APD to see what she could find out from Larry Hays. Hoo-boy, I thought. When she's too angry to tell me when she's leaving, she's really mad.

Lieutenant Hays worked in homicide and he'd been my late husband's partner and best friend. After Tommy died Larry took on the role of my brother/protector. For a private investigator, having a friend on the force was a huge bonus. If Larry hadn't worked on the Randazzo case, he'd know who had and would be able to give C.J. all the inside dope.

Talking to Larry was another good way for C.J. to get

over her anger. If she could talk shop with him—she'd chill out fast.

I tidied up my desk, set the answering machine, and left.

But instead of going home, I found myself heading to the Randazzos'. Something about Marta pushed my buttons and I had to see if I could find out why.

Marta Randazzo wasn't particularly glad to see me, but she didn't slam the door in my face. She just said, "Come in, if you like." I followed her down the hall to the den.

Once again I had the feeling I'd been in this room before, the Indian colors and Kachina dolls and arrowheads were so familiar it was spooky. I refused the drink she offered and sat down.

Marta certainly didn't look like a woman who only a few hours ago had learned of her husband's death. Her makeup was impeccable. No red eyes or tears. Her whole demeanor was changed, she acted poised and self-assured. She picked up her glass and drank, standing regally by the fireplace, and then stared at me over the rim. "You expected tears?" Her tone was defiant.

"Everyone handles grief differently."

"I can't pretend grief when there's nothing there. I can't pretend when deep down I'm glad Tony's dead."

Suddenly, I was ten years old again and memories came flooding back. My mother and I were at my aunt's house, in her living room decorated with Indian artifacts. Decorated much like this room was.

I could even hear my mother's voice. It sounded tearful and sad. *"Everyone handles grief differently."*

I recalled Aunt Patsy saying, "I can't pretend grief when deep down I'm glad Stoney is dead."

My mother said, "But, Patsy, I don't understand. What did you do?"

Both of my aunt's eyes were blackened and she had a plaster cast on her arm. I'd never seen anyone look so defiant. Aunt Patsy said, "I killed him. I got his pistol and I shot him. I just couldn't take the beatings anymore. Not with this baby coming."

"Shhh," said my mother turning to me. "Jenny, why

don't you go play outside. Aunt Patsy and I need to talk grown-up stuff."

I could now remember everything I'd blocked out. My aunt being arrested, and there was a trial or something. Later, she was sent away, probably to a women's prison. She didn't even come to my mother's funeral three years later. Maybe she couldn't if she was in prison, but as a child I didn't know that. I only knew how hurt I was because she wasn't there. I'd been crazy about Aunt Patsy and I guess I couldn't deal with all the emotional trauma and had buried it.

Until I met Marta Randazzo.

I looked at Marta. "You killed him, didn't you? You killed him because he beat you and cheated on you and you'd finally had enough. His affair with Sonja Bernard was the last straw."

Marta began shaking her head no, but I continued. "You wanted a way out."

"No," she said. And for the first time since I'd met her, she stood straight with her shoulders back. "He scarred Ellen Davis's face, but he wasn't sorry. He even laughed about it. Just like he laughed over what he did to me." Marta pulled her sweater up and off her head in one fluid motion. She was braless and I winced at the misshapen breasts and the hideous-red-surgical-scar tissue.

"See! See what he did to me?" She was crying now and could barely speak. "I—I killed him . . . be-because I didn't want him to get away with ruining another woman."

"But he didn't . . ."

"Y-you think giving Ellen Davis thousands of dollars could ever be enough? And it didn't even faze him. He was going to disappear. Move to another state and start all over. Start butchering women again. I couldn't let him. I—I had to stop him."

"So, that's why you had a blind spot about her. What did you do when she just up and confessed?" asked C.J.

"I told Marta I knew one of the best defense lawyers in Texas. I called Bulldog Porter. He came over and together they drove downtown to police headquarters."

I looked at C.J. "Thanks for not reminding me how right you were."

She shrugged. "What about Marta being stalked?"

"Randazzo probably set that up for his disappearing act."

"And Chris Lansen wasn't involved?"

"Bulldog wouldn't let Marta talk to me. I believe Chris dumped the body for her, but killing Tony was her own solitary act." I thought about that Dinah Washington song, then. "Marta sure had a front-row seat for her revenge."

REUNION QUEEN

By Barbara Collins

Her mood darker than the night—and the night was very dark—the striking blonde tooled the candy-apple Jaguar into the Marriot lot. She climbed out, pausing by the car, standing there like a modern-day gunfighter, red-nailed fingers slowly opening and closing.

With a smile bordering on a smirk, she walked toward the hotel, ground fog swirling up around her legs, red stiletto heels clicking on the asphalt, punctuating the thunder growling in the distance.

At the entrance of the modern, sterile building, she stopped and looked up.

Above the double-glass doors hung a homemade banner—WELCOME CLASS OF 1978—their fifteenth reunion; it flapped crazily in the breeze, as if trying to escape the imminent storm.

Her smile vanished, blue eyes clouded, as she gazed at the sign; the wind whipped long blond strands of hair around her face.

Lightning split the sky, and the world went white, then black. Big drops of rain began to pelt her, and the banner, its painted letters starting to bleed and run.

Her smile returned, and grew broader until she threw back her head, laughing, her throaty voice mingling with the thunder that followed.

She reached up and ripped the banner down, letting the wind take it.

Then she straightened her red lace dress, and adjusted each copious breast in the push-up bra, opened the glass doors, and walked inside.

*   *   *

Heather sat at a table with Linda just outside the hotel ballroom on the second floor. They were collecting money for the banquet tickets and handing out ID badges, which displayed each classmate's name above their old high school yearbook photo.

Heather leaned toward Linda, touching the other woman's arm intimately as if the two of them were best of friends, and giggled as if she were having a great time . . . but inside Heather was seething.

How did I get stuck on the goddamn door? she fumed. *I'm the fucking class president!*

Heather smiled sweetly at Linda, who was reciting recent bowling scores, like it was somehow important. She studied her classmate's face and concluded that no amount of plastic surgery could help. If *she* were Linda, she'd kill herself.

"Would you like to go bowling sometime?" Linda asked, under the deranged impression that spending the past hour with Heather made her a close friend—or a friend at all, for that matter.

"That sounds very entertaining," Heather answered. As in slicing and dicing a finger in the Cuisinart.

At the end of the carpeted corridor, three men burst out of the men's bathroom, laughing loudly, punching one another's arms. What was it about class reunions that regressed even a thirtysomething hunk like her husband into a nerdy teenager?

"Rick!" Heather called out disgustedly.

He ignored her.

So she hollered louder, "Rick! Come here!"

Her husband, tall, handsome, so perfect in his Armani suit, shrugged at his other two friends—a fat farmer and balding banker—and sauntered toward her.

Heather felt her face flush; how *dare* he be having a good time when she was so miserable!

"Where's Jennifer?" she snapped at him. "She was supposed to take my place fifteen minutes ago!"

He looked at her stupidly. "Haven't seen her, hon."

"Well, *find* her, damnit! I'm sick of sitting here!"

Out of the corner of her eye, Heather could see Linda shifting uncomfortably in her chair; Heather didn't want to alienate the woman—not just yet—she might need her vote.

Heather gave Linda a patronizing little smile. "It's just that, as *president,* I have other things to attend to," she explained.

Linda nodded and looked away.

Heather turned back to Rick. "Go . . . find . . . Jennifer, *dear.*"

"Okay, okay," he said, gesturing in a calm-down manner with both hands, "I'll go find her."

He winked at Linda.

Linda beamed.

"So *go,*" Heather said through clenched teeth. "And back off on the booze!"

"Yes, hon," he said and turned away.

Heather watched him move slowly down the hall, in no great hurry to accommodate her, which infuriated her further. Finally, Rick opened the ballroom doors, letting escape the loud, pounding disco music from their high school days, where it bounced off the walls in perfect timing with the beating of Heather's palpitating heart.

. . . ah ah ah ah stayin' alive . . .

The ballroom door slammed shut; the corridor fell into a strained silence.

Linda cleared her throat and asked, "I wonder who's going to be crowned Reunion Queen?"

Heather, pretending not to care, began to straighten the remaining badges on the table. "Whoever gets the most votes," she said, but thought, *It damn well better be me.*

After all, wasn't *she,* even after fifteen years, still the best-looking woman in her class? And Heather had gone to great lengths and expense to make sure that she was: trips to the tanning salon, weight-reduction classes, professional makeup and hair care (her shoulder-length brunette tresses completely untouched by gray—*now*), not to mention a six-month-long search for the perfect little designer dress. . . .

And for *what*? Heather thought sullenly, so she could rot out here, while everyone else was in the ballroom having fun?

Heather looked resentfully at Linda, whose mouth now hung open like a big bass being reeled in. What was the *matter* with her, anyway?

Heather followed Linda's stare to a woman who was ascending the stairs in front of them.

And Heather gasped—not because of the woman's hair, which was butter-blond brushing bare shoulders, or her porcelain face, its features almost too perfect, or her voluptuous figure, which bordered on Amazonian—but because the *bitch* was wearing Heather's designer dress!

Perfectly balanced on her high heels, the blonde undulated toward them.

"Hi!" she said.

Linda continued to stare at the woman, but Heather said pleasantly, "The Bimbo Convention must be at some *other* hotel." After all, this was no one Heather knew from school.

"Pardon me?" The blonde looked confused, which Heather considered redundant.

"This is a *class reunion*," Heather said, her voice dripping with insolence. "But then, I guess you couldn't read the sign outside."

The blonde flashed a dazzling white smile. "I'm afraid there *is* no sign . . . but I'm at the right place."

And she extended one hand, moving it over the remaining ID badges spread out on the table, like a fortune-teller picking a tarot card, and with a perfectly manicured fingernail, tapped one. "That's me!" she said.

Linda leaned forward in her chair. "Hilda?" she asked, stunned. "Hilda Payne?"

"Hello, Linda," the blonde said warmly.

With a squeal, Linda jumped up, ran around the table, and gave the blonde a hug.

"I can't *believe* it's you!" Linda said.

The blonde smiled. "It's been a long time. I'm sorry I couldn't make it back for the tenth."

"You . . . you look *wonderful*," Linda gushed.

"So do you," the blonde replied.

Gag me with a spoon, Heather thought. She studied the blonde, trying to mentally transform the homely girl on the badge into the gorgeous woman (all right, she admitted it) in front of her. But then, Heather really didn't remember Hilda much at all—or any of the other plain nonentities that had roamed the school hallways like cows, getting in her way.

"Are any of the other girls here?" the blonde asked Linda. "Mary? Diane?"

Linda nodded, her head jerking back and forth on her shoulders like a jack-in-the-box on a spring. "I can't *wait* until they see you!" she said excitedly.

And Linda began pulling the blonde by the arm down the hall toward the ballroom.

Heather stood up. "Hey, wait just a minute, Linda!" she said angrily. "Who's gonna look after the *table*?"

"How about you?" Linda shot back.

And the two women disappeared through the ballroom doors.

. . . heart of glass . . .

Heather slammed her fists on the table, rattling the cash box and scattering the badges.

Then, dejectedly, she slumped in her chair.

"But she's wearing my dress," Heather whimpered to no one. "She wearing *my dress*. . . ."

Rick leaned on the bar, a scotch and soda in hand, and surveyed the ballroom.

A few people had already taken seats at tables decorated in the school's colors—purple and gold—while others continued to mill around, trying to talk over the deafening disco music.

He hated those faggy songs. And he was embarrassed that his class had picked one of them as *their* song: "Disco Duck," for Christ's sake! Why couldn't he have been born earlier? Like his older brother, Ray, who was a senior in high school when the Beatles and Stones hit.

. . . she works hard for the money . . .

He took a drink, and shook his head. *She* should try working for a car dealership, he thought bitterly. Not that the work itself was hard. The hard part was having his wife's father own the business, and always being under the old man's thumb. Rick resented the hell out of him—*and* Heather, who talked him into turning down that pro ball draft offer to go into the family business.

Maybe that was why Rick was always looking for love in all the wrong places. . . .

His eyes locked with Jennifer's. The pretty, slender redhead was standing alone by the dance floor. He looked quickly away.

But then she was next to him, touching his arm lightly, wearing that hurt expression he detested.

"Look, Jen," he said carefully, not wanting his voice to carry too far, "sorry about last week. . . ."

"Can I see you tonight?" Her big brown eyes looked wet.

He avoided them, staring out across the room. "Maybe tomorrow," he said, and slowly moved away from her.

He *could* have seen Jennifer, if he'd wanted, but he didn't, because across the room, he'd seen somebody else. . . .

She was standing by the ballroom doors—an incredible creature. But surrounding her were some of the skankiest broads in the entire class; they were fawning over her, attending to her, like she was the queen bee and they were the drones.

Suddenly the gorgeous babe flashed him a smile.

Yeah! He chugged his drink, and set it on a table as he moved toward her like a magnet to metal.

. . . da ya think I'm sexy . . .

"Well, *hello,*" Rick said. "Come here often?"

She looked at him with sultry eyes. "Would you believe me if I said it was my very first time?"

He smirked. "No." He couldn't keep his eyes off her boobs; they looked like the real thing, not hard, fake implants like his wife's.

"I hope you're just trying to read my name tag," the blonde teased.

"Uh . . . yeah," he smiled, focusing on the badge's high school yearbook photo. God, what a dog she'd been!

"You don't remember me, do you?"

He shook his head. Not if she'd looked like that.

"Well," she smiled, "we didn't exactly have the same friends."

Flanking her, the drones glared at him. She could say that again.

"Come *on,* Hilda," one of them said. "Let's go find a table—by *ourselves.*"

"Perhaps I'll see you later," Rick said, reaching out, running his fingers sensuously down her arm.

"I'm almost sure of it." She smiled sexily. "Until then . . ."

She held out one hand for him to shake. As he took it, he felt something cold and hard in his palm.

He watched her as she wandered off with her friends. Then he looked down at the hotel key in his hand.

. . . *macho, macho man* . . .

He grinned.

In the ladies' lounge Jennifer reached for a tissue on the marble vanity and blew her nose. The bathroom was empty; everyone else was enjoying the prime rib dinner. She wasn't hungry.

She looked at herself in the mirror and hated what she saw: a desperate middle-aged woman helplessly in love with a married man.

With a sob, she turned away from herself. She felt like a drug addict—only the drug she was addicted to wasn't crack or cocaine, it was Rick. And even though her mind warned, "just say no," her heart refused to listen. . . .

She had been in love with him since high school, but he'd been a jock and she a bookworm, and he never noticed her. But at the ten-year reunion that all changed; he swept her off her feet—and onto her back—after she'd dumped her date, and he'd ditched his wife. And Jennifer had been hooked ever since.

Now five years later, her life was a mess. She didn't date. She had no friends—they had long ago tired of hearing her woes—and energy that should have gone into advancing her career went instead into the stagnant affair.

If she *only* had the strength to give him up! Yet, the thought of not seeing Rick—however sporadic and brief—threw her into a panic. . . .

The lounge door opened and that blonde, Hilda, entered—the one she had seen Rick flirting with earlier. Jennifer couldn't believe Hilda would even speak to Rick after what he'd done to her so many years ago. . . .

Hilda saw Jennifer and a small friendly smile formed. "Well, hi, Jen," she said.

"Hilda," Jennifer replied coolly, pretending to fix her hair in the mirror. How she envied this woman, who seemed so happy and in control of her life.

Hilda walked over to the vanity and with a sigh of relief, kicked off her high heels. Then she dumped the contents of her gold purse on to the counter, picked out the lipstick, and applied the blood-red color to her lips.

"Don't tell me you're still carrying the torch for that *creep*," Hilda said.

Jennifer turned away from the mirror; she didn't feel like discussing her situation with *anyone,* let alone some classmate she barely knew from high school.

She started to leave, but Hilda stepped back into her way.

"I know it's none of my business," Hilda said, her voice soft and reasoning, "but he's never going to leave Heather and marry you. Why should he? He's having his cake and eating it, too. You've got to face it."

Jennifer felt her face grow hot. "You're right, you know," she said. "You're absolutely right."

Hilda nodded smugly.

"It *is* none of your business!"

And she pushed past her.

"I'm glad my cousin Lenny isn't here to see you now," Hilda said behind her, almost contemptuously. "He thought you were the only smart, decent person in high school. I guess he was wrong."

Jennifer, her back to Hilda, hand on the door, hesitated. "I guess he was . . ." she said softly.

But instead of leaving, Jennifer looked over her shoulder. "I didn't know Lenny was your cousin."

"Not many people did, even though we were in the same grade together. We didn't have the same last name."

Jennifer walked back toward Hilda. She thought there was a faint resemblance. "Tell me, how is Lenny?"

"Dead."

The way Hilda said it, so casually, so flippantly, made Jennifer feel like she'd been slapped; if she hadn't been immediately filled with sadness and memories of Lenny, she would have verbally lashed out at the woman.

But instead, Jennifer said, "I'm sorry . . . and I'm sorry he didn't have a better life; he was even more lost and miserable than I was in high school. But he was a good friend." Then she asked, "How . . . how did he die?"

"He killed himself."

Jennifer looked down at the floor, then back at Hilda.

"I guess I'm not surprised," she said slowly. "But now I'll always wonder . . . if he and I had stayed in touch . . . friends listen to friends, you know. . . ."

"They should."

Jennifer waited until Hilda gathered up the contents of her purse on the counter, and put on her shoes.

They left the lounge and walked back down the corridor toward the ballroom.

As they passed the vacant table in the hallway, Jennifer said archly, "I heard Heather went home to change her dress."

Hilda smiled. "It wasn't too hard to find out what she'd be wearing tonight," she replied, opening the ballroom door. "After all, she'd told everybody in town."

. . . bad girls . . .

Bathed in the moonlight, Hilda stood nude by the open window in a room on the third floor of the hotel. One floor below, she could see her classmates, through the domed glass ceiling of the ballroom, still eating.

Muted music floated up to her.

. . . more than a woman . . .

There was a knock at the door.

She moved to the bed and slipped under the soft white sheets.

"Come!" she called.

A key fumbled in the lock.

The door opened, then closed, and Rick stood at the foot of the bed.

"We don't have much time," he whispered conspiratorially, unbuttoning his shirt. "My wife will be looking for me."

Hilda stuck out her lower lip, pretending to pout. "Too bad," she said. "I guess I'll just have to settle for what I can get."

Quickly, Rick removed the rest of his clothing; they lay in a heap on the floor.

"Come and get it, big boy. . . ." Hilda purred, patting a place next to herself on the bed.

. . . you're the one that I want . . .

Grinning like a kid Christmas morning, Rick climbed under the sheets, and pulled her roughly to him.

"What a bitchin' babe!" he said, his breath an unpleasant cocktail of cigarettes and booze.

He kissed her.

What a lousy lover, she thought.

He pulled back and peered in her face. "Look," he said, "I . . . I do remember you, now. And I hope you're not mad about that little joke . . . back in high school."

"Little joke?"

"You know . . . me pretending to invite you to the senior prom, and all."

"And all?"

She sat up in the bed, letting the sheet slide down to expose her firm, round breasts. She leaned toward him.

"Now *why* should I be mad?" she said, running one long red fingernail down his cheek. "It was just a harmless prank . . . and I think a person should be able to handle a harmless prank, don't you?"

He started to say something, but there was a loud pounding at the door.

"Hilda!" a male voice hollered. "Are you in there? Open the door!"

"Oh, my God!" she whispered frantically. "It's my husband!"

Rick jumped out of the bed. "You didn't tell me you were married!" he whispered back, seeming more annoyed than frightened.

She shrugged. "You didn't ask . . . besides, *you're* married."

Quickly she got out of the bed, snatched a red silk robe off a nearby chair, and put it on. "You've got to hide!" she said. "The last man Butch caught me with landed up in the hospital for six months!"

"Butch?" he said. "Oh, great! Wonderful! And just *where* am I supposed to hide in this dinky room?"

She came around the bed and grabbed him by the arm. "Quick!" she said. "Under the bed."

Rick dropped to the floor and tried to squeeze beneath the box spring but he was too big.

She shook her head. "Nope. Too narrow."

He stood up again.

"Here," she said, pulling him over to a wardrobe that stood against the wall, "get inside."

She opened the cabinet and pushed him in among the clothes and hangers, but the door wouldn't close.

"Nope," she said, pulling him back. "Too small."

"Why don't I just stand in the corner with a lamp-shade on my head?" he suggested sarcastically.

"Too obvious."

She looked toward the window.

"I know . . . climb out the window. You can stand on the ledge."

"Are you *nuts*? I'm not going out there!"

"Hilda!" the man bellowed from behind the door. "If there's somebody in there with you I'll kill the son of a bitch!"

Rick climbed out the window. Cursing, he inched his way along the ledge.

Hilda scooped up his clothes and threw them out after him; they sailed down, landing on the dome of the ball-room, attracting the attention of a few people who looked up, which was just what she wanted.

"What the hell did you do that for?" Rick asked, exas-perated, clinging to the wall.

"I can't have my husband finding your clothes! Now, don't worry, I'll get rid of him. Just stay put!"

"Like, where *else* would I go?"

. . . gonna fly now . . .

Hilda went to the door and opened it.

"Darling!" she said loudly. "I didn't mean to keep you waiting . . . I was in the bathtub."

A burly man in a Marriot maintenance uniform smiled and held out his hand.

She reached into the pocket of her silk robe and handed him a hundred-dollar bill.

Outside the window came a terrific crash, following shouts and screams.

Hilda ran to the window and looked down.

Below, on the ballroom floor sprawled Rick; he looked like a baby bird in a nest of glass.

"Sweet Jesus!" said the maintenance man, now stand-ing next to her. "You didn't say anything about anybody gettin' killed. . . ."

"How was I supposed to know he was going to fall?" she said, stunned. "I just wanted him *exposed*."

"He's exposed, all right," the maintenance man said,

looking down. He pointed a thick thumb at himself. "I'm outta here, lady," he said. "I don't know *you,* and you don't know me."

And he left.

She stepped back from the window, into the shadows of the room. "It was just a harmless prank. . . ."

Heather returned to the ballroom just in time to join the group of her classmates who were gazing up through the glass dome, giggling at something. She joined in with the laughter, at the sight of the naked man doing an ungainly tightrope act on the ledge of the floor above. Her laughter caught in her throat, however, as she recognized Rick, and then the group's glee turned to gasps as Rick fell, and they jumped back, as he crashed through in a shower of glass fragments.

She rushed to him.

Even before she knew if he was dead or alive, she bent near him where he lay, sprawled in a pile on his clothes and shards of glass. Those around saw only concern on her face, but her whispered words to her husband were: "This is the last time you humiliate me . . . I want a divorce!"

He could only manage a moan.

Later, she turned her back on him, as ambulance attendants arrived to tend to her husband's cuts, and walked regally away.

She was a queen about to be crowned, after all, with a court to attend. . . .

Hilda stood with her friends in the ballroom and watched as ambulance attendants carefully transferred Rick on to a gurney. Now that it was apparent Rick's injuries weren't life-threatening—falling on top of his clothes had kept him from being shredded—many of the spectators were snickering and laughing.

Jennifer walked up to Hilda. "You did that on purpose," she said acidly. "You set him up!"

"He set himself up," Hilda responded flatly.

There was a pause, then Jennifer blurted, "You're just full of surprises, aren't you?"

"Stick around. . . ."

A screech filled the room—feedback from the PA system—as one of the reunion committee members, a tall, lanky, sandy-haired man, spoke into the mike at the edge of the dance floor. "Everyone . . . please go back to your tables. In spite of this . . . unfortunate accident . . . the hotel will allow us to continue with our evening."

People began to return to their chairs. Several of the waiters were clearing away the last of the glass.

"I have the results of the ballots filled out during dinner," the committee member continued, holding up an envelope, "and the woman named Reunion Queen this evening will preside over tomorrow's pig roast."

A hush fell over the room.

He opened the envelope. "And the Reunion Queen is . . . Hilda Payne!"

Instantaneous squeals came from several tables, followed by loud applause.

Near the front, in a prominent position she'd taken, Heather stood amid her classmates, shocked; then she joined in, clapping, too loudly, her face frozen in a smile not even she believed.

Hilda walked slowly up to the microphone. She smiled and nodded at Heather, whose glazed smile seemed about to crack. Another classmate handed her a bouquet of red roses, and placed a small rhinestone tiara on her head.

She looked out over the audience: a sea of smiling faces.

"Thank you," she said, as the applause waned. "I think it's fitting that the girl who won The Ugliest Pig Contest at the prom fifteen years ago, be asked to preside over the pig roast tomorrow. . . ."

A few people laughed, but mostly, the smiles vanished.

"That's the problem with pranks," Hilda continued, "you can never be certain of the outcome. . . ."

The room was deadly quiet.

"I'll deliver this tiara, and these roses, personally . . . you see, I'm not Hilda. I'm Linnea. And before my elective surgery two years ago, my name was Lenny."

Hilda sat in a wheelchair by the window in her room at Fairview Nursing Home. Beyond the window was a breathtaking view of colorful flower gardens, rolling green hills, and a sky as blue as a robin's egg. But she did not see the scenery, her eyes remaining placid and dead—nor did she appreciate its beauty, for her mind was less than a child's.

"How is she doing today?" Linnea asked the nurse, a matronly woman with a kind face. They stood just outside the doorway.

Linnea had long ago stopped inquiring if her cousin's condition had improved since the attempted suicide; there was no reversing brain damage caused by carbon monoxide poisoning.

"She's been a little restless," the nurse answered. "I can't help but think it's because you've been away."

The nurse looked at the bouquet of roses and the tiara Linnea held in her hands. "She can keep the flowers," the nurse instructed, "but after you've gone, we'll have to take away the crown. I'm afraid one of our more agile guests might 'borrow' it. You understand."

Linnea nodded.

"We'll hold it in the office."

The nurse turned and left.

Linnea entered the room. "Hello, Hilda," she said softly, gently touching her cousin's arm.

The woman's body jerked a little, and the pupils of her eyes moved back and forth, like an infant's trying to make sense of its world.

Linnea sat in a nearby chair.

The afternoon sun streaming in the window moved in a slow arc across the room, as Linnea spoke in a soothing voice telling her cousin all about the reunion.

Finally, Linnea stood and placed the roses in her cousin's lap, and the tiara on the woman's head. She bent and kissed her.

In the parking lot, Linnea leaned against the steering wheel of her car and wept.

Then she wiped the tears from her face with the back of her hand, and started the car.

"Rock 'n' roll radio! Here's a disco blast from the past that will take you back, baby, to nineteen seventy-eight. . . ."

She wheeled the Porsche into the street.

. . . *I will survive.* . . .

SUBWAY

· ·

By S. J. Rozan

I got involved in the subway rapist case totally by accident. I happened to be heading for the subway station
that morning, when two police cars, sirens yowling,
squealed up around me. Four cops lunged out and
pounded down the steps. I pounded down right after
them.

At the bottom they rushed in the gate. I paid my fare
and made the platform in time to see them pointed to
the far end by a scared-looking man. I was right behind
them when they charged down the steps from the platform to the tracks.

That was about as far as I was going to go. It's not a
hot idea to run around in the dark with a bunch of cops
with their guns drawn, no matter how curious you are.
So I stood on the end of the platform watching, and I
heard a sound. A little, sad sound, beyond the edge of
the platform, in the dark, not far.

Other people must have heard it, but no one else was
moving. I listened again, then headed down onto the
tracks. Third rail, Lydia, I told myself, and stepped
broadly over anything that looked like it could possibly
have electricity running through it.

It was as disgusting down there as you'd expect, trash
and oily standing water that smelled like the drain when
the sink has a problem. A half-eaten pizza slice lay
against the track. I wondered if the third rail could fry
pizza dough.

As I squinted into the dark I pointed out to myself
that cops have flashlights. Way down the tracks I could

hear the slap of footsteps and the shouts of cop voices. Close by I heard nothing.

"Hello?" I called out tentatively. "Is anyone there? Are you all right?"

The sound came again, louder but still wordless. I edged toward it. It occurred to me to hope that, when they know there are cops running around, the TA stops the trains.

The tunnel wall on my right, dimly lit by widely spaced yellow bulbs, suddenly became black void. The little sounds, desperate now, got louder. I stepped into the blackness and saw, around to the right where you couldn't see it from the tracks, a weak suggestion of light spilling from what looked like a doorway. The little sounds were spilling from there, too.

The cops, surging down the tracks after the disappearing footsteps, had run right past this place.

My back against the wall, my gun drawn, I worked my way over there. I tried to do it silently, which is something I'm getting better at. When I got to the door I stopped for a minute, listened, then kicked the door and went in crouching, elbows straight, gun sweeping right-center-left.

I didn't need that. The small, foul room was empty except for a woman, bound, gagged, blindfolded, and half naked, making desperate little sounds in the corner.

Her name was Claire Morgan. I found that out a lot later, after I'd ripped off the blindfold, peeled the tape from her mouth, cut the rope that was biting into her wrists—I tried to memorize the knot for the cops; sometimes these things are important—and, while she covered herself as well as she could with the torn remains of her dress, stuck my head back into the tunnel and hollered real loud for help.

While help ran toward us I sat with her. I wrapped her in my jacket; she'd started to shiver. She clutched her knees, stared through blackened eyes at the filthy cement floor. "Bastards," she whispered. "Bastards, bastards, bastards, bastards, bastards—"

Cops and their flashlights poured into the room. I stood. "This woman needs help," I said, maybe a little extraneously.

The first cop in, a big, freckled guy who looked sixteen, narrowed his eyes and said suspiciously, "Who're you?" while a thin-faced woman cop knelt by Claire.

I told him, "Lydia Chin."

"What's that?" he demanded. Because my jacket was wrapped around Claire, the gun on my belt was visible.

"A Colt thirty-eight," I snapped. "It's licensed. I'm a private investigator."

"What're you doing here? This is a crime scene."

"And that's a victim," I said hotly. "She needs help."

The woman cop flashed a look at us. "You get a chance, Springer, you could call for a goddamn bus!" Her eyes met mine; sometimes being a woman comes before being a cop.

'Bus' is cop for 'ambulance,' and the young cop, flushing, called for one. He glared at me while he did it, as though all this, whatever it was, was my fault.

The EMS crew came and put Claire on a stretcher with a blanket over her and a tube in her arm. Officer Caccione, the woman cop, silently handed me back my jacket. We made a single-file line back onto the platform, where cops were taking names and statements from witnesses who waved their hands, contradicted each other, and described what they thought they'd seen about the guy who'd grabbed Claire from behind and dragged her off the end of the platform.

"Makes you wonder," Officer Caccione muttered to me.

"Wonder what?"

"Where the hell they all were when he was dragging her away."

In the end, all seventeen people on the platform gave statements, and I did, too, describing the room as I'd first seen it, the sounds I'd heard, the knot on the rope. The cops who'd charged down the tunnel after the sound of footsteps hadn't caught whoever was running away, but they seemed to have a fair composite description from the witnesses. Claire herself, attacked from behind and then blindfolded, had seen nothing.

"There may have been more than one of them," I told Officer Caccione, who was taking my statement.

She looked up sharply. "What do you mean?"

"Just before you came," I said, "she said, 'Bastards.' Plural, like that. 'Bastards.'"

"Ummm." She chewed the end of her pencil. "Another one waiting in the room?"

"Could be," I said. "I don't know."

"I'll pass that one. Someone'll talk to the vic in the hospital. You really a PI?"

"Uh-huh."

"Japanese?"

"Chinese. Chinese names are one syllable. Japanese names are usually more."

"That so?" she asked absently. "Look, keep yourself available, huh? I gotta go. Anything comes to you you forgot, call the precinct, talk to a detective on the case. Okay?"

"Okay."

She slipped my card into her notebook and stuck that in her pocket, then strode away with that rolling cop walk on those heavy cop shoes.

There wasn't much in the paper, so in a couple of days I stopped by the Sixth Precinct to see how the case was going. The detective on the case was a big-nosed sergeant named Kubelek, who was at his desk doing paperwork when I got there.

"Lydia Chin? Oh, yeah, Caccione's little door prize. The lady PI who happened to be in the station, right?" Kubelek leaned back in his chair. "Glad you're here. I could use something pretty to look at. 'Course *you* don't look old enough to drink. Jailbait, huh?" He winked at me.

"I don't drink. Sergeant—"

"So tell me, how did a nice Chinese girl like you get into a lousy business like yours?"

"I'm not so nice."

"Oooh, she bites. 'Scuse *me*." He sat up mock-businesslike at his desk. "So, what can I do for you, Miss Chin?"

"I was wondering how the case was going."

"Just in a sort of friendly interested way?"

"I was hoping you'd caught the guy."

"Nope." He made a parody of a sad face.

"Have you got any leads?"

"Depends on what you might call a lead."

Controlling my mouth, I switched tactics. "Have you

looked into the idea that there might have been more than one rapist?"

"Oh, right." He nodded, up and down, up and down. "Caccione told me what you thought the vic said."

"Thought? Sergeant—"

"Come on, Miss Chin. You found the vic, you were shook up—you know women are always unreliable witnesses in rape cases. Too emotionally involved, know what I mean?"

"No, I don't know what you mean. I'm a trained investigator, which means I can observe and remember—"

"Oh, I see. That's how come you figure you can tell the cops how to do their job?"

"I'm not doing that." I could hear my voice rising as my temperature rose. "This case concerns me and—"

"Actually, Miss Chin, it doesn't concern you. You were on the scene. Bully for you, sweetheart, that makes you a witness. If we need anything, we'll call you. Now I'm sure you're a very busy girl, so why don't you go out and investigate something?"

I started to say something I knew I would regret, but two other detectives pushed through the squad room door.

"Okay, Kubelek, cavalry's here." One of the new men pulled white containers out of a brown paper bag and lined them up on Kubelek's desk. I smelled ginger and scallions and old oil. The man looked at me and winked, then glanced at Kubelek. "Hey, are we interrupting something? We could . . ." He gestured cheerfully at a desk across the room, but made no move to go there.

"Nope," Kubelek said. "This is Miss Chin, girl PI. She was asking about the subway rapist case. Sorry I couldn't help you, Miss Chin."

"I am too." They had given me just about enough time to get my mouth under control. I turned to go. Then I turned back. "By the way, did you know too much Chinese food causes—oh, but probably you don't have to worry about that. It's the MSG," I explained, smiled all around, and left.

Well, I thought to myself, *almost* under control.

I was in my office catching up on my own paperwork and trying to convince myself that some things actually are none of my business when the phone rang. "Chin Investigative Services," I answered, first in English and then Chinese, because you never know.

"This Lydia Chin?" a woman's voice asked.

"Yes. Who's calling?"

"Isabel Caccione, Sixth Precinct. Remember me?"

"Of course. How are you?"

"I heard you got Eddie Kubelek scared to death. He thinks he's gonna get a heart attack or something."

"I'm sorry about that," I said meekly. "He made me angry."

"Actually I think he's afraid his dick is gonna fall off." She chuckled. "Kubelek's a pig. He thinks he was put on this earth to piss off women. He tell you anything?"

"He told me to go home."

"You work in Chinatown?"

"My office? It's on Canal near Elizabeth."

"Uh-uh. Too near the Fifth. I know some of those guys. How about uptown? Rusty Staub's, on Forty-seventh? That way I'm close to the F. I live in Queens," she added.

"Umm—fine." I tried not to sound as bewildered as I felt. "What for?"

"For a drink. My shift ends at eight. Eight-thirty good for you?"

"Sure," I said, and hung up thinking that if I was planning to stay in this business, maybe I should learn to drink.

Isabel Caccione, in a white sweatshirt with gold studs on it, was at a table by the door when I got to Rusty Staub's. She lifted a dark drink and waved it around so I'd see her. The tables there are the tall kind, and I climbed up onto the stool across from her feeling a little like a kid in the grown-ups' room. The bartender looked our way, maybe because he'd seen her drink waving.

"Rum and Coke," Isabel Caccione called to him. To me she said, "You?"

"Just club soda."

"That so?" She peered at me. "There's an Oriental guy I was at the Academy with, couldn't drink at all. Allergic. I think he was like Korean or something. You allergic?"

"Something like that. A lot of Asians can't drink."

"No kidding." She laughed. "Wish my husband had that. An Italian allergic to beer! Great."

She jumped off her stool and grabbed our drinks from the bar. When she brought them back I tried to pay her but she brushed me off. "Next round." She drained the remains of her first drink. "So Kubelek wouldn't give you nothing?"

"Nothing I wanted."

"Probably been years since he had anything any woman wanted." She drank her new drink and I drank mine. "They got a suspect," she said.

"They do?"

"Guy named Perry Aparo. Lives in the Village. Right in our own little precinct. They think this might be his third."

"Have they arrested him?"

She shook her head. "Put him in a lineup but nobody picked him out for sure." She added, "The vic was upset."

"That there was no definite ID?"

"Yeah. Well, wouldn't you be? Ask me, some of those citizens could ID him no problem, only they don't want to get involved." Her lip curled over those words.

"Why do the cops think it was him?"

"Aparo's full-time slime. He's been picked up more times than the garbage. He was chief suspect in another one, but he sleazed out of it. Knot was the same."

"Oh. Well, what do they do now?"

"Nothing."

"What do you mean, nothing? What about DNA? What about the witnesses?"

"I told you, no one was sure-sure. Or if they were, they wouldn't say. And they can't get DNA without a court order if he don't want to give it. They can't get a court order unless they arrest him, which they can't without probable cause. They got no conviction in the prior and no ID, they got no probable cause. Besides," she added, shaking her head, "they lost him."

"What do you mean, lost him?"

"He disappeared. After the lineup. He's scum but I guess he's not stupid."

"So now what?" I repeated. "What do they do now?"

"They wait."

"For what?"

"For him to make a mistake."

"You mean, to make a mistake doing it again?" I was horrified.

"You got it."

"What if he does it without making any mistakes?"

"Then they wait some more."

Isabel Caccione sipped her rum and Coke. I asked, "Is this why cops drink?"

She hit me with a sudden look. I almost reeled from the anger in her eyes. Then she muttered, "You got that right," and dropped her glance to the glass in her hand.

The air was loud with the voices of the gray-suited young men and navy-blazered young women who crowded the bar, admiring the moves of the football players on the TVS at either end and trying out moves of their own. The noise was like a glaring light, and I wished I were somewhere else.

"Why are you telling this to me?" I asked Isabel.

She looked at me for a moment, her lips pressed together, as though adding something up. "Why did you go see Kubelek?"

"I wanted to know," I said. "If they got him."

"What were you gonna do if I didn't call you?"

"I'm not sure."

"You were just gonna drop it?"

"No," I admitted. "Probably not."

Isabel didn't say anything. I got the feeling she was waiting for something more, so I said what every woman knows: "I mean, it could have been me."

"And so it sort of was, huh?"

I nodded.

She waited a little, sipping her drink. "Eddie Kubelek," she said. "He's not losing any sleep over this."

"What do you mean?"

"Well, for instance, a cop really into this could've figured a way to get a search warrant for Aparo's apartment. That might've helped, might not have, but it's something. But Kubelek's six months away from his pension. All he wants to do is to not rock the boat till then." She finished her rum and Coke. "Also, he's the kind of guy believes women are always asking for it anyway.

Also, Perry Aparo's a mean little sleaze who gave every cop trouble that ever took him up. Kubelek figures he don't need it. If he's lucky Aparo'll pick some other precinct next time, and some other gold shield gets stuck with it."

"Oh," I said softly.

Isabel's crimson nails scratched at a flaw in the glass tabletop. "Aparo's got a cousin," she said. "We got paperwork on him, too."

"And you think he might have been the second man?"

"Look," she said. "I don't think nothing. I'm a cop two years out of the Academy. Kubelek's a gold shield who don't like women. He finds out I'm even thinking about a case of his, I'm doing the graveyard shift at the Staten Island landfill."

Two young women twisted off their bar stools; two young men flashed twenty-dollar bills around. In a swirl of briefcases, handbags, and smiles, they all left together.

"Do you," I asked Isabel, as four other well-groomed men and women slipped into their places, "happen to have Aparo's address? And his cousin's?"

Wordlessly, she opened her shoulder bag and handed me a piece of paper torn from a notebook. The handwriting was full of wide, round strokes and the dots over the i's were circles. It held not only Aparo's address and that of a man named George Bryant, but Claire Morgan's as well.

Isabel suddenly looked at the thin old watch on her wrist. "Jeez, I gotta go. I told Tony I'd be home by ten. He gets like nervous if I'm late, you know?" She put some bills on the tabletop, jumped down off the bar stool. "Later," she said, and pushed through the glass doors, leaving me staring after her as the too-loud voices of men and women flashed around me.

The next morning I made my way through the bright and chilly streets of the Upper West Side to Claire Morgan's second-floor walk-up on Amsterdam. There was a long pause after I identified myself over the intercom. Then I was buzzed in, climbed the stairs, and found Claire Morgan watching through her partly open door.

She undid the chain when she saw it was really me, and stepped aside to let me in. While she clicked and clinked all the locks and chains I looked around. It was a studio apartment with a kitchenette, a pullout couch, a table with two chairs that matched and one that didn't. Cornflakes and milk were congealing in the bottom of a bowl on the table and the sink was full of dishes.

"It's kind of messy." Claire Morgan shrugged and hunched on one end of the couch. The bruises on her face were beginning to fade from purple to green; cuts were healing on her wrists where the rope had been.

"How are you?" I asked.

She shrugged again, twisted a strand of brown hair around her finger. Then, in a low voice, she said, "Lousy. I'm doing lousy, if you really want to know."

"I'm sorry."

"Yeah. So's everybody."

I didn't know what to say to that. I wasn't even sure why I'd come. A bus wheezed by on Amsterdam, below.

"They arrested somebody?" she asked. "You come to tell me they arrested somebody?"

"No," I said.

"They had that one guy. None of those fuckers would identify him. I was in the room with them, before the lineup. They know which guy. I could see it. But when they got in there, they wouldn't say. You know that?"

"I knew they let him go."

"So now that's it? That's just it? They know who he is but sorry, that's just too bad?" Her voice broke.

I said nothing.

"They could have stopped him," she burst out, her eyes suddenly blazing. "Those fuckers."

"Yes," I answered. I thought of that wet, stinking room I'd found her in. "But I guess they were afraid."

"Of what?" She was strident now. Her hands jerked in the air. "The cops said there were seventeen of them. There was only one of him. What the hell were they afraid of?"

"Claire," I said, trying to speak quietly, to calm her down, "was there only one of him? Afterward, you said 'bastards' to me. Do you remember that? Was there another one?"

She dropped her eyes to the floor. After a moment, her voice much softer now, but still shaky, she said, "See, I don't know. I don't remember."

"You don't remember?"

She shook her head. "The last thing I remember is being yanked down these stairs. I banged my ankle and it hurt, and my shoe fell off. After that the next thing I remember is you." Her hand went back to twist a strand of hair. "And even you and the cops and the hospital, it's not that clear. See, that's why I can't identify him or anything. I don't even know! I don't even know how many guys did this to me—!"

Starting to cry, Claire slammed her hand into the arm of the couch, stood, turned away, turned back. "Listen." The hot flush in her cheeks made the healing bruises look worse. "Listen. I mean, thanks, you know, you were the one who found me and everything. But maybe you should go now?" Her mouth quivered with the effort of holding back tears.

I stood. "Is there anything I can do?"

She shook her head without looking at me. Rapidly, she went to the door, opened all the locks and chains. As soon as I was in the hall she shut it again. I heard the chains clinking as I left, and I heard her sobbing.

The next place I tried was Perry Aparo's. Riding downtown on the subway I held a swaying stainless-steel strap and admitted to myself that I did know why I'd gone to see Claire Morgan. I'd wanted her to say, "I'm fine." I'd wanted her to say, "Oh, don't worry about me, I got over it. So they can't arrest him, so what? They'll get him next time. It's cool." I sort of amazed myself. For the first time in my life I'd actually wanted someone to tell me something was none of my business.

No one answered when I buzzed Aparo's Charles Street apartment, so I buzzed other apartments until someone let me in, and then I went up and banged on his door. No one answered when I did that, either. I thought of trying to pick the locks, but he had three, and there wasn't anything I was really looking for. And anything I found wouldn't be admissible in court anyway. Maybe I'd come back later, if my next stop was a washout, too.

Aparo's cousin, George Bryant, lived over on Fourteenth Street, near Eighth Avenue. Not really so far away. I walked, past the small cafes and shops that filled the ground floors of the low brick buildings, past the park where shrieking children chased one another in the chilly fall sunlight.

I hadn't had a gag ready for Aparo, but partly that was because I hadn't expected to find him. For his cousin I was better organized, which was a good thing, because he answered my buzz, and then my knock.

"Yeah?" On the head that stuck itself out of the apartment door the hair was thinning, but the neck and arms bulging out of the T-shirt were almost furry.

"I'm looking for Perry Aparo," I said as nastily as I could manage.

"Yeah?" he repeated. "So what?"

"Don't give me that crap. You're his cousin, Bryant, right? You know where he is?"

Cousin Bryant squinted at me. "Who the hell are you?"

"It's none of your goddamn business, except you're his cousin, so I'm going to tell you." I like this sort of gag: it gives me a chance to use the kind of language everybody in New York seems to use but me. "I work for a guy Perry owes money to. My boss doesn't like to be owed. Maybe Perry forgot that, so I came to remind him."

Bryant relaxed against the door frame and snickered. "You gotta be kidding. You're an enforcer? For who, Ho Chi Minh?"

"You in that war?" I sneered back. "A lot of big white men got blown away by a lot of little Asian women. I'm a Tae Kwon Do black belt and a small arms expert—" Exaggeration in a good cause being a duty and not a crime, I opened my jacket enough for him to see my gun, "—and I have a few other specialties I'd hate to have to show you. But that's all beside the point. If my boss decides your cousin needs to be disciplined, I won't be the one who comes for him. I don't do dirty work anymore. I got promoted. I'm just here to give him a polite warning. So where the hell is he?"

Bryant picked something out of his teeth. "You're out of your mind, lady. If I knew where he was I wouldn't tell you, and what the hell makes you think I know?"

I changed the subject slightly. "The cops are looking for him, too, I hear."

He scowled. "What, for that rape bullshit? I heard about that. They picked him up and let him go. They got nothing."

"On you either?"

"What?"

"I hear you helped him out with that."

"What are you talking about?"

"He didn't do that rape alone, so they say. You two have a good time?"

"Jesus, you really are crazy." He shoved the door abruptly. I stuck my foot in it before it closed, blessing Doc Marten, wherever he was.

"Look, pal," I said. "If you ask me, rapists are the worst scum there is. If my orders allowed it I'd blow you away right here. But I will tell you this: if your cousin goes to jail for something you and he did, and my boss doesn't get paid and he can't get to your cousin, that leaves only you. It's a lot of money, and my boss is a nasty son of a bitch. Get it?"

"Hey," Bryant said. "I didn't do whatever the hell you and your boss think I did, and I got no idea where Perry is, so why don't you just buzz off?"

"The guys the boss sends out now," I said, "the ones who replaced me? They're really weird. They're into things with eyeballs and eardrums. One of them was telling me the other day that it's impossible, absolutely impossible, to walk if you lose both big toes. Did you know that?"

"Christ! Get out of here, lady. Just beat it. What the hell is this?"

"This," I said, handing him a business card, "is my phone number. Perry better use it soon. *Goddamn* soon," I added, just to see what that sounded like coming out of me. I yanked my foot from the doorway so fast that Bryant, leaning on the door, had to grab it to keep it from slamming. Then, as I spun and stalked away, he slammed it resoundingly anyway, as though that's what he'd meant to do all along.

I guessed it probably was.

You might think being small, young, Asian, and a woman, I'd have trouble in a field where three-quarters of the professionals are middle-aged white male ex-cops.

Well, not usually. Mostly, I'm invisible, so totally non-threatening people don't see me at all, or don't take me seriously when they do. That can be very useful.

But on the corner of Fourteenth and Eighth, where all the middle-aged white male street people hang out, a small young Asian woman can't easily slip into the background. I made a long call from the corner booth to my own office phone, window shopped in the liquor store until I could name fifteen different vodkas, and juggled phantom appointments in my appointment book. I waited at the bus stop until the bus came, and then I didn't get on it. I had decided I had about three more minutes before one of the guys who'd been leering at me for a while came close enough that I'd have to slug him, blowing my cover; then what I'd been waiting for happened. George Bryant's apartment house door opened, and George Bryant came out.

He crossed the street, and I followed him, and it turned out that was as far as he was going. On the corner was a dingy doughnut shop whose rattling vent perfumed the sidewalk with sugary grease. Above the doughnut shop was a twenty-four-hour pool hall, which you got into by a door next to an alley. Through that door went George Bryant, looking, at the very least, annoyed. I didn't think I had much chance of slipping up there unnoticed, so I watched and waited. Bryant came out very soon, crossed the street, and went back home.

No one else came out and Bryant stayed home. My best guess was that that meant he hadn't found his cousin, or else that there was no one in the pool hall he could hustle. I had no way of knowing, and when a middle-aged white male street person with a caramel-toothed grin told me I was looking fine, I told him he was looking pretty good, too, and left.

I went back to my office and waited for Perry Aparo to call. Sitting around waiting for things drives me absolutely crazy, and he didn't call. Around lunchtime I went out and bought steamed dumplings from the stand on the corner; later I went over to the dojo and took the afternoon class, which is only for the higher ranks and is all sparring. Both times I hurried back to the office to check the machine, but nobody, it seemed, wanted to talk to me.

Evening came and hit that purply time when the green and yellow and blue neon lights really blaze, just for a few minutes. Disgusted, I was about to call my mother and see if there was anything I should pick up on the way home, when the phone rang under my hand.

I grabbed it, told it who I was in both languages, and waited to see who it was.

"Lydia?" A direct woman's voice got directly to the point. "Isabel Caccione. You seen Perry Aparo?"

"No. I thought this might be him calling, but I guess it's not."

"Why would he call you?"

I told her how I'd set up the cousin. She didn't speak for a moment, when I was through. Then she said, "God. Maybe you are nuts. Anyway, stay away from him, but if you hear from him, let me know. We're looking for him."

"How come?"

"We got a stiff we think might concern him."

"A stiff? A body? Whose?"

"One of the witnesses."

That took a second to register. "Witnesses? From the subway?"

"Right. Shot dead a couple hours ago. In the hallway of his building where he lives. Lived," she corrected herself conscientiously.

"And you think Aparo might have done it? Why would he do that?"

"This was one of the guys came to the lineup. He didn't finger him, but he came close. I told you, between you and I, I think they probably all could. Sometimes guys like that change their mind. Perry's been around long enough, he knows that. Maybe Perry's just don't want to have to worry."

"So he just killed him?" This was a little hard for me to take in.

"Hey, he grabbed a girl he never saw before, beat her up and raped her. It surprises you he'd shoot a guy just to save himself some trouble?"

"No," I said, "no, I guess not," though the truth is that that sort of thing always does surprise me.

Isabel had said they had a stakeout at Perry Aparo's apartment, and also at George Bryant's, in case he could lead them to Aparo. That didn't leave anything for me to do, so I called my mother and I went home.

I fidgeted all evening, annoying my mother, who suggested that if I concentrated on my domestic duties I would find my life more satisfying, as well as more virtuous. I took her at her word, and was up to my rubber gloves in a pail of hot soapy water washing out kitchen cabinets when the phone rang.

"Isabel," said Isabel. "We got another one."

"Another what? Another murder?"

"Uh-huh. Another witness in the Morgan case, dead as a doornail. Shot like the other one. You got any protection up there?"

"I—what kind of protection? Me?"

"He could know your name from the papers. If he figures out it was you came to see his cousin, you could be in deep doo-doo."

It wouldn't be hard to figure out, either, I thought: I'd given the cousin my card. "Well, I have a gun."

"Do me a favor, don't shoot nobody if you can help it. You want protection? I'll tell Kubelek. He's got us all running our tails off tracking down the other witnesses, to get them protection until we get this over with. God, is he pissed off, too. You want?"

"No. No, thanks. It would be harder than you might think for a white guy to sneak up on me in Chinatown, and having a cop hanging around me would be unbelievably bad for business." Something suddenly occurred to me. "Isabel, what about Claire?"

"We went up there," Isabel said. "I went myself. She told me to go to hell."

"She did?" I realized I wasn't really surprised to hear that.

"She said we didn't do her no good before, and she didn't want nothing to do with us. Also, she laughed. She said she was the one person he didn't have to worry about, because she was the one person there couldn't identify him." Isabel paused, then added, "She didn't look too good."

"No, she was sort of a wreck when I was there. But

what are you going to do? You can't just leave her un-
protected because she tells you to."

"Citizen's right to privacy is serious business."

"Isabel—"

"But," she interrupted me, "a citizen don't usually
notice an unmarked unit parked outside their apartment."

"Good," I said. "Thanks."

"Yeah. You take care of yourself, okay?"

"Okay. Wait," I yelped, as Isabel was about to hang
up. "Hey, wait. How does he know who they are?"

"What?"

"The witnesses. How does Aparo know their names?
I thought you guys kept that kind of thing pretty confidential, especially from alleged perpetrators."

"I don't know. You can find anything out, you look
in the right place. Aparo's been around enough police
stations. He knows procedure. I don't think it's that
hard."

"Isabel, I'm a PI. I have a license to know things a
regular person isn't supposed to know, but every time I
call a police station for some information I get hung up
on. Unless," I said, thinking out loud, "unless I happen
to know a cop who'll give me what I'm looking for."

"What, Kubelek?" She sounded surprised. "No way."

"Why not?"

"An asshole is one thing. A dirty cop's another."

"You can't be both?"

"Kubelek can't. I told you, he just wants to stay out
of trouble until he can take his pension and ride off into
the goddamn sunset."

I was about to say more, but I know enough cops to
know that sticking together is an important part of what
they call The Job. Isabel might have her own thoughts
about Kubelek, and about justice. I'd seen where her
thoughts about justice could lead; and she might, within
the closed-door privacy of the cop world, be willing to
act on her thoughts about Kubelek. But I had the feeling
I'd just been shown the wall between her world and
mine.

"Okay," I said. "Let me know if anything happens,
will you?"

She said she would, and we said good night.

* * *

While I was finishing the cabinets I had a thought. Maybe my mother was right about the virtues of domestic chores. I rinsed my bucket and my gloves and called the Sixth Precinct.

"Caccione? Hold it." I held it; the by-the-book voice came back. "Caccione's out. Want to speak to someone else?"

I didn't know who else to speak to, and if I was right about Kubelek, it might not be a good idea to speak to anybody else.

"Thanks, no." I clipped my gun back on my belt and got my black leather jacket from the front hall closet.

"Ling Wan-ju, it's the middle of the night," my mother complained. "Foolish girl! Where are you going?"

'Foolish' is actually a kind of translation of the Chinese word she used. "I'm going out, Ma. I have to work tonight."

"Work! You call it work, to go out in the middle of the night dressed like a man, with a gun, consorting with people it's humiliating even to be seen with—"

"Uh-huh." I kissed her, and shut the door on the speech about how my brothers all have *real* jobs, even Andrew, who photographs vegetables, for Pete's sake. I missed the second half, where she gets into the part about letting my hair grow, dressing like a girl, and finding a husband, but it's okay: I've heard it before.

Three people sat slumped over coffee at separate sections of the doughnut shop counter when I came out of the subway at Fourteenth and Eighth. A couple of men shared a bottle on the steps of the bank; another slept, or had already passed out, nearby.

The door to the pool hall was heavy, and creaked open onto a steep, uneven flight of steps. As I climbed, the rough, dry smell of cigarette smoke rolled down from above.

Everyone turned to look as I walked in. 'Everyone' was about a dozen men, most playing pool at four tables, one drinking Budweiser at the counter with another who leaned on the cash register and drank his own Budweiser. The cigarette smoke was as thick as the silence.

"Yes, Miss?" the guy at the cash register said, with no smile. The men at one table went back to playing pool. The others watched me. There must not be much excitement in their lives, I decided.

"Perry Aparo," I said loudly, looking around.

No one spoke.

I tried again. "Is one of you bastards Perry Aparo?" That didn't sound quite right to me, but the way these guys were looking at me pushed my worries about my English grammar into the background.

The cash register guy sucked in some Budweiser. "None of these bastards, lady. Aparo's not here. So who're you?" He had an out-of-focus tattoo on his forearm, and longish greasy hair.

"Lydia Chin," I said, still loud. "I don't know how much trouble he thinks he's in, but it's about double that. Where do I find him?"

The guy shrugged. No one else spoke, and they all seemed to be closer to me than when I came in. I hadn't noticed until now how warm it was in here, or how bright the bare fluorescent lights were.

Finally a skinny guy missing some teeth offered. "Try his apartment." A couple of them sniggered.

"Thanks," I snapped. "You're real sharp. Send me your résumé. Now: Aparo's in trouble. I'm a private eye, I know some people. I can help." Well, I didn't say I could help *him*. "And if anybody has any suggestions— any *intelligent* suggestions"—I glared at the gap-toothed guy—"about where I can find him, it could be worth your while."

I flipped a card onto the counter; wonder of wonders, it didn't slide off. With a contemptuous look around the room, I left.

Footsteps began at the top of the stairs as I was reaching the bottom. I'd half expected that, so I stepped outside and waited.

It was significantly cooler outside. I breathed in some refreshing Eighth Avenue air. The gap-toothed guy pushed through the creaky door and spotted me right away.

"Hey, honey, wait." He smiled like a broken comb. "Listen, we were funnin' you up there. I'm Perry Aparo."

I looked him up and down. "Bullshit." I hoped my mother's ESP wasn't on.

"C'mon—"

"Don't waste my time." I turned to go.

"Awright, awright." He grabbed my arm, put himself in front of me again, smiling ingratiatingly. "Okay, so I'm not him. But I know where he is."

I didn't believe him, but it's important to follow every lead. "Where?"

"Now, come on, honey, you said it was worth my while."

"Fifty bucks," I snarled. "When I find him."

"Oh, it don't have to be that." He stepped in very close. "It don't have to be money."

Hot garlic clouded out from the gaps in his teeth as he leaned over me, still holding my arm.

I stomped on his instep.

He yowled. "Goddammit, you bitch!"

I yanked my arm away, stepped back.

I've made mistakes before. The two I made this time were to step across the mouth of the alley, and to figure a guy like this wouldn't have any friends.

And maybe they weren't his friends, the two street people in the alley cuddled up to the Dumpster. It might be they just decided to help him out as a gesture of goodwill. New York is that kind of town.

Whatever their reasoning, one of them grabbed me. He tried to haul me back, off balance. I spun around, to steady myself, and gave my arm a quick twist. That broke his grip; but Toothless, behind me, bear-hugged me and lunged, pushing me into the alley as the third guy snatched at my ankles. I crashed to the ground, breath knocked out, Toothless pinning me. Gasping, I bit a hand I found in my face as I felt the sharp pain of fingers yanking on my hair. I was pulled and shoved and scraped along the ground deeper into the alley; I landed a kick but it didn't seem to matter.

The hot stink of garlic came back as Toothless laughed and slobbered on my neck, twisted my head in his hands, planted kisses on my face. I still couldn't breathe. I fought my hand inside my jacket but I couldn't get to my gun.

Someone else got to one, though. A shot rang out,

and a woman's voice shouted the most beautiful words I ever heard: "Police! Let her go!"

Weight lifted off me; a knee dug into my chest as someone tried to scramble away. I grabbed at a leg and brought Toothless down, feeling a small thrill of satisfaction as he crashed hard enough into the Dumpster to shove it a few feet down the alley.

I drew some rasping breaths, realized my head was pounding. My eyes closed, but the world began to sway. I knew that wasn't a good sign, so I forced them open.

Toothless and his buddies lay facedown on the alley pavement, as I dimly remembered the wonderful voice telling them to do. A skinny form in street clothes held a gun, two-handed, on the pack of them. I blinked. I'd thought there were only three, but a fourth lay facedown, too, near where the Dumpster had been.

"You!" Isabel Caccione called to me. "Lydia! You okay?"

"No," I said. "Can I shoot them?"

"No way. You can cuff them if you want to." She tossed me a pair of handcuffs from the handbag over her shoulder.

"What are you doing here?" I climbed, a little painfully, to my feet.

"Following you."

"Me?"

"Cop who brings in Aparo makes a dynamite collar. All the gold shields are chasing around following leads. I figured following you was a surer thing."

"You get promoted to plainclothes?"

"I'm on my own time. This is a biggie, I told you. You gonna cuff them or what?"

I cuffed Toothless and one of his buddies together by the ankles—people have been known to run away attached at the wrists. The other guy, the one who'd grabbed me, seemed dazed and fairly tame, lying facedown with his hands behind his head. As a police siren approached on Fourteenth Street I went to inspect the fourth one, who hadn't moved.

I found out why. "Isabel?" I said. A squad car squealed up behind her. "Isabel? This one's dead."

Two cops piled out of the car. Isabel flashed her

shield, then waved her gun at the men on the ground. "May be a weapon. Haven't read them their rights."

One of the new cops droned on about their rights as Isabel stepped cautiously over to where I was.

She peered into the face, gray and unmoving, of the guy whose body had been hidden by the Dumpster. She swallowed, looked at me. "This one's Perry Aparo."

Perry Aparo had been dead for at least a day. The Medical Examiner told us that, and also that he'd been shot, which was probably what killed him. A lot of people told people things that night. Sergeant Kubelek, who'd been hauled out of a serious poker game when his case suddenly got hot, told me he'd yank my license. He told Isabel she was in bad trouble for discharging her weapon when the perps (as it turned out) didn't have one. She told him to go soak his head. The two guys in the alley told us they hadn't done anything. Toothless, as he was stuffed into a police car in handcuffs, told me I was a hot babe and would I give him my number for when he got out? I told Kubelek why I'd been at the pool hall, and he told me I should have goddamn called him with any information I had on a fugitive's whereabouts. I almost told him I would have if I'd trusted him even the tiniest little bit, but I told him instead that if I were him I'd be wondering where Aparo's cousin was right now.

"Yeah?" he sneered. "Thank you, Miss Chin, we appreciate your help. So happens we've got a surveillance on Bryant. I'm gonna go get him as soon as I'm done here. He hasn't left his apartment all evening. Wish I could say the same for you."

Blood surged to my face. "So do I! You weren't the one who got dragged and kicked and mauled and drooled on—" Isabel put a hand on my arm. I stopped talking and took a deep breath before I started to cry.

"Oh, Christ," Kubelek muttered. "Caccione, get your pal out of here before she leaks all over everything. Then get your ass back to the precinct and wait for me there. You got an outhouse full of paperwork to fill out, doll. Should keep you busy all night."

As we left it took all my self-control not to sock Kubelek right in his snide grin.

*   *   *

A few blocks away Isabel stopped at a deli and got us cups of hot reviving liquid—coffee for her, tea for me. We opened the lids as we sat in the car by the curb.

"Told you to be careful," she said gruffly, her eyes on the night-lit New York street.

"You didn't stop me," I objected.

"You're saying you would've listened?"

"No." The lemony tea warmed its way down into my fingertips. "You could have told me you were following me," I complained.

She looked at me. "You gotta be kidding. That's ridiculous." She laughed.

She was right, it was totally ridiculous. Her laugh was infectious; I began to giggle. In no time we were rollicking, snorting, trying not to spill our drinks as we wiped our eyes. We blew our noses, calmed, tried to speak, and were shaken again by explosions of laughter the way the kettle is shaken by bursts of pent-up steam.

"God," said Isabel finally, her voice a little weak. "I almost peed my pants. Tony'd love that, huh? Sorry, honey, I wet the car." That started her off again, and me with her, until we were wrung out, and she was able to put the car in gear and roll us down Seventh Avenue.

For a little while we didn't speak. When she turned up Canal toward Chinatown, I said, "What do you figure? It's the cousin?"

"Must be." Isabel nodded.

"Why'd he kill Aparo?"

"My guess? Aparo wanted to give it up. Every cop in New York looking for him, he can't stay loose for long. He figures he's got a fifty-fifty chance of getting off on the rape, and if he ditches the gun they can't tie him to the witnesses getting killed. So he's gonna bring himself in and rat on the cousin. Make a nice deal, probably serve six months. The cousin don't like this arrangement, so blam!—he shoots him dead."

"Maybe he didn't even kill the witnesses," I said. "Maybe the cousin did, to keep Aparo from getting nervous that someone might change his mind and do a solid ID. It might not have occurred to him that that would put more pressure on Aparo, not less. He didn't strike me as a particularly bright guy."

"No, not particularly."

"So now what?"

"It's up to Kubelek. Probably he brings him in for questioning, tries to get him to trip over himself. If that don't happen, he's got to find something else he can use."

"You think he will?"

"Will what?"

"Well, before, you told me he wasn't going to bother about this case."

She glanced over at me. "Different case. The rape, he went through the motions. This is homicide, maybe multiple. Nice collar to go out on. Yeah, he'll bother."

Isabel dropped me at home. I felt uneasy, as though something was not quite right, but I didn't know what, so I thanked her for saving my life and she said I was welcome. I went upstairs, put all my clothes in the piles for the laundry and the cleaner and the shoemaker. I took a long, long shower, scrubbing three times with soap and a washcloth to make sure not an atom of those men stuck to me. I threw the washcloth in the garbage and went to bed.

I was dragged from the deep, soft darkness of sleep by the memory of my own words, repeating over and over in my head. I heard what I'd said myself hours ago and I knew what was wrong. I grabbed the phone by the bed, called the precinct and asked for Isabel, trying desperately to clear the sleep-fuzziness from my brain as I waited for her.

They couldn't find her. "She's here somewhere. Want to leave a message?"

"How about Sergeant Kubelek?"

"Went home."

"I thought he was interrogating a suspect."

"I wouldn't know. Who's this?"

I told him, and told him where I was going, so he could tell Isabel when he found her. Noting—because I couldn't help it—all the places where I ached and stung, I got dressed, clipped my gun to my belt, and went out.

The sky was turning a resigned gray when I paid off the cab driver, got out at the corner of Eighty-fourth and Amsterdam. Yesterday's trash was sifting across the sidewalk, and I felt terrible. I knew I was right, but I felt terrible.

There was a much longer pause than last time after I rang Claire Morgan's bell; I had to ring it twice. Claire finally answered, in a small tired voice. Then she told me to go away.

"No," I said. "Claire, I have to talk to you."

"I already know, he's dead," the tinny intercom said. "They told me."

"There's more than that."

"I can take care of myself."

"I know."

I guess it was the way I said it. She let me in, and when I got to her apartment she let me in there, too, and when she turned around and pushed the door shut behind her I saw she had a gun.

It was a revolver, held in one white-knuckled hand, pointed at me. It wavered a little, as though she wasn't sure of the best thing to do with it.

"You figured it out, didn't you?" Her voice scraped up out of her throat. "Damn it! Why did it have to be you?"

"Give me the gun, Claire." My heart was ricocheting in my chest; none of my martial arts body-control techniques were doing me any good. Belatedly, I remembered the unmarked unit Isabel had said was stationed outside Claire's building. I'd probably walked right by them. "It can still be all right. Give me the gun."

"All right? All *right*?" she shrilled. "It won't ever be all right again! And I'm not going to stop yet. There are fifteen more bastards out there, and I'm going to get every one of them. You know? Every goddamn one!"

I spoke evenly. "You need help, Claire. A doctor." And a good lawyer, I thought.

"Help! This isn't when I need help. That was when I needed help! When seventeen bastards watched this guy choke me and drag me and rape me and beat the shit out of me. I could have used help then!"

"You remember the whole thing, don't you?" Establish rapport. Keep them talking. No one will shoot you while they're talking to you. "There was only the one guy. You do remember that."

"Yeah. And I shot him first. But you were going

around telling everybody what I said, so I had to pretend like maybe there were more."

"But you meant the witnesses, when you said 'bastards.' That was who you meant."

"Sure as hell. It sure as hell was. And I swear to God I'm going to get every one of them."

"Claire—"

"Shut up! Just shut up! I can't think when you're talking to me. I've got to figure what to do now. You're not going to stop me, no way. But I don't know what to do."

"Please don't shoot me, Claire." It was a risk, but I took it.

"No." Her eyes brimmed with tears. "But I don't know what to do."

"Give me the gun." I took a step toward her.

She didn't lower the gun, but her face seemed to soften just a little. It might have worked; but a police siren sliced through the dawn silence.

"No!" Claire shrieked as a car door slammed below us. "No!" Her eyes were wild. "Get out of here!" she screamed at me. "Just go! Get out, get out, get out!" The gun jerked in her hand and an explosion rocked the room. Splinters flew from the door frame beside my head.

I yanked the door open, rolled into the hall. It slammed behind me. Another bullet whined through the door and rained plaster from the ceiling.

Isabel burst through the door downstairs, revolver drawn. Two other cops pounded up the stairs behind her as she yelled, "Police! Hold your fire!"

There was a short silence. The cops and I all stopped moving. Then, as Isabel, crouched against the wall, was about to bang her fist on the door, we heard another shot.

This one didn't come through the door. Its roar wasn't loud enough to block out the muffled thud that followed it. And the loudest thing of all, after Isabel pounded on the door two, three, four times, calling out Claire's name, was the silence.

Later, after the paramedics, the neighbors, the other cops, and the Medical Examiner, after the body bag, after Kubelek's nastiness and after lots and lots of questions, Isabel and I stood alone on the sidewalk on Amsterdam.

"That was what it was?" she asked me. "How long Aparo had been dead?"

I nodded. " 'At least a day,' the Medical Examiner said. "That means he was already dead when I went to see the cousin. If the cousin killed him why did he go out looking for him?"

"We don't know that's why he went out."

"No. But it started me thinking. And I realized that if Aparo was dead a day, there wasn't much time between the witnesses' deaths and his. In fact he could have been killed first—and he was, according to Claire."

I couldn't go on for a minute after I said Claire's name. I looked up the street, watched the traffic go by, people with goals and reasons. "And then I started thinking about the witnesses—how Aparo got their names. If you were right about Kubelek, then that was a problem. But Claire was at the lineup, and those were the witnesses who were killed first. I wasn't sure what that meant, but it just all bothered me. I went to bed thinking about it. And I woke up smelling that alley, and tasting that disgusting man, and hearing you ask me if I was all right, and hearing me ask you if I could shoot them."

"Damn," Isabel half whispered. She kicked at something, nothing, on the curb. "Goddamn it. I should have seen it."

"How?" I asked. "What could you have seen? I only saw it because of what happened to me."

"About the cousin. About the time of death. I should have seen that."

"I don't know." I shook my head. "Maybe we both should have seen it. Because we're women. Because of how it made us feel to know what happened, and it didn't even happen to us."

She nodded. Her dark, thin face was drawn and tired. She took out her car keys, jingled them in her hand. "Thanks for making me look good to the brass, anyway."

Kubelek's lieutenant had come out on this call, too, and I had played up Isabel's part in rescuing me twice. I had to do a little dance to avoid a lecture on keeping my license, but everyone must have been too tired for that, except Kubelek, who looked like enough of a fool already that he kept his mouth shut when we got to that point.

"Why wouldn't I?" I asked. "I don't know that much about being a cop, but I think you're a really good one. If you had Kubelek's job this wouldn't have happened." I added, "And when you have it, it won't."

She grinned a tired grin at that. "You got that right." She swung the car keys by their ring. "C'mon, give you a lift home?"

"No," I said. "I'm going to walk around for a while. Just sort of walk, you know?"

"Yeah," she said. "I know." She got into her car. "Well, take care of yourself. Give me a call sometime, okay?"

She pulled from the curb, joined the traffic moving north on Amsterdam. I waved; then I turned the other way, headed south. It was a long walk back to Chinatown, but a long walk was what I felt like.

HOT PROWL

· ·

By Mary Wings

5:12 P.M., February 19, 1992,
124 Bonnieview Drive, San Francisco

I had been watching my tape and scribbling down numbers to the steady bubbling of the crock-pot brewing dinner in the kitchen when I heard it. A cross between a smash and a thud against the steady pattern of rain. I went into the living room where he jumped as I entered. The remote slipped from my palm as I froze.

"Why did you have to be home?" he growled. He had a semiautomatic gun in his right hand.

He made a rush for me, pulling a ski cap over his face. The cap had been waiting on top of his head, it glistened with water drops as he pulled it down. His face would only be a flash of pink in my memory, a speaking blur. But I would never forget his voice. It turned out he talked a lot.

He slammed me up against the wall and I heard my nose crack on the plaster.

"I don't want any trouble," I reassured him when I could breathe, my lips pressed against the wall. I didn't want him to know I was in pain. He swung me around by one shoulder. I looked up the barrel of his gun, to the ski mask behind it.

"Into the kitchen." His mouth was a mobile circle, issuing commands. I did as I was told. He was a mezzo alto and he pointed the muzzle straight at me. Like a magic wand the gun moved me into the kitchen toward a corner of the room where the pantry door was firmly shut.

He was a medium-size white man between twenty and

253

thirty, I figured. Some brown hair was sticking out from the eyehole in his cap. I quickly turned my eyes away from his face. I didn't want to die.

He was hopping on his feet like a fighter getting ready for the ring, like a man on drugs.

"This is great," the ski mask said as his eyes pored over the contents of my living room, the Beta Cam camera with enhanced chip. The AMPEX audio mixer. He had made his haul for the week. I was the only problem, me and the rain outside that had begun to pour. It hadn't rained in a long time and I hadn't thought about my gun in a long time. It was sitting in my drawer. What was I supposed to do, wear it around the house? Sit down to my dinner with a shoulder holster?

I hadn't thought about men with guns for a while. I was glad I hadn't thought about them. Now it was going to start all over again. The ski mask's eyes blinked; I realized I'd been staring at him, the only two fleshy spots that moved in the ski cap, two holes, organs of intelligence guiding a predator.

I could see in the hallway that he'd taped one of the small panes of glass on the front door and broken it. He must have reached around and let himself in. The rain picked up; it was coming in sheets now.

"Now, look, I'm just going to lock you up in the pantry, lady. I don't want no trouble. You really made my day here." His eyes twitched over all the black plastic and shining knobs still visible from the living room. "So let's just keep calm."

"Don't rip the cords out of the wall of that deck there. It's hell getting replacements," I advised him, my heart pounding.

"Sure, thanks," he said ripping the cord off one of the telephones instead, yanking it out of the wall and coming toward me. I was shaking, violently.

"Sit the fuck down, lady," he growled. I sat down on the hard kitchen chair and stared at his dirty tan suede jacket, dark grease stains at all the skin contact points, the collar, the sagging pocket from which he had drawn the gun. It was at my eye level.

"First I'm going to get you all settled down here," he explained. I moved my eyes away from his mouth, the lower lip that curled over the knitted material. I looked down at the semiautomatic. It wasn't going to be easy tying me up and keeping the gun in his hand. I considered making a move but the little red dot in front of the hammer told me the safety was off.

"Close your eyes," he commanded, putting the barrel against my head. I felt the cold metal through my thin hair. My bowels moved. He reached behind him for the knob of the pantry door. It turned but the door was stuck. He crouched down behind me and started tying my hands with the cord.

"Okay, you just be good here, I won't put you in the closet. If you don't interfere with my business here this will all work out fine. I've had enough trouble today." I felt his fingers on my arms pulling the telephone cord tighter. I winced.

"Listen, I ain't going to rape you. I'm not a sicko," he reassured me. "Even though you're pretty cute." His sweaty palms tangled with mine as he fumbled.

Swell, I thought, and with his knot expertise in a minute we'd be holding hands.

"And all that technical stuff in there is really going to help me out here," he explained from behind me, "if that goddamn fucking rain doesn't hold me up."

"Ouch!" I yelled, as he'd pulled my arm back hurting the healing scar on my chest.

"Sorry," he mumbled, looking up at the blurry black-and-white images flashing on the monitor. We heard a clap of thunder outside. Rain was pounding on the skylight in drumbeats. The big branches of a pine tree waved above us.

"What's all this camera stuff?" he asked, "What are you some kinda movie director or something?"

"I teach video. San Francisco State."

"Video, well excuse me, lady. I just go to the movies. Now what kinda movies you make?"

"Nothing you've ever seen," I said.

"What, you think the only time I been out at night is driving a cab or something?"

"No, I wish you had seen it. That's all I mean. If I'd made a big film you would have seen it. And then I would have a production company and all this equipment wouldn't be in my house, and my house would have a security system and you wouldn't be there stealing it."

"Yeah, I guess you're right about that. Things are tough all over. But you should know I've seen a lot of *film* in my time." He picked up the gun and waved it in the air. "Now how about you and me watching one of your movies."

"What?"

"I mean, let's take this stuff with all the numbers off and watch something else."

He looked at a box on top of the television. "That a movie you made?"

"Yes," I said, my heart sinking.

"You and me can just relax in a chair and watch a movie and wait till this rain lets up." I watched as he popped the tape in and worked the controls until the titles came on.

"How come those numbers are still there?" I was glad he was focusing on those numbers.

"They're for editing purposes later; see I'll probably cut out some bits and put them further up, in the next section. You'll see," I said in the tones of my instructor voice. Well, I thought, the better he knows me, the longer I spend with him, the less likely it is that he'll shoot me.

An image came on the screen. The camera followed the back of a fat woman lumbering down the street. Her black knitted pants were much too tight; rolls of flesh jiggled as she walked. The camera was close up on her posterior now, moving in front of her we rounded her huge belly. A sports sack tied around her waist looked like a colostomy bag.

"No wonder you don't make any big movies," he said. "Who wants to look at a fat cow like that?"

The camera moved slowly upward and her right hand came up from below hip level, across those mounds of flesh and we, the camera, the burglar and myself, all looked down the barrel of her Smith and Wesson revolver.

5:15 P.M., February 19, 1992
Police officer Laura Deleuse
It hadn't rained for a while in San Francisco. The first

rain always brings up oil on the streets, car skids, petty fistfights. It made the air cleaner anyway and gangs tended to stay inside.

The car was idling and I was in a bad mood. Darrell and I weren't speaking and we got this reporter on a ride-along. Interested in female cops. Special feature article for a Filipino weekly. I'd already introduced her to my sergeant who still spoke tagalong and a black female lieutenant. Now we were in the car waiting for my partner Darrell.

"So what's the difference between burglary and robbery?" she asked folding her legs gracefully in the back seat. She'd worn a two-piece suit for the occasion; it wasn't going to do for the rain, but then she had to stay in the car anyway. That was the agreement.

What was Darrell doing in the locker room? I wondered. I thought maybe he was waiting till the rain let up. So me and the reporter could get acquainted and fog up the windshield a little. Her eyes had a nice sparkle but I wasn't in any kind of mood.

Darrell was angry because I didn't go to the memorial service of his ex-partner last weekend. I had problems of my own. I'd been to enough funerals lately but Darrell wasn't into understanding. Or letting go. Now we couldn't fix it because we had this reporter in the car.

"Burglary. Okay so you want to know about burglary as opposed to robbery?" I asked her and my words took on the easy rhythm of the random raindrops landing on the hood of the car. I watched her get out her steno notebook.

The reporter asked me about robbers and burglars I'd arrested, about their character. I sighed and held myself back. Public relations and all that.

"Your robber and your burglar are basically two different kinds of people. Your burglar isn't into contact. He's secretive, furtive. He wants the goods and the last thing he wants is you," I said.

"What? Oh. I'm saying, 'he' because I have never run across a female burglar. Well, except kids. Kids are used to squeeze in small places. And women work the bars to sell the goods. Fifteen, twenty dollars for equipment that's worth ten times that. Car stereos go right over the bar.

"Robbery's something else. Robbery is committed against a *person*." I sighed. Why didn't she just read the penal code. I'd be glad to send it to her. Why didn't Darrell hurry up? "Burglary is breaking and entering. Someone who enters a structure, any kind of structure. Be that your home, or your trailer, tent, aircraft, or other vessel with the intent to steal."

Darrell got in the car and we just nodded to each other. He introduced himself to the reporter. He could just be heard over the rain.

We started driving up Mission Street just past Army where a produce store owner was quickly taking piñatas down from the awning. The red crepe paper skirt of a mermaid was nearly soaked. My eyes flicked over the storefronts and the bar doors open despite the rain.

In between the slapping sounds of the windshield wipers the reporter asked me what happens if someone burgles an occupied house. I hesitated. Why didn't Darrell do some of this work? I looked over at him. He was stony faced. Eventually he took out a toothpick to use between his teeth. Thanks, Darrell.

"What if there's somebody home during a burglary?" she asked, an edge to her voice. We weren't making her job easier, I thought. I started to feel more sympathetic toward her.

"I'd say ninety-nine percent of burglars never encounter a human being. They're not stupid people. But if they're unlucky and somebody's home, it's called a 'hot prowl.' You'd have to be pretty stupid to burglarize an inhabited dwelling. All you have to do is ring the doorbell. Or you know those phone calls when you answer and somebody hangs up?"

The reporter shuddered. She didn't need to write that down. The radio started squawking. We listened to it for a while. I pulled over to a little Lebanese grocery store where Darrell always got a pack of cigarettes and a hard-boiled egg.

"Hey, pick up some coffee beans for me, would you?" I slipped Darrell a five-dollar bill. I put the car into park and watched him run quickly into the store through the rain.

"Have you been on any burglary calls when someone's

been home?" the reporter was asking me. Darrell was loitering in the grocery, making the owner nervous.

"No," I said. "But a lot of people will come home when their house has been worked over by professionals and they'll find their personal possessions all over the floor and big kitchen knife out on the counter. That's because if you do happen to come home and the burglar has a situation on his hands he can use the knife as a weapon against you.

"It's a big thing among burglars not to bring a weapon," I continued, slowing my words so she could relax a little while scribbling. "Ups the degree of burglary. From second to first. Longer prison sentence. He's a career junkie and wants as much time on the outside as possible.

"The last thing he wants is contact. If you come home and you got a hot prowl on your hands you'd better believe he's got that knife ready. But I'll tell you." I leaned back and looked at her. She looked back. Something unusual in those eyes. "There's more than one person who's opened their front door, saw this stranger running at them full speed with their butcher knife in his hand, and then ran right by them and straight out the door."

The reporter's face lit up. They love this kind of detail. I always wonder why people like the seamy side of life. Curiosity? Like healthy animals circling slowly around sick ones, not touching, just looking. Or was it just her job?

I thought about mine. I was tired of patrolling the Ingleside trying to hold back the tide of crime. It was like shoveling shit into the wind.

I would be a blip on the street forever, I thought. Not married to a cop, no cop brother, father and not even Irish.

Darrell got back in the car. He started peeling an egg; the smell permeated the interior, as he knew it would. I hated it when he ate eggs in the car.

"Burglars aren't social," I told the reporter with a sidelong glance at Darrell. "They got a career to protect. Of course, that's not the case with your basic jumpy sociopath. They're not what you'd call your career burglar.

"Your basic sociopath isn't concerned about the finer points of law or the point of his life. He's got an IQ the level of room temperature. He's just waiting to go inside; let's hope he doesn't get you in the process."

5:25 P.M., February 19, 1992, 124 Bonnieview Drive, San Francisco

Blam! The fat woman in the video unloaded the weapon at the screen. The burglar pushed the power button on the monitor. Her image shrunk to a pinpoint and was gone. But the burglar was pacing back and forth, agitated.

"What kinda stuff you messin' around with here lady?" I looked up at his eyes and mouth, the moving holes within the black ski mask.

"I dunno," I said. I had wanted to get away from sexualizing guns. The feminine gun in the little beaded handbag, the eyes with the eye shadow and long lashes behind the sights. But eyelashes wouldn't matter to me anymore. What mattered was guns. And mine was sitting in a drawer. The ski mask took a long look at me. I looked away.

"I don't like it, I don't like it one bit." His voice rose. His hands were twitching at his sides. I didn't know if he meant the video or the fat woman or my trying to desexualize guns. I felt like he could read my mind.

His gun was back in his right pocket. Then suddenly his hand was up high in the air, I was watching it come down, hearing it crack across my cheek, my neck seemed to crack with it.

"You got any guns here, lady?"

"No," I said. "No, I swear." I looked away from the mask. It could tell I was lying, I was sure.

He considered my answer while looking at his hands. They were shaking. His knees seemed to be trembling and he reached behind him to steady himself on the kitchen table.

"I'm not lying to you," I said. I could hardly speak. I was hyperventilating. It would be better to talk a bit, get my voice back. I would try to be more normal, I thought with the one part of my brain that wasn't thinking about dying. "There's about forty dollars cash in my purse, the equipment, no jewelry worth mentioning."

"Good, that's good," he said, but he didn't feel good. The burglar reached his hand into his left pocket and pulled out a vial with brown powder in it. He unscrewed the cap and tapped some of the powder onto his finger, put his finger up to the fleshy hole in the middle of the mask and snorted. I had to do something here. I couldn't just sit in the chair anymore, I thought. I would just die in this chair. I watched him take the drug. I had no idea if it would be an advantage that he was stoned.

But his hands stopped twitching and he stopped dancing on the balls of his feet. He sat down, leaning into the back of the chair, waiting for the drug to take effect. His profile with the ski mask made him look like a pawn in a chess set. We listened to the rain pounding on the skylight together.

"Where you from?" the ski mask asked.

"Philly."

"Hey, me too." His words had trouble escaping his lips. I knew he'd had too much. Whatever that brown powder was, he hadn't learned to control intake.

"Go to the Italian Market?" I asked.

"Yeah. Where the peaches come in tissue wrappers and they yell at you if you touch them." The long globe of his head bobbed up and down in slow motion, his words coming separately, like beads on a string.

Then he heard the bubbling. The Crock-Pot lid was jiggling with escaping steam. All his frantic energy seemed to return, as if he'd never taken the drug. He sprang out of the chair. It wasn't heroin, I thought, discouraged. It would be something else, something synthetic, angel dust.

"Hey, what's cookin'?"

He looked over to where the Crock-Pot was gently gurgling. Then the mask looked up, squinting into the skylight.

"I could just make myself at home here." He sat down and put his long lanky legs on the kitchen table, moving aside my Minnie and Mickey Mouse salt and pepper set with his engineer's boots. I could see the tread pattern and little bits of soil and pine needles stuck to the bottom of them.

Those damn pine needles, I thought; I'd been sweeping them out of the house all week. Pine needles. Would that be the last thought I'd ever have? Sweeping pine needles. It wasn't a bad thought.

Agatha would be arriving in twenty minutes for dinner. I strained my head to look behind my back, turning my wrist to try to see my watch. He noticed.

Suddenly the Crock-Pot didn't look so good to him.

"Expectin' company?" He picked the gun up and pointed it at me.

He pulled the hammer back.

"No," I lied. "I mean, not for a while."

He threw the semiautomatic on the table and it spun past Minnie's clownish high heel. The muzzle was pointing straight at my chest. He picked up a cookbook from the kitchen table. "Oil-less Diet," he read and opened the cover. "Yeach."

The phone in the living room rang. The pupils in the ski mask fixed on me as we listened to my own message on the tape. *"This is Naomi Grielli. Thanks for calling, I'm fine now, but can't come to the phone. Please leave a message. . . ."*

The burglar and I both stopped and listened to the voice after the beep. It was Agatha. She was canceling dinner. Her car had broken down in the East Bay. She couldn't make it across the bridge in time. And she knew me well enough to know not to come too late.

"I hope you didn't put the okra in yet," she advised. *"It really turns into mush if you cook it so long. And I won't be able to bring the garam masala. That's the only thing that saves those parsnips."* She sighed into the tape. *"Do your best with cumin and garlic. I'll call later tonight."*

The burglar released the hammer of the semiautomatic and put it back on the table. It was still raining hard outside.

The eyehole of the ski mask winked at me. "Maybe I'll stay for dinner."

5:25 P.M., February 19, 1992
Police Officer Laura Deleuse

The three of us watched shoppers going in and out of the Safeway. A little kid was selling candy bars in front of the automatic doors. Darrell got out of the car to buy one.

"Jewelry. Some burglars have that kind of sparkle in their eye," I continued. "We're not talking about your cat thief Robert Wagner kinda guy. Black turtleneck pirouetting over rooftops. We're talking junkies who have to bring in fifteen hundred a week. What they have to do to get it is not a pretty picture. Although some of them know their way around the better antiques. Only take rugs over a hundred years old."

"Do many get caught?"

"Not a high closure rate on any of your professionals. You figure for every four times they're arrested they've done maybe two hundred, three hundred burglaries." Darrell got back in the car. He had the candy bar but he put it away and I knew why. It would be difficult to eat it without offering it to both me and the reporter. Darrell had manners. "Sacred Heart High School Peanut Butter Melt Away," the wrapper had said.

5:40 P.M., February 19, 1992,
124 Bonnieview Drive, San Francisco

The telephone cord was loose. He hadn't tied my hands together very well. I could wiggle my fingers up into my palms under the cord. I could probably just slip the whole thing off. I looked over at the burglar. He was reading the diet book again. He'd forgotten his plan about putting me in the pantry.

He threw the cookbook on the table. It barely missed the semiautomatic. His motor responses were clearly affected by the drug.

The safety was off on the semiautomatic. But there was something weird about that gun, the way it spun past Minnie Mouse's shoe.

He went over to the Crock-Pot and took off the lid, leaning back quickly when the steam seared his ruddy skin.

"Smells good," he said.

"It's okra, tofu, seaweed, and parsnips."

"You shittin' me," he said. He stuck in a wooden spoon that was lying next to the Crock-Pot and scooped some of the steaming food into his mouth.

"Fuck!" the mask screamed and leaning over the sink, cooling his burned tongue with tap water.

I froze. My fingers had loosened the telephone cord

behind my back so that I could easily slide the nylon up and down.

"Shut the fuck up, stupid bitch," the mask mumbled even though I hadn't said anything. "Too bad for you Agatha ain't coming for dinner. Maybe it's too bad for me too, ha, ha, ha. You ain't bad lookin' though."

He went to the cupboard and got himself one of my Fiestaware plates, a bright aqua, and a soup spoon. He ladled some of the hot food onto the plate and laid it steaming on the table. The white and brown mush steamed on the bright aqua circle. He stood and watched it.

The gun lay next to the food, the muzzle was aiming at the plate, at him, at his crotch, which was just at table height.

5:45 P.M., February 19, 1992
Police Officer Laura Deleuse

"What about *your* war stories?" I asked Darrell in front of the reporter. He shrugged. He was being just peachy tonight. I matched his stony silence and all three of us listened to the rain for a while.

The radio came on and we listened and then it went off. Darrell didn't do anything with his candy bar. He knew better than to smoke in the car.

5:45 P.M., February 19, 1992,
124 Bonnieview Drive, San Francisco

"You got anything good in that pantry?" the burglar asked. I didn't answer.

He walked toward me and I quickly slid my fingers back under the cord. The cord still appeared to be around my wrists. His gun was on the table. He was walking past me; I could feel his dirty suede jacket brush my arm when he stopped. He looked down at my shirt where my one right breast seemed to pull the material away from the flatter left-hand side.

"Hey, you ain't got no tit," he said.

"You think that's news to me?"

"Stop shittin' me. And hey, you quit looking at my gun." He backed away quickly, picking up his gun suddenly and never taking his eyes off my face. The little semiautomatic flopped into his palm.

"Is that *your* gun?" I asked, and his hesitation told me almost everything I needed to know.

"Well it's my gun now, lady," he said, waving it a few times in front of my face. Without meaning to, he gave me a good look at the thing. A good enough look to see that there was no magazine, no clip in the handle. That was almost good news. Then came the bad. He walked behind me into the pantry, he grabbed the knob and pulled at it. The door was warped from the moisture and stuck in its frame. But with a hard pull he got it open and the room was filled with an odor sweeter than any market in Tunisia.

"SHEEEEEEEIIIIIIT!" he screamed and my heart sank. "PAYDAY BABY!" he leaned back out of the pantry and gave me a big hug, that horrible dirty suede covering my blouse like skin of a sick animal, pulling the scars across my chest.

5:45 P.M., February 19, 1992
Police Officer Laura Deleuse

"Stop here, I want to make a phone call," Darrell said. It was a hard night for him, I could tell. He needed to talk, but that was his problem. The rain had let up and he was on the street, moving his eyes all around while he spoke to somebody on the end of the line.

The reporter waited until he picked up the horn of the pay phone to ask me.

"Have you arrived at any homicide scenes?" she asked.

"No," I lied. I didn't want to tell her. We sat in the silence, watching Darrell on the phone, his weight on one foot and then the other. Darrell was going to try and get me to do all the relating tonight, I thought stubbornly. Homicide. I looked at the reporter. She was biting her lip. It was a nice lip and I didn't think she should be biting it, but I didn't want to be the only one filling up the air space in the car either.

"Would you like to work homicide?" she asked.

"Sure," I said. But it wasn't likely. Homicide inspector? Not in my lifetime. In my twelve years on the force there have only been two appointments for inspectors and neither was for homicide. The chief has to appoint you specifically to homicide.

And I had a lieutenant who didn't like me. For some reason he thought I was a hippie and I just couldn't shake it.

All that plus a vindictive mayoral administration where heads had a way of rolling easily along the corridors of the Hall of Justice. Patronage and revenge. No, I'd never make homicide inspector.

At least inspectors are governed by a civil service exam now. It used to be that all the inspectors were grandfathered in by the chief. Appointed.

I thought about the night I first met up with those dinosaurs. They usually came from cop families and couldn't make the lieutenant's or even sergeant's exam. So there were some bonehead homicide inspectors with only a police lineage to recommend them. Yes, I'd met those goons.

It involved this prostitute who worked Capp Street. Her street name was Streak because she had this white streak of hair just in one spot. She was young and the rest of her hair was dark. Made a very pretty impression.

Usually someone loses the pigment in their hair when they sustain a blow to the head. At least, that's what it usually means in someone that young. Concussion, she'd gotten hit with a heavy object, something like that.

Apparently she'd picked up this cabdriver and he'd taken her to his flophouse room. We received the call and when we came on the scene we found her dead on the floor with a bullet in the middle of her forehead, just under that silver streak. Her face was covered with powder and there was a lot of blood and scalp and gray matter on the floor underneath all her long hair.

The cabbie was shrugging his shoulders and saying he didn't know what had happened. He also twitched a lot and hadn't shaved in a few days. Streak had been scraping the bottom of the barrel.

We called over the inspectors who were on night duty. A great crowd of dinosaurs, they'd all been dining at one of their favorite Irish places when dispatch reached them.

Irish juice has run deep in the department since the first officers hit the street in 1849 in long button-down coats. These boys didn't get where they were by being born yesterday. They were born a hundred years ago.

So they've gotten the call and they came into the flophouse room. Still a few after-dinner cigars stuck in their mouths, totally AB, alcohol breath, and generally continuing to have a good time.

Saw the girl, saw the cabdriver and immediately identified with him. He told his story in the best boy style, shrugging his shoulders. *Those expendable trashy women, you just never know what self-destructive thing they'll do next.* They all had a good headshake about that's the way it goes sometimes.

I couldn't believe it. I saw the cocaine on the mirror on top of the refrigerator. Never got put in the report. The cabbie's story was that it had happened when he went out to the store; he came back and found her dead on the floor. I didn't see any beer, or brown paper bag, or anything lying around that indicated that he'd made a trip. The cigarettes he was smoking one from a pack that was half full and his hands shook like he'd be lucky to hold onto the steering wheel another six months.

Those goons didn't even ask. They just clucked their heads and walked out, engaging in some little pissing on the tree contest about gunshot wounds to the head and who'd seen the most gray matter.

Fucking well-juiced dinosaurs. Patronage jobs. Most of them are retired now. Thank God. New blood is slowly coming in. Still it won't be mine.

So who leaves a prostitute alone in a room, anyway? Why would he bring her up there? Since when don't cabbies park in bus stops and run in to your local convenience store for whatever. Yeah, sure, tell me he went out to get a condom.

No, the way I figured it, they had some kind of fight. She either tried to steal the gun, or he tried to use it against her, or she was ripping off his drugs. Or he'd been pimping her and she was holding out his percentage.

Somebody was trying to rip something off from somebody and she got shot in the head. And those goons never even bothered to find out.

What bothered me so much about it, yeah, the young woman in her prime and all that, but what was her future anyway? What bothered me was the cabbie. He's still out there somewhere, driving around, picking up whores and carrying a gun with less to keep him from shooting it. Those homicide inspectors gave him a pat on the back.

Long forgotten by everyone but me. Would I tell our back seat cub reporter?

I looked back at her, nyloned knees crossed, she was looking over her notes carefully. Shorthand. Maybe she floated up from the typing pool. It couldn't have been too easy for her either, getting ahead in a male world.

"We usually stop for dinner around eight," I said.

We'd go out to dinner with the reporter and if we were lucky nothing would happen tonight. Then I would go home at about 2:00 A.M. to my house whose floor joists were being eaten away by termites.

When I wake up in the morning I'll have coffee with my roommate who has just gotten thrush. It was the first symptom he'd had since he'd been diagnosed HIV positive one year ago.

It was also something I didn't feel like Darrell needed to hear.

5:50 P.M., February 19, 1992,
124 Bonnieview Drive, San Francisco

The burglar was still exclaiming his good fortune and I was breathing heavily from the sudden pain I'd felt, including a sinking heart.

In the pantry, hanging upside down were three five foot tall, limp but verdant plants. An arrangement of long thin bright green leaves, pungent, with long powdered flowers on the ends, pointing at the floor. The burglar had discovered the best sensimilla harvest I'd ever had.

Resin was coating the hairs on his arms as he embraced the plants, adding aroma to the skin of his jacket. I breathed in deeply, just as he did.

"Where are the fuckin' garbage bags, lady?" he said.

"Third drawer under the sink."

He got out a roll and quickly tore off a few bags, one ripped down the middle; he swore at it.

He worked quickly, putting the gun in his pocket, cutting down the plants, one by one. He got up on a chair, trying to break off the green stalks but they resisted. Then he put the branches across his legs, forcing them to bend. The gun bounced against his hip, almost falling out of his pocket. I watched him frantically trying to control those plants, making them behave. The white garbage bags were punctured by the sinewy green stalks.

He kicked one of the bags across the floor toward the kitchen door. Then another. He followed the last one punching the sack with the toe of his foot. His toe came in contact with the wall through the bag. That must hurt, I thought. He seemed to get angrier. He kept on kicking until I saw the wall begin to give way underneath his shoe until he punched a good-size hole into the sheetrock.

Then he got down on his hands and knees and stared into the hole. There was something very wrong with him.

I don't want to die, I thought. I didn't want to be thinking about not wanting to die. I wanted to get his gun.

He scuttled into the pantry for the last few bags running past me, the gun hanging heavily in the dirty suede pocket where he'd forgotten about it. The handle of the gun loomed out of his pocket, almost touching me at shoulder level.

I made my move, whipped hands from behind, beeline for the weapon, palm around the handle.

He scarcely noticed that my hands were untied, in front of me and taking the gun in his pocket. I stood up and stepped back, my finger finding the trigger. He smiled nervously. Guns make all the difference.

"Hey, lady, guess what!" The ski mask was grinning as he hoisted a bag of pot over his shoulder.

"Yeah, I know what." I put his ski mask head right between the sights. "The safety is still off and my finger is on the trigger and you have a big bag with my pot in it."

"It ain't loaded." The mask smiled and laughed at his joke.

"No, wait a minute. You don't really know that, do you. You don't know that because it's not your gun."

"Yeah but there's not a magazine in the thing."

"There could be a bullet, one last bullet in the chamber." I moved the gun slightly out in front of me. Abdomen height. I remembered the position. Close in.

"Do you know how many police officers have wounded

themselves, gun professionals shot themselves with semi-automatics? It's because there's no way to tell if there's a bullet in the chamber. Now you may have taken the magazine out, but are you absolutely sure there isn't one left in the chamber? And are you willing to bet your life on it?"

I looked at his eyes and it told me all I wanted to know. I was right. He hadn't checked the chamber. I took a deliberate step away from him, never moving the gun off of him.

"Sure I know there's no bullet in the chamber, man, I loaded it myself." The mask grinned, but his hands were trembling, the plastic sack with all the pot in it shuddered.

Suddenly he turned and lunged toward me, but I took a step back faster and was out of his reach, pulling the hammer back. He heard the metal click. His hesitation meant I had him.

"You do that again, I'll shoot," I promised. "And I know how." I tried to keep my hands steady. If I had a bullet I had only one. I couldn't waste that last bullet. "You stole this gun, didn't you? You probably stole it this morning." I saw on his face that my words were true. "I could smell that it had been used recently. And certainly someone didn't use it on you or you wouldn't be here. So you just took it off of whoever and took out the magazine and thought that was that. Didn't you?"

"I didn't think nothing," the mask said sullenly.

"Sit down."

He glared at me.

"Sit the fuck down or I'll shoot you, I swear. I don't have that much to lose," I found myself saying. But neither, I thought, did he if he had actually shot someone earlier in the day.

My lips became small and tight and I looked at him without blinking and I said, "If you try for this gun I'm going to pull this trigger." I thought about my chest, about my illness. I thought about the scalpel of the surgeon that cut off my breast, about jury trials and pulling the trigger. "*You* sit the fuck down," I growled.

He pulled a chair up to the kitchen table. My intended dinner was already cool on the plate in front of him. The parsnips had turned into gray mush, the okra had burst open spilling its bitter seeds throughout, the slimy leaves entwining with long black strings of hiziki seaweed.

Those horrible stupid diets, the terrifying fear that the chemo wouldn't work. That moment when they took off the dressings and I looked down at my own body and couldn't believe what had happened to it, the weeks after the operation when the wound was so big I thought it could never heal. But it did. And I did. And I wasn't going to eat okra parsnip seaweed tofu meals anymore. He was.

"Eat," I said.

"What? This?"

"Eat!"

"Fuck no, man," he whined but I yelled louder. "Eat!" I was getting hysterical, and I didn't want him to think I was losing control. But the threat of my losing control would help him obey me, obey the possibility of that one bullet still being left in the chamber.

He lifted up the spoon and dove it into the mass and a lump of tofu shuddered its way into the utensil, covered with okra seeds. It came toward his mouth and fell inside. I saw his lips quiver and tears sprung to his eyes, the ski mask moved above his face and he grabbed his stomach. He was going to vomit.

I moved to where the other telephone was, keeping him carefully in the sights, but he was so busy trying not to puke he didn't notice at first. It was easy enough to dial 911. I said my address. I said to come immediately. I said "gun" and hung up.

I looked back at the burglar. He'd finished vomiting. His mask moved slowly from side to side, like he was adjusting his neck but then he was onto the balls of his feet and flying at me through the air.

The filthy suede flapped at his sides like the wings of a sick bat, his arm outstretched, aiming to push the gun away, but he wasn't fast enough.

I didn't even think about whether there was a bullet in the chamber. There wasn't time. I stepped back and pulled the trigger.

5:55 P.M., February 19, 1992
Police Officer Laura Deleuse

It had stopped raining and it was getting dark. Then the call came over the radio.

"In the Ingleside. A priority. 459. Hot Prowl. Roll Call 3 Henry 3. 124 Bonnieview Drive."

That was us. The address was near the top of Diamond Heights. The reporter was trying to appear calm, but she was clinging on to the handholds in the back seat and something like a smile played across her lips.

Arrived at 6.02, way up in the hills. Hate those kind of calls. People with hillside houses and expensive, easily fenceable goods. Two TVS and one for the kids. Everybody with their own computer. A high-end Macintosh for Dad. Throw in a few VCRs, some jewelry and some cash. And an attitude that doesn't make the job easier. They have the kind of life where they feel like bad things shouldn't happen to them.

When I arrive there that's the kind of mood they're in. Pissed off at me for not doing my job, for not protecting them from what's just happened. Even when they have French doors because the little panes of glass are so pretty and easy to break into. Houses way off the street, front doors hidden down paths of gnarling vines with rose blossoms and fragrant night-blooming jasmine.

I told the reporter to stay in the car, since Darrell wasn't saying much to either one of us. She looked gravely disappointed, but what did she expect.

I walked down a long flagstone pathway under the trellises that arched above me loaded with old, well-established vines. Small, security-useless fairy lights lit the flagstone steps leading down to the redwood shingled house. A big pine tree loomed above the roof and spilled wet needles down all along the path. Everybody up in the hills emulated this Snow White and the Seven Dwarfs kind of architecture and landscape, but it wouldn't be a fairy tale when we got there. The 911 call that came in had mentioned a gun.

Darrell and I pulled our weapons out as we stood on either side of the pretty French door. He gave me a look that I knew and it fixed a lot of things that were wrong with the night.

I won't let it get in the way, his look said and I knew for the next moments he would be totally on my side.

Someone had knocked out one of the panes after tapping it. Someone who was probably still inside.

The wind played with the copper patinaed tubes of a

wind chime. Darrell put his hand through the broken pane, reached up, and turned the knob.

In the hallway we heard a regular swishing sound. We crept along the wall and aimed our weapons into the kitchen. A forty-year-old white woman was diligently sweeping her floor. At her feet lay a man in a ski mask. He was bleeding. She was careful not to let the bristles of the broom touch the gathering pool of blood underneath his hips.

"Oh, you're here!" she said, smiling nervously, leaning the broom up against the wall.

I thought about how I would write it up in the report. We'd entered with our guns drawn, but holstered them immediately.

A man in a ski mask lay wounded and unconscious on the floor. He needed an ambulance. A semiautomatic Walther lay on the kitchen table.

I took a good look around the place; there was a lot of fancy camera equipment and televisions. A familiar pungent odor was in the air, mixed with gunpowder. A kitchen chair was circled with telephone cord. A gooey gray mound of food on an aqua plate was sitting on the table.

A pantry door was ajar. Inside, strings were hanging down from the ceiling. Somebody had kicked a hole in the wall in the kitchen and a lot of white plastic bags with escaping vegetation were littering the floor, along with some pine needles she'd been trying to sweep up.

The woman, about five foot six inches tall, about forty years of age, was holding a broom in her hand. She didn't look healthy and she identified herself as Ms. Grielli. I picked up the weapon from the kitchen table with my handkerchief. There was no magazine in it; the chamber was empty.

The burglar's head was resting on a white plastic bag filled with marijuana and there were other plastic bags piled by the kitchen door. He had a spoon clutched in his hand. He had a fairly strong pulse. She'd hit him in the upper thigh.

Darrell went to call an ambulance and support; I leaned down and carefully pulled the ski mask off his head. I recognized him. I'd seen that face before. Another revolving-door customer of the city jail. He had a rap sheet as long as his dick and I'd had the unfortunate opportunity to see that, too.

Ms. Grielli claimed he was an armed intruder and had tied her to a chair. I saw no reason to dispute this.

He would be charged with first-degree burglary, possession of narcotics, and possible kidnapping. I couldn't wait to meet him again in court.

Ms. Grielli claimed that the intruder had entered the premises with intent to burgle and upon seeing her, drew the gun. According to her statement she managed to get it away from him as he burgled her apartment. She knew it didn't have a clip in the handle but was aware of the possibility that there might be a bullet left in the chamber.

She claims to have gotten the gun from his pocket and then called 911. He attacked her and she shot him.

"And then I just stood there and didn't know what to do," she said with a quick little laugh. "So I started sweeping." She picked up the broom and put it back in the pantry and closed the door. The floor wasn't clean yet.

She showed me a WW II Browning semiautomatic in a locked box with current registration, supporting her story that she was familiar with the workings of semiautomatic pistols. She said she had been mugged in her driveway in October 1987. The armed robber in that case had never been apprehended.

After I took my report I saw no reason to take Ms. Grielli into custody. I found no evidence that contradicted her story.

I spent some time talking to her. She didn't appear to be terribly shaken, just nervous. In fact, she seemed proud of having disarmed the man and shot him. It was a gutsy thing to do; the odds were against her but she beat them.

Ms. Grielli appeared to have some health difficulties. She had that burned-out radiation look; hair that was only fuzz covering her head. I hoped she kept beating the odds.

Officers Chu and Scappichio arrived on the scene and escorted the prisoner to the ambulance and to San Francisco General Hospital.

The suspect will be arraigned one week from now,

held on charges of burglary 459, kidnapping and possession of narcotics. End of report.

"Got a friend you can call to come over tonight?" I asked Ms. Grielli. She was looking better, the color was coming back into her face.

"Yes," she said. "I think I'll have my friend Agatha come over and spend the night." She indicated a house next door. I could see the lights burning inside. A few curious neighbors would probably be outside.

"Want me to go over there with you?" I asked.

"No," she said, "I'm just fine now, I really am." I believed her.

Darrell was outside, waiting for me just in front of her door. I walked to the door and on second thought returned to the kitchen where she was leaning into the sink, pouring the gray congealed contents of a Crock-Pot down the garbage disposal.

"And Ms. Grielli—" She turned around. She was smiling as she threw the gelatinous matter away. "They might want to come to your house for questioning," I said. "So you'd better give your floor a good vaccuming." I nodded toward the pantry. She looked at the closed door and her eyes slid back across the floor where pine needles and other vegetation littered the black-and-white linoleum.

"No problem," she said quietly. We stood there for a moment in the silence and then she flipped a switch of the garbage disposal. We both watched as the gooey gray matter disappeared into the city's sewer system. She was a nice lady, but maybe she needed cooking lessons.

7 P.M., February 19, 1992, patrol car, San Francisco Police Officer Laura Deleuse

I got back into the patrol car. The reporter leaned forward over the seat rest and asked quietly, "Officer Deleuse, tell me what happened in there," she said. "I mean all those white garbage bags coming out of the house. I saw the other officers put them in their car."

"Narcotics," I said. "Marijuana."

"Was that what the burglar was trying to get? What happened to the woman? Was she shot?" The woman sounded almost hopeful.

"She disarmed a thief and shot *him*. Haven't seen many of those."

"She did!" the reporter crowed and took out her steno book.

"Listen," I said, "it's dinnertime and for a half hour I'm off duty."

"Sure, sure," the reporter said. "Sorry." She tucked her steno book back into a neat little leather handbag. The clasp closed with a click.

I thought about all the ways people needed drugs. Chemotherapy patients. My roommate whose insurance wouldn't cover his AZT. Junkies that don't have a life anymore and don't think twice about taking a few people along with them.

I looked at the reporter. I could see in the streetlight that she was prematurely gray. I thought about the prostitute, Streak, the cabbie and the detectives who didn't see the cocaine on the refrigerator, the detectives who didn't care. I hoped I was a different kind of cop.

Darrell was finished with the radio. He was in a better mood and I was glad. He was talking to the reporter about a restaurant review he'd read in the *Chronicle* last week. Patricia Unterman, the restaurant critic, had recommended the curries of a Thai restaurant right here in the Ingleside district.

Darrell liked green curry. The reporter preferred Pad Thai noodles. I looked forward to little potatoes and coconut sauce and hoped that nothing else would happen tonight.

THE MAGGODY FILES:
TIME WILL TELL

By Joan Hess

"Mary Frances was so excited I could barely get her hair rolled," Estelle Oppers said as she reached for the basket of pretzels on the bar. "She was as jumpy as a long-tailed cat in a room full of rocking chairs, and I finally had to threaten to get a towel and tie her down."

Ruby Bee Hanks smiled as she envisioned Mary Frances Frank, who wasn't even five feet tall but had more energy than one of those nuclear power plants. "Well, you got to admit being named Teacher of the Year is an honor. I don't know how she's faced those teenagers every morning for forty years and tried to get them interested in poetry when they were more interested in one another's britches. Back in my time, we sat on opposite sides of the room, and—"

"The award is gonna be presented at the cafeteria this Friday evening. I told her to come by that morning and I'll recomb her hair for free. She was real pleased." Estelle nodded smugly at her reflection in the mirror, real pleased by the undeniable generosity of her own gesture.

Harrumphing under her breath, Ruby Bee came out from behind the bar to take another pitcher of beer to the only customers, a trio of truckers in the back booth. Business at Ruby Bee's Bar & Grill was slow these days, but so was everything in Maggody, Arkansas (pop. 755). These days, at least, everybody knew where Arkansas was on the map on account of the new president (*not* between Oklahoma and Texas, as the old president had said), and Ruby Bee was hoping that tourists might start flocking like cowbirds now that summer was approaching. Jim Bob Buchanon seemed to feel the same, since he'd repaired the dryers at the Suds of Fun Launderette and put a fresh coat of paint on the front of Jim Bob's SuperSaver Buy 4 Less. This very morning she'd watched Roy Stivers setting out brass lamps and cracked washbowls in front of his antique store, and Brother Verber down at the Voice of the Almighty Lord Assembly Hall had changed the letters on the portable sign to read: STRANGERS WELCOME; FREE ADMISSION TO HEAVEN. This wasn't to say the collection plate wouldn't be passed under their noses several times, but at least he wasn't selling tickets at the door.

"I already knew about all the details concerning the ceremony," she said disdainfully as she returned. "Benjamin called me yesterday to say he wants to have a surprise party afterward at their house. He was supposed to come by at two to talk about the menu." She consulted the neon-trimmed clock behind her. "It's already after four. I wonder if he's still coming."

Estelle snorted. "I wouldn't hold my breath. Poor Mary Frances had to wait most of an hour before he picked her up. I'd have been hotter than a pepper mill, but she said she was used to it after all these years. She admitted he was always late when they were dating in college and she should have known there was no way to change him. The only reason she didn't wait at the altar was that she told him the wrong time for the wedding. He was at the hospital when Sara Anne was born, but Mary Frances was in labor so long her mother had time to drive down from Saint Louis. When Ben Junior was born, he didn't get there until she was back in her room and the baby was in the nursery. Imagine it taking him more than three hours to get to the hospital!"

"She's a saint to put up with him all these years. Maybe I ought to call him at his office and remind him about our meeting. Do you recollect the name of his insurance outfit in Starley City?"

Estelle did, and pretty soon Ruby Bee was asking to speak to Benjamin Frank.

The secretary's sigh hinted at years of frustration. "He's not here yet, Mrs. Hanks. He called more than an hour ago to say he was on his way, so I'm hoping he'll be here before Mr. Whitbread gets fed up and leaves. There's a lot of business at stake." She sighed again, but most likely not for the last time.

"It don't take an hour to get to Starley City," said Ruby Bee, feeling sorry for the secretary and the unknown Mr. Whitbread. "I could be there in fifteen minutes."

"Mr. Frank has good intentions, but he'll think of errands along the way and pretty soon he'll be on the other side of the county talking to a client or over at the cafe drinking coffee. He won't even notice that he's late."

Ruby Bee asked her to remind him of the meeting, then hung up and mentally adjusted Mary Frances's halo. "How can someone be like that?" she asked Estelle. "If I was Mary Frances, I'd have long since ripped out my hair and taken to wandering around town in my underwear like Cornwallis Buchanon did before they packed him off to the county old folks home."

"She said they've never heard the opening hymn at church or seen the credits at the picture show. She used to invite folks for supper, but she finally stopped on account of Benjamin getting home about the time everybody was saying good night. Last year they were supposed to visit Ben Junior all the way up in Alaska, but they got to the airport late and missed the flight. She cried for a week because she was gonna see their new grandbaby for the first time and Ben Junior had booked them on a three-day cruise as a Christmas present. Of course the airline wouldn't refund the money for the tickets because it wasn't their fault, and Ben Junior lost the deposit."

"There ought to be one of those twelve-step programs for folks like that," Ruby Bee said with a trace of tartness, "but they couldn't hold their meetings. Everybody'd show up too late."

They were busy commiserating with Mary Frances when the door opened and Benjamin Frank came striding across the dance floor. He was a big man, his face crinkled, his gray hair clipped short, his grin stretching from ear to ear, his teeth as white and even as could be bought anywhere. He had an unfortunate fondness for plaid and polyester, but the overall effect was dapper, if not chic. "How're the two prettiest ladies in Maggody today?" he called. "I keep waiting to hear you've both eloped with handsome millionaires from Farberville. If Mary Frances didn't keep me on a short leash, I'd be showing up on your doorsteps with flowers and candy to beg for a peck on the cheek."

Ruby Bee gave him a pinched frown. "You said you were coming at two o'clock, Benjamin, and your secretary was expecting you an hour ago."

He winked at Estelle as he sat on the stool beside her. "You sure worked magic on Mary Frances's hair this morning. You ought to open a hair salon in New York City and run those fancy boys like Vidal Sassoon right out of business."

Estelle patted her own festive red beehive. "That's right kind of you, Benjamin," she said, unable to stop herself from simpering. "A lot of folks don't realize that cosmetology is an art, and—"

"About the party," inserted Ruby Bee. "What kind of food do you want me to fix?"

He beamed at her. "Everybody knows you're the best cook west of the Mississippi, Ruby Bee. You decide on the menu, and don't think twice about the price. I'm so proud of Mary Frances for being the Teacher of the Year that I get misty just thinking about it. I want this party to be real special. The ceremony starts at seven, so we'll most likely leave by six-thirty. You can bring the food then and get everything all set out in the dining room. I'll leave some balloons and crepe paper streamers in a sack on the back porch and be eternally grateful if you could tape 'em up."

"We'd be delighted," Estelle said just as if she were the one catering and not just tagging along out of habit. "Mary Frances will be downright thrilled when she steps through the door."

"But we aim to be at the high school at seven," said Ruby Bee. "Mary Frances won't get her award until everybody's done making speeches, but I don't want to miss a minute of it." She paused to give him a piercing look. "And you don't, either."

"I'll be sitting in the first row," Benjamin said as he slid off the stool. "I promised her I'd be home and in the shower by six o'clock, and ready to escort her whenever she's finished getting gussied up. I guess I'd better head on to my office. My secretary gets irritable if I'm late."

Ruby Bee waited until he was gone before she said, "I'd get homicidal, myself. Do you realize he never once apologized for being late?"

They resumed commiserating with poor Mary Frances, who'd taught countless teenagers to recite poetry but couldn't seem to teach her husband how to tell time.

I'd given up trying to whittle a chunk of wood into something remotely resembling a marshland mallard and was dozing away the day in the Maggody PD, where I was the one and only P. Once upon a time I'd had a real live deputy, but now I had a beeper. I also had an answering machine, but I'd quit checking messages after I realized the only person using it was my mother, Ruby Bee, and every last one of her messages began with a treatise on how much she disliked talking to a machine. What I really needed was voice mail, I decided as I monitored the progress of a spider across the ceiling. "To gripe about my schoolmarm hair, Press One. To gripe about my aversion to lipstick, Press Two. To gripe about my lack of a social life, Press Three." It would never work; there weren't enough buttons to handle Ruby Bee's litany of my sins.

The telephone interrupted my whimsical reverie. After a few scowls in its direction, I picked up the receiver and reluctantly conceded that the caller had reached the PD.

"Arly, this is Mrs. Jim Bob," said a familiar but not welcome voice. "I am fed up with those junior high boys cutting across the back of my yard on their way to Boone Creek. Not five minutes ago they tramped right through my begonias, and when I went onto the porch and told them to get off my property, one of them used an obscenity."

"No kidding?" I said with the proper degree of incredulity. "Do you want me to shoot 'em? I've still got four bullets in a box in the back room."

"No, I want you to go down to the creek and give them a lecture about trespassing and disrespect for their elders. I'd do it myself but I have to fix a green bean casserole for Eula Lemoy, whose back is bothering her. It won't keep me from watching for your car to go down the road within the next five minutes, Miss Chief of Police."

"I'll probably go ahead and shoot 'em," I said, albeit to the dial tone. Mrs. Jim Bob's a royal pain, but Jim Bob's the mayor and therefore, at least technically, my boss. In order to avoid a tedious lecture at the next town council meeting, I hung the CLOSED sign on the door and drove down Finger Lane to the swimming hole to see if I could persuade the miscreants to find another shortcut.

Said miscreants had moved on. I gazed at the bubbly brown water, remembering some moonlit nights of my youth when hormones had bubbled as loudly. The sun was warm, the breeze laden with earthy rawness of spring, the birds twittering and flitting in the branches, the squirrels nattering at me. Manhattan, where I'd led a tumultuous married life, has art galleries and opera, but there are some scenes that are a sight more elegant.

It occurred to me that I needed to stake out the swimming hole for an hour or two, just in case the miscreants returned. In order to survive the ordeal, I needed provisions along the lines of a ham sandwich, potato salad, a bag of cookies, and a big cup of iced tea. All of this was available at the SuperSaver deli, where I could also find a tabloid filled with wondrous stories of alien lobbyists and sexual aberrations.

Such are the exactitudes of law enforcement in a town where nothing ever happens, I told myself as I parked in front of the store and started inside. I detoured to greet the figure almost hidden behind a cart piled high with sacks of groceries.

"Congratulations, Mrs. Frank," I said, resisting the urge to scuffle my feet and duck my head as if I were telling lies about uncompleted homework. She hadn't been a tyrant in the classroom, but even fifteen or so years later, with white hair and faded blue eyes, she radiated a measurable dose of the same authority.

"Thank you, Arly. I must say I'm tickled pink, although I don't know if I'm more excited about the award or my retirement. Forty years is a long time to attempt to instill a lively interest in dead poets."

I couldn't argue with that. "Well, congratulations again," I said, edging toward the door.

"Forty years of bells and tardy slips," she continued in a musing voice, "to be followed by who knows how many years of waiting for Benjamin. That's what I'm doing now. My car's in the shop, so I'm at his mercy. Do you know how long I've been standing here?" Her voice tightened and her eyes narrowed as she regarded the rows of parked cars. "Over half an hour, that's how long. Benjamin promised to pick me up at four sharp, which is why I went ahead and bought ice cream and frozen orange juice."

"Would you like me to give you a ride home?"

"That's thoughtful of you, Arly, but surely Benjamin will be here before too much longer. It simply never occurs to him that other people dislike waiting for him. I've grown accustomed to it after all these years, but now that I'm retiring, I wonder if I'll be able to handle it."

I was eager to get back to the creek, take off my shoes and let the mud slip between my toes, stuff my face, read about two-headed babies in the Amazon rain forest. "I'll be clapping for you on Friday," I said in one last attempt to extricate myself from the conversation.

"But Benjamin won't," she said, talking more to herself than to yours truly. "It won't matter how many times I tell him how important this is, how many times I beg him to be there at seven o'clock. He'll cross his heart and swear he'll be there, but he won't, and he'll be wondering where everyone is when he arrives two hours later. This may be the most important event in my life—an acknowledgment of all my years of teaching and the beginning of what's supposed to be our golden years together. He really should be on time." She took an orange from a sack and squeezed it until the skin burst and juice dribbled down her white fingers. "He really should."

Something was dribbling down my back that wasn't a source of vitamin C and I was ready to forget about my picnic and flat out flee to my car. I'd known Mary Frances Frank for a good many years, but this was my first glimpse of her as a vindictive Munchkin. "I'm sure he'll make it this one time," I said.

"He'd better," she said. "Otherwise, he'll be very, very sorry . . . this one time."

By Friday I'd corralled the miscreants and bawled them out, cleaned the back room of the PD in a paroxysm of seasonal madness, and given some consideration to dust-busting my efficiency apartment above the antique store. Only my penchant for chicken-fried steak and cream gravy saved me, and I was devising ways to idle away the afternoon as I went into the bar and grill.

"Thought you said you'd be here at noon," Ruby Bee said in an unfriendly voice.

I didn't much worry about it, in that she's no more predictable than the weather—and this was hurricane season, after all. "Did I say that? I could have sworn I said I'd be here around noon." I appropriated a stool and gave her a beguiling smile. "How about the blue plate special and a glass of milk?"

"How about you learn to be on time?" muttered my mother, although she did so while stomping into the kitchen.

I sat and waited, listening placidly to the wails from the jukebox and the conversations from the booths along the wall. Now that it was no longer legal to shoot help-less birds and hapless mammals, the hot topic seemed to be the slaughter of large mouth bass and crappies. At least it was preferable to brands of toilet bowl cleaners.

Estelle sat down beside me as Ruby Bee came through the kitchen doors. "I guess we're all excited," she said.

"I guess we are," I said, although I had no idea what she assumed was exciting us. I myself was a little choked up at the sight of the plate Ruby Bee was carrying, but I'm a patsy in such matters.

Ruby Bee banged down the plate in front of me. "Has Mary Frances decided what she's going to wear to-night?" she asked Estelle.

"Her beige linen suit. She wanted to buy a new dress, but her car's still at the shop and Benjamin didn't get home yesterday in time for her to drive to Farberville. I wouldn't have liked to have been him when he finally got there. Mary Frances's eyes were flashing when she told me about it this morning, and I can imagine what all she said to him. They may have been married for forty years, but his lateness is starting to get on her nerves."

"I heard something interesting," Ruby Bee said. She glanced at me to see if I was listening, then moved down the bar so she and Estelle could share the big secret. The two often mistake me for someone who cares. "I heard," she continued with the muted subtlety of a chain saw, "that Mary Frances made up with her brother just two days ago. After all these years of not speaking, she upped and called him, and then borrowed Elsie's car for the afternoon and went to visit him."

"She didn't say one word to me," Estelle said, clearly stunned by the magnitude of the revelation. "Not one word, and there I was recombing her hair for free!"

"Elsie promised not to tell anyone, but we were talking about the award ceremony tonight and she let drop that Mary Frances invited her brother and his wife."

"What about the credenza?"

Ruby Bee nodded somberly. "She gave it to him. Here they've been fighting like dogs and cats over it since their mama died ten years ago, refusing to speak to each other at the family reunions, paying lawyers to file lawsuits, and sitting on opposite sides of the church at weddings and funerals. All of a sudden she's willing to give him the credenza just to make peace with him. He went to her house and picked it up last night. I was flabbergasted when I heard that."

I halted a forkful of mashed potatoes halfway to my mouth. "I don't understand why you're treating this like the collapse of the Soviet Union. Maybe she wants to begin her retirement without any lingering feuds."

Estelle pondered this while she ate a pretzel. "Nope, this credenza is mahogany and it's been in the family for three or four generations. We're not talking about a sewing box or an end table worth a few dollars. Roy Stivers appraised it back when Mary Frances and her brother were dividing the estate, and he said he hadn't come across a nicer one in all his born days."

In that I wasn't sure I'd recognize a credenza if it nipped me on the butt, I resumed eating.

Ruby Bee resumed gossiping. "Elsie was miffed when Mary Frances brought the car back all covered with mud. It seems her brother is working on that new stretch

of highway that's supposed to replace Highway Seventy-
one if they ever finish blasting through the mountains.
Mary Frances wanted to hose off the mud, but Else said
not to bother on account of it wasn't right for the
Teacher of the Year to be washing cars. They almost
had an argument over it, but Mary Frances insisted Elsie
come over for coffee and homemade doughnuts this
morning. Elsie ain't all that hard to mollify."

"Mary Frances is gonna be real hard to mollify if Benjamin's not on time tonight," Estelle said. "She told me
she was going to teach him a lesson once and for all.
Do you reckon she'll say something in her speech?"

"She can't say anything folks don't already know."

The discussion wandered at this point, and so did I.
Not off to the trenches, mind you, or even off to deter-
mine the dimensions of the credenza and delve into the
mystery of why a woman might want to make peace
with her brother after ten years of estrangement. The
grapevine was more than capable of producing a tidy
solution sooner or later.

Where I wandered was out to the skeletal remains of
Purtle's Esso station, where I could run a speed trap
to make a little money for the local coffers and, more
importantly, read a magazine. At five o'clock, I went
back to the PD and tucked away my radar gun, called
the dispatcher at the sheriff's office to find out if I'd
missed anything newsworthy (I hadn't), and was halfway
out the door when I noticed the blinking red rat's eye
of the answering machine.

Approach-avoidance reared its ugly head. Was it the
man of my dreams offering an escape to a Caribbean
island? Was it a lawyer in Manhattan calling to tell me
my ex-husband was so overcome with remorse that he
was sending the money he owed me? Or was it the
pope?

I pushed the button.

"This is Ruby Bee Hanks, and I don't know why I
bother to call over there when all I ever get is this rude
machine. I don't know what the world's coming to when
people can't bother to answer their own telephones."
There was a sharp inhalation before she took off once
more. "Estelle and I are going out to Mary Frances's
house just before the ceremony to get everything ready

for the party. We won't get to the cafeteria until right at seven, so you need to go over early and save us seats on—"

The machine cut her off before I could, although it was close. I locked up and walked across the road to my apartment, having been warned much earlier that Ruby Bee's Bar & Grill would not be serving supper to the likes of me or anyone else. I could survive on a can of soup, since I'd be having chocolate cake and champagne punch within a matter of hours, I assured myself as I showered and changed into a skirt and blouse in honor of the honoree.

I figured I'd best get to the high school fifteen minutes early in order to secure the best seats. Would Benjamin Frank be thinking the same thing? From what I could gather, the only place he'd get to on time was his own funeral—unless Mary Frances Frank did indeed teach him a lesson as she'd vowed. The adage about old dogs and new tricks came to mind, along with her comment that he would be 'very, very sorry.'

Abruptly I got it—credenza and all. My fingers felt numb as I finished buttoning my blouse, grabbed the car keys, and sprinted down the stairs and across the road. Mary Frances had not been making peace with her brother; she'd been making a deal. It was nearly six-forty, which meant Ruby Bee and Estelle were in as much danger as Benjamin Frank, and if my car balked, all three were in for one helluva surprise party.

I squealed out in front of a pickup truck and jammed down the accelerator. The Franks lived in a farmhouse several miles out of town on a passable county road. Six forty-two. Ruby Bee and Estelle might already be there, taping up streamers and setting out the punch bowl. Benjamin might be there, or still at his office in Starley City. Six forty-five. Mary Frances had no idea Ruby Bee and Estelle might be in the house. Six forty-eight.

I turned off the highway and tightened my grip on the steering wheel as I bounced down the road. Six-fifty came and went. Biting down on my lip, I went even faster and therefore came within inches of crashing into the back of Ruby Bee's car in the middle of the road. Dust caught up with me as I leaned my forehead against the steering wheel and waited for the adrenaline to abate.

Ruby Bee stood up on the far side of her car. "What in tarnation's going on?" she squawked. "You liked to kill the both of us! Driving like a madman on a narrow road!"

I got out of my car and clung to the antenna until my knees quit knocking. "Where's Estelle?"

"As any fool can see, I had a flat tire. She went on ahead to see if Benjamin can come help us change it and get all the party food into the house. At this rate, there's no way we'll be at the cafeteria on time."

Six fifty-eight. "How far is it?" I demanded.

"You're antsy this evening," she said, her hands on her hips and a disapproving look on her face. "It's nearly a mile further, and Estelle's wearing high heels, but she should be getting there by now. If you'd stop gawking and loosen these lug nuts, we won't need Benjamin's help."

"Is he there?"

"Now how on earth should I know a thing like that?"

We both turned and looked up the road a split second before an explosion rocked the sky, the sound reverberating across the valley like distant cannon fire. Black smoke and an orange haze appeared above the trees. It was seven o'clock.

Mrs. Jim Bob stood behind a podium, her hands clutching the edges as she leaned into the microphone. "And our only hope for the future lies in the moral education of our youth, who need to learn about respecting their elders and staying out of their begonias," she was saying as I came into the room.

"Excuse me," I said, "but there's been an accident. I need to speak to Mrs. Frank." Scanning the faces in the audience, I hurried up to the front row as Mary Frances Frank stood up. I asked her to accompany me to the back of the room.

"There was an explosion at your house," I said, then stopped, ignoring the murmurs of uneasiness and Mrs. Jim Bob's shrill comments about being interrupted.

"I thought I smelled gas," she said without hesitation. "I mentioned it to Benjamin this morning, and he said he'd call the gas company. It's a good thing nobody was home."

"Then your husband is here?"

"Well, I believe he ought to be on his way by now. He called from his office at six and assured me he'd go by the house to take a quick shower, then come right here. I made a point of reminding him how important it was for him to be here at seven, then arranged for Mrs. Jim Bob to give me a ride." She regarded me with a level expression. "He may be running a few minutes late, but he should be here any minute."

"It's already seven-thirty," I said. "I had to wait at your house until a sheriff's deputy arrived to take over. The volunteer fire department is on its way, but I'm afraid there won't be anything to save. It was a powerful explosion. My first thought was dynamite."

"Why were you out that way?"

"I went to warn Ruby Bee and Estelle to be away from the house at seven o'clock. Benjamin arranged a surprise party for you after the ceremony, and they were delivering the food on their way here."

Her face turned as white as her hair. "Oh, no . . . I didn't know. I had no idea. Were they injured?"

I gave her the look she'd given me years earlier when I'd tried to explain that my dog ate my term paper. "You're damn lucky they weren't. Ruby Bee had a flat a mile from your house, and Estelle went ahead to ask Benjamin to give them a hand. If she hadn't lost a heel, she might well have lost her life."

"Thank God," she whispered.

"Benjamin's car was in the driveway," I continued coldly. "He must have been running late. If he'd been here as he promised, no one would have been hurt in the explosion."

She looked up at me, her eyes welling with tears, her lips trembling. "I told him over and over how important it was that he be here at the cafeteria at exactly seven o'clock. I really did."

I believed her. I really did.

DUST DEVIL

· ·

By Nancy Pickard

The father of the child pulled back the vertical blinds that hung at the window of his law office, and stared at the merciless sky that glared back at him from above downtown Kansas City. The sun was a branding iron, scorching the Midwest wherever its rays touched the earth. In this, the hottest August on record, the temperature had broken 100 degrees for twenty-one days running. Newspapers warned parents not to leave their children or pets in cars, the city pools were so full a person couldn't dive under water without hitting somebody's legs, in airless rooms old people died for lack of fans.

The private investigator who was seated in the room inquired, "Look like it could rain?"

The man at the window, Chad Peters, didn't bother to answer the question that was on everybody's lips. He wasn't looking for rain. He was looking for his three-month-old son, Brook.

"My wife stole him from the hospital," Peters said, as if the private investigator hadn't spoken.

"Your wife's name?"

"Diane." His voice was hard and cracked, like the scorched earth, and it shook with a rage that rivaled the heat of the drought. "Diane Peters. If she's still using my name. If not, she might use her maiden name, Brewer. Diane Brewer. She was going to abort, but I got a court order preventing her from doing it. By the time her lawyers got that reversed, she was too far along in her pregnancy. And then what does she do, she steals the baby she didn't want to begin with. I'm the one who

290

wanted the baby, not her. My son Brook wouldn't be alive if it weren't for me. I don't even know if he is still alive. . . ." He let the blinds fall, plunging his office into artificial coolness and light, and he turned his face away.

The private investigator watched him. He judged Chad Peters to be around forty years old, already a full partner with his name on the door. Peters was tall, slim, a good-looking man, but not likable in his grief; he held himself upright and rigid as a dam, as if afraid that if somebody touched him it would poke a hole in his defenses, and all of his emotions would come rushing out in a drowning flood. The private investigator didn't like him, but he felt sorry for him, all the same. Losing a child to the other parent, that was tough on anybody. When the man had himself under control once again, he looked back at the private investigator. Peter's eyes were red-rimmed, but his flushed cheeks were dry, as if the heat of his anger had dried his tears before they could fall.

"Find them for me," he said. "I'll give you your advance, and expenses, and whatever it costs beyond that, but I'll tell you, the last investigator I hired took my money and ran with it. I never heard from him again after the first couple of phone calls. What I figure is that he found her, and that Diane talked him into letting her go. She's capable of that. Diane would screw an ax murderer if she thought it would hurt me somehow." His glance at the private investigator was aggressive, offensive. "How do I know you won't screw me, too?"

"You don't, but I won't."

Peters shrugged, as if he were past the point of expecting any good to come of anything. "What's your name again?"

"Ken, Mr. Peters. I'm Ken Meredith."

"I can't remember anything anymore. I don't know where to tell you to look, either. I'll give you the names of her family and friends, everything I gave the other guy, I'll give you any information you need, and I'll warn you as I warned him—"

Meredith cocked his head, always interested in warnings.

"Diane is nuts. She's an overgrown flower child, a twenty-seven-year-old hippie who's too young even to know what that means. She didn't want me, she didn't want our child. Too conventional. Too bourgeois. Of course, she also didn't want to use birth control pills while we were married," he said bitterly. "Too much risk of cancer, she said. You run a greater risk of getting run over by a truck on the highway, I said. It's not your body, she said. Which is the same thing she said when I stopped her from having the abortion. It may not be my body, I said, but it's sure as hell my child. I don't know how far she'll go to spite me, but . . ." Peters shook his head. "I'm afraid . . ."

"Of what, exactly?"

"That Diane will abandon my son. Or kill him."

"Kill her own child?"

There was a moment of silence, and then Peters said, "What do you think abortion is, Mr. Meredith?"

"What do I do when I find them?"

"Call me, but not if it means letting her out of your sight. If you so much as suspect that she'll run with him again, then take him."

"Steal the baby, just grab him? I can't—"

Peters interrupted him. "She has no rights."

Meredith was not convinced, but he thought of something else that settled the argument for him. "Okay, but it'll cost a lot more if I have to do it that way."

"Of course." The father of the child pulled back a slat of the vertical blinds and stared outside again. Meredith could barely hear his next words. "Everything costs more than you think it will."

The grandmother of the child, on the father's side, showed the private investigator her son's baby book.

"This is Chad as a baby; I'm showing you this because he looked just like my grandson. I got to see Brook in the hospital before she stole him away. Brook is a beautiful baby, just like his daddy was—look at all of that dark hair! I remember the doctor joking. He said, 'Mrs. Peters, if we'd given him a haircut, you wouldn't have had to have a C-section!' Take this picture with you, Mr. Meredith. If you find a baby who looks like this, it's Brook." She was a young and pretty grandmother, and she gazed at him with sad hope in her eyes. "Maybe you could have some copies made? Put them up in truck stops, or something?"

"Where do you think she took him, Mrs. Peters?"

She sighed, and he watched the hope fade from her eyes as the breath escaped from her mouth. "If there were still such a thing as a Haight-Ashbury, she would have taken him there. She was so strange and emotional all the time, Mr. Meredith, I always suspected she must be on drugs. I don't know why Chad married her, although she's pretty, I'd have to say that she's very pretty. Chad always wanted a family, especially children. That could be one reason he married a woman so much younger than he is. And maybe he thought she was fun for a while, so much younger and freer in her behavior, you know."

She was working her wedding band, rubbing it up and down on her finger. Her eyes filled and her voice cracked on her next words.

"I think my worst fear is that she'll sell him, for money, for drugs."

"She isn't a very responsible person," her best friend confided to the private investigator, as they sat together in her kitchen drinking sun tea from an iced pitcher she had set on the table between them. "I told the other guy that, too. I'll be straight with you, like I was with him. I love her like a sister, but she was always a little crazy. Like she'd fall for these guys, and she'd just move in with them after one date! Crazy. Nobody does that anymore. It's not . . . responsible. AIDS, and herpes and serial killers and all that. You can't trust people like you used to. But Diane always trusted everybody." Her mouth twisted into an expression of wry bitterness. "At least she did until she met Chad. He taught her that there are people in this world you can only trust to use you. He's like that, incredibly controlling. You'll do things Chad's way, or else. Diane was always so flaky, she must have looked like somebody he could mold, you know? Like turn her into this sweet, obedient little wife." The best friend looked up at Meredith, and laughed. "Boy, was he wrong."

"Why didn't she want to have the baby?"

"Why should she?"

"What?"

"I said, why should she want to have one?"

"I don't know. I thought every woman did."

"No." She didn't say it in an unfriendly way, but just as a statement of fact. He felt a little amazed at that.

"Then why did she keep it and run away with it?"

Her best friend smiled. "He was really cute."

"The baby? Is that the reason, because he was so cute?"

"I don't know, it could be. You probably think she's a bad person because she didn't want to have a baby and because she wanted to abort it. But she isn't. She didn't love Chad and she didn't want to have a baby, especially with him, that's all. You could say that when she *met* her baby, she fell for him." Her best friend grinned. "I told you, she was always falling in love at first sight. So just because she didn't want him before, doesn't mean she might not want him when he got here. Sure, she ran away with him, but it wouldn't be the first time she ran off with some guy."

Ken Meredith found himself feeling very confused, as if he'd wandered into a thicket of femaleness where he was lost without a map. He thought of the first PI, and pictured him running off with nutty Diane Peters and her baby. She'd keep him around only until they spent the money, that's what she'd do, and then she'd split again. Although, if she was half as good looking as her pictures, maybe that wasn't such a bad way for a guy to make a fool of himself, even if it was just for a little while. Meredith felt like laughing. The heat was getting to him, he decided. He sucked an ice cube into his mouth, to chill himself back into reality.

"But she took him away from his father," he said, talking around the melting cube.

"Well, of course," her best friend said, and then leaned forward to add patiently, as though to someone slow and stupid. "Chad's a lawyer, you know. Chad got custody, in the divorce settlement, and Diane gave up all visitation rights, because she didn't think she wanted the baby. He would have taken the baby away from her forever."

"The baby she didn't want, right?"

"Before. Not after." She screwed up her face so that

she looked very intense, as if she were trying to convince him of something. "Mr. Meredith, can you imagine how it'd feel if other people *made* you grow a baby inside of you?" She touched her hands to her abdomen. "It'd be horrible." Her long fingernails scraped the fabric of her yellow shorts. "You'd feel like you wanted to tear it out of you with your bare hands."

"Then why didn't she just go ahead and abort it?"

"Chad told her he'd send her to prison."

Meredith doubted that could happen, but he wasn't sure, so he just said, "Where'd she go with the baby?"

The best friend leaned back, and grinned again. "I'm going to tell you?"

Meredith sighed. He wondered if the other PI had also felt like strangling this woman, if she had said that to him, too.

"No, really," she said quickly, as if sensing that she'd gone too far. "Honestly, I don't know, although it's true that I wouldn't tell you if I did. But I don't, really."

"What's she using for money?"

The best friend shrugged. "From the divorce. And she's got a car, she could go a long way." The last phrase was accompanied by a swift, sly glance, as if she hoped to persuade him that it was useless to look.

"Mr. Peters is afraid she might abandon the baby."

She looked angry. "No way."

"His mother thinks she might sell the baby for drugs."

That produced a laugh. "Yeah, right."

"But you said yourself that she's irresponsible."

She rubbed her nose and thought about it. "I guess . . . I guess what I'm afraid of is that she won't have the sense to keep him out of this heat. What if she goes into a grocery store, or something, and she leaves him sleeping in her car? You know what she said to me one time? She said, I don't see why you couldn't just leave a baby in the house for ten minutes while you ran to the grocery store. Can you believe that? My God, I told her, in ten minutes—less than that—a house could burn down!" The best friend nibbled on her lower lip. "What if Diane does something dumb like that? He could . . . die . . ." She looked up at him, the laughter gone. "Okay. Well, I don't know where she went, but she loves nature. She always wanted to live on a farm, out in the country. You might look there."

He thought of all the Midwest, most of it countryside, all of it baking under the 104-degree sun, and he shook his head, and smiled. "You couldn't be a little more specific?"

"Well, you might try the Flint Hills," she said. "Diane thinks it's beautiful out there." The best friend shuddered. "Gives me the creeps, all that open space."

"Thanks," he said, getting up. By advising him to "try the Flint Hills," she had narrowed it down to only about a couple of million acres of open country.

"How'd you get to be a private eye?" she asked him.

Abruptly, he sat down again. The best friend was attractive and he was divorced and loath to go out into the 100-plus heat again. "I ought to warn you that I'm not really a very nice person," he said, surprising both of them. "What I do, sometimes it's shitty, like spying on unsuspecting people, like that. You might think, well, if a husband's playing around, he's got it coming, but you might be surprised to find out that he's the nice one, and the wife who hired me, she's the bitch. Or maybe it's the husband who hired me and he's a jerk, and his wife, the one I'm following around, she's okay. But I'm working for whoever's paying me, that's the bottom line for me."

"You think Chad's a jerk?" she asked him, smiling a little.

"No, no, I didn't say that. You wouldn't have a beer, would you?"

Ken Meredith figured that the first investigator had also gotten a line on the possibility that the mother and child were hiding in the Flint Hills. According to Peters, the first guy had made his last report from a Rodeway Inn on I–35 at Emporia. Said he was following a lead. Meredith had laughed to himself when he heard that: sure, we're all following leads, even when we're sitting on our butts in air-conditioned motel rooms watching HBO. What the first guy had followed was the money, Meredith figured, and he'd followed it right on down the road.

In the first couple of days after getting the job from Chad Peters, Meredith followed his usual routine for dis-

dred dollars' worth of canned goods, diet Cokes, and other imperishables.

That told him she was staying around there, somewhere within driving vicinity of Council Groves. To figure out where, he sought the help of the sheriff.

The sheriff showed Ken Meredith a map of the county and pointed out to him the locations of empty and abandoned buildings. "If she's not staying with friends someplace, or if somebody hasn't taken her in, then my bet is that she'd holed up with the baby in one of these vacant places," the sheriff said. "Some of them are in falling-down condition, I mean she'd have to be crazy for sure to live in one of them, but one or two of them are nice places that belong to absentee landowners. Like this ranch—" He penciled an X on a thin line of road on the map. "I suppose she could be camped out, but I think somebody'd notice her, where they wouldn't necessarily if she kept inside of one of these old barns or houses."

By the time he was finished at the sheriff's office, Ken Meredith had a map and a list of rural addresses and directions on how to get to each place. He also had instructions to include the sheriff's office in any action he might be forced to take that might require legal, possibly armed, assistance.

It was easy, he thought, as he got back into his car, when you knew how to do it. He was so damned hot, though, and annoyed at this woman for running away and causing him so much aggravation in such miserable weather. He pictured himself spending the next days driving for miles over dirt and gravel roads, raising clouds of brown dust. What if his car overheated out in the middle of nowhere? What if he busted an oil pan or a tire?

Meredith could almost sympathize with the other private investigator for taking off with the money and saying to hell with the selfish bitch.

The mother of the child climbed the hill behind the cabin every day, sometimes carrying Brook to the top in a papoose sack strapped to her back, other times climbing alone while the baby napped in the cabin. The hill was her Indian lookout, where she'd found an arrowhead that she wore around her neck on a string like an amulet.

The cabin she called her "safe" house. When she'd found it, it was empty except for a broken-leg table and a leftover wooden stool. Diane had cleaned its filthy kitchen, the bathroom, and all the rest of it. There she settled in with Brook, stocking the cupboards with the pans, food, and supplies she purchased after she fled from the hospital, making beds on the floor for both of them out of stolen hospital blankets and thrift store sheets.

Nobody bothered them. Sometimes she longed for the sound of traffic, for a telephone, and especially for a television. At those moments, she felt ashamed of her weakness. Then she reminded herself that she loved the cabin, its isolation, the eerie quiet, the pitch-dark nights that made her feel as if she were as courageous as the early prairie mothers.

She even loved the heat and dryness of the drought.

It seemed, on some days, to evaporate her, so that she felt as if she'd disappeared entirely. On other days, it baked her into a calm, stolid passivity that felt like endurance. The two of them, mother and child, had themselves and Diane's full breasts and canned goods in the cupboards and the cabin and the enveloping, comforting heat.

One day after lunch, in the third month of their disappearance, when the baby was asleep in the cabin, Diane climbed to the top of the hill. The brown grass, hard and prickly as straight pins, crackled under her tennis shoes so that she felt as if she were climbing a tinfoil mountain.

As she climbed, the sun felt like a warm body pressed against her, sweating against her, and it filled her with a different, but very familiar kind of longing. At the top, she stripped out of her halter top, her jeans, her panties, even her shoes. Stepping carefully on the flint pebbles and the grass that cut her feet, she stood on the hilltop, feeling like a tiny, invisible speck of life in an immense, dying landscape.

She could see no one.

No one could see her.

She lifted her arms above her head, so her hair fell down her back, and she closed her eyes and faced the sun. She hummed, the sort of tuneless song she thought an Indian woman might have hummed, a propitiation, and a prayer of gratitude to the sun.

The heat embraced her.

After a moment, she turned her face away from the sun and opened her eyes.

Down the dirt lane, dust was moving.

A deer? Diane lowered her arms to her sides, smiling at the thought of a deer—perhaps the antlered stag she had seen—and herself alone on the prairie, two natural creatures in a wilderness. . . .

The dust moved, and cleared, and she saw a man walking down the dirt road.

The shock of seeing a human being on the lane was so great that for a moment she didn't move. Then she dropped to the ground, wincing as the sharp grass and rocks bit her bare skin. Frantic with haste and fear, she worked herself back into the halter, jeans, and shoes, leaving the panties where they lay. When she looked up again, the man was closer, walking without any sound she could hear, keeping to the shade of the cottonwood trees, but coming steadily, as if he had a purpose in mind.

From behind the old tractor, with shaking hands and racing heart, she observed him.

He was tall, thin, with straight brown hair that shone when the sun hit it, as if it were greasy. The man wore city shoes and cheap-looking trousers and a short-sleeve blue shirt, opened three buttons at the neck so that his white T-shirt showed beneath it. He kept to the shadows, walking with his eyes on his shoes, except that every few seconds, he glanced up at the cabin. He didn't look at the top of the hill. Was that because he had already spied her there?

"Who are you?" she whispered, her mouth gone as dry as the ground around her.

With a single long stride, the man stepped out from the shade of the cottonwoods, and began the long walk up the driveway. Diane strained to hear the sound of gravel under his shoes. Why would a stranger walk up her gravel drive in the middle of the broiling day? There were many possible reasons, but only one likely one. She stared at him so hard her eyes squinted to slits in the sun, as if she were trying to probe through that long skull into the reasons he held in his brain, as if she were trying to will him away, away! He had a long, tired face, and he looked angry, as if the heat had provoked him.

She watched him walk up the two steps to the back door.

Now he stood between her and the baby, and she felt it acutely. The three of them were in a line now—Diane crouching at the top of the rise, the stranger at the door, and the baby sleeping in the cabin.

Ken Meredith cupped his hands, making binoculars out of them, and peered through the window that was set into the back door of the little cabin. He couldn't see into the dark interior, so he drew back and walked around the house, trying to look into the other windows. But they were all curtained against the sun. Or against somebody looking in them, and maybe seeing something hidden in there?

Instead of knocking, he placed his hand on the doorknob.

"What are you doing!"

Startled, he turned quickly and looked toward the sound of the woman's voice. He saw her now, standing at the top of the rise behind the cabin. At first, he thought he was hallucinating in the heat, because what he thought he saw was a wild-haired, copper-skinned Indian woman above him. But then he saw that it was Diane Peters, all right, and that she was holding a good-size rock in her right hand.

He held his hands high, open wide, to display innocence.

He had the unnerving feeling of having aroused something ancient and primitive from deep within the flint hills of the prairie. He was not normally an introspective man, or even a sensitive one, but Meredith knew fear when he saw it, and raw, dangerous fury.

He put down his hands, easily, appeasingly.

"Ran out of gas, ma'am. Use your phone?"

His heart beat twice before she said, "You'll have to go somewhere else."

The private investigator pretended to slump against the back door screen. "I don't think I can," he called tiredly up to her, and smiled as charmingly as he knew how. "Ma'am, I've already walked about five miles in these darned shoes, and if I don't get a drink of water, I'm going to die right here on your stoop. Please, If you could even make the call for me, I'll leave, and wait back down the road for the tow truck."

"I thought you said you ran out of gas."

He coughed into his hands before he squinted up at her again. "I don't know for sure that's the problem, ma'am. Could be a dead battery, or maybe it's just this heat that killed it, you know how cars are, they're like us people, can't take too much pressure." He smiled again, inviting her to smile down, to climb down the hill to him.

Instead, she shifted her weight, lifting the rock for a moment as she did so.

Instinctively, Meredith stepped back, though he tried to disguise the movement as meaningless and as casual as a man shaking dirt out of his shoe. But he knew that she had seen it and recognized that no man with just an empty gas tank on his mind would move so quickly, so defensively.

"Go away," she said in a tough voice.

He pursed his lips, as if he were thinking that over, but then he shook his head at her, almost sadly, as if he were disappointed in her.

The man suddenly cocked his head toward the cabin.

Oh my God, Diane thought, he's heard the baby.

One of his hands disappeared from her view, and she realized he was opening the cabin door.

Through the open windows, filtered through the curtains and the dusty screens, came the crying sounds of a baby waking up. The man shot her a look that had cunning in it. Quickly, he turned his back on her and faced the door.

"No!" Diane screamed. "Stay out of there!"

She ran down the hill at him, and reached the stoop just as he was about to shut the door in her face. Diane shoved her weight at the door, forcing it open.

"Damn, lady!"

The door pushed Meredith backward, and he was laughing a little, as though in astonishment at her strength. "Now hold on, Diane, let's just talk about this . . ." His arms flew up to protect his head as she flung herself at him with the rock. ". . . your husband's got a right to see his baby. . . ."

The baby began to wail in the bedroom.

"No!" She brought the rock down on the side of Meredith's face. Blood ran into his eyes, blinding him, and then into his open, astonished mouth, choking him. "No, no, no!" With every scream, she struck him, until he slumped to the floor.

Her hands lost their strength, and the rock fell out of them.

The man was still breathing.

After a moment, Diane stepped over him.

She washed her hands at the sink, and then ran to the screaming baby. With the stranger out of her sight, around the bend of the L-shaped room, she nursed Brook back to tranquillity,

"I will never let anyone take you away from me."

She whispered it over and over, in a singsong, like a lullaby.

The idea had come to her as she had lain in her own blood on the delivery table, the very moment they laid at her breast the baby that Chad had forced her to bear, and which he would now force her to give up forever. She had stared at the tiny face and thought: This is what Chad wants more than anything else in the world. And suddenly she had known what to do. She would take the baby! By running away with the child, she would make Chad suffer every day for the rest of his life. Lying on the delivery table with the baby in her arms, Diane had felt the first stirring of love . . . and the vicious, soul-deep satisfaction of perfect revenge. Nobody will ever take this child away from me, she had sworn at that moment. Nobody. Ever.

While the baby kicked his legs happily on the cabin floor, Diane pulled the unconscious man deep into the cold, damp darkness of the storm cellar where the other man's body lay, and then she walked out and bolted the door. This time, she didn't take his wallet to see what his name was, or how old he was, or to see if he had any pictures in his wallet of a wife or little children. This time she didn't want to know anything about him, not even if he carried a private investigator's license, like the first one. She did remove his keys, however, and then set out walking until she found his car a half mile down the road. She drove it into the same barn where her own car was stored, and then abandoned the vehicles to the owls and rats. Back at the cabin, Diane scrubbed the linoleum floor, while her jeans and halter top soaked in cold water in the sink.

In the morning, the baby giggled at the sight of the deer in the pasture.

The drought carried on into September.

In Kansas City, Chad Peters hired a third private eye, this one a former cop by the name of Ed Banks.

In the country, every day after lunch, Diane climbed the rise behind the house. The heat was such that she began taking her clothes off inside the cabin and going naked in the afternoon. The sun baked her skin to brown and warmed the milk in her heavy breasts.

At the top of the rise, she raised her arms to the sun, her hair fell down her back like an Indian blanket, and she closed her eyes. When she opened them, she gazed down, looking for dust devils blowing up the long, dirt road.

AMONG MY SOUVENIRS

By Sharyn McCrumb

The face was a little blurry, but she was used to seeing it that way. She must have looked at it a thousand times in old magazines—grainy black-and-white shots, snapped by a magazine photographer at a nightclub; amateurish candid photos on the back of record albums; misty publicity stills that erased even the pores of his skin. She knew that face. A poster-size version of it had stared down at her from beneath the high school banner on her bedroom wall—twenty-odd years ago. God, had it been that long? Now the face was blurry with booze, fatigue, and the sagging of a jawline that was no longer boyish. But it was still him, sitting in the bar, big as life.

Maggie used to wonder what she would do if she met him in the flesh. In the tenth grade she and Kathy Ryan used to philosophize about such things at slumber parties: "Why don't you fix your hair like Connie Stevens'?"—"Which Man From U.N.C.L.E. do you like best?"—"What would you do if you met Devlin Robey?" Then they'd collapse in giggles, unable even to fantasize meeting a real, live rock 'n' roll singer. He lived a glamorous life of limousines and penthouse suites while they suffered through gym class, and algebra with Mrs. Cady. Growing up seemed a hundred years away.

When Maggie was a senior, she did get to see Devlin Robey—when you live on Long Island, sooner or later your prince will come. Everybody comes to the Big Apple. But the encounter was as distant and unreal as the airbrushed poster on her closet door. Devlin Robey was a shining blur glimpsed on a distant stage, and Maggie was a tiny speck in a sea of screaming adolescents.

She and Kathy squealed and cried and threw paper roses at the stage, but it didn't really feel like *seeing* him. He was a lot clearer on the television screen when she watched *American Bandstand*. After the concert, they had fought their way through a horde of fans to reach the stage door, only to be driven off by three thugs in overcoats—Mr. Robey's "handlers," while Devlin himself plowed his way through the throng to a waiting limousine, oblivious to the screams of protest in his wake.

They cried all the way home.

Maggie was so disillusioned by her idol's callous behavior that she wrote him a letter, in care of his record company, complaining about how he let his fans be treated. She enclosed her ticket stub from the concert, and one of her wallet-size class pictures. A few weeks later, she received an autographed eight by ten of Devlin Robey, a copy of his latest album, and a handwritten apology on Epic Records notepaper. He said he was sorry to rush past them like that, but that he'd had to hurry back to the hotel to call his mother, who had been ill that night. He hoped that Maggie would forgive him for his thoughtlessness, and he promised to visit with his fans after concerts whenever he possibly could.

That letter was enough magic to keep Maggie going for weeks, and she played the album until it was scarred from wear, but eventually the wonder of it faded, and the memory, like the albums and fan magazines, was packed away in tissue paper in the closet of her youth, while Maggie got on with her life.

She took business courses, and made mostly B's. She thought she'd probably end up as a secretary somewhere after high school. It was no use thinking about college: her parents didn't have that kind of money, and if they had, they wouldn't have spent it sending her off to get more educated. Since she'd just end up getting married anyway, her father reasoned, wasting her time and their savings on a fancy education made no sense. Maggie wished she could have taken shop or auto mechanics like the guys did, but the guidance counselor had smiled and vetoed the suggestion. Home economics and typing: that's what girls took. He was sure that Maggie would be happier in one of those courses, where she belonged. Now, sometimes, when the plumbing needed fixing or the toaster wouldn't work, Maggie wished she had insisted on being allowed to take practical courses, so that she wouldn't have to use the grocery money to pay repair bills, but it was no use looking back, she figured. What's done was done.

The summer after high school, Maggie married Leon Holtz, who wasn't as handsome as Devlin Robey, but he was real. He said he loved her, and he rented a sky-blue tux and bought her a white gardenia corsage when he took her to the senior prom. There wasn't any reason not to get married, that Maggie could see. Leon had a construction job in his uncle's business, and she was a clerk at the Ford dealership, which meant nearly six hundred a month in take-home pay after taxes. They could afford a small apartment, and some furniture from Sofa City, so why wait? If Maggie had any flashes of prewedding jitters about happily-ever-after with Leon, or any lingering regrets at relinquishing dreams of some other existence, where one could actually know people like Devlin Robey—if she had misgivings about any of it, she gave no sign.

Richie was born fourteen months later. The marriage lasted until he was two. He was a round-faced, solemn child with his mother's brown eyes, but he had scoliosis—which is doctor talk for a crook-back—so there were medical bills on top of everything else, and finally, Leon, fed up with the confinement of wedded poverty, took off. Maggie moved to Manhattan, because she figured the pay would be better, especially if she forgot about being a clerk. She was just twenty-one, then, and her looks were still okay.

After a couple of false starts, she got a job as a cocktail waitress in the Red Lion Lounge. She didn't like the red velvet uniform that came to the top of her thighs, or the black net stockings she had to wear with it, but the tips were good, and Maggie supposed that the outfit had a lot to do with that. She was twenty-seven now. Sometimes, when her feet throbbed from spending six hours in spike heels and her face ached from smiling at jerks who like to put the make on waitresses, she'd think about the high school shop classes, wondering what life would have been like if she'd learned how to fix cars.

"You want to bring me a drink?" He smiled up at her

lazily. The ladies man who is sure of his magnetism. *You want to bring me a drink?* Like he was conferring a privilege on her. Well, maybe he was. Maggie looked down at Devlin Robey's blurring middle-aged features, and thought with surprise that once she would have been honored to serve this man. Would have fought for the chance to do it. But that was half a lifetime ago. Now she was just tired, trying to get through the shift with enough money to pay the phone bill. She'd been up most of the night before with one of Richie's back aches, and now she felt as if she were sleepwalking. She stared at the graying curls of chest hair at the top of his purple shirt, the pouches under his eyes that were darker than his fading tan, and the plastic smile. What the hell.

"Sure," she said with no more than her customary brightness, "A drink. What do you want?"

When she brought back the Dewar's-rocks, he was reading the racing news, but as she approached, he set the page aside and smiled up at her. "Thanks," he said, and then after a beat: "You know who I am?"

It struck her as kind of sad the way he asked it. Hesitant, like he had heard "no" too many times lately, as if each denial of his fame cut the lines deeper into his face. She felt sorry for him. Wished it were twenty years ago. But it wasn't. "Yeah," said Maggie, smoothing out the napkin as she set down his drink. "Yeah, I remember. You're Devlin Robey. I seen you sing once."

The lines smoothed out and his eyes widened: you could just see the teen idol somewhere in there. "No kiddin'!" he said, with a laugh that sounded like sheer relief. "Well, here . . ." That ought to be good for a twenty, Maggie was thinking, but as she watched, Devlin Robey pulled the cocktail napkin out from under his drink and signed his name with a flourish.

"Thanks," said Maggie, slipping the napkin into her pocket with the tips. Maybe the twenty would come later. At least it would be something to tell Kathy Ryan if she ever saw her again. She started to move away to another table, but he touched her arm. "Don't leave yet. So, you heard me sing, huh? At Paradise Alley?"

She told him where the concert had been, and for a moment she thought of mentioning her letter to him, but the two suits at table nine were waving like their tongues might shrivel up, so she eased out of his grasp. "I'll check on you in a few," she promised, summoning her smile for the thirsting suits.

For the rest of her shift, Maggie alternated between real customers and the wistful face of Devlin Robey, who ordered drinks just for the small talk that came with them. "Which one of my songs did you like best?"

" 'I'm Afraid to Go Home,' " said Maggie instantly, and when he looked puzzled, she reminded him, "It was the B side to 'Tiger Lily.' "

"Yeah! Yeah! I almost got an award for that one." His eyes crinkled with pleasure.

Another round he wanted to know if she'd seen him in the beach movie he made for Buena Vista. She remembered the movie, and didn't say that she couldn't place him in it. It had been a bit part, leading nowhere. After that he went back to singing, mostly in Vegas. Now in Atlantic City. "They love me in the casinos," he told her. "The folks from the 'burbs go wild over me—makes 'em remember the good times, they tell me."

Maggie tried to remember some good times, but all she found was stills of her and Kathy Ryan listening to records and talking about the future. She was going to be a fashion model and live in Paris. Kathy would be a vet in an African Wildlife Preserve. They would spend holidays together in the Bahamas. "You want some peanuts to go with that drink?" Maggie asked.

At two o'clock the Red Lion was closing, but Devlin Robey had not budged. He kept nursing a Dewar's that was more water than Scotch, hunched down like a stray dog who didn't want to be thrown out in the street. Maggie wondered what was wrong with the guy. He was rich and famous, right?

"Are you about finished with that drink? Boss says it's quittin' time."

"Yeah, yeah. I'm a night owl, I guess. All those years of doing casino shows at eleven. Seems like the shank of the evening to me." He glanced at his watch, and then at her: the red velvet tunic, the black fishnet stockings, the cleavage. "You're getting off work now?"

The smile never wavered but inside she groaned. Tonight had seemed about two days long, and all that kept her going was the thought of a hot bubble bath to soak

her feet and the softness of clean sheets to sink into
before she passed out from sheer weariness. So now—
twenty years too late to be an answer to prayer—Devlin
Robey wants to take her out. Where was he when it
would have mattered?

"I'm sorry," she said. "Thanks anyway, but not tonight." *Maybe ten years ago, but not tonight.*

The one answer she wouldn't have made back when
she was Devlin Robey's vestal virgin turned out to be
the only one that worked the charm. Suddenly his half-
hearted invitation became urgent. "I'll be straight with
you," he said, with eyes like stained glass. "I'm feeling
kind of down tonight, and I thought it might help to
spend some time with an old friend."

Is that what we were? Maggie thought. *I was twenty-
five rows back at the concert; I was on the other side of
the speakers when WABC's Cousin Brucie played your
records; and while you were airbrushed and glossy, I was
wearing Clearisil and holding the fan magazine. We were
friends?* She didn't say it, though. If Maggie had learned
anything in seven years as a cocktail waitress, it was not
to reply to outrageous statements. She shrugged. "I'm
sorry," thinking that would be the end of it. Wondering
if she'd even bother to tell anybody about it. It wouldn't
be any fun to talk about if you had to explain to the
other waitresses, bunch of kids, who Devlin Robey was.

"At least give me your phone number—uh—Maggie."
Her name was signed with a flourish on his check: *Thank
you! Maggie.* "I get to the city every so often. Maybe I
could call you, give you more notice. We could set something up. You're all right. You ever think about the
business?"

No. Show business offered the same hours as nightclub waitressing, and besides she couldn't sing or dance.
But Lana Turner had been discovered in a drugstore, so
maybe . . . After all, who was Maggie Holtz to slap the
hand of fate? She tore off the business expense tab from
the Red Lion check, and scribbled her name and phone
number across it. "Sure. Why not," she said. "Call me
sometime."

She patted the autographed cocktail napkin folded in
the pocket with her tips, wondering if Richie would like
to have it for his scrapbook. Or maybe she should put

it in his baby book: *the guy I was pretending to make it with the night you were conceived.* Two scraps of paper; one for each of them to toss. She figured that would be the end of it.

It wasn't, though. Four nights later—four a.m.—the Advil had finally kicked in, allowing her to plunge into sleep, when the phone screamed, dragging her back. She'd forgotten to turn on the damned answering machine. She grabbed for the receiver, only to reinstate the silence, but his voice came through to her, a little swacked, crooning, "I'm Afraid To Go Home," and she knew it was him.

"Devlin Robey," she said, wondering why wishes got granted only when you no longer wanted them.

"Maggie doll." He slurred her name. "I just wanted a friendly voice. I got the blues so bad."

"Hangover?"

"No. That'll be after I wake up—if I ever get to sleep, that is. Thought I might get sleepy talking about old times, you know?"

"Old times."

"I lost big tonight at the tables. I played seventeen in roulette a dozen times and it wouldn't come up for me. Seventeen—my number!"

She caught herself nodding forward, and forced the number seventeen to roll around in her memories. Oh, yeah. " 'Seventeen, My Heaven Teen,' " she murmured. "That was your big hit, wasn't it?"

"I got a Cashbox Award for that one. S'in the den at my place in Vegas. Maybe I'll show it to you some time."

"Wouldn't your wife object?"

She heard him sigh. "Jeez, Trina. What a cow. She was a showgirl when I married her. Ninety-five pounds of blonde. Now she acts like giving me a blow job is a major act of charity, and she's in the tanning salon so much she looks like a leather Barbie doll. Not that I'm home much. I'm on the road a lot."

"Yeah. It's a tough life." She pictured him in a suite the size of her apartment. Maybe one of those sunken tubs in a black marble bathroom.

"It's not like I'm too keen to go home, you know? I have a daughter, Claudia, but jeez it breaks my heart to see her. She was born premature. Probably 'cause Trina was always trying to barf up her dinner to stay skinny. She's never been right, Claudia hasn't. Brain damage at birth. But she always smile so big when she sees me, and throws her little arms out."

"How old is she?"

"Twelve, I guess. I always picture her when she was little. She was beautiful when she was three all over. Now she's just three inside. Her birthday is the seventeenth of June. My lucky number. Seventeen."

"Not tonight, though, huh?"

"No. Tonight it cost me plenty. I shouldn't bet when I'm loaded. Loaded drunk, I mean; the other kind is never an issue. I like to be with people, though. I'd like to be with you. You don't have an ax to grind. You're not like these glitter tarts here, running around in feathers, can't remember past nineteen-seventy-five. You're good people, Maggie. Look, can I come over some time?"

"I bet you get lotsa offers," said Maggie, hoping somebody else would take the heat.

"I like you," he said. "You're real. Like my kid. Not just some hardass in the chorus line with a Pepsodent smile and an angle. I've had a bellyful of them."

She shouldn't have let him tell her about his kid. It made her think of Richie, and made her think that maybe Devlin Robey hadn't had it all his way like she'd figured. All of a sudden, he wasn't just some glossy poster that she could toss when she tired of it. He was a regular guy with feelings. And maybe she owed him. After all, she had used him as her fantasy all those years ago. Maybe it was time to pay up.

"Okay, like Tuesday? That's when I'm off." She could send Richie to her folks in Rockaway. They kept talking until his voice slurred into unconsciousness.

"Your monogamous john is here," said Cap the bartender, nodding toward table seven.

"Yeah," said Maggie. She'd already seen Devlin Robey come in, trying to look casual. He came three days a month now, whenever he could get away from his casino gig. Sometimes it was her night off, and if it wasn't, he'd sit at number seven until closing times, nursing a Dewars-water, and trying to keep a conversation going as Maggie edged her way past to wait on the paying customers.

On her nights off, they'd eat Italian, which meant mostly vino for Devlin Robey, and then go back to her place for sex. Robey was only good for once a night, so he liked to prolong it with kinky stuff, strip shows, and listening to Maggie talk dirty, which she found she could do while her mind focused on planning her grocery list for the coming week, and thinking what she needed to take to the cleaners. She felt sorry for Robey, because he had been famous once, and the coddling he received as a star had crippled him for life. He couldn't get used to people not being kind anymore; to being ignored by all the regular folks who used to envy him. Whereas she'd had a lifetime of getting used to the world's indifference. But he had been her idol, and he had once stooped down to be kind to her, a nobody, with a beautiful, sincere handwritten letter. So now he needed somebody, so it was Payback. And Payback is a Mother. She thought about how famous he was while he grunted and strained on top of her. She pictured that airbrushed poster on her wall.

"Maybe you should charge him," said Cap, as she was about to walk away.

"I ain't on the game," said Maggie.

"Didn't say you were. But you're providing a service. Shrinks charge, don't they? And they got more money than you, Maggie dearest."

She shrugged. "Some things aren't about money."

"Well, if money is no object with you, you can leave early tonight. You might as well. It's dead in here."

He said it too loud. Devlin Robey heard him, and she saw his face light up. No use telling him she was stuck here now. Thanks a heap, Cap. At least Richie was gone—sleeping over at Kevin's tonight. Devlin Robey was already putting his coat on by the time she reached his table. "Boy, am I glad we can get outta here! I'm afraid I might have company tonight."

His face was even more like a fish belly than usual, and his eyes sagged into dark pouches. "What do you mean, company?" asked Maggie, glancing toward the door.

"Tell you later."

They went to a different Italian restaurant, but it had the same oilcloth table covers, and the same vino, which he drank in equal quantities to the usual stuff, and she had the angel hair pasta, less rubbery than that of the old place. He wouldn't talk about *company,* while they were eating, but he kept looking around, and he whispered, even when he was just talking to her. She had to get him back to her place—in a cab, because he was scared to walk—and get two cups of black decaf down him, before he'd open up.

"Tell me," she said, and she wasn't being Fantasy Girl this time.

"It's okay." He took a thick brown envelope out of the breast pocket of his suit, and laid it on top of the stack of *Redbook* and *Enquirer*s. "I got it covered, see? Most of it anyhow. I think it's enough to call the dogs off."

"You've been gambling again," she said.

"Hey, sooner or later 'Seventeen' will sing for me again, right?"

"So you owe some pretty heavy people, I guess."

He shrugged, palms up. "It's Atlantic City. They're not Boy Scouts. I was supposed to meet them tonight with the cash, but I was a little short. Had to come up here, hock some things. Borrow what I could from a home boy, and hope I got it together before they came looking for me. Now I'm okay. I can take the meeting. It's not all there, but it's enough to keep me going. I wrote a note with it, promising more next week. I got record royalties coming."

Maggie's eyes narrowed. "Why'd you want to see me?"

"Not for money!" He laughed a little. "Maggie, this is way out of your league, doll. You just keep your stash in that cookie jar of yours, and let me worry about these gentlemen. I just came to see you 'cause I love you."

He probably does, Maggie thought sadly as she led him to the bedroom. He can see the reflection of the record album poster in my eyes.

It was past two when she got up to take a leak. Robey had been asleep for hours, sated with sweat and swear words. She saw the envelope lying on the coffee table, and scooped it up as she passed. Might as well see how deep he's in, she thought. Was saving a fallen idol part of the deal? Maybe she could talk him into getting counseling. Gamblers Anonymous, or something. She wondered why dead and famous were the only two choices some people seemed to want.

She didn't go back to bed. When Robey woke up at nine, she gave him aspirin and Bloody Mary Mix for his hangover, and a plastic cup of decaf for the road, but no kiss. He was headed back to Atlantic City, still too sleepy and hung over for pleasantries. Devlin Robey was not a morning person. Neither was Maggie Holtz, but this morning she was wide awake. She sat in front of the television, listening to the game shows, but watching the phone. It rang at five past noon. The answering machine kicked in, and after it said its piece, she heard Devlin Robey's famous, not-so-velvet voice, now shrill in the speaker. "Maggie! Are you there? Pick up! It's me. Listen, you know that envelope I told you about? The one with the cash in it. Listen, I must have left it at your place. There are some gentlemen here who need to know I had it. Could you just pick up, Maggie? Could you tell them about the cash in the envelope, please? It's important."

She heard another voice say, "Real important."

Maggie picked up the phone. "I never saw any envelope, Devlin," she said. "Can't you just stall those guys like you said you would? Till you get some money?"

She heard him cry out as she was replacing the receiver. She set the brown envelope back on the table. There were a lot of hundreds inside it, but that wasn't the point. Some things aren't about money. It was the letter that mattered, the one he wrote to the gamblers asking for more time to pay in full. That wasn't anything like the handwriting she'd seen on his other letter, the one she'd received so long ago containing an apology from "Devlin Robey." So she really didn't owe him anything. She owed herself a lot of years. She wondered how much it would cost to go to trade school, and if the bills in the brown envelope would cover it. Maggie wanted to learn to fix things.

TANTALIZING MYSTERY ANTHOLOGIES

MYSTERY ANTHOLOGIES

☐ **MURDER ON TRIAL** *13 Courtroom Mysteries By the Masters of Detection.* Attorney and clients, judges and prosecutors, witnesses and victims all meet in this perfect locale for outstanding mystery fiction. Now, subpoenaed from the pages of *Alfred Hitchcock's Mystery Magazine and Ellery Queen Mystery Magazine*—with the sole motive of entertaining you—are tales brimming with courtroom drama. (177215—$4.99)

☐ **MURDER FOR MOTHER by Ruth Rendell, Barbara Collins, Billie Sue Mosiman, Bill Crider, J. Madison Davis, Wendy Hornsby, and twelve more.** These eighteen works of short fiction celebrate Mother's Day with a gift of great entertainment . . . a story collection that every mystery-loving mama won't want to miss. (180364—$4.99)

☐ **MURDER FOR FATHER** 20 Mystery Stories by Ruth Rendell, Ed Gorman, Barbara Collins, and 7 More Contemporary Writers of Detective Fiction. Here are proud papas committing crimes, solving cases, or being role models for dark deeds of retribution, revenge, and of course, murder. (180682—$4.99)

*Prices slightly higher in Canada
